INTERFERENCE

S. L. LUCK

This is a work of fiction. Names, characters, places, and incidents either are the product of the author's imagination or are used fictitiously. Any resemblance to actual persons, living or dead, events, or locales is entirely coincidental.

Copyright © 2021 S. L. LUCK

All rights reserved. No part of this book may be reproduced or used in any manner without written permission of the copyright owner except for the use of quotations in a book review.
For more information: info@authorsluck.com

FIRST EDITION

www.authorsluck.com

ISBN: 978-1-7771652-2-2

Cover design by ebooklaunch.com

OTHER NOVELS BY S.L. LUCK

Redeemer

Authors need reviews! If you enjoy this novel, please consider giving an online review at your favorite store.
Many thanks!

Check out my short stories and blog at
www.authorsluck.com

For Chris, because buses run on diesel.

—

My gratitude goes to my first reader, Jen, who tells me if I've got a winner, to Diane for her cultural insight, and to my editor, C.B. Moore, for her sharp eye.
Huge thanks to all of you.

PROLOGUE

Harold Ridgeway woke knowing it would be his last day on earth. Polk County, Texas, was suitably cloudy this morning, with the bitter winds of Hurricane Xavier departing much too slowly, but even that would not stall his death.

They were as bent on his execution as he had been on those murders, and he knew that after eleven years inside Polunsky's paint-peeled, sunlight-deficient walls, no one would mourn him. His transfer to A-Pod three months prior told him his options were exhausted, so he accordingly prepared for death. Harold didn't pray, as others had before him, for he knew that he was beyond salvation. The devil had been his companion much longer than Jesus, and that alone sealed his fate.

Instead, Harold took solace in the memory of those dark nights of delicious terror. In his new surroundings, with his high, slit window and emaciated mattress and cold floor and leaking roof, Harold meditated on screams and clutchings and last breaths, consuming these recollections almost orgasmically, sometimes actually so. It required little effort to take him back. By now, he had returned so often that all he needed was to close his eyes and bite his thumb. The taste of that dirty part of his flesh evinced flashbacks of necks and lips and body parts of all colors, sizes, and genders that

1

rigored as he watched, fascinated, and this release was what he presently settled into to calm his nerves.

Rising as his breakfast clanged through the door slot, Harold yawned and stretched. He turned the twenty-seven deaths over in his mind and briefly considered admitting to the other nine. The hope of new information could stay his execution, though not indefinitely, and while his depraved existence at Polunsky hadn't been constructive for anyone, something inside Harold rallied for more time. It was there, the *thing*, the enduring urge that had ravaged his youth and planted strange impulses that had dominated his life. Harold wasn't sure if the thing was part of him or of some spectral deity, but it was there, invading his brain, twisting his motives, rotting his ambitions. The thing stuffed his ears with reassurances, like a gentle pat on a dog's head. Then it grew impatient and filled his mind with a darkness he had come to rely on. Harold had requested no visitors today, so he turned to the *thing* now, if only to have an understanding companion. *You there?* he wondered inside his head.

The *thing* unfurled itself, spreading wide until all space that was not the *thing* was shrouded inside him. She liked to be called Pandora, but Harold was too selfish to understand that. Narcissistic hosts, the best hosts, could be compelled to do many things except recognize the notion of self in others, and while Pandora *could* make him speak her name, the effort was beneath her. He had already given her what she wanted, hadn't he?

He'd given her terror and death and the kind of melancholy that not only filled her tanks but also kept her satiated for longer periods than when she was with Pickton or Dahmer or Gacy. Harold held on, pushing his victims to the edges of death, then brought them back, repeatedly extending their torture (and Pandora's rapture) until the very last filament that held them to life was snuffed, as if by a whisper. Pandora sensed his anxiety. It filled the chambers of his heart, the marrow of his fifty-two-year-old bones, his cartilage, his blood, the vitreous of his eyes. Pandora stroked him, letting the weight of her presence soothe what was left of his soul, and thanked him for his service. She would stay with this one until the very end. *I'm here*, she conveyed.

I'm not sorry for anything, he imparted, *and I don't feel wrong about that.*

Pandora let him reflect while she poked around his memory so she, too, could relive those moments. She went back to the first, a young nurse walking home from a late shift with her nose in her phone. Harold had followed her for six blocks, lurking behind bushes and fences and cars, until the woman entered a small clutch of trees along a shortcut between the sidewalk and an older residential area. Once she had departed the reach of the streetlights Harold sprang at her, clamped his hand over her mouth, and pulled her into the bushes. Barely an adult himself, Harold was not prepared for how viciously she fought, and he sustained long scratches across his face and deep bite marks on his hands. She'd almost torn off his pinky finger when he finally knocked her out and carried her to his car for the long drive to his grandmother's farmhouse in Hillsboro. There, in the quiet of the night, with his grandmother's hearing aid on the night table as she slept, Harold dragged the woman to a disused pig barn. Then he woke the nurse and let his urges reign.

That evening had rejuvenated Pandora as it would have a relapsed addict. That first taste of death, long since overdue, fortified the deepest part of her being, and she knew at once that she had chosen well with Harold. He wasn't premature like many of the others, and he faced no moral dilemma because darkness was already present in Harold long before Pandora had even reached him, perhaps since birth. This allowed her to fuse quickly and securely, and she stayed with him, growing stronger with every kill, while Harold himself leaned into their interdependent companionship. *Remember Barbara?* Pandora asked him now. *She almost got you, you know.*

A thin smile cracked Harold's lips. He recalled his second, an older accountant out for an evening run. Harold hadn't realized how fit the woman was until she broke free from his hold, running like the devil down the empty streets of Fort Stockton's industrial zone. He had the rusty taste of blood by the time he caught up with her, along with a dozen broken blisters and a number of gouges from clumsy jumps over stored equipment. He'd been purple as a grape when he squeezed through that last opening between a loader and the wall of a metal fabrication outfit, catching Barbara by her ponytail. *She was a tough one,* Harold agreed to Pandora. For a long while, they dwelled on their time together. Laughing, howling, arousing each other with thoughts of Stephen, Paulina, Max, Olga, Felicity, Dorothy, Elijah, and the others; they spent the hours this way, until Harold was finally escorted to the cage for his strip search. He removed his jumpsuit and let it fall to the floor while too many sets of eyes scoured his skin, his insides. *Will you stay with me?* Harold asked Pandora, feeling the first real pangs of apprehension since his incarceration, not because *his* time had run out but because his time with *Pandora* had run out.

I will, Pandora told him.

Where will you go after me?

INTERFERENCE

This Pandora could not answer, for Harold was a rare breed. He was loyal and eager and never hesitated when given a command. Unlike others who fought her occupation, Harold welcomed Pandora's presence, and though she'd dabbled unenthusiastically with dozens of other potential hosts since his incarceration, she always found them lacking. She didn't much care for the ones who acted mechanically, who didn't enjoy their adventures together. It was like having an unappreciative lover, and while Pandora might have settled for such affairs in her early years, she now often longed for foreplay and those naughty after-moments when her hosts shared their often unexpected delight. Harold was a good lover this way. She never had to ask him. If anything, it was Harold who initiated their hunts and their subsequent gloating. She would miss him. At last, she regarded the circle of apprehensive uniforms crowding her host and pushed outward, sending a small jolt through their shoes and up their feet. Instantly a collective shriek rang out.

"What the hell was that?" McMurty wailed, skipping off his feet. The smallest of the six, he felt Pandora's strike the most severely.

Robinson, the longest-serving guard at Polunsky, lifted each foot and inspected the bottom of his shoes. "Call the warden and get someone to check the generators. Maybe the storm's messed with the electrical." McMurty hurried away.

A crisp new prison uniform was given to Harold, and he quickly covered his nakedness for his transport to the Wall. But before the cage door could open, Pandora flung herself upward. Bolts of light shattered the overhead fluorescents above the cage, beside the cage, down the hall, in every prisoner's cell, *bang, bang, bang, bang*, until all lights were extinguished and they were thrust into darkness. Sirens

5

blared, men shouted, radios buzzed, footsteps retreated, advanced, fumbled about, the whole prison in a fury of panic. Through the commotion, Harold's curiosity came soft and clear to Pandora. *W-was that you?* he asked.

Pandora flexed herself again, nudging the guards, poking the prisoners, jabbing the warden himself. Screams normally reserved for the men in the chamber now erupted violently here, there, inside the walls where free men and sentenced men shared a rare common experience. Alone in the cage, however, Harold was the only one untouched. Pandora now reached tenderly for him. *I had to do something,* she insisted, and that was enough for him, for he knew that had she orchestrated his escape, his freedom would be short-lived and they would not hesitate to gun him down. After all Harold had done for her, she couldn't let that happen. No. She could not. She would not let them take him the way they wanted. Instead, she wrapped herself around his heart and pressed her appreciation into him. Pandora coiled tight, tighter yet, more and more, until the steady beats of Harold's heart faded softly away. She stayed like that for some time, and when the lights finally came back on, she released Harold's body to them. Then, lamenting his death, Pandora went to find a new host.

1

George Torres yawned. In the pre-dawn darkness of a breezy October morning, he stopped his bus in front of the Best Western Hotel and kept the engine running as he waited for his passengers. Already awake for the better part of two hours, George had consumed two cups of coffee and was contemplating a third when the hotel manager Fiona Anderson knocked on the door. She hopped back as the door swung open and George stepped out. "Morning," he said, his view of Fiona momentarily obscured by the fog of his breath. "Full house today, Fi?"

Fiona's small shoulders were drawn up to her ears as she shivered in her thin suit. She tapped her clipboard with a pen. "Almost. You got thirty-nine today. There was some stomach bug that has eight of them down or you'd be crammed. Want me to bring them out?"

George said, "I need to hit the washroom first, and you got any of that brew from last time? The dark stuff? I could use another cup."

"Sure do." Fiona nodded. "You do your thing and I'll give them their envelopes while they wait. They're a lively group today." She laughed, her own breath spurting mists of grey from the heat of her mouth.

7

Inside, George hurried to a restroom stall, wincing a little as he urinated. Suffering from a long-simmering urinary tract infection, George had just begun his antibiotics and regretted his reluctance to visit a doctor every time he encountered a toilet. This time was no different. He held his urine at the onset of pain, again and again until he stood in front of the toilet for a solid ten minutes. He knew that coffee was no help, but he needed it to drive and so it put him in a predicament between unemployment or pain. To no great relief he chose the latter, and as he zipped up his fly, George wiped the beginnings of a tear from the corner of his eye. He strode to the small café beside the reception desk, poured himself a large black coffee from the self-serve carafe, and joined Fiona in the lobby. Thirty-nine pairs of tired eyes looked back at him, eager to board the bus. "Hi all," George said jovially, tipping his coffee cup toward them. There were greetings and shouts and whistles from old men and old women, ready to rest their bones in the plushy bus seats.

Fiona said, "Let's hope you're all this happy on your way back from the casino."

Chuckles and familiar groans rose from the group. Fiona conducted one last attendance check and put them into George's capable hands for the two-hour drive to Fauville, where southern Ontario's largest casino sprawled along Lake Huron waiting for the gamblers' deposits. The European styling of the small city regularly drew visitors from across Canada and many northeastern states, with the larger hotels in Garrett, Ontario, hosting weekly charters and offering discount accommodations. George had been assigned to the Best Western departure going on five years, collecting groups from the building at seven a.m. sharp every Wednesday and Saturday, and by now he knew the route to the Huron Casino so well he felt he could drive it in his sleep. Still, he sipped his coffee and greeted his guests while they boarded his bus.

"Morning, Georgie," Rose Mayberry cooed, wiggling her fingers as she passed him. George suspected the high color of her cheeks had little to do with the chill, as Rose had not only been a regular of his since her husband passed the previous year but had also slipped George her phone number on three separate occasions. After his divorce three years earlier, George enjoyed his newfound bachelorhood, and though he often missed female companionship, the idea of Rose in his bed didn't arouse much affection in him. She was kindly, yes, but nattered so loudly that her voice could not be suppressed even when he cranked the music all the way up.

"Hi Rosie," he waved at her and swung his eyes behind her to Ned Chambers, who was struggling up the stairs with his walker. George rushed to the man and adjusted the angle of the contraption to make it easier for Ned.

"Oh, thanks George. I guess I'm still not used to this thing," Ned said a bit uncomfortably.

George put a hand on Ned's shoulder. "Don't worry about it. I'll be needing one of these things soon enough so the practice is good for me."

Together the men navigated the steep steps inside. George folded Ned's walker and put it behind his seat, then he sat and greeted the remaining passengers as they passed by, secretly compartmentalizing them by their hair. There were nineteen baldies, thirteen grays, four who still dyed their hair blond, two bottle brunettes and one who looked much too young to be in company of the rest of the group.

George pulled his headset over his own gray head and adjusted the microphone. "Test, test," he mouthed into the mic, adjusting the volume. "Morning folks. Looks like Earl and Ginger have brought themselves a stowaway today."

All eyes swung to the young woman in an aisle seat between Earl and Ginger Cheevers.

Earl's thick hand waved up to George. He cupped a hand beside his mouth, calling out from the center of the bus, "Taking the granddaughter to the casino. She turned nineteen last week!" The woman's cheeks flushed as Earl pointed at her and a wild crescendo of cheers rushed her way from every direction.

George said, "Well happy birthday, young lady. I'm sorry to say that since you're beside *that* guy, you've already lost, but we wish you luck anyway." Good-natured hoots and hollers rang out as Earl was patted on his back from many sides. "Now, now, settle down, folks. Don't beat him before the casino gets his money."

Another swelling of cheers and chuckles filled the bus, subsiding when George ran through the short itinerary. By the time he reached the mandatory safety presentation, not a single passenger was paying attention. Then they were off. With a hydraulics hiss, the bus pulled away from the curb. They passed the Delta, the Holiday Inn, and three small bed and breakfasts before leaving the curve of the water. Smells of fresh bread and sweet coffee came at them as they neared a twenty-four-hour bakery, where George adeptly swung the bus around so they could see the river while they departed the city. With the sun emerging over the water on their right, the passengers settled, relaxing old bones in familiar company, eventually letting their eyes shut, their heads tilt, their mouths fall open with the comfort of sleep.

Soon, the day was bright. Colors of autumn bloomed in the fields, on the trees, in the steep banks of the Callingwood River; the rich reds and bright oranges and enchanting golds of falling leaves reflected like drops of honey on the moving

INTERFERENCE

water. George turned the radio on, already set to 103.9, Garrett's only classic rock station. Led Zeppelin's "Stairway to Heaven" had just begun. He hummed to himself, driving slowly, taking his time.

A sudden slap of wind gusted against the side of the bus. George redirected the wheel. Again the wind pushed. Wiping the crust from the corners of his eyes, George straightened and focused on the road. Another blast of air now stirred the passengers and George tightened his spine, alert to the strange weather. The misleading sunshine toyed with the bus, threading it through wild mechanisms of pressure, thrust, and extraction until purses were tossed and wallets were thrown and eyeglasses were jostled. George switched his mic on again.

"Looks like we're going to have a bit of a rough ride today, folks. I don't know where that came from, but I think we better tighten our belts. Please put your chairs u—"

The bus rocked violently, its rear skittering across fresh leaf-litter into a lane of oncoming traffic. George yanked on the wheel. Rose Mayberry screamed. Prayers were thrust to the Lord, the sign of the cross was made in the front seat, the second, the third, the fourth. Passengers prayed to God, to Buddha, to the Creator. Ernie Stiles, a devout atheist, called for his cat, Domer, to somehow rescue him. With great effort, George clamped the wheel right, more right, left, more left, until the wind slowed and the bus once again settled.

George adjusted his headset, which had almost fallen off his head. "You all right there, folks? I'm going to pull over and conduct a safety check. Please do not unbuckle until I have stopped the vehicle. I repeat, do not unbuckle until I have stopped the vehicle."

11

He glanced into the rear-view mirror. No major harm done, though behind him Rose looked green with nausea; the vomit bag Simone Gladriuk pushed at her was subsequently filled. George looked back to the road. Three blocks ahead, on the other side of the Callingwood Bridge, there was a gas station where they could safely stop.

George said, "We're going to stop at the Petro up ahead and see how everyone is doing. Sit tight and I'll have us parked in no time."

Usually, George was fanatical about turning the microphone off. One wet sneeze on his second shift fifteen years ago had taught him the importance of inhibiting his communication, but his current anxiety scrambled his senses, and he inadvertently left the line open. Shaking, George brought the bus past the football fields on the left and began his trek over the Pacifica Inlet on the right. Wind patted the carriage, so George eased off the accelerator. They were going ten kilometers less than the speed limit, but George was a safety guy, and he was not inclined to risk another gust as he entered the bridge. Slowly, slowly, the bus advanced onto the platform and as they passed the first connection plate, George's heart fluttered with apprehension. He did not know why this happened; only, there was a feeling that came to him, something like dread, something like foreboding, something like intuition. He shuddered, trying to shake the feeling away but as he looked down at the rush of water in the angry river far below, his stomach soured. Hands tight on the wheel, George took his guests further over the water. The short span of the inlet was of no consolation, for George felt the stirrings of an encircling evil so deeply that his bladder convulsed, and the sharp sting of urine caused him to gasp.

INTERFERENCE

"You all right there, George?" Bernard Clemmens leaned toward him from his front aisle seat.

Before George could respond, wind lashed the carriage. Bernard hollered as an SUV smashed into the side of the bus. George veered left, left, left, anywhere but right, missing one car, two, three, speeding in their direction from the oncoming lane. Again, George brought the bus back into the lane, only to be slammed by another gust, another blast, another squall. The bus rocked. Rose vomited. Ernie shouted his cat's name. Earl and Ginger reached for their granddaughter. Ned Chambers fainted. Spotting the end of the bridge just a few hundred meters away, George hit the gas pedal. From the opposite direction, a semi truck hauling three shiny new tractors suddenly veered into their lane. George swerved away. The semi swerved away. Wind thrashed from the left, from the right, down the center of the bridge, on all sides of every vehicle, of every cable. Then—just as George regained control—the semi hit.

Terrible waves of inertia cut, sheared, rammed, sliced, and smashed glass, steel, fabric, bodies. If George had been looking, he would have witnessed the bus snap one of the bridge cables as it breached the guardrail. If George had been looking, he would have noticed the view of the road escape his windshield and the dark panorama of the Callingwood River bloom in its place. If George had been looking, he would have seen Ernie and Bernard slide down the aisle and hit the windshield as the bus tipped over the side of the bridge. George would have seen purses and wallets and jackets plummet and mount the windshield. He would have heard shrieks and wails and the sickening sound of bones breaking. He would have smelled the failure of bladders and bowels, the rupture of Styrofoam coffee cups, the expulsion

13

of many stomachs, the first wisps of diesel. But George did not see, hear, or smell any of this before they hit the water. He was already dead.

2

Sylvia Baker adjusted the collar of her jacket. In the frigid corner of the guard shelter where she huddled waiting for the children to arrive, she shivered, regretting her decision to volunteer for another year. It always happened this way, though. When the freshness of spring softened the grievance of winter, and when the splendor of summer tempered the hardship of rainy months outside, Sylvia gave in. *She was the best*, they said. *They needed her*, they said. *Westgate Elementary couldn't do without the city's best crossing guard*, entreated Joan Meyers, the school administrator.

Then came the cards from the children and letters from the parents and, this past year, even a letter and gift from Mayor Falconer herself, commending Sylvia for twenty-five years of volunteering. Their gift was strategic, of course. Presently, it was on her back doing its damnedest to keep her warm and the wind out, and as she pulled up her zipper and tightened her hood, she vowed this year would be her last.

In the amber cast of the early morning, she peered across the street at a townhome, from which the glow of a television beamed between unclosed curtains. Three heads covered her view of the screen, but one shifted slightly as it leaned onto a nearby shoulder. Sylvia squinted, spying a breaking news report in an alarming red block at the top of the screen. The heads moved again. Sylvia stood to get a better view but felt a gentle tug at the front of her vest.

"Morning Mrs. Baker," a small voice said.

"Good morning Charlie." Sylvia nodded to the young boy and stepped out of her shelter, sucking in her breath at the sight of his red ears. "Shouldn't you be putting your toque on, young man?" The boy shrugged indifferently. Sylvia plucked Charlie's blue hat from his side pocket and stuck it on his head, patting it over his ears. "Now, isn't that better?" she asked.

The boy was too busy blowing breath clouds to answer her, so she squeezed his hand and told him to wait on the sidewalk while she prepared the road. Wind slapped her back, her face, the thin layer of her pants as she paused in the middle of the road where she held up her stop sign. Two cars slowed then stopped as they waited for Charlie to cross but his head was turned in the direction of the townhomes, all windows now bright and active with television broadcast. A third car stopped. A fourth.

"Charlie Zabrowski, start walking before they run out of gas!" Sylvia called. The boy scurried past her and with an aimless wave, entered the school gate and disappeared beyond the front doors.

Quickly, she turned back to the guard house, using her boot to sweep out an accumulation of leaves that had blown inside. The next twenty minutes went like that: sweeping, stopping, shivering, hustling kids across the breezy street. She recovered fallen mittens, hats, homework, hairclips, and even a shoe when Logan Biles followed too close and stepped on the back of Misty Heywood's ankle. The littlest ones, Sylvia's favorites, always came late, as the junior and senior kindergarteners were last to begin their day in the library at the

16

front of the school. Sylvia was often invited to join them while they took turns reading aloud.

She stretched her neck, rolling her head along her shoulders as the day slowly, slowly began to warm. Down the block, she spotted five little heads bobbing toward her. At once, two broke out running, laughing, and racing each other. A mother called for them to stop. They ran faster. A father called for them to stop. They picked up speed, the wind devilishly pushing against their backs. Sylvia stepped out from the guardhouse. Her voice boomed through the wind. "Ronnie and Bobbie! You heard your parents!" The boys slowed, elbowing each other as the rest of the group caught up. Gusts swelled around her head, against her eyes, over the tight line of her mouth. It grew stronger, buffeting Sylvia from all sides as she waited for the last stragglers, two pairs of sisters, to join them at the corner. "Hold on to your hats!" she instructed the nine tiny faces squinting up at her. "And wait here."

The children shook with cold while Sylvia looked left, right, left again. Traffic picked up so the process was slower but then Sylvia's legs began to tingle. Small pulses of numbness ran from her toes, then to her ankles, then her knees and to her hips. She felt a light prickling in her ribs, in the cartilage of her shoulders. There was something like the gentle touching of fingers against her brainstem and for a moment, Sylvia felt an intrusion akin to a stranger unlocking the door in the middle of the night. The faceless thing crawled inside her, first superficially, then scratched and dug and finally clawed into the septum that separated her physical self from her spiritual self.

Sylvia sniffed, glaring down at the children behind her. Many cars passed as the children waited. The lingering parents exchanged looks. New heat began to rise in Sylvia's body and as she took a little girl's hand, the child recoiled at her touch. Sylvia snatched the girl's hand back, pulling her into the busy road where cars now streamed steadily in all directions. The girl whimpered, trying to remove herself from Sylvia's hot grasp.

"Hey!" The father of one of the children called to them but Sylvia had lost that part of herself that could respond. "Hey!" The father cried again, running toward them while a mother held the other children back.

A slow trickle of blood fell from Sylvia's nose. The girl screamed as Sylvia dragged her further into the street. A horn blared. Another. Tires screeched. Parents shrieked. Sylvia's head turned into the traffic.

And then she collapsed.

3

Ed Norman cradled his cup of peppermint tea as he sat in his wheelchair and watched the giant maples shed great swaths of leaves onto the wide lawn of Southbridge Retirement. It had been his home for the better part of six years, and Ed enjoyed a comfortable camaraderie with the nursing staff and most of his fellow residents, who sat watching the leaves with him in the common area.

From behind bifocals and glaucoma and cataracts, many sets of eyes rose upward, targeting the slow descent of leaves until they hit the ground. Teas were sipped, blankets were snuggled, and sweet biscuits were nibbled thoughtfully amid occasional expressions of delight or awe.

The morning wind that had battered the windows and shook the veranda had abated as suddenly as it began, and now the residents gathered appreciatively as their anxiety returned to other parts of their psyche. Footsteps plodded up behind Ed, and then a flat hand found and cupped his shoulder.

"Thought the roof was going to go there for a while," Chester Collins said, his eyebrows cresting to the middle of his liver-spotted forehead. "What do you think that was? Sign that winter's coming, or maybe we're getting what's left of that hurricane ... the one by Texas, what's that one called again? Xanadu?" He pushed a plate of cheese and crackers at Ed and sat down beside him.

"Xavier," Ed corrected him. "But we're too far north for that, Chester. I think we're in for an early winter. Wouldn't be surprised if the lawn is white in the morning."

"Ah," Chester said, slapping Ed's shoulder. "I don't feel it in my bones yet." He rolled his shoulders, tested his knees, splayed his fingers, experimenting. "I think we got three or four weeks yet. Let's hope you're wrong, Eddie."

Ed's own body was no weather gauge as Chester's was. Unlike what many of the other residents experienced, he felt no pain in his joints with the changing of the weather. While the omens of snow and rain crept up and clung to their cartilage and tightened their tendons, Ed was physically unaffected. He could move as he wished without great effort or pain, though sluggishly, as expected. Seasonal difficulty was not seasonal at all for Ed since his affliction reposed inside him every day that he continued to live. It was inside his brain, had been there for twenty-three years and refused to leave. That nagging, disagreeable feeling that was so much worse than any physical malady: doubt.

His first experience with heaven was seventy-two years ago, when he and Bessie were both fourteen and she had come charging at him in her new roller skates. Ed had just left Tucker's with a bag of nails for his father when he heard screaming behind him. There, coming down the long slope of sidewalk in a rustling pink dress, hands flailing, knees buckling, hair swishing over her face, Bessie yelled for him to get out of the way. Her warning had the opposite effect, for instead of dipping away from the sidewalk, he stood captivated, clutching his bag of nails as Bessie barrelled toward him. Even from a distance, even with the brunette flag of hair across her eyes, even with her dress blown sideways and the ivory hem of her underpants perilously exposed, he thought he'd seen an angel.

The instant Bessie smashed into him, they toppled together onto the sidewalk. His bag of nails flew and their knees and elbows were cut and their faces were rashed, but Ed saw in her the remaining years of his life. Her green eyes shone with tears, and in his stupor he went to brush away the wetness on her cheek, only to deposit a dark smear of blood under her eye from an unnoticed cut along his thumb. If she hadn't worried over him, maybe he could have walked away and forgotten her. Maybe. But she fretted and fussed so much that by the time she had him back on his feet and a tissue on his bleeding hand, Ed knew he was in love.

Bessie was all things good and all things right. Whereas Ed's own family wasn't of religious disposition, Bessie insisted on it. "God is all things good and all things right," she would tell him, and that had stuck with Ed. He grew to understand that it was true. Like Bessie, God gave him purpose, gave him redemption, and prescribed a way of living that made sense to Ed. It was through Bessie that Ed found the Holy Redeemer Church, where he would first be parishioner and then administrator with what he came to believe was divine business acuity.

For many years, Ed had no complaints, as God really was all things good and all things right. Then the church burnt down, with Father Pauliuk's own wife Donna and his curate, Stu Kline, trapped inside. He tried to see their terrible deaths as Divine Purpose, but the rationale felt wrong, all wrong. It wrenched at him, loosening the convictions he thought had irrevocably tightened with Bessie's gentle guidance over time. It made him wonder. It made him think. It

21

made him sick. But Bessie, always stronger than Ed had ever been, insisted that understanding was not anyone's to have, and that God had His way.

He prayed for answers, got none. Even as his convictions receded, he talked to the Lord, invested himself in the church, in its people, in its doctrine. So it was that little by little, Ed felt his beliefs gather again, tightening with time and with the loosening of memory. Had Ed died before Bessie, he would have gone to God with open arms and with steadfast love. But three years after the Redeemer fire, God had taken Bessie in her sleep during a weekend with the grandchildren. In an instant, all the things that fortified Ed, all the things that made him what he was had gone, and so began his life of purgatory.

"You okay there Eddie?" Chester squeezed Ed's shoulder.

Ed sniffed and sipped his now cold tea. "Huh? Yeah. Sorry, Chester. Was just thinking. Hey, you making the float again for the parade this year? I heard Miles Simpkon is bent on trying to outdo you."

A gravelly laugh erupted from Chester's throat. "Ha! That guy, I'll tell you, he's never going to stop until he gets that ribbon, Eddie. Three years first place, but I'm going for four and, let me tell you, this one's going to be a zinger, Eddie, the best one yet. We got hydraulics this year! My son's been working on it all summer."

The glow of pride spread across Chester's face, wide across the teeth and temples. For the next three weeks, this face would boast and pique and delight in the making of Southbridge's annual float. Around every corner and at every gathering, this face would fill in even the smallest spaces of solitude with news of ingenuity and cunning and unimaginable grandeur. How Chester lived to hear the ladies gasp and feel the men nod on appreciatively, his stories expanding to fit the depth of their loneliness. So great was the buildup that Southbridge's first-place achievement each of the last three years had been anticlimactic and secondary to the production itself. Ed now reflected that the three weeks leading up to the Garrett Fall Festival were the only three weeks of the year he could actually stand to be around Chester, which now made him say: "Can't wait to see what you've come up with."

Chester leaned so close that Ed could smell coffee on his breath and see specks of crackers between his teeth and on his lips. Chester said, "We got a dragon this year, Eddie. Fire and ice, *big-bang sha-boom* type of stuff that'll blow their socks off. Jeremy made it so the head and tail move. Fire as high as the sky! We'll have to keep the kids back at least twenty feet or they'll roast!" Chester's hand went to his forehead. "Maybe we need a sign or something, huh? Yeah. A sign." Chester's eyes drifted in thought, then fell on the cluster of residents gathering around the television.

"My!" Hattie Freemont's mouth dropped open.

"No. No. No." Albert Humphrey sank his rear onto the coffee table, spilling Dorothy Davis' pear juice. Neither of them paid any attention while his seat grew wet and the plastic tumbler rolled to the floor.

"It can't be!" Dorothy cried, her eyes on the screen, only the screen.

Ed turned toward the television, where the residents collected with gasps and moans and great inhalations of grief. "What is it?" Ed asked, rising now.

Chester's chair slid back. He rushed toward the other residents, pushing his way inside the circle where he could see. "What happ—Eddie! Get over here! Look at this! Isn't that ... yes, yes, there's his number on the back. 5-8-7. God,

23

it's George's bus. It's George's bus in the water! Eddie! Look at it! Oh, just look at it!"

The sound that escaped his lips was felt by all of them and the collective shudder that whirred through the room brought the three on-duty nurses, Georgia, Sam, and Paul rushing to their charges.

Ed squeezed past Hattie and Dorothy. The vision on the screen was a frantic revolution of terrible coverage. The bus in the water. The tarp-covered bodies on the riverbank. The firemen. The paramedics. The police. The mayor. The divers. The wailing onlookers. The bus in the water. The tarp-covered bodies. Someone beside Ed vomited. Another fainted. Ed wiped his eyes. "My Lord. My Lord," he panted, though he wasn't conscious of whom he was speaking. "My Lord," Ed repeated, unaware that he had suddenly crossed himself.

"That's Sonja's boy!" Albert said. "Don't let her see this. Don't! Keep her away from the TV. Someone, go, go, GO!"

He thrust a hand toward the door, the quiver of his Parkinson's noticeably pronounced. Dorothy and Hattie sprang from the room as if their feet were on fire. With the sixteen decades between them, the women called upon speed they hadn't used in years.

Then Garrett's most famous reporter, Jessica Chung, appeared on screen, her microphone shaking in her usually steady hand.

"Folks, today marks one of the darkest days in the city's history. What you are about to see is not for the faint of heart. If you have children, we ask that you turn your screen away from them or send them to another room. If you have health issues, we ask that you consider your well-being before you continue with our broadcast. I will give you a moment to do what is right for your family before I proceed." She fell quiet, her knuckles pressure-white, the muscles in her jaw twitching as she waited. She drew in a deep breath. "Thank you for staying with us. We are in front of the Callingwood Bridge where Fauville Tour Bus number 587 travelling from the Best Western to the Huron Casino has breeched the guardrail and crashed into the river. Authorities have confirmed thirty-one deaths, with eight unaccounted for and one survivor, whose identity authorities are not releasing until all affected families have been contacted. A command center has been assembled at the Legion on Fifth and Alice Avenue. Family members and friends are asked not to call the hospital or emergency services but visit the command center for information on their loved ones. I repeat, do *not* call the hospital or emergency services. Concerned family members are asked to go to the Legion on Fifth and Alice for more information."

The Legion's address appeared in a red block at the top of the screen, along with a phone number to the command center. "I bring you now to a witness of the terrible tragedy, Mr. Carl McLeod. What can you tell us about the accident?" She swung her shaking microphone over to Carl, who had just finished blowing his nose.

Carl's hand went to his head as he dragged unsteady fingers through his hair, his eyes going wide with recollection. He pointed away from the reporter. "I was approaching the bridge from the other direction in my truck, heading toward the bus behind that semi over there." He pointed to the crumpled front end of the semi, then put a hand over his mouth to contain a sob. The reporter waited and eventually he went on. "The wind just came out of nowhere. It had to be the wind because I felt it. I could barely keep my own truck on four wheels. But then … then there was a big gust and the guy ahead of me ended up in the oncoming lane. I don't know how to explain it better than that. I've never seen anything like it."

"That must have been horrific to see," Jessica led.

"Terrible. Just terrible," Carl agreed. "I'll never forget it. Those people … my God … those poor people. The bus driver never had a chance." He looked upward, trying to control his tears.

Somewhere behind Ed, a swish of footsteps rushed toward the women's ward. At ninety-six years old, George's mother, Sonja Torres, was one of the oldest residents at Southbridge, and Ed knew that news of her son's accident wouldn't go lightly on her. The woman had survived her husband and a daughter who died of cancer in her mid-thirties, but as resilient as Sonja was, George's almost certain death in his mid-sixties would render the woman completely alone. Ed's own experience with loneliness was not as vast since he still had three grown children and five grandchildren to visit him, but they were transient tethers to an impermanent world. *Lose those and you might as well give up*, Ed thought, his heart aching for Sonja.

Wet pants and all, Albert Humphrey stood, shaking his head. "I can't watch this. I just can't." He pushed out of the crowd and left the room.

"Turn the channel," Chester said for all of them. "Turn it off." His eyes slipped to the coffee table in search of the remote.

In a voice soft and sorrowful, a woman at the back of the room said, "We must pray."

The new resident whom Ed couldn't name, directed them to bow their heads. Everyone obeyed.

"Heavenly Father, we pray for the souls of this tragedy and we ask that you keep them and their families in Your divine care."

INTERFERENCE

She went on, but while the heads were bowed and the eyes were closed and the lips moved, Ed quietly left the room. A flurry of activity awaited him in the hallway, where uniformed employees were scuttling between Sonja's room and the nurse's station.

"You can't do that!" A nurse's voice broke into the hallway. "Don't Mrs. Torres, please don't!"

As Ed came to Sonja's door, he saw Hattie and Dorothy huddling in the corner in tears while Sonja Torres, old as she was, assaulted them with cups and saucers and books and pictures and even a bedpan.

The small black nurse, Georgia, raised her voice. "Stop Mrs. Torres! Please stop." Georgia pinned down the woman's arms, but Mrs. Torres spat and wailed for her son.

Ed caught Hattie's eye and beckoned her to the hallway. She pulled Dorothy along behind her. Gently, he said, "Let her be. She just needs some time. Who knows, George might be okay after all," he offered hopefully, even though he didn't believe it to be true. Noticing the exasperation on Hattie's face, he added, "It's a good thing the news came from you and not someone else. She'll appreciate that one day. You've done a good thing, don't worry your hearts over it."

The women let out small, agreeable sobs and departed to Hattie's room while the biggest on-duty aid, Paul, brushed past them and hurried into Sonja's room to help Georgia. With a last look at the commotion, Ed slowly ventured across the building to his own room, taking his time, enjoying the movement without the limitation of his wheelchair, which he reserved for longer excursions.

The room was cool, so Ed closed the window and took a sweater from his closet, sliding his arms through the thick wool and buttoning the front before easing into his recliner.

27

He pulled a blanket over his lap and turned on the television. This early in October, Ed would normally expect news of the weather and of the upcoming Fall Festival, which drew tens of thousands of visitors every year, but Jessica Chung's serious face dominated every station. He turned now to the local weather channel, where a feed of the week's forecast wound over the screen. At the bottom, no surprise, news of the bus accident led the bottom scroll, followed by a short reminder of the upcoming Fall Festival, and directing viewers to local banks and grocery stores to purchase advance admission tickets. Ed sighed and turned off the television, reflecting on the hardships of life, when he felt a pain in his chest.

4

Pandora woke with her new eyes. In the hospital room, machines beeped and visitors whispered, and she looked outward from Sylvia Baker's face while a woman in scrubs and a tall, blond man in a dark suit spoke quietly at the foot of her bed.

In moments like these, when she awakened inside a new host, she felt strange and almost never at home. Harold had been the exception, but he was no more, and as she inspected her new body, Pandora felt a bitter disappointment so deep she wondered if she would ever recover. Harold, her Harold, her favorite host, was gone, and in her haste for another, she had been jittery and lost control, recklessly pushing out and drawing attention where she most needed secrecy.

But, oh! That bus had felt *good*. She hadn't meant for such public executions, but they were a salve for her rage, for her heartache, and she would deal with the repercussion if it ever came. Only twice before had she been found out. Once in Prague, when a group of distraught mothers rightfully suspected Pandora of preying on their children. An unfortunately accurate reading from a fortune teller led the women to perform a ridiculous séance which gave Pandora the hiccups until she departed the area. The second time, in Africa, where Pandora had taken to collapsing mines, residents of a local village

29

declared the presence of a ghost and sought a powerful medicine man to excise Pandora from the foreman she'd taken upon. With a white-painted face, the man shook antelope horns, swung snake skins, crushed bat jaws, and ate the intestines of a lizard. Mumbling fast, his voice rose to great crescendos, then abruptly dipped as he beseeched the gods, the spirits, and the prophets to expel the evil in the mines. Pandora's first reaction was to laugh at the witchcraft, but then she was struck as if by lightning. Once, twice, a dozen times Pandora was thrashed and stung and burned. She felt a tearing and ripping of the thing that held her to earth and though she fought back, her wounds grew deeper, verging on totality until she finally fled.

That was her quickest departure, on which she now reflected, feeling her new toes, her new arms. This was a body she could hide in. It was a body that looked small and fragile, unimportant, and unambitious. Pandora couldn't ask for better camouflage unless she'd assumed a child's body, but since those raised too many suspicions, she settled for Sylvia Baker. Unnecessary as it was, she liked to fill her body's lungs with air, test its capacity, and presently she did so. Where Harold's lungs were capable of great uptakes, thick tar residue prevented much from Sylvia. Her cilia were so coated that Pandora's sharp indrawn breath was an exercise in pressing sludge, and her small chest rose and fell only slightly but with monstrous effort. No matter. In fact, this made her disguise all the more genius.

Pandora was smiling at her own cunning when a voice said, "I think she's waking up. Mrs. Baker? Sylvia? Can you hear me, Sylvia?"

"Mother?" inquired another voice, and then Sylvia felt a gentle hand on her ankle.

They were unaware she was awake, so she pretended to stir at the sound of their voices. Pandora twitched Sylvia's pinky finger, her big toes, her shoulders, then she fluttered her eyelids and swayed the woman's nicotine-yellowed neck. She mumbled something they couldn't understand and slid her eyes open. At once, the being that was Sylvia reacted to the sight of the man and Pandora let her reach for him.

"Troy?" Sylvia croaked, her throat dry and with the bitter taste of medicine.

"You had us worried," Sylvia's son said, reaching for her hand.

His was a good face, angular and handsome, and Pandora thought that, had she been an actual woman, or at very least a human, she might have wanted this man. As he stood beside her, she took in his blueness of his eyes, the sharpness of his bones, and the shadows of his skin, white here, darker there, so that he looked both dangerous and benevolent, at least in this light.

"I'm glad you're okay, Mother." His formality was unexpected but not entirely unusual. Still, he squeezed and kissed Sylvia's fingers and looked on as a caring son would.

Her response required a motherly touch, so Pandora allowed Sylvia to speak. "Oh, Troy. My boy, my sweet boy." She leaned forward and accepted a hug. Warmth spread from Sylvia's middle. The feeling was an unpleasant massage to Pandora. Instances of love—the *feeling*, the receiving—all damaged her by degrees, whereas hate and fear and malice, those delicious treats, fortified everything that Pandora was. As Sylvia adjusted to Pandora's residence, Pandora would allow what she could, but as with pockets of air in a new pair of gloves, the fit would have to be adjusted and the air eventually let out.

31

The woman beside Troy came forward, setting a clipboard on the side table. "Mrs. Baker, I'm Dr. Tanti. You can call me Adhira. How are you feeling, Mrs. Baker?" The doctor's large brown eyes were inquisitive and concerned.

"W-what happened?" Sylvia asked.

Dr. Tanti's lips pressed together tightly, preparing for difficult conversation. "You had a stroke, Mrs. Baker. You are lucky to be alive."

"A stroke? I—I don't remember that. I—" Sylvia put a hand to her mouth, then stopped, her eyes widening at the sight of her other hand. "Why can't I move my arm? Why can't I move my arm? Troy?" Ineffectually, she willed it to move, and let out a gasp when it remained still.

Troy sat on the bed, pressing a hand against his tie to keep it in place. "You had a stroke, Mother. Everything will be all right. I've already taken care of it." His eyes swung to the clock on the far wall.

Confusion swirled across Sylvia's half-paralyzed face. The left corner of her mouth ticked outward with agitation while the other side, the other eye, the other cheek, drooped without motion. "Taken care of what? I don't know what you mean. I'm—how long have I been here?" She looked at Dr. Tanti, her dull, straw-colored hair flat against her sweaty forehead. "How long?"

"It's okay, Mrs. Baker," the doctor said. "The important thing is that you are here now, in our care. We do need to run some more tests on you, however."

"What for?" Sylvia asked, panic rising through her disused throat. The sound was cracked and whirring, like an old motor starting up.

"We know you've had a stroke, Mrs. Baker, but we haven't yet been able to say with confidence which kind you've experienced. Can you tell us how much you remember?"

Sylvia gazed at her blanket, trying to recall her last moment of consciousness. Pandora didn't intervene, for this was a test of the woman's strength. The less she remembered, the weaker she was and therefore easier to control. "I was at work. At the school," Sylvia mumbled. "That's all I know. That's all."

The doctor leaned forward, shining a pen light into Sylvia's eyes. "Anything after that?" Sylvia shook her head.

Troy said, "Do you remember the girl, Mother?"

Sylvia's face was blank. "A girl? Which one? I see a hundred girls every day at the school. Can you be specific?" With her face half immobilized, her words were slurred; hundred became *hunred* and specific became *pacific*. Dr. Tanti pressed two fingers to Sylvia's dead wrist, timing her pulse against the wall clock. "Did something … happen to a girl?" She sucked in her breath, "Did a car …? Did something happen, Troy? Did I … oh please tell me nothing happened!" Fear stole over the woman and she began to shake.

Troy squeezed his mother's fingers and said, "Everyone's all right, Mother. Nothing happened." He gestured to the doctor, who inserted a needle into Sylvia's intravenous line.

"We're going to give you something to help you relax, Mrs. Baker. You're safe here and everything is going to be all right. Just some tests, and when you're clear, we'll have you off to Southbridge. Won't that be nice? I hear the residents just love it there." Dr. Tanti smiled and retrieved her clipboard, scribbling as she talked. "You know, you're lucky to have a son like Troy. Most people wait for months to get in that place. Sometimes years."

"Southbridge? The *home*, Troy? You want to put me in a home?" Sylvia's jaw fell open and her lips began to quiver. "I'm too young for that. I'm barely over seventy! I can

33

recover, can't I?" She looked at the doctor, who was now holding Sylvia's chart to her chest, her face full of pity.

Dr. Tanti said, "All things are possible, Mrs. Baker. In my years practicing medicine, I've had more than a few patients surprise me. The human spirit cannot be underestimated. I can tell you're strong and this will serve you well in your recovery, but I cannot promise your life will be unchanged. You may recover quickly, or it may take some time. The tests may tell us some, but again they may not. So far, we're at a loss as to the cause of your episode. Your CT and ultrasound have come back clear. We found no clots, so we can safely rule out an ischemic stroke and there is no apparent bleeding, so we can rule out a hemorrhagic episode. So far, we've found no apparent cause of your stroke; we only know that you've had one. Our goal here is to ensure you're stabilized and not at risk of another episode, and then begin rehabilitation as soon as possible. Most stroke patients are discharged within a week, but with a plan for further rehabilitation. Heartland is an excellent clinic, but it's short term. Your son connected with Southbridge for your continuing care *after* your stay there. Southbridge has an excellent partnership with Heartland so, to be fair to your son, it was a natural choice." Dr. Tanti's speech was smooth, as though she had recited the same words to many other people, many times before.

"Troy?" Sylvia's eyes fluttered at her son.

He sighed. "It's for the best, Mother. I'm in Toronto and you're all alone here. Who's going to take care of you when I leave?" Troy inspected the cuffs of his shirt and tugged them straight.

"I—" Sylvia started but suddenly found she had no answer.

INTERFERENCE

"You have friends in Southbridge, Mother. You'll be happy there." Troy patted her leg, positive reinforcement for her future obedience.

Sylvia pulled herself up and considered the doctor and her son, the people intent on her incarceration. There was a fog in her head that she tried to push back, but it wouldn't entirely go away. She clenched her teeth, needing to say what she had to say before sleep took her again. "I'm a grown woman and I can decide for myself what's best for me. What about home visits? Tammy Giroux had them when she was in that accident. Why can't I do the same?"

A vein in Troy's jaw pulsed and he faced her with annoyance. His tongue slid over his teeth and when he finally spoke, his words were short. "You're right, Mother. You do have a choice, but I'll worry if you're alone again. Do you want to make me worry, Mother? Is that what you want?"

Sylvia's jaw shuffled left and right as though she were weighing a great decision, testing the taste of it. "Well, I … of course not, Troy. You know I don't like you to worry. I was just thinking it would be good to try, you know, since I'm still young." Her eyes went to her son, who appeared troubled. Troy's brows knit together, and his mouth pouted the way it would for as long as she could remember. His beautiful baby face was no gift of his father's, it was of Sylvia and Sylvia's mother and grandmother.

Presently, that smooth-skinned, radiant face drew her in and dismantled her resolve the way it always did. The fog was heavier now, and her son was closer. The combination of the two drained what remained of her strength.

She said, "But I'll try it for you, Troy. It might be okay if I try it for a little, just a little, and then if I don't like it, I can go home, right, Troy? Does that sound okay to you?" She held her breath, waiting for him to speak.

35

Troy fingered the sharp line of his jaw, considering her proposition. After a time, he said, "It's your choice, Mother. If this is what you want, I think it's the right thing to do. Try it out and see how you like it. I'll make sure the house is ready if you decide to come back." As he kissed the top of her head, she inhaled the scent of his soap and of his expensive cologne and wondered where he had come from and where he was going.

It was when Dr. Tanti cleared her throat that Sylvia realized the other woman had not left the room. "I'll check on you again tomorrow, Mrs. Baker, but I was wondering if I can see your son for a moment in the hall?"

"Go ahead," Sylvia said to Troy. "I'm getting sleepy anyway. You'll come back later?"

"Sure thing, Mother," he said, advancing to the brighter lights of the corridor.

Sylvia saw his profile, lean and angular, against the backdrop of the light and was again struck by his beauty. The beauty that she and his father Adam had made forty-one years ago. That she wasn't a grandmother yet was of no concern to Sylvia because, looking at Troy and the way Dr. Tanti smiled up at him and the way the passing nurses glanced at him, grandchildren would come, and she still had many years to enjoy them.

She smiled as the air around her grew heavier and her limbs, dead and alive, fell into a peaceful stillness. For a time, she watched her son in the doorway and before Sylvia closed her eyes, she thought she recognized an exchange of phone numbers.

5

Greg Huxley was exhausted. In all his years as an attending physician at Garrett General, he'd gone without sleep, gone without lunch, gone without showering for the better part of a day, sometimes two, but he had never delivered the news of so many deaths to so many families in such a span, all before noon.

Shortly after sunrise, the bodies had rolled in. They came in ones and twos, until additional ambulances were dispatched from Sarnia and London, when they came in a dozen at a time. Most were dead on arrival; the others had been intubated and defibrillated. Their limbs were tied into tourniquets, necks were braced, and displaced parts were gathered and hurried into coolers, few of which were assigned to the correct owner.

Almost all victims had drowned in the river. Some had their pulses return weakly after hands and mouths and machines manically worked life back into them. But even after the great effort, the pulses eventually faded away in surgery rooms, in hallways, in screaming ambulances, on the riverbank. In addition to the thirty-three bus passengers who had so far been recovered, two men and one woman who had dived into the water to attempt a rescue had also died, caught on the tangle of metal below the surface. Further rescue attempts by locals were then swiftly thwarted by Chief Dan Fogel, who ordered an immediate perimeter and called in OPP's dive unit to locate the seven missing passengers. All in all, the worst mass casualty the city had ever experienced.

He stood now in the lone survivor's hospital room, praying she remained stable, hoping to give at least one family some good news. Huxley himself had repaired the fracture in her skull, and he watched her now as the ventilator moved oxygen into her lungs, the steady push of air through tubes something he'd grown used to over the years. Although surgeries like these were usually dispatched to larger hospitals out of Toronto or Hamilton, her condition when the paramedics had brought her in required immediate attention. Huxley's steady hands had guided him well during the four-hour surgery, masterfully locating and extricating segments of the girl's depressed skull. How she would fare, he didn't know, but the fracture was relatively small, and the girl's pupils reacted swiftly to his light out of surgery, so he was optimistic; exhausted but optimistic.

Huxley observed the girl's eyes again, relieved when the green fringe of her irises bloomed large as her pupils constricted. The nursing team had done a fine job cleaning her up. Her freckled skin was mostly rid of blood and dirt, save for a small purple-black patch beneath a thicket of red hair they hadn't shaved. Their lone survivor, a symbol of resilience, a symbol of hope, had to survive, and Huxley was determined to ensure she did.

Though it was late and he was tired, so very tired, Huxley would stay at the hospital tonight in case he was needed. He yawned, looking over Anabelle Cheever's chart one last time. It wasn't in his nature to touch patients outside of professional attention, but he did so now, reaching for Anabelle's hand, maybe to squeeze his strength into her, maybe so she knew that she wasn't alone. This small body was the city's hope, and Huxley felt compelled to extend the support of fifteen thousand others through the touch of his fingers.

When Huxley took her fingers between his palms, a sizzle of pain tore into him as though he'd been shocked. He recoiled, wondering if one of the machines had somehow polarized the girl. Again he reached for her and again the same pulse ran through his skin.

He hailed the nursing staff, and soon there was a flurry of activity around Anabelle. Machines were checked, tubes were studied, and connections were examined, all the while zinging and stinging the working hands any moment they touched her.

"Something's wrong," Huxley said to his team.

"But she's not in distress, Doctor. Her vitals are good, responses are good. Unless it's the equipment, I don't know what to tell you. Let me just—" The ICU's head nurse put a stethoscope to Anabelle's chest and gasped at the prickle to her ear. "She's *electrified!*"

Huxley frowned. "Impossible. We just worked on her. This didn't happen when she was in surgery." His fingers worried through his grey hair, then he pointed to the five other beds in the unit, where patients unrelated to the bus crash recovered. "Examine the other patients and equipment and get someone from maintenance here. We've got to figure this out. Someone stay with her, but don't touch her unless absolutely necessary, understand?"

Three nurses nodded back at him, then Huxley ran to the nursing station, where he sped through a litany of numbers and explained the situation. Moments later, neurologist Dr. Adhira Tanti appeared, along with cardiologist Dr. Abebe "Abe" Nkosi and laboratory technician Jennifer Bailey.

At once, Abe strode to Anabelle's bed, readying his stethoscope. "You know that what you are suggesting is impossible, Huxley?" Abe regarded Huxley as if he were mad. Huxley himself suspected that Abe was not so far off.

"Of course it's impossible, but it's happening anyway. See for yourself," Huxley said, gesturing to Anabelle. "But be careful." He stepped back.

Abe's eyes went to Dr. Tanti, their shared look full of disbelief. With a shrug, the doctor placed the stethoscope against Anabelle's chest. "Ah!" he cried, flinging himself away from the patient in a mad scramble that knocked Anabelle's monitor and IV pump. His glasses fell to the floor. "Impossible! This can't be, Huxley. This can't. Her organs would malfunction. Her heart would fail. In her condition, the girl would *die*." Abe's hands went to his bald head, sliding down to the thick pads of his dark cheeks as he considered the mystery of the situation.

Dr. Tanti plucked Abe's glasses from beneath the supply cart and handed them to him. "You okay?" she asked.

Abe nodded and examined Anabelle's monitors. "Thank you, doctor, I'm fine. Just an unexpected shock. Our patient, though, I don't know what to make of this. Look at her readings. Heart rate, good. Blood pressure, systolic a little low but not especially concerning. Oxygen, in normal range. Respiration, good. Vitals and ECG, otherwise healthy. How curious." He thought then to touch the monitor, figuring the contraption would be electrified as well, but it wasn't.

"She can't deliver that magnitude of current. If anything, it's one of the other machines. Have you tried disconnecting her and going manual?" Dr. Tanti asked Huxley.

"Not yet," Huxley said. "I wanted your opinions first."

INTERFERENCE

The lab technician stepped forward holding her kit. Her eyes narrowed. "Have you tried wearing gloves? Maybe that would help."

Huxley scratched his chin. "It's worth a shot."

"Grab me a small, please Melissa," Dr. Tanti instructed the ICU's head nurse. "I'd like to try."

The nurse hurried away and returned with two pairs for the doctor. "Just in case," she said nervously.

Adhira accepted the gloves with a reassuring nod. The fit was snug, but twice she worked her fingers into their chambers and snapped the material at her wrist. As Huxley, Abe, the lab technician, and the nursing staff looked on, Adhira said, "There doesn't seem to be any issue from the machines, otherwise you would have been zapped when you touched them, Abe, but let's start there." She reached for the monitor and tapped it quickly. Getting no reaction, Adhira placed her palm on the side of the machine. "Nothing here," she reported to the group of onlookers.

Next, Adhira tapped Anabelle's IV pump, then her ventilator, then her catheter, receiving no response from any of the equipment. With pinched fingers, she squeezed Anabelle's IV line and felt nothing. Slowly, she went to the girl's head, where Adhira put two gloved fingers to the outside of her surgical bandage. Current raged through Adhira's fingertips, up the tendons of her wrist, along the muscles in her arm, her shoulder. Adhira shook violently, unable to remove herself from the shock until she was pulled away by Huxley, who gasped when he touched her.

Though she was a practicing Hindu, Adhira often fell into Christian cursing. "My God," she said to them. "What *is* this? How can this be? Huxley? Abe? The girl is electrified. What … what do you make this?" Her head spun toward the other doctors, then to the nurses, then to the lab tech.

41

"Someone call for me?" Morley Sanders, Garrett General's maintenance engineer, hastened into the room with his toolbox, breathing heavily from too many cigarettes and too many pounds. He wiped his forehead, blinking at them. Without pause, Huxley relayed Anabelle's condition to Morley, whose pinched face registered confusion, disbelief, and finally shock. He said, "Well, now, that can't be right. The *patient* can't be permanently electrified; we're good conductors of electricity, but to produce a continuous charge of that magnitude is impossible. The bed, though. Maybe there's a loose wire hitting it somewhere. Have you looked?"

The group searched. Eyes went behind the bed, over the monitor, around every light, every outlet, every cable.

"Nothing, huh?" Morley slid his tongue beneath his bottom lip, squinting at Anabelle. At length, he asked, "Mind if I see for myself? I got to tell you, I feel kind of silly about this. If it's all right with you, I'd like to see what kind of shock we're talking about here. It might help me figure out where it's coming from."

"I wouldn't recommend it," Abe said, crinkling his nose at Morley's outreached hand.

"Maybe with thicker gloves?" Dr. Tanti suggested, ignorant to the concepts of electrical study.

Morley said, "It can't be that bad, or she wouldn't still be here. I'm no doc, but her monitor doesn't scream danger to me. If you let me just …"

As Morley reached forward, Huxley captured his arm. "Three of us got the zing of our lives when we touched her. I can't let you do this."

"What do you expect me to do without knowing what it is I'm supposed to be doing? Look, you've warned me, so you're covered. I'll sign anything you want, but I can't help you unless I locate the source. *She* might not be it, for all we know. Maybe it's the bed. Maybe it's not, but you've got to let me see what we're up against before I go calling my guys about it." Morley puffed out his chest, feeling them discharge their collective superiority at him until he threw his hands up. "How am I supposed to help her then?"

Dr. Nkosi peeked at Huxley, whose reluctance was obvious. He said, "It's not safe for anyone to touch her but she's going to need care. We simply cannot care for her in this state, so we need to figure this out. The girl will die if we don't."

"Do you have gloves with you, Morley?" Adhira asked. "I wonder if a different material will work."

Morley dug into his toolbox and presented to them a pair of mechanical gloves. "They're more for light electrical work, but seeing that they're thick and your gloves didn't work, maybe I'll give these a try."

The doctors exchanged looks. Huxley's shoulders sagged. "Are you sure about this, Morley?"

"Hell, no, I'm not sure about this, but we've got to try, don't we? If I can just figure out where the source is, then we can help her." He drew on his gloves and, under their watchful eyes, approached Anabelle's bed. Morley led with his pinky finger, lowering the thick bulb of his knuckle slowly toward the footboard. Like a striking snake, he touched the metal so quickly his arm was a blur to their observing eyes. "Nothing wrong here," he reported to the doctors, now testing the headboard, now siderails, now the mattress itself. He let out the air he'd been holding, sensing that the doctors were pranking him.

"Careful," Abe warned as Morley's index finger drew toward Anabelle's wrist.

Morley pulled back once, twice, feeling ridiculous for doing so. He dared not look back, for he knew the doctors were waiting on him. Instead, he swiped the sweat from his brow and leaned closer still.

"Well," he quavered, "here goes nothing." Morley tapped Anabelle's wrist.

Lights surged in the room, brighter and brighter until the overhead tubes shattered in a great spray of glass through their covers and onto the people below. Glass flew into the lab tech's eyes, onto Dr. Nkosi's head, and onto Huxley's cheeks, where shards pricked him like needles and drew a saddle of bloody dots across his nose.

Though covered in glass, Anabelle remained unresponsive. Bleats of terror and cries of pain swept through the sterile environment, and soon other cries in other rooms were wakened throughout the unit. Monitors shrilled. Nurses ran to their patients. But the doctors stood, looking at Morley in a heap on the ground.

6

The wail of an alarm clock woke Dan Fogel. He hammered the thing quiet at least three times before the motel's reception rang him for his scheduled wake-up call. Then he rubbed his tired eyes and groaned to the bathroom, where he fell asleep on the toilet for another twenty minutes with his shorts around his ankles. It was his cellphone that woke him next. However tired he was, twenty-three years of police work ingrained in him the obligation to answer, at whatever time and during whatever circumstance. He pulled his shorts up, splashed cold water on his unshaven face, and toweled his hands on his way to the bedside table. "Fogel," he coughed into the phone.

"Dan? You up?" Constable Sarah Cardinal's voice was muffled by the clatter of voices, the clicking of keyboards, and the ringing phones.

Dan picked the alarm clock he'd battered from the floor and spied the time. "I'll be there in twenty, Sarah. Hold them for me, will you?"

"Will do, boss," she said. "I'll have your coffee ready."

His shower was too quick, and the water was too cold, but Dan let it wake him and prepare him for another awful day. Yesterday, he hadn't even had his first sip of coffee when the gates of hell opened and unleashed its terrible fury onto

45

his city. Forty-two dead and another barely alive. He sighed into the water, then took some into his mouth, drinking, until at last he turned the water off. He wrapped a towel around his waist and turned. The man looking back at him was old now, with dark hollows under his eyes, and deeply grooved skin on his forehead, on his cheeks. The grey hair, once passable for the suave fringe of a cool hipster, was now like that of an unkempt fisherman, lost long at sea.

Before Brandy slid him the divorce papers, Dan had healthy color to his cheeks. He was lean and well-kept and turned as many heads as his team arrested. Now, after two months in the Sunset Motel and copious amounts of greasy takeout, the man in the mirror looked pudgy and nauseated.

He slid a comb through his hair, wondering what Brandy was doing. If she was still waking to Shane, or if she had moved on to another man with the intent of incapacitating him too. Dan rolled his shoulders, stretched the tension from his neck, and dressed quietly, wishing Tom Widlow were still alive and still chief and could handle this for him. Tom's death of lung cancer six months before lavished a sorrow on the department so deep, Dan still hadn't recovered. How to heal an ailing team from the loss of one of the greatest leaders of all time? Dan didn't know; he only knew that he could never fill the footprints Tom left.

Outside, the sky was gray and heavy with moisture. Umbrella-swinging pedestrians hurried to their places while the last currents of morning traffic slowly abated. In his cruiser, Dan quickly reviewed his schedule while the vehicle warmed. Another day of hell awaited him, and he sighed deeply as he ran through his press conference notes.

Already late, he closed his book and was about to pull from the parking lot when something thumped against his door. He depressed his brake and peered into the back seat.

Again, the door was struck, but Dan saw nothing and no one that could explain the sound. He set the car in park and curled his fingers over the door handle, ready to inspect the exterior of the vehicle, when the wide, snapping mouth of a German Shepherd smashed against the glass mere inches from his face.

Dan cried out as the dog hit the cruiser again, scraping the window with its teeth. The dog's tongue slithered wildly against the glass, and soon the animal's mouth was bloody and one of its teeth broke loose. Enraged barks and the clattering of nails drew the attention of onlookers, and now unprotected pedestrians ran for shelter, pointing at the breeze of fur warring against the police car.

Dan engaged the radio. "Dispatch, this is 222."

Crackling came from the radio. "Go ahead, 222."

The dog flew at Dan's face, shaking the glass. "I've got a 10-91V out at the Sunset Motel on Brighton. The animal has me trapped in my vehicle."

"Sunset Motel on Brighton. Copy."

Dan looked at the dog, presently rearing for another strike. "He's going to bust into my vehicle. 10-33. Repeat. 10-33."

Clutching the radio on his shoulder, Dan's other hand found his taser. Inching backward, the dog snarled, yapped and braced its paws, its mean eyes targeting the space behind the fragile glass where Dan trembled. Slowly, he unbuttoned his holster.

Just then, a door behind him opened and Dan saw in his mirror a small boy. The boy looked at the dog attacking Dan's cruiser and froze. From the open door came no adult to usher the boy away, and Dan knew that if he didn't do something, the dog might go for the boy. As if sensing Dan's

47

thought, the German Shepherd's ears pricked up and his focus moved from Dan and to the boy. Too slowly the boy backed up, and too quickly the dog turned its body, so Dan did the only thing he could think of. With the flick of his thumb, he turned the siren on.

The dog yelped as a flash of blue and white lights stung its eyes and the heavenly-high wail of Dan's siren punctured its ears. At once the animal calmed.

From across the street, a woman came running. "Tally!" she cried. "Tally, you get back here!"

Her shrill voice carried through the sound of the siren and through Dan's closed vehicle. He worried that the woman's panic might stir the animal again, but the rage that previously thrummed inside it was gone. Obediently the dog called Tally wagged his tail and trotted to his owner, a contented tongue lolling from the side of his mouth.

Dan unrolled his window an inch and watched the dog submit to the woman as she connected a leash to its collar. "Your dog almost got me there, ma'am," he said through the opening.

"I'm so sorry, officer. I'm so sorry. He's usually not like this. Honest. I don't know what got into him. He's never done anything like this before." Her small face drew up to Dan's window, where she saw patches of Tally's fur and spots of Tally's blood on the glass. Squinting, she inspected her dog's smeared saliva on the widow. The woman's fingers went to her open mouth. "Oh! Oh no! Oh, officer! Did he—?"

Dan nodded, nervous as he opened his door and stepped out of his cruiser. "I'm fine, ma'am, but you need to keep a leash on him. I have to ask, was he spooked by something? Or maybe he hates law enforcement? We get some of those every now and then, but you don't look like the type to train

INTERFERENCE

a dog like that." Staying close to his open door, Dan regarded the animal curiously. Tally sat panting, tilting his head up at Dan, then he whined and rolled onto his back.

"He wants you to pet him," the woman said with a tremble in her voice.

"Two minutes ago, he wanted to eat my face," Dan told her, puzzled.

Large, worried eyes stared back at him. "Am I in trouble, officer?"

The dog whined, his rump rubbing against the pavement as his tail wagged. It *looked* friendly, Dan admitted to himself, and maybe because he was tired, maybe because yesterday's events had knocked the sense out of him, he knelt down and ran his fingers over the dog's belly. Soft yips of pleasure came from its mouth, and before Dan could remove his hand, the dog licked his wrist.

"He *seems* peaceful enough," Dan said. "But I'd like to have our animal control pay you a visit and get their thoughts on him. If they clear him, and if you cover the damage to my door, I think we're settled. Does that sound fair to you?"

The woman nodded, and Dan recorded her information. Sirens rushed nearby, flooding the parking lot with more red and blue lights as the help Dan had called for finally arrived. He silenced the sound with a wave of his hand and bid the woman a better day. Then he returned to his car and called Sarah to apprise her of his situation and tell her that he was on his way. He would not regret using the dog as an excuse for being late.

As expected, the press was savage. Where previous conferences had the usual lineup of local reporters, today's conference produced affiliate journalists in droves for papers

49

from Toronto, Montreal, and Ottawa to cities as far away as Edmonton, Vancouver, and even Detroit and Chicago. It was a spectacle, and Dan was in the center of it. In other cities, homegrown reporters might engage sensitively in the wake of tragedy, but Garrett's own Jessica Chung, keenly aware of extra cameras and wider audience, drew upon her holding in the city and dragged the ordeal into something more appropriate for a referee and a three-count. Why hadn't Dan had any answers yet? she asked. Why had it taken so long to recover the bodies? Would more people have survived if Dan's team had responded sooner? Why was there police presence around the lone survivor? Did Dan really believe he was doing enough? Would former Chief Tom Widlow have handled the situation any differently?

While Jessica hadn't used Dan's actual name, she might as well have bent him over and kicked him in the ass in front of everyone, then stabbed him in the gut with one of her stilettos. She was brutal, and by the end of the conference, Dan had a raging headache.

When he finally lumbered into his office, Sarah rushed in and thrust a glass of water and two Tylenol before him. "What a bitch," she said, watching Dan swallow his pills. She took his glass and shook her head. "I don't know how you do it, Dan. If I were you, I would have kicked that woman's ass out the second she opened her mouth."

He sighed into his chair, slumping his chin onto his cupped hands. "That's why they pay me the big bucks. *Chief Shit-Putter-Upper.* I should get a new nametag, don't you think?"

"You deserve a fucking medal for that one. How does she come up with that?"

INTERFERENCE

Dan shrugged. Twenty-three years on the police force and most of his interactions with journalists had been amenable, but since the Holy Redeemer cold case had been solved after a two-decade delay, there were suggestions of information withheld that could have otherwise prevented the deaths of three more people. While Phil Beecher and his team at the *Garrett Gazette* were understanding of the precinct's position, Garrett's CGTV, a small-market independent station with a staff of seven and audience consisting mostly of seniors and other isolates, took the department's reserve as a slight against media. In the three years since, their ruined relationship had the station taking every opportunity to portray the Garrett Police as incapable, incompetent, self-important and—the worst, Dan thought—as generally unconcerned with the wellbeing of the city's people.

He'd hoped that, given the scale of yesterday's accident, Jessica Chung would have deferred to the tenets of empathy and understanding, but she came at him with her barbed questions and didn't stop until a reporter from the *National Post* suggested none too delicately that Jessica herself might need counselling. The collective chuckling that filled the room was the only bright spot in his day, and he recalled it now, if only to soothe his headache.

He said, "Everyone has their defects. My mother used to tell that to me and my brothers whenever she'd hear of one of us getting in trouble at school or failing an assignment. She'd say, 'Everyone has their defects, but the winners turn them into strengths.' I'll always remember that. Ms. Chung might give *me* heartburn, but she's someone's winner, I think. Besides, that station is going to hate us no matter what we say, so there's no reason to poke them, if you get me."

51

A response was on Sarah's tongue, but then something whacked against Dan's window. When he swung his chair around, he saw a patch of feathers stuck to the glass.

"I'd say that makes at least two of us with a headache today." He leaned toward the window and laughed to his constable, then jumped back as another bird hit the space five inches in front of his eyes. It slid down the window and fell to the ground.

Sarah came beside him and looked out. Yesterday's wind had subsided to a slight breeze and the afternoon sun was already beginning its descent, but the field behind the station was otherwise bright and calm.

"Must be the weather," she said, and then she was blinking at the face of a duck headed straight for the window. "I think it's going to—" she warned when the duck hit the glass.

Dan stood and they both stumbled backward as the impact split the glass into a spiderweb of cracks.

"You got some bird food on the windowsill?" Sarah asked.

Dan shook his head. "But the way this day is going, I wouldn't be surprised if an elephant came next." He picked up his phone and called Marty's Glass, explaining the need for an urgent repair. "Put something on it. I don't care what. Anything that will keep the birds away."

"You're the sixth one this morning," Marty told him. "I don't know what's happening out there, but it seems like all those fellas want to be inside today. I got two different schools with geese inside them, the TD bank on Weller was hit by an eagle, Boomer's front window was shattered by a crow, and two apartments on Mitton were damaged by sparrows. Sparrows! Can you believe that? Something's in the air, I tell you."

"Have you seen anything like this before, Marty?" Dan asked, his previously receding headache now resisting the pills.

"Not in many years," Marty told him. "Fifteen or twenty years ago we had quite a few strikes when that Hurricane Ivan ran through the coast down there. Something about it affected the air currents up here that'd done it to them. Busiest month we've ever had." He was chewing on the phone, and Dan pulled the receiver away from his ear.

"Maybe it's that Xavier storm near Texas," Dan reasoned aloud, remembering the news he read before he'd finally fallen asleep in the morning. "But I think it's already over, isn't it?"

"Nor sure about that." Marty swallowed. "It's hurricane season anyway. There's always a storm somewhere, but if it keeps going like this, I'm going to run out of stock. Ah, well. That's how it goes sometimes, huh? Anyway, I won't keep you, Dan. I'll have Tina measure the window this morning, but we likely won't be ready to install until tomorrow if it's standard, a week if it's not. We can close it up in the meantime, though," Marty said helpfully.

"As soon as you can get it done, Marty, we'd be grateful," Dan said.

"You got it," the man responded, and Dan ended the call.

Occupied with the phone, Dan hadn't realized Sarah was still in his office until she cleared her throat. "You want me to ask Jesse about this?" Her jaw worked at a piece of gum she had been chewing since she entered his office, and she blew a small bubble that popped almost instantly.

Sarah's husband, Jesse Cardinal, was the city's only animal control officer. Occasionally, such as in the case of a

53

wandering bear or moose that strayed too far from home, protection officers from the province might assist Jesse, but not for something as small as a few birds.

Dan said, "Ask him about the birds and have him do an animal check at this address for me." He held a small slip of paper between two fingers and gave it to Sarah, who regarded the paper with a raised eyebrow.

"The dog?" she asked.

Dan nodded. "Yup. Tell Jesse to be careful. That dog would have torn me apart had he got to me. One minute he was wild, but then … Lord help me if he wasn't calm and friendly and wanted a belly rub. I don't know what to make of it, and I don't know what that dog's going to be like when Jesse sees it, but make sure he's prepared. Tell him to bring Johnny if he can."

The constable rolled her eyes. "He hates working with his brother, you know that."

"I don't know why he doesn't get off his ass and hire him already. He needs the help and he's got the budget. Nepotism aside, Johnny's a good worker. He was great when we had him over the summer."

One of five interns the department had engaged during the recent summer months, Johnny Cardinal proved himself to be responsible, eager, and showed an infinite willingness to work hard. Unlike many graduates, he was flexible and self-motivated, and his ability to intelligently engage with Aboriginal communities was a great benefit to the department. Barely over twenty, the kid was mature and exhibited a great deal of promise. Dan himself liked the kid, but he also understood Jesse's rationale for not wanting to hire him for animal control: Jesse was good, but he was also tragically narcissistic.

"He's young, Sarah. Right now he's puffing his chest, but that'll blow over eventually. Hell, I was probably the same at his age."

"Impossible," Sarah disagreed.

Dan shrugged. "Whatever the case, Jesse's going to need help. I need this done today."

With a reluctant sigh, Sarah swung her small body around and left Dan's office, her ponytail swinging rhythmically against her back. As she left, Dan's mind swept again to the vision of the bus in the water and to the length of divers, firemen, paramedics, and constables carrying the bodies up the embankment, and then to the crowd of sobbing citizens. He pinched the bridge of his nose and spread his thumbs hard and wide over his eyebrows, trying to squeeze the images away, but they wouldn't budge. Those thoughts, still there, still lurking, intermingled with impressions of snapping dogs and charging fowl. Bodies, beaks, and barks clashed inside Dan's head, and it took the ringing of his phone to finally yank him from the melee.

"Fogel," he answered distractedly.

Over the line there was a murmur of low chatter and the mechanical sounds of steady beeps and a powerful ventilation system. "Dan," Greg Huxley breathed steadily into the phone. "We have a problem."

7

In the dim light of his office, Greg Huxley flexed his fingers around his stress ball and looked out over the grounds of the hospital, three floors down. Though it was not yet dinner, the day had grown dark, and Huxley could see the glow of lit cigarettes in the hospital's small smoking area in front of the emergency department, near the parking lot. He watched them for a time, seeing the intensity of the lights grow, recede, snuff out—when the flames of other lighters and matches spread their glow before new faces desperate for relief.

Somewhere a man cried, and Huxley returned to his desk and Anabelle Cheever's file. Had it not been for the issue of the girl's electrical charge, there was little doubt the girl would live. The surgery was successful, and her vitals were strong. Even the slight dip in Anabelle's blood pressure had remedied itself. For now, she was an induced coma, as was common practice after the surgery she'd endured, but eventually the medications would have to be reduced and Anabelle would have to be wakened. Huxley estimated that would happen sometime in the next few days, perhaps a week, but the more immediate problem was how to care for Anabelle when she couldn't be touched.

INTERFERENCE

His mind turned to the image of Morley on the ground. How quickly the man had fallen. As Huxley touched the tender abrasions on his face, he reflected on his fortune of not ending up on a gurney like Morley. He, too, would live, but given the man's health, the cardiac arrest he'd suffered would likely mean immediate retirement once he recovered.

Never before had a patient stumped Huxley like Anabelle Cheever. Most conditions could eventually be reasoned by science, but no matter which studies he returned to, and no matter which colleagues he consulted with, Huxley found no answer or even hint of an answer for Anabelle's situation. At a complete loss as to how to proceed, he spent the last two hours emailing his familiar counterparts in Toronto, Montreal, Vancouver, Philadelphia, and New York and waited for their responses. He wasn't expecting much, but anything they gave him would be more than he had now. Lastly, he called Dan Fogel both to explain the situation of the lone survivor and to engage a protection detail to the ICU after one of the nurses found reporter Jessica Chung nosing around the nursing station after she had been escorted out only twenty minutes before.

He waited for Dan now, closing his eyes for a moment when his phone rang. Three minutes later, a tired-looking Dan Fogel was escorted to his office by one of the security guards, who quickly and wordlessly departed.

"You've seen better days," Dan said, shaking Huxley's hand.

"As have you," the doctor responded. "Maybe we call it a career and hit the road to Vegas?"

Dan groaned. "I wish, but I'm sure the shit would find us there, too."

57

"Isn't that the truth," Huxley agreed. "Can I get you anything? Coffee? Water? Something stronger? I don't keep anything in my desk, but my colleague in pediatrics does." He winked at Dan.

"Wish I could, but it would probably put me out, I'm so goddamned tired. Haven't seen this kind of hell since that fire, but this is worse, so much worse." The quick silence was heavy on them, and the two men sighed. Dan said, "It's good to see you, Greg, but I have to admit, I'm not sure I believe what you told me on the phone. Outside of the movies, I've never heard of such a thing."

"I hear you. It *would* make much more sense on a screen, but right now it's on the fifth floor in our ICU. We had to move three other patients from that unit to our cardiac unit and fly two to Toronto just to make room. I'm not making this up. I wish to God I was. Her whole body is a live wire." The doctor's cheeks puffed wide as he blew out a long breath.

Dan saw the seriousness in Huxley's face but couldn't reconcile the story with the factions of reality. "I want to believe you, Greg, but it sounds like fiction to me. You're telling me she's a conductor of electricity?"

Huxley shook his head. "We're *all* conductors of electricity, but from what we can see," he paused to steady his next words, "she seems to be a *generator* of it."

"You've got to be kidding me."

Huxley pulled at his bottom lip. "Originally, we thought the charge was coming from her monitor, but now we're sure that isn't the case. Nothing from the IV pump, either. The only other thing connected to her body is her collection bag. I don't know about you, but I've never heard of electric piss, and we can change the bag, no problem."

58

INTERFERENCE

"Can I see her?" Dan asked.

"I insist you do. Maybe if you believe me, you can wrangle up your own kind of help and figure out what the hell is going on. I tell you, Dan, I'm this close to calling the Feds." He thrust his thumb and forefinger out to the police chief.

Dan leaned backward in his chair, recoiling at the idea of outside intervention. While he felt that good policework required teamwork, he also knew that inputs with ego *and* superiority often halted progress, sometimes completely. To Huxley, he said, "If you feel the need, Greg, I'm all for it, but remember what they did when you called them in for that Smith boy? The one with that stuff on his leg that was making him hallucinate? They damn near shut down the city when the kid just had a reaction from that pit in Tar Vat Bay. They wanted us to block a five-mile radius around the city. What a nightmare that was."

"Terrible way to end a family vacation."

Huxley recalled that the kid hadn't told his parents he'd fallen near the tar pit, so it was three days later when they returned home that the boy began to hallucinate. The boy was at the age where baths were avoided at all costs, so the toxins had plenty of time to leach into his skin. Unaware, Huxley had ordered every blood and diagnostic test he could think of, but they had all returned inconclusive. Eventually the boy began to improve, but then his little sister, who had no previous symptoms, fell into a coma shortly after he was released from the hospital. Their parents had also developed nausea so severe they had to be hospitalized. Huxley had consulted with professionals across the continent, and when investigations inside the Smith family home provided no further information, he alerted the Public Health Agency.

59

Concerned with the possibility of virulent transmission, the PHA had just convinced the minister of health to authorize a lockdown on the city just as the source of the trouble was discovered. Not only had the Smith boy fallen into toxic tar, but his little sister had collected several containers of the material during a family hike. The "black slime" she subsequently took home and played with led to the hospitalization of her entire family.

Until Anabelle Cheever, the Smith family had been his most difficult professional experience, and he now called on that experience. "We both want to avoid that, Dan. It's absolutely a last resort, but we can't discount it completely. The law compels us to do what is right, no?"

Dan said. "We'll do what's necessary, but let me ask you this: *is* she contagious? Whatever she has, or whatever is happening to her, are any of your other patients like that? Any symptoms of ... electrification?" Immediately Dan felt ridiculous for saying the word, for playing into a situation that made no rational sense.

"No, but that doesn't mean it can't happen."

"If you ask me, none of this can happen."

"You're right on that one, but it is, and we have to deal with it, which leads me to the main reason I called you. Chung's all over this place. She's practically in the nurse's laps. We've asked her to leave and had her escorted out, but she just keeps coming back. She snatched a stack of patient files right off the fifth-floor nursing station, and our guys had to trap her in the stairwell to get them back."

On the other side of Huxley's desk, Dan's eyebrows went up. "You still have her?"

The doctor shook his head. "No. She sweet-talked a new guard who let her go. He's looking for a job, if you want him."

"I'll pass."

There was a shuffling of feet in the hallway outside Huxley's door, but he ignored it. "Ms. Cheever needs some protection, I'm afraid. Can you swing it?"

"We can do that." Dan reached into his pocket. His fingers fluttered quickly over his phone as he typed a message to Sarah, then he looked up at Huxley. "I'll pay a visit to the station, too. Sometimes a warning in uniform is all it takes. Even TV folks have hearts if you look close enough."

"I appreciate that. I—"

Beeps and bells and bellows rang out from the other side of Huxley's door, then the doctor's phone rang. He looked at the number on the screen and lifted the receiver to his ear. He hadn't uttered a single word when the voice on the other side of the line hollered loud enough for Dan to hear. *Everywhere ... cats ... inside.* Slowly, slowly, Huxley drew the phone away from his ear. Then he rose from his desk and went to the door. Sensing trouble, the police chief followed the doctor into the hallway, where bullets of fur were zipping down the corridor, flashing into rooms, bounding over chairs, and thrashing into panicked nurses and horrified patients.

"What the bloody hell?!" Dan cried. He thought to draw his gun but quickly holstered it. Instead, he whipped out his phone and called Sarah, directing her to send a squad of officers and animal control to Garrett General. He stepped back into Huxley's office as a large tabby zoomed past his legs, a length of IV tubing dangling from its mouth.

"Who let them in?" Huxley shouted down the hall, but everyone was too busy fending off cats to answer.

Dan shook an orange cat off his leg.

One of the nurses tossed her apple juice at a charging Persian and it scrambled away. This gave Huxley an idea.

61

"The supply closet!" he called to Dan and led him six doors away to a public restroom, beside which was a small room.

The doctor fumbled with his key, glad he had had the foresight to take them from his drawer. Growls and hisses and shrieks resounded behind them, and soon the men were armed with mops and a bucket full of water, which they now rolled out in front of them. A whizz of black shot toward them. Huxley dunked the end of his mop into the water and whipped it at the cat. Great splashes of water hit the cat's face, and its nails skittered against the floor as it retreated, meowing angrily.

Dan saw the hasty withdrawal and dipped his own mop into the bucket; now both the doctor and the police chief were dashing down the halls, swinging their wet weapons this way, that way, corralling the wayward animals into a corner near the elevators. Without warning, a bell rang and the farthest doors opened to the faces of two elderly women swaddling large bouquets of flowers in their arms.

"Gah!" one of the women cried, dropping her flowers as seven cats rushed into the compartment. Quickly, she pulled her stupefied companion from the elevator just as the doors closed on the frenzied felines.

Huxley ran to the nursing station and hailed help to Elevator B at all levels, then he ran back to the elevator Dan was guarding.

A breathless nurse rushed to them and clutched his wrist. "You got them all, thank God, but we've got more on the fifth and maybe a dozen in the ER. Can you get them?" He bent forward with his hands on his thighs, panting. Blood dripped from his left wrist, where he'd been bitten by a cat.

"You all right, José?" Huxley asked him.

The nurse nodded. "But I can't leave the floor. Three of them attacked Brenda, and she's getting treated for a severe

INTERFERENCE

allergic reaction, so we'll be short until we get cover in. You go, I'll watch the elevator," he said.

In the middle of the corridor at the nurses' station, the phone began to ring, but all the nurses were in patient rooms or receiving medical treatment themselves. From behind the desk, something began to beep, but that, too, went unanswered.

Then the instinct which had carried him through many years of tough police work surged through Dan. He instructed the nurse. "Call security and have them lock the elevators down, but make sure there are no people inside; then watch this door, and whatever you do, don't let them out if they make their way back. Get a bucket of water; that will send them scrambling. Hux, we need to stick together. Which floor has more people?"

"The first, our ER, of course. The fifth is where our ICU is, but we only have one patient there: Ms. Cheever." His eyes swung over the police chief, who was suddenly overcome with indecision.

Finally, Dan said, "We can't leave her."

He led Huxley back to the supply closet to fill another bucket of water. Even inside, the sirens sounded close, so near to the hospital that they seemed part of the facility itself. Sarah's voice erupted from the radio on Dan's chest, and he knew that help had arrived.

"Dr. Huxley! Dr. Huxley!" José rushed from the nursing desk waving his arms as Dan and Huxley rolled their buckets out of the closet. "You"—he breathed heavily— "you don't have to go to the fifth anymore."

"Why not?" Dan asked the nurse, whose wrist was still bleeding freely.

"They're all dead, sir," José told him. "The cats. I think they've been electrocuted."

63

8

From inside Sylvia Baker's sleeping body, Pandora felt the itch. The feeling crawled over her like a newly hatched sac of spiders. She felt a tingle in places that never tingled and prickles in places that never prickled.

The sensation was uncomfortable not only because it provoked the same grating irritation of human mosquito bites in hard-to-scratch places, but also because the feeling portended an upheaval she'd experienced only once before, with the medicine man.

She'd made the mistake of taking his witchcraft lightly and remembered now how he had whispered to a crow, sourced its cunning, and targeted its dark flock upon her. Until then, Pandora had been able to control anything with a heartbeat, anything that breathed, but the medicine man had siphoned that power with his chantings and burnings and swingings, and then she'd felt what she thought she would never feel: discomfort. The birds had started slowly, nagging at her spaces, pulling her togetherness apart, and, unfamiliar with the sensation as she was, Pandora had actually thought it signified a strengthening of her power. How naïve.

While she came to understand that she was immortal, she also knew that her immortality was predicated on human acquisition: she needed hosts to survive. Her existence

64

outside of the human body was great, but eventually she became malnourished and ineffective. When the itch first came, she thought that perhaps whatever deity made her had finally put in what was left out, and that she might never need a host again. She realized her foolishness the moment the itch became pain, a realization that almost came too late. Presently, she sought outside of herself, looking for the medicine man, but he was far away in Africa, where his powers couldn't reach her. No, some other force was working to disconnect Pandora, but she wasn't sure who or *what* that was. She only knew that it was close.

Centuries ago, after her experience with the medicine man, she would have fled from whatever lurked after her. But Harold was gone, and Pandora was alone. He was the first one she'd ever really grieved, and that sorrow had to go *somewhere*. She would channel her heartache, that terrible thing, first into discovery and then into, well, death—of course. That would make her feel better. It always did.

While she didn't necessarily require rest, rest she did once Sylvia's son Troy left the hospital. She would have preferred him to stay longer so she could get better acquainted with the darkness she knew was within him, but something about the bus accident gave Pandora the rare sensation of exhaustion. Death was her fuel, but the fuel in Garrett was low-grade and unsatisfying, so Pandora settled more deeply into Sylvia's body where she might slowly recover.

She wondered at her problem until an unfamiliar stirring rose inside her, constricting her cells and then stretching them apart. Near. Far. Tight. Loose. Up. Down. At amusement parks before she weakened a cable or loosened a belt or removed a bolt, she had seen riders experience what she now felt. Their vomiting and the bile coloring of their skin would be Pandora's too if she were of the flesh. She did feel their loss of control, however, and that brought on a terrible fear, inadvertently making Sylvia shake. The woman stirred but didn't wake, so Pandora reached outward, seeking the source of their problem. Out and away and through walls and around corners, up staircases, down elevator shafts, inside roofs and through doors went Pandora's ethereal fingers. Kneading, exploring, she investigated. The response was feral, frenzied in a manner that made little sense, as if a filter had been placed over her unfailing sight. The interference was jarring.

That's what it was—interference. With the medicine man, she could still see, could still hear, but this new thing, whatever it was, obscured her. Another deity, perhaps? God coming to banish her? Pandora pushed at the thing, but it didn't budge. Again she raged at it, collecting all her energy and one, two, fifteen, thirty times she attacked the thing, but the thing went on as if Pandora had done nothing at all. In her normal state, the thing would have been obliterated by such an effort, but in her emaciated condition, it was like bubbles hitting a mountain; nothing moved, and Pandora was left winded. She collapsed into herself, recovering with nibbles of Sylvia's soul, when the door slowly opened and something entered.

Light sliced into the darkened room as the door fell wide by the rush of a small animal. Pandora, in Sylvia, sat up. The woman rubbed her eyes, swinging her new attention to the door, the foot of the bed, the chair in front of the far wall.

"Hello?" Sylvia Baker said. From under her bed, something hissed. "Hello?" Sylvia said again, pulling her blankets to her chin.

INTERFERENCE

Awaking alone in a hospital room was bad enough. Awaking alone in a hospital room with a dead arm and an animal hissing under the bed was much, much worse. She reached for her right hand and pulled her arm away from the edge of the bed and over her stomach, then she reached for the call button hanging from a cord near her left ear.

Growling erupted beneath her. Sylvia shrieked. She pawed the button and accidentally knocked it off the bed. It cracked against the floor.

Skittering over the floor towards her feet, the animal snarled.

"Help," Sylvia croaked, but her voice was still not strong enough to yell. "Help," she whispered again.

The blanket was tugged from her hands. Then the stomach-emptying sound of nails scraping against metal told her the thing was climbing onto her bed. She looked at her monitor and began slapping buttons. Green lines blipped. Blue lights flicked. White numbers vanished and returned, vanished and returned, a high tone rang out and angry sounds rose forth from the thing crawling up the foot of her bed.

Sylvia pounded the monitor again and again until the tones from the machine were bleeping and ringing, and she was sure someone would come running. A paw rose and gripped the mattress, and for a moment, Sylvia tilted her head at the inconsequential thing. But when a second paw seized the blanket, it brought with it bright spots of blood that soaked into the sheet. Then a cat's head sprang up and dropped someone else's finger beside her foot.

She screamed. Fear thundered up her throat and she scrambled her half-paralyzed body off the bed, taking her monitor and IV bags with her. The crash sent the animal away, then it turned and paced toward her. Too slowly, she

67

tried crawling away from the cat, but it was on her, pawing at her face, cutting into her neck, scraping the delicate skin from her arms. Sylvia drew her knees to her chest and covered the top of her head. She closed her eyes and prayed. Then she felt wetness on her face and the cat scrambled away.

Sylvia looked up and saw the silhouette of a man with a mop in the doorway. Seconds later, another man entered the room with a looped pole. Her eyes adjusted to the brightness behind them, and then she recognized two former students of Westgate Elementary: Dan Fogel and Jesse Cardinal. Even with her stroke, her memory hadn't failed her, and she was thankful for the police chief and the animal control officer.

"Oh, thank you! Thank you!" she cried into the floor. "Thank you," she whimpered again.

Dan hit a switch on the wall and light flooded the room. Crouched low, Jesse dashed past him to the supply cart in the corner, under which the cat huddled. It hissed, spat, growled, *moaned.* Jesse leapt back as paws sliced at his foot, then he carefully leaned over with his pole and moved it toward the cat while Dan blocked the doorway in case the animal decided to bolt.

"You ready?" Jesse asked without looking away.

"I've got the door," Dan said.

With her head against the floor, Sylvia had a clear and terrible view of the cat. It looked at her with bulging, mean eyes and then swung its head to Jesse's pole at its back. The supply cart shook as the cat went wild. The pole whipped in Jesse's hands, up, down, back, lashing around while the cat struck at it, hit it, bit the loop with its bloody jaws. The supply cart tipped over and then a quick step forward gave Jesse a better angle. He lunged the loop over the cat's neck and yanked the pole back to tighten his hold. Minutes later, Jesse

68

secured the cat in a carrier and hauled it to his van with the others, then went back inside to collect his pole.

"It's okay Mrs. Baker, it's going to be okay," Dan comforted Sylvia as Jesse entered. Over his shoulder, Dan said, "See if you can find her a nurse, will you? There's got to be someone who can help her."

Jesse nodded and was gone.

Tenderly, Dan raised Sylvia so that she sat with her back against the wall. He was untangling her IV line when two nurses sped into the room and lifted Sylvia from the floor.

"We've got you ma'am," the nurse with a messy ponytail said. Her hair slid over her eyes as she helped her partner settle Sylvia back onto the bed, and she ineffectually blew upward until her hands were free enough to tuck it back behind her ears. "Now that the circus has departed, I think we'll all have a better night. Let's get you checked out. Do you have any pain?"

Sylvia's bones ached and she rubbed her hip, whimpering when her fingers found painful spots. The nurses tugged at Sylvia's hospital gown to examine her injuries. The men looked away and Sylvia saw them begin to retreat, but she held up her good arm to stop them.

"I might have died if it weren't for you two," she told them. "Thank you, boys, for saving me."

Her voice crackled and she began to cry. Inside, Pandora laughed, knowing that one flick in the cat's direction would have flattened it. Of course, Pandora was unaffected. The cat had caused her no pain, no suffering, but Sylvia's suffering gave her much relief. She felt ten times stronger, exponentially more energetic. With a shaky hand, Sylvia reached out to the men.

Dan strode to the bed and squeezed her fingers. "My pleasure. All those days I ran across the street when I was younger, you probably saved my life at least a hundred times. Might have been flattened if it weren't for you. And I prefer dogs anyway." He smiled down at her.

Jesse, too, stepped to Sylvia's bed. His past experience with the crossing guard had been fleeting, as his mother preferred to drive him to school when he was a boy; but the times he did encounter Sylvia, she had always given him a warm smile and gently guided him and his friends across the street while inquiring about their day. He now regarded her for the first time since arriving at the hospital, her thin hair, her droopy face, her gray eyes, and his outstretched hand snapped back. From inside Jesse arose a warning about the woman. The appreciative, dimpled cheeks that were meant to be kind felt false, so much so that they caused him to flinch. Whether it was the Spirits or his own intuition, he didn't know, but Jesse sensed a great and terrible evil inside the woman.

Her arm reached further for him, her spindly fingers seeking his own, but Jesse bowed with tight lips. "I've got cat pee all over me, sorry," he said quickly, and slid out of the room.

Well, this is interesting, Pandora thought. *Jesse* ... She reached outward ... *Cardinal. Jesse Cardinal. Iroquois. Oneida. Son of the Standing Stone. Nature's own. Strong spirit girdled with human flesh. Definitely a challenge.* Was *he* the cause of her trouble? Did *he* call the animals to insanity? It wasn't Pandora, though she did think their frenzy was entertaining, even delicious, but the conduct suggested another power at work. This she couldn't have. While the nurses worked on Sylvia, Dan excused himself from the room. Then Pandora, too, drifted out the door, down the hallway to the parking lot where the police chief was trying to catch up with Jesse.

"Hold up!" Dan panted after him. "Jesse, wait!"

Jesse opened the door to his van and flung the catch pole inside. He paced, rubbing his temples, smoothing the dark thatch of hair that hung below his neck. His shoulders were tense as he swung to look at Dan.

"Why'd you take off like that?" Dan asked, pressing the stitch from his side.

"That woman's evil."

Dan's frowned. "What are you talking about? She's probably the sweetest woman in Garrett. It's been a wild night, Jesse, but I think you should go home and get some rest."

Jesse shook his head. "I felt it, Dan. I *felt* it. There's something not right with her." He saw the skepticism on Dan's face and when the other man didn't speak, Jesse sighed. "I don't know, maybe it's the shitstorm that's got to me. That crash yesterday. The cats today. I mean, you ever see anything like this? Thirty cats just up and decide to attack a hospital? How the fuck did they get up all those floors?" He wiped his forehead. "I've been doing this for, what, thirteen, fourteen years now, and I tell you, I've never seen anything like it. Johnny said that the ones on the top floor were all fried up like they were electrocuted. Is that right?"

"That's right," Dan said quietly.

"You don't seem surprised."

"With all that's happened over the last two days, I wouldn't be surprised if Jesus brought coffee to the station."

Jesse's face flexed with irritation. "You want to tell me what the fuck is going on, Dan? Do you know something?

My brother was up there, for God's sake. What if something happened to him?"

Wind whispered over the men, sweeping cool air up their sleeves, down their collars, over their faces. Darkness overtook the day's gleam, and little could be seen beyond the bright cones of the lamp posts—but still Dan looked out into the field surrounding the hospital. With a great exhalation of breath, he said, "I don't know what's happening, Jesse, honestly I don't. There's a situation on the fifth floor that we can't explain, and I don't know if it has anything to do with the animals behaving the way they are, but I suspect it might. I can't tell you why because I don't know myself. Right now, I have no answers to explain any of it, but I promise you that I'm going to try, and I'll need your help for that."

"Go on," Jesse said.

"Do you have any guesses as to why those cats behaved the way they did?" Dan asked, but Jesse shook his head. "How 'bout the birds that hit my window this morning? That dog that attacked my car?"

Hair blew over Jesse's eyes and he raked it back. "Your guess is as good as mine. I checked out the dog like you asked, but, honestly, he was the friendliest thing I'd ever seen. Took some blood, so we'll see if the vet finds anything there. As for the birds,"—he shrugged— "maybe it's the weather. I've heard that radio signals can mix them up. Hormones can do that too, but we're talking different species, so I don't think that's it. Maybe it's something in the water? Have you looked into it?"

"Not yet," Dan admitted. "But I'm going to give Mayor Falconer a call. She might know if there's been a change in the system. Water, electrical, or otherwise."

Through his open window, indignant growls stretched into the night, so Jesse got inside and started the van. He rested his elbow on the window frame and said, "I'll let you know if we find anything with the cats."

"And I'll let you know if I find anything through the mayor," Dan told him. With a double pat on the side of Jesse's van, Dan stepped back and watched the taillights disappear in the darkness.

For a time, Pandora stayed with Dan, considering. She knew it would be to her benefit if she let him continue his investigation. Hell, he might even figure out her problem before *she* did, and wouldn't that be something? Harold would have howled at the idea, and she, too, now chuckled a little. As the police chief found his way back to the hospital, Pandora followed in companionable silence, then returned to her host. They had things to do.

9

The beginning of autumn's first snowfall floated softly on the other side of Ed Norman's window. In the morning light, with the awakening sun shining brightly through the trees and the new snow falling like glitter over the empty parking lot, Ed peeked at the healing incision just below his left shoulder. Though his skin was loose—sagging in places, bunched in others—they had done a good job patching him up. Tenderly, he touched the area where they had inserted his pacemaker. He couldn't feel an electrical pulse there, as they said he likely wouldn't, but still his fingers fluttered over his sensitive skin.

How close he had been to Bessie just a few days ago. Had the bus accident not happened and the nurses not proceeded to check in on every resident after Jessica Chung's shocking news broadcast, Ed might have been where he most wanted to be. Instead, he'd woken in Garrett General three days before with mechanical parts and the same debilitating longing that refused to go away. He rolled his shoulders now and lifted himself out of bed, thankful to be back in his own pyjamas, with his own slippers, in his own room at Southbridge.

His robe was where he'd left it hanging behind the bathroom door, and he shuffled slowly that way, taking his time on the toilet, then slipped the familiar comfort on. Ed tied

74

the fleece belt loosely around his waist, splashed water on his cheeks, and smoothed the top of his head. He clicked his tongue at the apparition in the mirror, noting the grey sheen of his skin and the deep cavities under his eyes. He looked like death, wanted to be dead, but was sadly still alive. He sighed and made his way to the kitchen for breakfast.

"Eddie!" Hattie Freemont raised her coffee cup in greeting and slid a chair out for him.

She was sitting with Dorothy Davis and the new resident who had led the impromptu prayer session after the news of the bus crash. Ed didn't feel up for company, but Hattie was one of the kindest residents at Southbridge, so his guilt led him to the table where the other women shuffled their plates and cups aside to make room for him.

"How are you feeling Eddie?" Hattie put a gentle hand on his shoulder as he sat and hung his new cane against his chair.

"Like a robot," he said.

"I hear you got a pacemaker," the new woman said, and she set her fingers over his own. "It's a bit strange at first, but before long you won't even know it's there. Trust me." With this, she slid aside the collar of her blouse and showed him her own scar.

Ed lifted his eyebrows. "Doesn't look so bad," he said, seeking the coffee Hattie was passing him with the hand the other woman had grabbed.

"Of course it's not bad. There are much worse surgeries to have, Eddie. Do you mind if I call you Eddie, or would you prefer Ed?" She blinked at him through round, thick glasses.

"Ed, Eddie, either works for me," he said. "But what should I call you?"

"Oh! My manners have gone with the weather, haven't they? I'm Evelyn, but most people call me Evie." Her hand went to her mouth as she tittered. "Look at that, Eddie, we *rhyme*. Isn't that something?" He felt her inspecting him now, so he looked away and poured cream into his coffee, stirring while they inquired about his surgery.

"Don't remember it," Ed said, and that brought a laugh from the women.

"Same with my hip replacement," Dorothy leaned forward with her cup clutched to her chest. "But I tell you, recovery was hell. Took me almost three months to walk around the block again but after that, I felt better than I did in my thirties. I wouldn't have been able to do yoga again without it. It'll take time, Eddie, but I'll bet you'll be even better than before." Coffee spilled against Dorothy's chest as she spoke, and her eyes swung down to inspect the damage. "Now if only there was a surgery for clumsiness."

"Sign me up!" Hattie roared and the faces across from Ed became wet with laughter. Ed joined their fun with a chuckle, then excused himself to fill a plate.

"You sit back down, Edward Norman," Dorothy ordered immediately, snatching his cane from him. "You've got three perfectly good women right in front of you. Let us do what we were made to do. Do you see any children around here?" Ed shook his head, uncomprehending. "Then how are we supposed to get all of our mothering out, huh?"

Ed held out his palms. "I'm fully capable. I don't want to bother you."

"It will bother us if you don't let us help you." Hattie's hands went to her hips. "Now, what will it be, Eddie? Toast? Eggs? Oatmeal? They got some of those cinnamon buns you like."

"You drive a hard bargain." Ed sighed into his chair. "I'm supposed to have toast or oatmeal. Either of those will do."

"Cinnamon bun it is." Evie grinned, sweeping away to the serving station on the other side of the room. Ed watched her depart, and that's when he felt Hattie and Dorothy's eyes on him.

"What?"

"Lucky you have a pacemaker there, Eddie," Hattie observed slyly.

"Yes, but only because Chester just showed up."

From the corridor, Chester Collins strolled toward them, chest high, chin higher, so obviously full of brag that Ed turned, pretending not to see him.

A moment later, Chester was beside their table. "I guess a man's gotta get a mechanical heart to get a woman around here," he said, slapping Ed's back.

"Just a pacemaker," Ed replied, realizing for the first time that Chester had his jacket on. "Where are you off to so early?"

Evie returned with Ed's food, but Chester snuck one of the cinnamon buns from the plate before she could protest. "They're for the patient!" She smacked his hand.

"He should be eating oatmeal anyway," Chester looked down at Ed and elbowed him, bringing a fresh wave of pain to Ed's shoulder. "I'm helping him, ain't that right, Eddie?"

"A regular Mother Teresa." Ed winced.

As he pried the cinnamon bun open, steam rose from Chester's hands and he blew at them until he finally popped a piece into his mouth. He chewed, open-mouthed, then said, "Working on the float today. Testing the hydraulics for the dragon's neck, and if all goes right, we've got to start covering the skeleton. We got a lot of work yet. Tons. More than we've ever had. After George's bus—well, you know— Perry said this year's festival has to be the best or he doesn't want us around next year. Can you imagine that? Firing volunteers? I mean, he's gone nutso if you ask me. By the time this is all over I might need a pacemaker too. Maybe *then* I'll get the ladies."

Hattie, Dorothy, and Evie averted their eyes, then Dorothy fingered one of the pearls on her necklace, thinking. "Why so much work? What's Perry got going on this year?"

"Too damn much, as far as I'm concerned. We've got all the usual things, but he wants more of everything. Lights, food, games, events, big enough to make everyone forget for a while, you know? I guess I can't blame him, but it's running me ragged. Haven't had a second to shit. Sorry, ladies, but you know what I mean."

"Why, we'd be glad to help you." This came from Evie, who was too new to Southbridge to understand that spending any time with Chester was enough to actually *want* dementia.

Hattie and Dorothy exchanged nervous looks with Ed, but Chester, oblivious, said, "Yeah?" A speckle of food flew from his mouth onto Ed's glasses, which he promptly removed and cleaned with a tissue from the pocket of his robe.

"Of course we'll help," Evie said for the four of them. "We've got nothing better to do today but watch the snow come. I think the fresh air would be good for us. Just a little, though, we don't want Eddie to overdo it."

"Fantastic! You're sure taking a load off my shoulders. You ladies couldn't be prettier, but I think we need to give Eddie a few minutes to clean himself up. Anyone want more coffee while we wait?"

INTERFERENCE

In his recent condition, Ed felt in no mood to go to the fairgrounds with Chester. His incision was sore, and his heart attack had given him a tiredness that settled in his bones. The day called for watching weather and watching TV. So he opened his mouth to decline but saw new excitement on the women's faces that caused him to relent. He said, "Give me twenty." Ed stood and carefully made his way back to his room.

His shower was hot and loosened his joints. He took his time, after a while sitting on the bench and hanging his head to let the water prick the tenderness from the back of his neck. Oh, how he wanted to stay in bed and sleep and never wake up. He figured that's what the trick was for some residents at Southbridge; by resisting fellowship, they could lie in wait of the Long Sleep, tuck themselves into their bed caskets and hum their requiems until their hearts stopped beating. Bessie wouldn't have wanted that for him, though. She would have been appalled if Ed succumbed to his own loneliness, so he dried and dressed himself in his warmest flannel shirt. His legs slid into his pants like shriveled beans into windsocks, and the fabric belled against his skin as he returned to the waiting faces of his friends in the foyer. Weak though he was, he felt an unexpected eagerness forming inside him when Evie passed him a tumbler of coffee and hooked her arm under his, lending her strength as they excited the building to Chester's waiting car. Chester picked his teeth behind the wheel while Hattie opened the front passenger door, gesturing for Ed to sit.

"A man could get mighty lazy being around you three," Ed said, leaning on his cane as he lowered himself beside Chester in the front.

"He's just milking it, ladies. Aren't you Eddie? Pacemaker's nothing. You want hurt? Try open-heart surgery. They cut me right through my breastbone when I lived in

Calgary. See that?" Chester unzipped his jacket and unfastened the top two buttons of his shirt, showing them a long purple scar in the middle of his chest. "Twenty years later and the scar is just as bad, and you know what? When Jeannie was alive, she didn't do half the fussing over me that you three do over this guy. A little tough love will heal him quicker than you can say boo." He chewed on his toothpick, watching Dorothy, Hattie, and Evie settle in the back seat, while Ed unrolled the window to free himself of Chester's bad breath.

Soon they were out of the parking lot, progressing slowly over the newly iced streets. Chester took the long route, avoiding the graffiti-splashed, overdosed length of Mitton and instead proceeded north along Oak Street, between Garrett's best-kept stretch of heritage homes. All five of them had been in many of the homes they now passed, with the women remarking on the décor they remembered and the men comparing the sturdiness of their frames to the increasing fragility of subsequent development.

They had just turned onto Campbell when a dog ran out in front of them. Chester slammed the brakes to avoid hitting it. Five heads were thrust forward, five heads jerked back and ten hands braced for impact as the wheels slid against the asphalt. Everyone relaxed when the car skidded safely to a stop.

Dorothy's palm went to her heart. "Oh! That gave me a shock! Good thing you're watching the road, Chester. You okay, Eddie?" From the back seat, her hand slipped over his shoulder.

"Pacemaker's working." Ed laughed uneasily. "I'm all right; you folks? Chester?"

INTERFERENCE

"He came out of nowhere!" Chester took his hands from the wheel to fix the hair that slid from his bald head, patting it gently back into place and then swivelled to look at the three spooked women. "Good thing I got winter tires, or Eddie's face might've wrecked my dash." He patted the glove compartment and started forward again. "I tell you, there's some mighty strange things going on these days. Bus crashing, animals charging, and they've got some girl in the hospital spitting electricity. You hear about that?"

"Nonsense," Hattie swiped her hand out. "You're just telling tales."

"No shit," Chester told her.

"Glenda's front windows were broken by squirrels two days ago," Dorothy said of her daughter. "I didn't know that squirrels could do that."

"They can't," Evie said. "But anything is possible if the good Lord wills it."

"You said a girl is … what now?" Dorothy asked.

"Electric, at least that's what Morley's daughter told Jeremy's wife. He was helping some docs with a machine or something in the ICU, and I guess a patient zapped him."

"You mean a machine zapped him," Ed said.

"No, no. That's what I'm trying to tell you. It was the *patient*. Something about her skin being charged, I guess. The story's wild, but Morley's been in the hospital ever since. They made Alison sign a confidentiality agreement, but she told their daughter and their daughter told Jeremy's wife. Think it's the apocalypse?"

"Don't go scaring people, Chester," Ed warned.

Chester turned to Ed. "Would I lie about something like this?"

"Maybe you heard wrong," Hattie offered helpfully.

81

"My ears may be old, but they're not plugged. I'm telling you exactly what I heard, I swear."

"Well, there's got to be some other explanation for it." Dorothy fidgeted with the clasp of her purse and pulled a roll of mints out, doling them to Hattie and Evie, then two to Ed, who passed both to Chester. She said, "You know as well as I do that death scrambles the senses. Did Morley or Alison know of anyone who died on that bus? Maybe the family's having a moment? Grief can make people say some pretty strange things. When Bob died, I wasn't myself for a long time. Took the grandkids out to the animal farm near London maybe two months after, and wouldn't I be damned if a sheep sounded exactly like him? There it was, four legs, tail, chewing weeds, covered in wool, and I swore right then and there it was Bob. They had to tear me away from that place. Of course, I *knew* it wasn't him, I knew that, but I wanted to believe he was still with me. Grief is the best imaginator."

"Not sure about that," Chester said dismissively.

Moments later, the fairgrounds bloomed into view and fresh excitement overcame them. Gravel and new snow dusted up against the car as it left the asphalt and entered the long and winding approach to the pavilion at the far end of the field. Old eyes looked appreciatively at the expanse around them, and they were just nearing the parking area when Chester said, "Hey, did you hear we're getting another resident next week?"

"Who?" asked Hattie.

"Delmer Baker's widow, Sylvia. She was a crossing guard at the elementary. Remember her?"

10

Light flooded Dr. Adhira Tanti's off-site office as the sun rose behind her desk. In the large picture window, snow brighter than her eyes could handle drifted from the sky and fell on the on the small courtyard where employees of the medical center took their cigarette breaks.

She turned the blinds to dim the light and pressed her fingers to her temples. It had been another hard night. For the last week, she'd spent every waking hour at the hospital. Not only did she have Annabelle Cheever to contend with, but also an unusual spurt of episodes among patients that she could not explain. Dialysis patients were in and out within an hour, as opposed to the usual four. Adjustments to their machines were fruitless, as the process seemed to operate by its own volition, yet recipient patients appeared unaffected by the speed. Eleven expectant mothers, including three who were several weeks from term, experienced the same progression of contractions at exactly the same time, and gave birth at exactly the same second, sending nurses, doctors, and midwives scrambling to keep up. There were two occurrences of spontaneous remission in pediatric cancer patients, four incidents where victims of unrelated traffic accidents endured horrific psychotic episodes, and a God-awful day in the emergency room when thirteen children were seen for the sudden onset of grand mal seizures. Now, as Adhira rose from the leather couch normally reserved for visitors, she smoothed the front of her blouse and twisted her waist to stretch her spine. She didn't enjoy sleeping at the office, but neither could she part from it. Especially now.

Adhira folded the thin throw blanket she used for occasions like this and tucked it neatly against the wall on the back of the couch. Then she slid her tired feet into her shoes and began another day by asking her assistant, Chad, to bring her a latte with a double shot of espresso. She fixed her days-old makeup while she waited, noting with more than a little disgust that the layers did nothing but make her look slightly vulgar. She needed a shower and she needed rest, but neither of those would come for a while; hopefully this evening, if the chaos stopped.

There was a soft knock at the door and then Chad entered with her coffee. "Morn—" He stopped and surveyed her. "You look like shit, boss babe. Screw the latte, it's not going to help you. Get an anesthesiologist here to put you to sleep, okay?" He gave her the coffee and put his hands on his hips.

"If you can find one willing to do that, make the call," Adhira said, sipping fast.

"Any luck with Ms. Electric?" he asked.

"I wish you would stop calling her that," Adhira scolded him. "And, no, we still don't know how or why it happened. Have we heard back from NCT?" She asked the question knowing that her former colleagues at the Neurology Center of Toronto were habitually slow to respond to their correspondence, mostly because they despised being taught their own profession by her sophomoric assistant. His confidence mostly played in Adhira's favor, but the rare occasions when it hindered her, she regretted having such high tolerance for his impertinence.

Chad shook his head and propped an elbow on the arm wrapped across his chest. He pinched his chin, looking at her with what appeared to be pity. "They haven't responded to any of your calls, and only one of your emails. I don't know why you bother with them."

Adhira ignored his tone. "Was it Mac?"

"Who else?"

"What did he say?" Her eyes swung to the decades-old, framed picture on her shelf where she and Tyler Macklund posed together at a small dinner party to celebrate the completion of their PHDs.

"He said that he's empty without you, that he hasn't had a good lay in years, and he's left his wife and kids so you can be together."

Adhira spat out her coffee. "Not funny," she said.

Chad wiped his shirt. "He said he'd look into it. That was literally everything."

She took a brush from her purse, smoothed her hair into a low twist, and pinned it into place. "Did he even read my emails? Never mind. Call him again and tell him it's urgent. And get me another coffee to go."

While Chad pivoted back to the reception area, she made her way to her personal washroom where she brushed her teeth and rubbed a wet towel over her armpits, wishing she had insisted on the installation of a shower when she'd leased the space.

Soon, with another coffee in hand and Chad assaulting her with plumes of cologne he knew he was not allowed to wear, Adhira coughed her way outside. Her car was parked near the side entrance but she walked past it, very much

85

needing the exercise to clear her head. An accumulation of snow made the sidewalk slippery, but Adhira kept to the wind-bared track along the right and presently she felt the cool air rejuvenate her. She knew it wouldn't last. It would dissipate three blocks ahead, where chaos awaited in Annabelle Cheever's hospital room.

Purposefully she took her time, proceeding from the cluster of pharmacies, orthotic supply stores, and various diagnostic buildings, past a quick-service coffee shop, and into a 7-11 where she bought a pack of cigarettes that she would try not to smoke. She was almost at the entrance to the hospital when, behind her, a horn honked. Adhira turned and saw Sylvia Baker's son, Troy, waving from the window of a black sports car. Even with her impressive salary, Adhira knew that she couldn't afford a car like Troy's, so she couldn't help but marvel at his profession as she waved back at him. "Morning!" she called cheerfully.

He pulled aside and stopped at the curb. "I'd offer you a ride, but it looks like we're both here already," he said when she caught up to his car.

"Thanks anyway." Adhira smiled, feeling a blush rise from her neck and into her cheeks. At least they were outside, where she could blame it on the weather. "I'm sure your mother will be glad to see you today," she said.

"I'm not so sure about that. She really doesn't want to go to Southbridge," he said, and then Adhira remembered that she was to sign Sylvia's discharge papers this morning. Besides her photographic memory, Adhira never forgot a face or an appointment in her entire career—a propensity which sustained her through eight years of university—so the realization she'd almost missed something brought a wave of anxiety that stung her nerves. She made a mental note to

INTERFERENCE

confirm her schedule with Chad once she got to her office at the hospital while she waited for Troy to park. A moment later, his tall silhouette rose into view. He wore a similar dark suit to the other she'd seen and a crisp white shirt underneath. A long jacket flapped above his knees as he walked, carrying a cup of coffee in a gloved hand. Where Adhira's breath was visible in the chilly morning air, Troy's exhalations were clear but for a slight fog near his lips when he spoke. "I'm glad I caught up with you. The incident the other night … I was expecting more information."

Adhira's memory flashed to their exchange of phone numbers in Sylvia's room but at once replaced this with the recollection of the directive to inform patient families about the cats. She had called Troy to explain the situation because, well, she did have his number and though it was not the use she'd actually intended it for, she felt their previous connection might inoculate the hospital against unwanted action. As they walked, she said, "Yes, that. Let me apologize again, Mr. Baker."

"Troy, please," he insisted.

"Troy," she acquiesced quickly. "I know it's little consolation since Sylvia is being released today, but I can assure you that we take patient safety very seriously. We've never had an incident like this, and I'd be the first to resign if we ever do again. We still don't know what possessed them to attack like that. Our security footage has them entering through several doors. I could maybe understand one getting into the building, if there was some smell that attracted it or if it were being chased, but not so many at various points of entry at the same time. There simply isn't anything to explain it." He held the door open for her as they entered the hospital, where they paused near the information desk. Adhira

87

turned to face him. "We're working with law and animal enforcement as well as our security team to try and understand how and why this happened so we can prevent similar occurrences in the future. I'm so sorry about the scare your mother had, I really am."

He stared down at her. "I appreciate your honesty, Doctor—"

"It's Adhira," she said.

"Adhira," he pronounced in three overdrawn syllables. "I do appreciate your honesty and I don't question whether my mother was in good hands, but I suspect there's something you're not telling me."

Adhira blinked. "I don't understand."

Troy's eyes swung around the atrium, from the small gift and flower shop to the cafeteria, then to the inner balconies, up, up, up, to the top floor. "I heard about your patient," he admitted, and then his blue eyes narrowed on hers.

"Why don't we talk in my office?" she offered. He turned away to put his coffee cup in a can near the elevators and she followed, feeling slightly stung that he'd held his knowledge back until now.

When he faced her again, the sharp angles of his face were softened by the lowering of his chin. "You misunderstand my intention, Adhira. I'm offering my support. I'll be in the city for some time helping my mother manage her affairs. Since I'm here and since you have a situation that could put you in legal jeopardy, I'd like to offer you confidential advice, gratis of course."

Garett General already had a very capable team of lawyers, as most medical facilities did, and though the hospital's CEO Cliff Henderson would be the lead on legal proceedings, Adhira considered Troy's offer with a twinge of elation. She could first find out what he knew, offer just enough to optically display restraint, and then maybe parlay the informal consultation into something more personal, if only for a short while. Adhira was okay with that. In her line of work, relationships with non-medical partners were fraught with the frustration of work days that never ended and work nights that superseded all other commitments. She said, "I appreciate your offer. We already have legal counsel, as I'm sure you're aware, but an off-the-record conversation couldn't hurt. Maybe over dinner?" She tried to sound casual, but in the tired and greasy state she was in, she realized her invitation might appear desperate to him.

The side of Troy's mouth slanted upward. "I could do that."

Three hours later, Adhira had discharged four patients (Sylvia among them), consulted on the potential recovery of a near-drowning victim, visited two Alzheimer's and three pediatric patients and though it was already noon, she still hadn't eaten breakfast. Sighing, she slumped into her chair, removed her shoes, and closed her eyes. She was used to being busy, but the weight of the last week had drained her usual stamina, so she was snoring in minutes. Then dreams about to materialize were shucked away by a knock on her door. *Go away*, she thought, nauseous with exhaustion. The soft flesh of her eyelids curtained down once more, but the knock came again before she could ignore it. "Yes?" she groaned.

Abe Nkosi turned the handle and entered with Greg Huxley in tow. Both men looked like she felt. Their faces were blighted with the hollows typical of end-stage cancer patients, and even Dr. Nkosi's dark skin appeared sallow and pale. The whites of Huxley's eyes were a disturbing shade of red and neither man had used a razor for some time.

"Tell me one of you has won the lottery and chartered a plane to Jamaica for us."

"Next best thing," Abe replied, setting an oil-stained paper bag on her desk.

She didn't need to open the bag to know Abe had brought her a croissant from his wife's bakery. The doctors took the two seats in front of her desk and sat quietly as Adhira tore the bag open and ate the pastry too quickly to taste it. "If you ever leave your wife, let me know," Adhira eventually said.

"You can have her whenever her mother comes to visit." Abe shrugged.

The pastry hit Adhira's stomach, waking it and making her even more hungry, but instead she sipped from her water bottle while the other doctors sat silent. "You want something from me," she said.

Leaning his elbows on the edge of Adhira's desk, Huxley drew in a long breath through his nose. His lips tightened. "We have a solution for Anabelle Cheever that we want to run by you."

"Go ahead," Adhira replied. She hadn't forgotten about Anabelle Cheever, nor would she ever; she just hadn't got to that dilemma today.

"It's been almost a week now, and we're at the point where we have no choice but to move her. We simply have to. We've done what we could to ease the pressure on her body by changing the elevations of the bed. One of Morley's guys rigged it so we could slant it and ease lateral pressures, but we can't be sure she doesn't have dozens of bedsores under there. She needs to be cleaned, I need to check her incision, her IV line needs to be changed, her parents are wild with anxiety. They're threatening legal action if we don't figure this out."

"Have you reached out to Public Health yet?" Adhira asked carefully.

Huxley said, "I've given enough to cover our asses but not enough for them to come running. If our idea doesn't work, I've really got no choice but let them take over."

"Cliff is insisting on it," Abe said of the CEO when Adhira raised her eyebrows.

She looked at the two of them—the way they bit their lower lips and fiddled with their hands and worked their jaw muscles—and knew that she wouldn't like whatever it was they were about to suggest. "What's your plan?"

"Have you ever had a dead battery in your car?" The question came from Abe.

"Who hasn't?" Adhira scoffed.

"Ever had to jumpstart it with booster cables?" Huxley joined in.

"I'm not sure what you're getting at."

Abe cleared his throat and settled his elbows on his knees, clasping his hands together as he spoke. "We consulted with our electrical engineers and they compared it to us like a dead battery, only Anabelle's battery is the working one. *She* is the working car with a full charge and right now, her cables—essentially her whole body—are live with nowhere to go. Electricity always wants to get to the ground, and we need to help it get there. I know it's going to sound ridiculous, but we need to ground her. The engineers suggest—bear with me now—they suggest hooking her up to booster cables and directing her charge to a bank of batteries."

"What?"

91

Huxley padded his palms on Adhira's desk before she could object. "It's our only option right now. The engineering team reached out to all the auto wreckers in town to obtain old batteries. They've secured a station outside with a few hundred of them, and they're ready to try it. The only thing is, we can't be sure if the batteries can handle it. They might be fine. Or they might explode."

Suddenly Adhira's mouth was very dry, and she took another sip of water so she could speak. "Have we blocked the area off?"

"Just finished," Huxley reported.

Adhira pressed her knuckles to her lips, her mind turning over all the possibilities of what could go wrong. "Could the power fail?"

"Nothing's impossible, but they don't believe so," Abe said.

Adhira frowned. "I don't know about this."

"The generators are working," Huxley reported.

"We can't compromise the safety of hundreds of patients for the well-being of one."

"I can't remember a time when you didn't at least *try* to keep a patient alive," Huxley remarked.

"That's not fair."

Papers fluttered across the desk as Huxley threw his hands up. "She's going to die, Adhira. You want to be the one to tell the city that they're going to lose their only survivor? Be my guest." His mouth clamped shut.

Doctor Nkosi, generally more reserved than Doctor Huxley, glanced at his co-worker and, on this occasion, attempted to engage his rational side by slipping a hand over Huxley's shoulder and squeezing it. "None of us wants that," he said gently but firmly, then turned to Adhira. "We've already run this by Cliff. We have his approval as long as we unanimously agree that this is the right course of action. That's why we're here. If you feel our solution puts too much risk on the hospital, then we have to accept that. I, for one, wasn't so sure myself, but I am also not an electrician. I had to remember that we wouldn't ask an electrician into the operating room, just as they wouldn't seek our advice for wiring a building. I know it's an impossible decision, but its one we have to make. If we don't try, Anabelle Cheever will die. The way they described it, the solution sounds like it could work, so I am willing to meet the absurdity of the situation with an equal resolution." He sat back and waited for Adhira to respond.

"Cliff actually agreed to this?" she asked. Both men nodded.

Adhira's eyes went to the ceiling as she sought an answer that wasn't of the earth. Nothing up there presented itself while she stared, so she sighed heavily and set her eyes back on the other doctors. "I can't believe I'm going to say this, but how exactly do they suggest we hook our patient into a bank of car batteries?"

11

The weekend street was filled with the uninhibited energy of Garrett's school children enjoying their first snowfall of the season. The morning flakes that came softly were by afternoon eddying around ankles, over curbs, through fences, across windshields, and melting on the tongues of small open mouths.

Sarah Cardinal, having just urinated on her ninth pregnancy stick of the last four months, carefully set her test on a folded piece of toilet paper and eased her apprehension by sitting on the bathroom counter to watch the outdoor festivities from her second-floor bathroom window. She wound her hair through her fingers while a group of children rolled the makings of a snowman across the inner courtyard of their townhome community. Beside this, smaller children were sweeping snow angels into the ground while yet another group, joined by three teenagers, were erecting what looked to be dueling castles. Twice she went to look at the stick but held back to avoid the disappointment she knew would surely come.

A snowball hit the glass in front of her face and Sarah flinched, nearly falling from the counter. Outside, her husband stood with a bag of groceries in one hand and a snowball in the other. He waved up at the window and whirled around

94

to huck it at their neighbor's eight-year-old son. The boy brayed with laughter and then Jesse was surrounded by five, eight, thirteen kids blasting him with ice rockets from his ankles to his cheeks. The platoon disbanded giddily when Jesse calmly set his groceries down and, with his arms over his head, rushed at them, kicking up snow. Even from the distance, Sarah could have sworn his eyes were wet when he looked up at her before entering the house, and she reflected that they may be the only happy tears he would cry today.

How they wanted a baby. They hadn't been trying long, only six months or so, but somehow they'd both naively thought it would be easy and that they would be pregnant overnight. After many nights and many days, however, Sarah and Jesse were still just Sarah and Jesse. Last week, she had even sought council from Elder Nikonha, who reassured her that she was fertile and that she would have more than one child. Jesse also regularly sought advice from their elders, and when Sarah conveyed Elder Nikonha's assurance, he told her that he wasn't worried because the Elder had told him the same thing. Now, as she heard Jesse setting his keys on the entrance console, Sarah silently prayed their Elder was right.

From the bottom of the stairs, Jesse called to her. "Got your ice cream," he said. "But I wouldn't eat it until after we get back or you'll be cold all day." Quick steps led him to the top of their small condominium, where he found Sarah sitting on the bathroom counter. He kissed the top of her head and pointed out the window. "You should have joined us out there."

She squinted her eyes shut and thrust the pregnancy stick at him. "You look at it. I can't."

Jesse saw the stick in her hand. "Again? We're going to go broke with the amount you spend on those things. This is the

95

third one this week, Sarah." He plucked the test from her fingers and looked at it. "Remind me again what we want to see."

"Two lines," Sarah blurted. "You know it's two lines, Jesse. Don't be like that."

Laughter rumbled up Jesse's throat and he pinched her big toe to make her open her eyes, but she squeezed them shut. "You sure you want to know?" Jesse teased.

"Only if it's good," she told him. "If it's not, then throw it out the window at one of those kids."

"That's a terrible thing for a mother to say."

"I don't care."

"Also terrible."

"Jesse, will you just—" And then she realized what he'd said. Her eyes sprung open. "Did you say *mother?*"

"Maybe I did." Jesse smiled. "But how will you know if I throw the test outside?"

"Give it to me," she ordered, reaching behind his back.

He held her, wrapping himself around her flailing arms. He kissed her neck, stroked her head, and nodded their answer into her.

"A-are you sure?" Sarah stuttered against Jesse's chest, and then he put before her eyes the two lines they both had been hoping for.

She thought momentarily of taking another test just to be sure but remembered she had used the last of tests in the bulk pack she'd purchased. She would get her doctor to confirm the pregnancy after the weekend, but she knew she would never really be content until their baby was in her arms. When Jesse released her, she saw that his face, like hers, was wet.

From a drawer below where she sat, Jesse took a hand towel and wiped his face, then dabbed Sarah's cheeks. He said, "I knew Nikonha was right. Nothing to worry about

96

INTERFERENCE

but a baby. Now we have about twenty minutes before we have to pick Johnny up. Should we try again, just to be extra sure?" He nodded toward their bedroom.

Twenty-two minutes later and with color flushing their cheeks, they were in their car, progressing slowly from the moderate tenements, past the snow-covered off-leash park, over two sets of train tracks, and onto the unplowed beams of the Novadale Bridge. An oncoming car, travelling too quickly onto the bridge, slid momentarily into their lane but Jesse feathered the brake pedal and managed to stop while the other car corrected its path and passed them with an apologetic wave from its driver.

Sarah admired Jesse's control, knowing that her own instinct at one time would have been to press the brake too fast or veer toward the guardrail. The responses she had previously employed during traffic duty resulted in three damaged cruisers at the beginning of her career. Thankfully, her previous chief, Tom Widlow, had seen past her nascent defensive driving tactics and, rather than fire her, invested heavily in driver's training. As they passed the bridge, Sarah remembered her former boss with gratitude and put her hand to her stomach as she looked out over the departing river. Soon they were at Johnny's apartment building. Here, too, children were scampering over snowbanks, diving into newly erected fortresses, dodging snowballs, rolling their bodies over fresh surfaces.

Jesse pulled into the visitor parking area and called his brother. After a time, he hung up and dialed again, scowling at Johnny's balcony. "I'll bet he's still sleeping," Jesse grumbled.

97

"This late?" Sarah said, spying the time on the radio. *2:02 p.m.*

"I told you he didn't want to come."

"Maybe he's in the shower."

"Hungover, more likely."

Sarah patted his shoulder. "Give him a break. He's still young. We were like that, too, remember?"

"We were never as bad as he is. You know, I don't think he cares about anything." He sighed, and then a snowball hit the windshield. Beyond the sliding splat of snow, Johnny grinned.

They watched as Jesse's little brother, knapsack in hand, dusted up snow while he made his way to their car. In the periphery, a young mother who had been building a snowman with her children stopped rolling long enough to admire Johnny. She smoothed back her hair, blinking at him while her children cried for her to keep rolling, keep building. Sarah laughed. Jesse rolled his eyes as Johnny got into the back seat. New flakes of snow clung to Johnny's shoulder-length hair and he shook it, spraying the back of Jesse's neck. "Merry Christmas," he joked.

"Did you bring the tape?" Jesse asked without preamble, swinging out of the parking lot and onto Simon Avenue.

"Tape, hammer, pliers, three pairs of scissors, zip ties, stapler, gloves. Dad wanted me to bring the staple gun too, but I told him we wouldn't need it," Johnny said, settling his wide shoulders against the seat.

He smelled faintly of alcohol, as they'd suspected he would. Johnny gave everything he had to everything he did: school, work, women, amusement. There was nothing mediocre about him and no matter how much Jesse tried to steer his brother into respectable adulthood, Johnny wouldn't be hurried. He would do everything his own way or no way. While he sat in their backseat bragging about his latest exploit in which three women tore one of his shirts trying to count his abs, Sarah wondered which portions of the Cardinal genes their baby would inherit.

"Whatever you didn't bring, I'm sure Dad will," Jesse said, because their father always remembered whatever they forgot. Keys, school assignments, examination dates. The boys relied on his memory as they grew from toddlers to teens, and depended on it even more as men, though it was now Johnny who benefitted from it the most. It was their father who didn't need a reminder to chauffer their car-less son to and from work, to and from pleasure. It was their father who purchased Johnny's gifts for their mother, whatever the occasion, and it was their father who reminded Johnny when and where he was expected for interviews—thanks to which he was never late. That same memory would come in handy today, when he joined his sons at the fairgrounds to oversee the construction of their entry for the annual parade. This year they were assembling a pie-making scene with three bears, two beavers, and a moose. Johnny himself had shot two of the bears, which his father was bringing in his trailer, along with the rest of the animals.

In his rear-view mirror, Jesse spied a scratch near Johnny's chin. He touched his jaw, remembering their time at the hospital. "That still from the other night?"

Johnny nodded. "Fuckers got me good. Yours heal up yet?"

"Almost all gone. I didn't get it as bad as you. Make sure you put some ointment on that, okay? Or you'll end up in the hospital too. Cat bites can kill you."

"Yes, Dad."

"I'm serious."

The brothers brooded while Jesse drove. The sky had become white with snow; wind folded it over the road, onto the sidewalks, bunching it up on the shore of the Callingwood River beside which they now cautiously moved.

"Did you get their test results yet?" Johnny asked.

"All came back clean. Not a single one with rabies. No toxoplasmosis. No infections of any sort. Same thing with the birds. Still waiting to hear from the city on the water samples, but besides the change in weather, I can't figure it out."

"So you won't need me then?" Johnny's eyes slipped away from the front seat to his phone as he messaged Cassandra, one of the women he'd been with the night before.

"Do you have something better to do?" Jesse said, and immediately felt Sarah's eyes on him.

The silence in the car was heavy. Jesse knew his brother would rather mooch off their parents than work. The good people they were, they indulged his whims without protest, but Jesse couldn't permit him to take advantage of them any longer. He was about to say as much when Sarah's mouth fell open and she pointed at the river.

"The water," she gasped. "It's ... gone."

Past Sarah's pointing finger, the brothers looked west where the water of the Callingwood River had seemingly evaporated. Once submerged weeds, now limp against the riverbed, lay as flat as rocks among air-gasping fish that flailed as they searched for water. Where snow collected, gathered, amassed on the streets and in the fields, here it was absorbed into the earth the moment it landed. The draining was sudden and fierce, for they had not remembered it this way yesterday, nor earlier when Jesse passed the river on his

100

INTERFERENCE

way to pick up Sarah's ice cream. This was new. Like the birds. Like the cats. Like the bus crash. Their city was going to hell—or was already there.

A collective gulp bubbled from the car. Ahead, several vehicles had pulled over to gape at the river, and more than a few people were outside taking pictures with their phones. Whatever misery their city faced, the rest of the world would know within seconds.

"What the fuck?" Johnny unrolled his window, but the lowering of the glass did not change the sight. As far north and south as he could see was the cadaver of Garrett's longest and widest river, its grey-green insides now on full display, releasing its old life into the earth. Weeds hung over dead-wood scatter like skin on old bones, and even the river's many teeth, exposed in knockouts of shells heaped from its center to its sides, were lifeless. As the wind blew and the snow fell, the Callingwood River resembled a kilometers-long crater fringed in snowbank.

Sarah took her phone from her purse and called Dan. To Johnny, Jesse said, "Call Mayor Falconer and ask her to meet us at the fairgrounds."

For once, Johnny immediately did as his brother asked.

12

Light sliced through Sylvia's living room blinds, spotlighting the dust that had settled during her hospital stay in the small house she had enjoyed for over forty years. Now, as she entered her home for the first time in a week, she smelled the sourness of disuse and her stomach turned.

She knew her return would be emotional, but the knowledge didn't lessen the pain. She leaned on her cane, stepping inside while Troy impatiently grumbled behind her that he was cold. This visit had been hard won, for Troy had wanted to take her from the hospital directly to Southbridge where, he insisted, there were no memories that might make her yearn for home and set her recovery back. But she wailed in his car until the tympanic vibrations began to hurt them both, and Troy grudgingly relented.

Sure, her own son might have threatened to toss her out of the car if she didn't stop screaming, but Sylvia would use whatever faculties she had left to get what she needed. Her baby boy was her life, but he was also the source of all her difficulties, besides the stroke.

Nothing between them was ever easy. Even in her fragile state, the tenderness expected by other parents from other children in similar situations was absent in Troy. He just didn't have it in him. Where her friends' grown children

102

were helpful and thoughtful and supportive, Troy was un-sympathetic and inconsiderate. His current behavior was not new. As a child, even with her adoration and Delmer's, Troy had never been warm to them. What infant despised hugs? What toddler didn't want to be tucked in at night or kissed on the forehead or coddled when sad or sick? Only Troy. Still, he was hers, and as he finally entered the house and went to the kitchen, disinclined to assist her up the stairs, Sylvia loved him.

"We're supposed to be at Southbridge in an hour," Troy said, hanging his jacket on the back of a kitchen chair.

"I won't be long. I just wanted to see it. You'll keep it for me until I come back?" Sylvia asked the question because although Troy had previously told her he was going to look after the house, she noticed that the hallway carpet was missing and that her collection of porcelain figurines was, by the look of the tape and paper on her side table, in the process of being packed into a box.

"I can get you a good price for it, you know."

"You said, but as I told you I intend on coming back. This is my home, Troy, and I won't be pushed out of it. A few months at Southbridge and I'll be able to take care of it myself again. Then I'll be out of your hair." Of course, only half of her face said this. When she most needed to assert her independence, her words were muffled and weak.

From the kitchen, Troy brought a glass of water which he drank as though he couldn't speak without it. Sylvia watched the lump of his Adam's apple pitch upward while he emptied his glass, then he set it beside her remaining porcelain ballerina and sighed. "I'm not sure you understand what it took to get you in there, Mother."

103

Only, Sylvia did know: not much. That Troy was well-connected was no secret, and he liked to remind her of this every time she requested something of him. He pressed upon her how important it was to not overuse his resources, but Sylvia had long suspected that her few requests required little more than a phone call, email, or text message. She knew that after twenty years in the high-flying legal stratosphere in Toronto, Troy got whatever it was he wanted and that only grudgingly did his comfort extend to her. Her flesh and blood looked down at her now, waiting for her to respond. She said, "I appreciate your help, Troy."

She left him then, struggling up the few stairs to her bedroom. Here, too, things were missing. The four-poster bed frame that Delmer had made was still there, as were the matching dresser and night tables, but the mirrors were gone. So were the pictures of their old cat, Lucy. Rage did not boil up inside her like it used to when Troy showed his true colors, but she did feel a tightening around her heart. This, Pandora liked very much.

As her host opened drawers and closets and stuffed outdated clothes into a large suitcase, silently crying so as not to agitate her son, Pandora released herself to visit the handsome devil on the first floor. Absorbed by his phone, Troy was typing a message while Pandora watched. Generally, she found humans boring. They were predictable and fragile. Only a few were engaging enough to stay with, and only Harold had actually excited her. His appetite for death had almost superseded her own, and though Pandora did not expect to find another like him, there was something about Troy she found intriguing.

After Harold's death, when she was most impulsive, she might have taken this man instead of Sylvia—but in her core, Pandora suspected Troy would not be taken or, more importantly, *led* easily. Unwilling lovers did not make for companionable relationships. Weak partners like Sylvia, however, could be controlled into lengthy relations, and that was good enough for now. Still, she preferred Troy close. She didn't know why but a peek inside might reveal her answer, so she closed in on him now. Troy had finished his message and was slipping his phone into his jacket. His shoulders crested as he rested his hands on the kitchen island, and Pandora saw an enticing spot just above his collar, at the back of his neck, through which to make her entry. She stretched at him eagerly.

And was blocked.

Troy's fingers went to his neck as though he was slapping a mosquito. He whirled around, seeking the thing that had touched him. Pandora pressed again, but encountered … *resistance?* This could not be. She whacked him. Troy frowned and cracked his neck. His eyes veered to the corner, the other corner, the patio door, the old cupboards behind him. Then he cleared his throat and, for the first time in all her millennia, Pandora *sneezed.* It was the most appropriate word for the momentary sensation of her atoms releasing their attraction. For an infinitesimal slice of time, Pandora was not Pandora. She had lost control.

"Hello?" Troy said aloud, but Pandora did not answer him. Instead she circled him, wondering if *he* was the source of her exhaustion in the hospital, if *he* was the interference she'd felt in Garrett. "Mother?" Troy called up the stairs, but Sylvia was already on the main floor bathroom gathering her cosmetics bag.

"Almost done," Sylvia said a little tearfully, peeking her head out of the bathroom door.

"Were you in the kitchen?'

"Am I not allowed in my own kitchen now?"

Troy studied the house. Other than the crows fighting over the neighbor's trash and his mother limping through the living room, there was no sound, yet Troy listened. Only when Sylvia finally banged her way outside with her suitcase did he finally take his eyes from the kitchen.

The drive to Southbridge was quiet. Sylvia chanced to turn the radio on, and Troy grimaced at the oldies stations she preferred until she changed the channel to a local news report that caught their attention.

"You heard right, folks. The Callingwood River has drained. Officials are working to find the cause of the issue. Our very own Mac Thomas is reporting from the Sixth Street Bridge with more information. What can you tell us, Mac?"

"Thanks Mia. As you can expect, the scene along the Callingwood River is chaotic. Emergency services have been deployed across the city to rescue citizens who have tried to cross the river on foot but have gotten stuck in the riverbed—including almost the entirety of Garrett High's junior wrestling team. Mayor Ada Falconer has warned that emergency services are stretched thin and has asked residents to stay away from the river as the disruption could be the result of an upstream blockage that might release at any moment. The mayor is meeting with City Manager Boyce Swinkley and Police Chief Dan Fogel to get to the bottom of this. In the meantime, those residents with boats still on the river are asked not to try to retrieve them. I repeat, Mayor Falconer has asked citizens not to retrieve their boats, as doing so could put you or your loved ones in danger at a time when emergency services may not be able to respond quickly. Back to you, Mia."

INTERFERENCE

Troy turned to another radio station, another, another. By now there was no music, only bad news. A boil water advisory was in effect until further notice, and residents near the water treatment plant were notified of a potential foul smell if the city's sewage couldn't be properly released. Then there were the reports of pets being lost in the mud and of children stuck up to their necks trying to rescue them. Local ecologists lamented the inestimable loss of the river's wildlife. The host of *Truth Radio*, Garrett's conspiracy talk show, suggested the river and the bus crash were the result of federal experimentation with satellite magnets while one of his guests rejected this theory and instead posited a rise of alien activity.

A block away from the assisted-living residence, Sylvia turned to her son. "Take me home, Troy."

He continued driving. "It's the best place for you, Mother."

"Listen, Troy. Did you hear what they're saying? Something's happening in the city. I should be home. I should be in my own home where it's safe." The functioning side of her mouth quivered.

The cord of muscles along Troy's jawline flexed as he turned into Southbridge's parking lot. Outside, a worker was shoveling the front walk while another was spreading salt across the sidewalk with a big silver scoop. A truck that had a blade attachment was on the homestretch of clearing the parking area, passing Troy and Sylvia with a wave as they parked. Troy shut the car off.

"You can't take care of yourself right now, Mother, and I'm unable to babysit you. I'm in the middle of the firm's biggest acquisition and I don't have time to carry you up the stairs or make sure you get enough fiber."

107

The sting registered on Sylvia's face through the angry red flush of her cheeks. She fumbled for the handle until Troy unlocked the door. Stumbling out of the car, Sylvia caught her hip on a metal pin, but she held back her cry. Her good ankle turned awkwardly as she spun toward the trunk. That, too, she held back.

Sylvia pounded on the trunk. Her weak hand slapped at it until Troy pressed a button and the door lifted, and Sylvia had to step back so it didn't hit her. She took hold of her suitcase, but it was heavy and the effort hurt her arm. Again she pulled until Troy quietly got out of the car, brushed her aside, and took out the suitcase. She did not say thank you after he brought it to the sidewalk. She couldn't, because he drove away.

While Sylvia's body drooped with emotion, Pandora wondered at her son, at Garrett, at the interference she felt in the hospital. Instinct told her to leave the city and find another host somewhere else, but something in Pandora also told her that she could not leave the city for the same reason that she was disturbed by it: there was a power here, perhaps equal to Pandora's own. If she didn't destroy it, it might destroy her. That's what evil things did.

Presently, Pandora observed Sylvia's struggle with the suitcase. The woman tried pulling it, tried pushing it, tried kicking it with her half body, her depleted strength. Sylvia slipped on a portion of the icy sidewalk that was not yet salted and fell to her knees. If Pandora were human, she might enjoy a hot bag of popcorn right now, but her fun was cut short when the man shovelling the sidewalk and the other salting it ran to her. A woman rushed out of the building and took Sylvia's suitcase, following the men as they worked together to bring a now sobbing Sylvia inside. Her hair fell against her sunken cheeks as she gave the receptionist her name and explained that she was there for a very temporary stay.

The receptionist understood Sylvia's stroke-mumbled words and nodded warmly. "Yes, you're here for our rehab program."

"Temporarily," Sylvia mumbled again, now leaning on the handle of her suitcase.

"Sure," the woman said. "Do you have your paperwork? Sylvia sniffed. "Paperwork?"

"Do you have someone with you who might have the paperwork?"

"I'm alone," Sylvia told her.

There was a clicking of keys on the receptionist's keyboard. She was chewing a large wad of gum that smelled like overripe fruit. "No worries. Okay, then. We'll get Georgia to show you to your room so you can get settled and help you fill them out, then she'll give you a tour if you're up for it."

A nurse barely taller than the reception desk appeared. Her smooth caramel skin shone with the health of youth and her big bright eyes radiated a gentleness that made Sylvia start to cry again.

"Oh, now, Mrs.—" Georgia peeked at the papers the receptionist slid over. "Baker. None of that, now. We've got nothing but goodness waiting on you, you hear? Healing, communion, and care, doesn't that sound good, Mrs. Baker?" Georgia slipped her hands around Sylvia and gave her a hug. Sylvia nodded into her, sniffling. "Let's get you to your room, Mrs. Baker. Can you walk, or would you like me to get you a wheelchair?"

"I can walk," Sylvia croaked as Georgia released her. Pandora hated hugs. More than anything in the world, she hated hugs. But she allowed Sylvia to be embraced because she needed her host to regain her strength. In the state she was in, Sylvia couldn't kill, and that would not do. If hugging the woman helped her recuperate, Pandora would let them squish Sylvia to death because, well, that would be fun too.

"To our left is the cafeteria and the common room, but we're going to go the other way, where the rooms are. Quite a few of our residents are out at the fairgrounds getting ready for the Fall Festival, but I'll be sure to introduce you when they're back. Do you have any hobbies, Mrs. Baker?"

One of Georgia's small arms was tucked lightly around Sylvia's waist while the other pulled Sylvia's suitcase behind them. They were walking a snail's pace, Sylvia knew, but her parking-lot expulsion had exhausted her, and since the corridor was empty she could safely spy into her neighbors' rooms without drawing attention to herself.

Her head swung left and right as they passed each door, many closed but some open. The rooms were brighter than she expected and she was surprised to see not hospital beds and clinical furniture but sofas and recliners, carved armoires, and plush carpets. The smell of cinnamon wafted from one room while Neil Young's "Rockin' in The Free World" was borne from another. A man reading a paper at a table in his room waved at them as they passed.

"That's Albert," Georgia explained. "He's always reading the paper and reminding us how uninformed we all are, but he doesn't know that by the time he gets the paper, it's already old news. Refuses to use the iPad his son got him for Christmas because he doesn't trust it. Thinks it's some sort of spy device." She chuckled conspiratorially. "You have an iPad, Mrs. Baker?"

Sylvia nodded. "I use it to play games the kids at school showed me. I don't think anyone's spying on me." Inside, Pandora snickered.

INTERFERENCE

"Well," Georgia went on, leading Sylvia to a room near the end of the hall. "Don't tell Albert you said that, or he'll try to convince you of it. With graphs." She winked, then turned toward a door beside which was a wall-mounted placard bearing Sylvia's name. "Here we are. Your home away from home."

"Temporary home," Sylvia added tiredly.

The nurse squeezed Sylvia's shoulder. "I know it's overwhelming, Sylvia. Do you mind if I call you by your first name?" Silently Sylvia nodded, and Georgia faced her and held her watering eyes with her own. "It's okay to be upset. It's a big change for anyone, but I want you to know that we'll do everything we can to make your stay enjoyable. Our rehabilitation program is one of the best in Ontario, and whether it takes you three months or a year, we're here for you. Who knows? You might even find you want to stay with us. I promise we're not bad when you get to know us."

Georgia opened the door to Sylvia's room, welcoming her inside with the motion of her arm.

"I—" but Sylvia couldn't finish.

"Is it okay, Sylvia?"

Sylvia's fingers covered her open mouth as she scanned her room. The hallway carpet that was missing from her house lay neatly at the foot of a simple oak bed, upon which her favorite duvet was folded. She was so angry with Troy that she hadn't noticed her pillows were missing, but here they were, four of them all fluffed up and ready for her head. The pictures of her and Delmer's favorite cat, Lucy, hung near her reading chair, and the porcelain figurines she thought Troy had packed away were here too, arranged on a side table Delmer made for her when Troy was just three years old. She looked around and saw her mirrors and

111

wedding pictures and knitting bag. Without warning, Sylvia began to cry.

Georgia's small hands rubbed Sylvia's back. "Did we miss anything? Your son brought these here last night. Is there anything else you wanted, Sylvia?"

"This is just temporary," Sylvia repeated.

Georgia set Sylvia's suitcase on the bed and opened the blinds to the sight of a snow-covered field and a scattering of large oak trees that were shedding the last of their leaves. "Well, while you're here, you've got one of our nicer views and great neighbors. You'll get to meet Eddie and Hattie when they come back from the fairgrounds later today."

With instructions on how to call the reception desk if Sylvia needed anything, Georgia departed and Sylvia took to the bed to rest her tired body, her tired mind. She was watching the end of the afternoon snowfall when she drifted into a dreamless sleep while Pandora began planning. In Southbridge, death would surely be easy picking, and Pandora figured her biggest challenge would be who to kill first: Hattie or Eddie.

13

As he collapsed into his usual seat at Boomer's restaurant, Dan Fogel felt the weight of the terrible week bear down on him. Exhaustion settled deep in his muscles, and even the smell of coffee being poured into his mug by his favorite waitress did little to stir his senses. To Nina's confusion, he ordered whatever she wanted to serve, as the energy to choose escaped him. It was in that bus, with those damn cats, in the ICU, and on the riverbed, where it most needed to be. He rubbed his temples and closed his eyes, smelling deep over his cup, only realizing his waitress was still there when she politely cleared her throat.

"You okay there, Dan?" Nina's eyes narrowed.

"Don't have a choice," Dan said, and sipped his coffee.

Nina stuffed her notepad into the pocket of her apron and sat on the edge of the bench across from him. "Brandy?" she asked of his soon-to-be ex-wife.

Their impending divorce wasn't a secret, as most news wasn't in small towns, but what made their separation especially notable was that his wife had been caught on camera in the middle of a blow job to Shane Carson of Carson Brothers Roofing. Unfortunately for all of them, this particular brother could shingle a house but could not figure out his laptop when he decided to record their private interaction and accidentally streamed it on his company's website. In truth, seeing his wife drooling over Shane's cock was a personal low for Dan, but for the first time in many weeks he hadn't given it a thought. Now reminded of it, he almost wished those cats had gone feral months ago and ripped Shane's balls open. To Nina he said, "My week was so bad I almost forgot about that."

"Is it that girl, then?"

Dan's head went up. "Come again?'

Nina poured more coffee into his cup, opened and added two creamers, and stirred it for Dan while she chewed her gum. "Earl and Ginger's granddaughter. The lone survivor? Rumor has it that there's some pretty weird shit going on with her. You've got a security detail covering her, right?"

Dan's throat went dry. Although he knew the news would travel, he had hoped that given the enormity of the crash, perhaps the city would temper its whispers, if only for compassion's sake. Obviously, death just fueled the speed at which the talk spread. He said, "We're keeping the media away from her, that's all."

"If you say so," Nina said, seemingly affronted that Dan didn't divulge more. She stood and tapped the table. "I'll have your order out in a jiff."

As promised, a beef dip and steaming bowl of chicken noodle soup was brought to his table a few minutes later. Nina departed while Dan sprinkled everything with pepper. His first bite didn't so much rejuvenate him as calm his ulcers, and he let it settle his stomach as he ate. By the time he was done with his sandwich, he was too full for the soup, so he asked Nina for a container.

From his booth, he saw the flash of headlights pull into the parking lot, then the bell over the door rang out to signify Boyce Swinkley's entrance. The shine from Swinkley's head reflected the restaurant's phosphorescent lights, and he wiped a few melting snowflakes from his skull with his forearm while he stomped his shoes on the floormat, scanning the restaurant.

Boyce found Dan's raised arm and made his way to the table. "Damn near got rear-ended on my way here. Roads are hell," he said, hanging his jacket on the rack at the end of the bench.

"So is the river," Dan retorted.

Boyce removed his fogged glasses and cleaned them with the hem of his shirt, putting them back on with a snort. "I tell you, Dan, something's happening here. I can *feel* it. A river doesn't just run dry overnight."

"Anything on your end yet?"

Boyce ordered coffee and a BLT from Nina, then shook his head. "Not a goddamn thing. Ministry's all over it, 'course. They've got people from New Brunswick to Saskatchewan trying to figure it out. Current theory is fracking gone wrong, but we've got none of that anywhere near that river, Dan. I'm still thinking it's those Baront guys. You know the slough that used to be near Jack Fisher's farm?"

"Dried up twenty years ago," Dan said.

"Didn't just dry up. Baront was drilling one of their gas wells near there. Won't say they drilled too shallow, but they drilled too shallow and fracked it. Lawyers saved their asses." His lips pressed together angrily.

His food arrived and he ate quickly while Dan settled both their bills. Together they left the restaurant, with Boyce joining Dan in his cruiser because it had better tires. Though it was early evening, the moonless sky had grown dark, and there was a chill that caused Dan to crank the heat. October snowfall wasn't unusual for the city, but it always seemed to

115

stun disbelieving residents as if shovels and snow tires and antifreeze were afterthoughts better employed in colder cities. As they pulled from Boomer's parking lot and headed north toward Garrett's municipal block and the mayor's office, unprepared vehicles slid past stop signs and skated anxiously away from other bumpers. Tired and stressed, they exchanged accounts of the last few days while Dan drove.

"You finally get that wrestling team from the river?" Boyce asked.

"Wouldn't be here if we didn't," Dan said. "Wasn't so bad. Joe had his engines in and out in an hour. It was that damn daycare that was a bitch. You'd think that with all the warnings that they'd stay away, especially a kiddie group like that. But no, they got to collect shells and rocks for their macaroni crafts. They were stuck so hard, one of my guys popped his knee trying to get a little one out. Ministry pulled the daycare's license this morning. Thank God." He tightened his grip on the wheel, remembering.

"It's hard to protect stupid, ain't it?" Boyce said. "I caught a fella taking pictures in our treatment plant this morning. Said the river is our fault and that he was going to prove that we're holding the water back just so we can increase taxes. Can you believe it? Damn near shit my pants when I ran into him."

Dan raised an eyebrow. "You want an officer on that?"

"Nah. I threatened to throw him in the sludge tank if I caught him again. He skedaddled pretty fast." Boyce drew a roll of antacids from his pocket and popped two into his mouth, chewing while breathing through his nose.

Before long, the brick and limestone façade of City Hall bloomed into view. The area was mostly empty, save for a scattering of holiday vendors making their last business of the

INTERFERENCE

day. Steam rose from booths selling hot chocolate, specialty ciders, and roasted chestnuts while aromas of pine, cinnamon, cranberry, and leather sprang from craft shacks displaying autumn décor, potpourri, candles, moccasins, and fur-lined mittens. In the center, a man playing a saxophone rose from his stool and began packing his instrument away. Dan parked, and as they walked through the departing crowd toward the mayor's office, chatter about the river and of the bus accident and of Anabelle Cheever was all they heard. "Let's cancel the Fall Festival and give them something else to talk about," Boyce suggested.

Dan shrugged. "Don't tempt me."

Down the sidewalk, around the shuttered fountain, and up the steps of City Hall they went. The building was usually closed by this time, but tonight, on the other side of the glass, lights were on, offices were open, and people were working. Through the revolving door, they were greeted by a security officer who directed them up the stairs to the second floor where Ada Falconer was waiting for them.

"Aren't you two a sight for sore eyes," she said, coming from around her desk to greet them. The woman could run marathons in stilettos, but now she was shoeless, in skirt and stockings, and with little smudges of makeup around her eyes. Her blouse was untucked, for which she made no apology to Boyce or Dan. She extended a hand to them and directed them to sit.

"What fresh hell have we been hit with today?" Dan asked. "The sky falling now? Maybe a volcano has surfaced beneath the city and we need to evacuate?"

Boyce and Ada shared a groan. She put glass bottles of sparkling water in front of them and said, "Same hell as this morning, though aliens could land at this point and it wouldn't faze me. How are you two doing?"

117

"Stretched, that's for sure," Dan reported. "We've got support from London—eight officers there—and another thirteen from Toronto. Ministry rented out the Best Western for their investigation and deployment teams and the Red Cross is holed up in the Clarion. I have two guys on that damn reporter too. We blink and she's got her nose where it doesn't belong, no matter how many times we toss her out. Last thing we need with all the shit that's been going on."

"Thanks for helping with that," Ada said.

"No trouble," Dan said.

Ada leaned back in her chair and sighed. "So, how close are we to solving this thing?"

"We're not," Boyce said. "But we're working on it. I wish I could give you a timeline on this one, Ada, but your guess is as good as mine. Best guess is someone drilled a hole through the aquifer and hit a cavity, but so far, the geologists haven't found anything that would support that. They might not know for weeks; hell, even months."

Ada frowned. "How does this change our water?"

"Not much, thankfully. We're already drawing from Lake Huron, but now our backup will be our sole source. I would keep the boil-water advisory for at least the week, until we get the reports back from the ministry, just to be safe, but it's the *output* that's going to cause us problems. The collection tanks will need to be emptied, but we now have no channel to do that. We're going to have to haul it to a disposal site. The MNRF is going to cut us a deal on this, for the time being." The Ministry of Natural Resources and Forestry had, in fact, been a huge support to Boyce, for which he was sincerely grateful. The city manager for going on thirteen years, Boyce was paid to prepare for emergencies, but he could never have predicted the immediate drainage of the city's primary

118

INTERFERENCE

water supply. While the ministry had graciously offered support, it was by no means a quick fix. Hauling the city's sewage required strategic planning and that precious commodity, time. They would get it done, but not so quickly that the city wouldn't stink to high heaven before they did.

He conveyed these concerns to Ada, who put her face into her palms. "Think we can get a deal on air fresheners somewhere?"

"A city that stinks together, links together. Our new motto." Dan smirked.

"I'll tell that to the Prime Minister," Ada groaned. "You know, this is not the kind of attention I was hoping for our city."

"Feds?" Boyce looked at Dan.

"Of course," Ada acknowledged. "They're just as interested as everyone else. You know how proactive they are when it comes to Canadians' water supply." Dan and Boyce nodded knowingly at her gibe. "Anyway, be sure to keep me updated. Working hours are out the window. I don't care if it's three a.m., I want to know if there's progress. The city needs some good news, whatever it is."

"Understood," Boyce agreed, while Dan tipped his chin.

Ada removed a packet of almonds from her desk drawer, ripped the corner open, and poured some into her hand. She plucked a few out of her palm and chewed them thoughtfully. "Dinner," she said, and took a drink of water. "Now for the crazy part. You know of the situation at the hospital?"

"Don't tell me there's dogs now," the police chief straightened, waiting.

"No dogs, they've had none of those problems since Jesse took them all away, but they've come to an impasse that you two need to be aware of."

119

Dan braced himself for bad news. "Oh?"

"The ICU patient needs to be moved. Her doctors have worked with the positioning of her bed to reduce the risk of bedsores, but they believe they're at the point where she almost certainly has them, potentially many of them. They are treating her with antibiotics just in case, but—and here's the bigger issue—she just had her skull repaired and they need to check her incision and run her through some tests. They can't do that if anyone who touches her gets electrocuted."

"Why don't they just ground her?" Boyce asked. "I'm no electrician, but isn't that the simplest thing to do?"

Ada shrugged. "Anyone who touches her closes the loop, or so the electrical engineers explained in layman's terms. You would think her bed does that, but for reasons beyond their understanding, it doesn't. They have a potential solution they want to try, however keep in mind there is absolutely no guarantee it will work. They're not anticipating any disruptions, but they've warned us just in case." She held her hand up when Dan began to object. "I know that's the last thing this city needs right now, but I also want you to imagine what would happen if we lost that girl. We have a duty to try everything we can to help her. Also, and pardon me for being a bit morbid here, *if* she passes, we don't know when her body will cease to generate electricity. Dead or alive, we have to figure this out, or our only hospital may lose its ICU."

"What are they proposing?" Boyce's face knotted in apprehension.

Her eyes swung outside, toward the closed shacks two stories below. Then she looked at them squarely. "Understand that I know this solution sounds absurd. I do. But it's the only one they've got. At eleven o'clock, they are going to

120

INTERFERENCE

clamp cables to Anabelle Cheever and hook her up to a battery bank. They're hoping that by drawing power from her to the batteries, it will temper the charge. I can't remember how they explained it, but that's the gist."

"You've got to be kidding me." Boyce's hands went to the sides of his bald head. His mustache twitched.

"I wish I was."

"What exactly does this mean?" Dan asked.

The mayor's cheeks swelled with a long push of air. She smoothed her dark hair behind her ears and removed her earrings. At last, she said, "We need to be ready for anything."

14

In the dark hours of a cold October night, after the city's streets were cleared of snow and local emergency service departments and Ontario's Independent Electricity System Operator (IESP) were apprised of potential electrical disturbances, Mayor Ada Falconer authorized Garrett General's plan for connecting Anabelle Cheever to the battery bank. Police, fire, maintenance, and medical teams were readied across the city while Garrett's bureaucratic complement, in the pressure-soaked City Hall, waited by phones and computers, set to respond to whatever awaited them. Now, on the deserted fifth floor of Garrett General, six brave souls assembled around the nursing station, reviewing their strategy.

Doctors Greg Huxley, Adhira Tanti, and Abe Nkosi listened attentively while Chief Electrical Engineer Bruce McKiskin, using the nursing station whiteboard behind him, briefed the team. He'd drawn a respectable stick figure of Anabelle Cheever in the hospital bed. Gray loops circled the figure's feet, and from this ran two red lines to the end of the bed and down to the floor, where they would meet the cables leading to the battery bank system outside.

"Now," Bruce explained, pointing to the top of the whiteboard, "if a conductor were to be connected in such a manner, it would feed through here and make its way to the bank system outside. The hospital's power system is designed to accommodate surges as they occur, but we can't be sure she won't overload it and impact the city's power grid. For this reason, we are going to switch to our emergency generators until it is safe to return to the city's grid network. It's not pretty work, by all means, but it's the best we could do given our time frame. Lakehead Power is ready to react to any outages; all we have to do is make the connection." A trail of sweat ran down the length of the engineer's back, and as he swung around to face them, they saw similar sweat marks down the front. He regarded their faces and said, "Can't say I've ever done anything like this before."

Abe leaned over and rested his elbows on the nursing desk. His finger air-traced Bruce's drawing as he mumbled the procedure to himself. "Take me back a bit. Won't she still be energized? How does hooking her up to the battery bank change our ability to treat her? And how are we to get the clamps around her feet? We've never been able to touch her."

"Good questions," Bruce said. "You're right, connecting generators of electricity to exterior sources do not render them powerless, but we think—now, this is our best guess—that channeling her power might help us to moderate, if not control, her charge. The bed itself *should* run a current because Anabelle is lying on it, but as you experienced yourself, it does not. This tells us that we are working with peculiarities that could actually work in our favor. As for how we're going to get the clamps on, I'll let Kate take care of that." Bruce gestured to the serious-looking woman beside Huxley.

Without delay, Kate gestured to a black oval near the bottom of the board. "This is our magic weapon. Most, if not all of you, have operated a drone at some point, so you will be more or less familiar with the technology. In this case,

123

your Canadian Tire or Walmart variety apparatus can't do much more than hover above our patient. Courtesy of the Canadian Military, we've secured a much more advanced drone with robotic capabilities. As Bruce earlier mentioned, the connection to Anabelle's feet must be made without connection to the floor. A drone is the only way to do this. The technology has been around for years, but with helicopters and power lines. This is just a smaller version of that."

"You can do this?" Adhira's face cramped with doubt.

"We've *already* done it," Kate explained. "While Bruce and his team completed the preparations here, Frank and I practiced a simulation on a dummy in that bed near the entrance." She motioned to the empty bed beneath a wall clock, toward which all heads turned. "Our wires weren't live, of course, but we did manage to get the clamps onto the dummy's feet. It's going to sound alarming, but it should reassure you that we use this technology when working with explosives overseas. I'm very familiar with it, and I've been working with this particular drone for over three years. We can do this." Her small shoulders and delicate face belied the authority within her, but the doctors nodded on appreciatively as she spoke.

Bruce said, "All of our teams are ready. We just want your agreement before we proceed." He capped the pen on his marker and set it on the bottom lip of the board, then he stepped back and rolled up his sleeves, waiting.

Huxley looked at Abe and Adhira. "Well?" he said.

Abe removed his glasses and rubbed the bridge of his nose. He put one of the earpieces to his lips and bit gently on it. "We have an extraordinary situation that requires an extraordinary solution. If we proceed, we don't know what will happen to the patient, but we do know that if we don't proceed, our patient will most likely die. Science has taught us that if we proceed through the conduit of fact, we can be reasonably confident of what we will see ahead, even in the dark. Your experience"—he gestured to Bruce, Kate, and Frank— "and our experience combined give me reasonable assurance that this will work. At the very least, we know that if this works her probability of survival greatly increases."

"And if she dies *because* of it?" Adhira interjected.

"I don't see this as any different from surgery, where there is *always* risk involved," Abe said.

The engineers quietly observed the doctors' deliberation. Huxley's hands went to the small of his back, then he drew his shoulders together and stretched his spine. "He's right," he said to Adhira. "This is exactly how we need to look at this. It's just a different kind of surgery. An electrical surgery, if you like."

Adhira dragged her palms down her face, stopping at her chin. "I wish they'd taught us how to prepare for this in medical school. I can't believe I'm going to say this, but if you two believe this is the right course of action for this patient, then I'm with you."

"I'll have them switch the generators on," Bruce said. Then he picked up the phone and ordered his team to proceed.

The next twenty minutes were busy with last preparations. Reporter Jessica Chung was again not-so-gently escorted out of the building, and calls were made, power was switched, and the battery bank was prepared. The drone was engaged, then it pinched Anabelle's blanket and pulled it off the bed so that her frame was revealed. The girl's body seemed to have evaporated with the removal of the blanket. So thin it was that the lumps and folds which could have been construed as her body were realized now as only pockets of air.

125

At the sight of Anabelle's gowned figure, Kate gasped slightly, and Frank looked away. Once more the doctors checked Anabelle's monitors before Adhira inclined her head, indicating that the engineers could proceed.

At precisely 11:05 p.m., the wires were drawn from the floor and connected to the clamps affixed to Kate's drone. Then Kate took the controller in both hands and lifted the drone from the floor. Six pairs of eyes followed the wires as they drew upward and hovered over Anabelle's bed, then six mouths closed with held breath.

The whir of the drone grated on them and Adhira cringed, wanting the sound to stop. She looked away, back at the bed, away, biting her thumbnail until her tooth broke through and she had to tear her ripped nail off with her other hand. The drone went lower, lower still, and then the robotic arms holding the clamps depressed their levers and the clamps opened over Anabelle's feet. As Adhira glanced back at the drone, Abe's fingers tightened over her wrist. She opened her hand to let him clasp it. Their dark skin was squeezed white. Huxley himself laid his fist on Abe's shoulder, then pressed his forehead to his fist.

Abe said to them, "Keep your eyes open for the miracle, we owe her that much." Huxley squeezed Abe's shoulder. Adhira squeezed Abe's hand. The doctors watched.

With steady hands and unblinking eyes, Kate navigated the drone to just three inches over Anabelle's feet. Steadily, she maneuvered the clamps onto Anabelle's feet and then released the levers.

The hospital went dark.

15

On the other side of the quiet city, Sylvia Baker woke with a scream. Despite the sedatives, sudden pain tore through the medicated membrane of her consciousness and flung her upright in a strange new darkness. Again she wailed, reaching with her good hand to the unlit spaces around her. Someone had hit her. Wetness curtained the lower half of her face and her fingers touched it now, feeling for tears or blood. A cone of light invaded her room, followed by Georgia, the nurse who had helped her with her suitcase just a few hours before.

The nurse squinted in the semi-darkness, took in the splatter of blood below Sylvia's nose, and slapped the overhead light on. Then she rushed to Sylvia, who was whimpering with confusion.

"Sylvia, darling! What happened?" Georgia's small arms went around the top of Sylvia's shoulders to give the older woman a quick hug before pulling away. "Let me get a look at that."

Sylvia's hands slid to the bloodstained blanket on her lap while the nurse inspected her face. Quickly, Georgia shuffled to the bathroom, wet one of the institution's towels, and dabbed the mess from Sylvia's face.

127

It wasn't so much the pain as the *anticipation* of pain that caused her to suck air through her teeth. "Owww," she sobbed.

"Well, now, Sylvia. I don't know how this happened, but you've got yourself a nosebleed. Do you remember bumping anything in your sleep? Maybe the wall or your headboard?" Georgia asked helpfully, squinting as she lowered her head to get a better look at Sylvia's nose. The nurse wiped Sylvia's face and pinched the bridge her nose with a clean segment of the towel.

Sylvia winced under the pressure. "I was sleeping when it happened. The pain, it just woke me up. This never happened at home. I want to go home." Her half-working lips pronounced home like *hobe* and the sound set fresh despair over her. Her shoulders slumped and she wept while Georgia held the towel to her face.

"You know, I used to get nosebleeds all the time when I was a kid," Georgia said. "My mom said it was because I picked it too much but, I tell you, it was dry as hell where we lived. I don't mean to use such language, Sylvia, but it was true. Farm fields north, south, east, and west, about sixteen hours from here and hot like you wouldn't believe. You want to know what we had out there? Nothing. No river. No lakes. Not a spring of anything. I swear we had to truck in ice just to have room temperature tap water. The thing that worked best for me wasn't pinching, it was always water. Hot water in the sink and my head under a towel over it. Kept me clean for days until the next one. You want me to put a humidifier in here, Sylvia?"

Only, Pandora knew that the humidifier wouldn't work. This wasn't a dry nose or a bedtime bump. While Sylvia reluctantly waded into the depths of sleep, there had been a stirring inside Pandora. She'd felt it creep up her exterior and make the thing that she was shudder; and Pandora *never* shuddered. She was reposing restlessly inside Sylvia, wondering at the intrusion, when there was a great drawing of energy that issued outward, away from her host and Southbridge to somewhere else. It … *hurt*. It was her first experience with pain, but what shocked her more was that she, Pandora, couldn't stop it. She wasn't averse to *Sylvia* feeling pain, necessarily, but not herself. Sylvia's bloody nose was Pandora's … what? Decomposition? Yes. Decomposition. That's exactly what it felt like. Whatever the interference was, it broke Pandora down and leaked her out of Sylvia's nose. Weakly, she gathered herself together, intent on figuring where the interference had come from. But first she needed her strength back, so she exited Sylvia and wound herself toward the next room, where Hattie Freemont was asleep.

While Pandora lurked, Georgia removed the towel from Sylvia's nose and inspected the flow. "It's stopped for now," she said to Sylvia. "Let's get you some fresh pyjamas, huh?" The nurse spun around and began pulling open the empty drawers, looking for Sylvia's clothes. Understanding, she spied Sylvia's suitcase in the corner, lifted it onto the reclining chair and opened it. She said kindly, "First days are always tough. You'll feel so much better when you're unpacked. I can help you with that tomorrow, if you'd like." She found a pink nightgown and gave it to Sylvia, then returned to the aide station so Sylvia could change. A short time later, with her nightgown and slippers on, Sylvia left her room.

"Are you okay, Mrs. Baker?" an aide Sylvia didn't recognize called out as she shuffled toward the recreation room.

From a door at the end of the corridor, Georgia emerged with a stack of towels in her hands. "I've got some fresh towels for you, Sylvia. How's your nose doing?"

Feeling like she was about to be guided back to her room, Sylvia said, "I'm not tired."

"You might feel better with some sleep, hun," Georgia reasoned.

At the scratching of slippers behind them, Sylvia and the nurses turned to see Ed Norman saunter down the hall, tying the belt of his robe. He smoothed his white hair so that it lay flat against his head. "Those two trying to get lottery numbers out of you?" he asked Sylvia.

Georgia giggled. "I still haven't won, you know."

"I can't make the numbers come up again, no matter how much I try," Ed said.

To alleviate Sylvia's confusion, the man behind the desk explained. "Eddie here is the biggest lottery winner we got. He won twenty-thousand big ones on the 649. When was it? This past February?"

"Beginning of March," Ed admitted. To Sylvia, he said, "I played the same numbers for thirty years. Win one time, and now I'm everyone's rabbit's foot. I swear, if those numbers ever hit the *big* one, there won't be a single loser in this building. I'm Ed, by the way. Call me Ed, Eddie, or Hey You, I pretty much answer to everything." He offered his hand to Sylvia's dead one and she shook it awkwardly with her good one. "Why don't you walk with me and I'll tell you the numbers? When I can't sleep I like to get myself some cocoa and watch the racoons try to pry the lids off the trash cans out back. We can see them through the window. Join me?"

He offered Sylvia his arm so earnestly that she took it without hesitation. Gloria mouthed her gratitude to Ed as they passed. Ed winked.

INTERFERENCE

They took their time through the building as Ed pointed to each door and explained a little about the residents behind them. There were Chatty Cathies and Nosy Neighbors and Boastful Braggarts. There were knitters, bakers, carvers, painters, gardeners, puzzlers, stamp collectors, scrapbookers, swimmers, walkers, photographers, and writers. It was a busy place, he asserted, where there was much to do if one had the will to do it. As an assisted-living home, Southbridge did just that: helped residents continue to enjoy life and do the things they liked best.

"I know it sounds preachy," Ed now confessed. "But I found that once I accepted the help, everything was easier, and I was much happier. It wasn't good for me to be alone. Here, I get to be around people. I can also escape to my room when they get to be too much." He lowered his voice a little. "I'll introduce you to Chester later."

A small laugh rose up Sylvia's throat. She hadn't laughed in so long that the feeling was foreign, but very much welcome. "I look forward to it," she said.

"Don't," Ed replied and, giggling, they proceeded to the kitchen. He drew a chair from the dining area and set it near the island.

Sylvia sat while Ed shuffled through cupboards and drawers, then to the fridge to get the milk. "Do you like it here, Ed?" she asked timidly.

Ed poured milk in a pot and turned the burner on. "I suppose I do. After my wife died, I stared at the living room wall until I forgot what the rest of the world looked like. My kids didn't like what it did to me, and *I* didn't like what it did to me. Being here, I still stare at the wall sometimes, but at least there's company to remind me that the world still exists. Depressing, but it's true. I have good days here, and I

131

know you will too. It'll just take some time, and then one day you'll find yourself in the kitchen in the middle of the night making cocoa for a new friend."

"I don't plan to stay," Sylvia said as she watched Ed stir powder into the pot. "My son put me in here for my rehab, but I'm going home once I'm done."

"It seemed like a prison sentence to me, too," Ed agreed. "You're in the Heartland Program, I take it?"

Sylvia nodded. "I start tomorrow already."

"They don't waste time, but that's a good thing. We really don't have any to waste, now, do we?" Carefully, Ed poured the cocoa into their mugs, adding three small marshmallows into each. Then they settled at a table near the windows where, as promised, trashcans were rattling under the weight of two raccoons.

"Do they ever get in?" Sylvia asked after a time.

"Not yet, but they still try every night."

"Did you hear about the river, Ed?"

"Who hasn't?"

"My son thinks it's a drilling mistake."

"Could be," Ed said. "Could be a blockage somewhere, could be Armageddon. Or maybe God was just thirsty." He blew over the top of his mug to cool it and took two quick sips.

"Are you a Christian?"

"I'm not *not* a Christian. Is that an answer?"

Sylvia held her cup against her chest. "I think everything is on a scale except math, science, and that. Either you believe or don't believe. Once that's settled, it's the semantics that tangle us up."

"I think there's a gray area in belief," Ed said honestly, openly, for the first time.

132

"I think that doubt is transient. When things are going well, we believe, but when things don't go well, we doubt. That's just our weakness come to mess with us, but that seed—of belief, I mean—never really goes away even if it seems like it. It's just planted so deep you can't see it. I've believed all my life, even when the rest of my family didn't. I don't know, it just felt good to me, even as a little girl. Does that sound silly, Ed?" Sylvia asked. "Gosh, this is the most I've talked with anyone since my stroke."

"Should I walk you back to your room?"

"Thanks, but I'm all right. I get dizzy from time to time, but I don't know if that's from stress or from the stroke. I like to be up whenever I'm feeling good." A trash can fell against the window and they saw through a spray of light the racoons pounce and scratch at it. Sylvia tapped on the glass as she had done many times to Troy's fish tank when he had them in his bedroom as a little boy. The raccoons turned to face the window. "They might be dirty, but they're sure cute," Sylvia said.

In the darkness outside, the racoons scattered and then hurled their bodies at the glass where she'd scratched. The animals drew back, gathered company, and then five of them were battering the glass. Six. Seven. Eight. Fourteen. The sound of claws scratching the window made them cringe, so with a flat palm Ed patted the window, hoping to scare the critters away. Instantly, teeth gnashed near Ed's hand. He stepped back, pulling Sylvia by the shoulder, spilling her cocoa.

"They … they must be rabid!" Ed gasped. Teeth and tongues gnashed the space in front of them, and soon it was marred a dark, wet red. From the centermost racoon's mouth spurted a tooth, yet the oblivious animal charged again. They heard a crack, and from the bottom of the windowpane, a thin fissure surged upward. Half-dragging Sylvia behind him, Ed dashed for the wall phone and picked it up. It immediately connected to the aide station and Ed stammered out the situation.

"Oh my God, they're going to break it!" Sylvia cried, moving as fast as her body would allow toward the corridor.

They hurried along until, suddenly, the room was quiet. Sylvia closed her eyes, clutching Ed's arm, but Ed stopped and chanced a backwards glance. "Would you look at that! They're gone, Sylvia. They've up and left!" He slapped his forehead, wondering if he had dreamt the whole thing.

Sylvia started to speak, but four aides were rushing past her to the kitchen, two of them with broom sticks.

They left the aides to their business while Ed walked Sylvia back to her room. "I'm afraid you've had the most exciting first night ever at Southbridge. Here I take you to see our raccoons, and they didn't want to be seen. They're usually much quieter."

"Beats staring at the wall," she reasoned.

"You're right about that," he chuckled. "You know, I think you're going to fit in real fine around here. You know where I live and that's Hattie's room right there." He released his arm from Sylvia's and pointed to Hattie's slightly open door. "Great lady. I think you'll get along well."

They said goodnight and began to turn toward their own rooms when Sylvia cocked her head. There was a sound coming from Hattie's room. "Do you hear that?" she asked. "Like a … a mouse or a whistle." She didn't want to infringe on the other woman's privacy, but something about the sound didn't seem quite right to Sylvia.

134

INTERFERENCE

"She's probably just snoring," Ed said. "She's got one of those machines for sleep apnea but sometimes she knocks it off in her sleep."

Sylvia did not look convinced, so Ed put his ear to Hattie's door, concentrating on the whistling sound, when his foot accidentally nudged the door a little more open. There, on the bed, was Hattie Freemont, face blue, eyes bulging and bloodshot, with the corrugated tube of her CPAP machine driven deep inside her throat. The whistling sound they'd heard was the machine trying to push air into Hattie's stomach. Ed's friend and Sylvia's new neighbor was dead.

16

Unbeknownst to the twelve hundred residents of Garrett's multi-family district, the power went out while they were sleeping and wasn't restored for eight hours, when the first wisps of dawn began to break above the horizon. Over morning coffee, the city's chatter involved a great deal of speculation as to the strange events, made stranger yet by distortions from the television and internet. The power, the water, the animals, the crash; all of it was sucked into the city's gossip vine and spewed from neighbor to neighbor, where it germinated in the sludge of conspiracy.

By the time Jesse Cardinal picked up his brother, a handful of protests had erupted against federal experimentation on municipalities. Briefly, a group of men blocked Jesse's car from proceeding to the command station between the fairgrounds and the Callingwood Bridge, until Johnny shouted out of his window that he knew where every one of them lived and that the syndicate would know too if they didn't move their asses.

After they proceeded past the parting men, Jesse cuffed Johnny on the back of the head. "The Native Syndicate? What the hell, man. You better not be messed up with them, or I swear I'll keep driving and drop you off in Indiana with Aunt Vicky. She'll set you straight."

"Chill, man." Johnny swatted the air in front of him. "They're no so bad. Politicians kill way more people, you know."

Jesse stomped on the break pedal and the car skidded to a stop near a group of uniformed onlookers by the command center. His nostrils flared at his little brother. "It's not funny," Jesse grumbled. "I need you to be serious. There's too much going on around here without me having to worry about you."

"No one asked you to worry about me," Johnny said flatly, waving to a group of three women in orange vests.

They continued to a flagged parking area, and Jesse turned off the engine. He squeezed the keys in his hand. "Want to know something? I think you'd be dead if I didn't worry about you. How many times didn't I get your ass out of trouble, huh? Mom and Dad keep bailing you out of shit, but they don't know the half of it. You're smart, damn you're smart, but you sure don't act like it."

"Good pep talk, bro. Next time remind me to bring ear plugs." Johnny slammed the door and the two brothers separately collected themselves to a Ministry of Natural Resources official. They gave their names and were directed to a tall woman with a clipboard in her hand.

"Myra Pearson, Provincial Emergency Operations," she shook their hands. "But just call me Myra. We've gone through the spiel with our earlier groups, so I'll just give you the short of it." She spun away from them and paced toward the river so quickly, they were almost jogging to keep up. Myra pointed at people working along the riverbank and many more on the riverbed itself. "Neon yellow are your emergency services, orange are ministry folks, and the bright green ones are your NGOs. You're going to be working with

137

them." She dragged a finger down her clipboard, turned the page, and tapped the top. "You've got the Animal Alliance of Canada, the David Suzuki Foundation, five municipal conservation societies, Ducks Unlimited, and about thirty local citizens. We estimate there's about eleven hundred birds stuck in the mud that need rescue. We also have two beaver habitats that will have to be relocated. Half a click down we've got a trapped moose and under the bridge there are some martens in a pile of deadwood that somehow heaped up and snarled them. The fish should be left for the wildlife but it's too much of a temptation in this case, so they'll have to be picked up. The mud is like quicksand if you're not careful with it. We're using snowshoes to distribute our weight, and I wouldn't go out there without them. They're right over there beside that box of vests. Any questions?" She blinked at them, waiting.

"I think we've got it," Jesse said for both. "Snowshoes, vests. Where do you want us right now?"

"You okay with picking up fish? It's not the most glamorous job we've got, but it's one of the most important." From under the bridge, a high whistle rang out and two men in hard hats waved Myra toward them. "Wish I could chat, but I'm being stretched today. If you need anything else, just go to the volunteer station near that tree." She left them.

They found gloves, garbage bags, and poke-sticks and grabbed their vests and snowshoes before proceeding to an unoccupied spot on the riverbank. This close, the thick smell of decay made them retch, so they put gum in their mouths before fastening their snowshoes to their boots. Tentatively, the brothers stepped out onto the riverbed. The mud sucked at their feet but held their weight, and they ventured further in the muck until Jesse stopped. "Stay close, okay? The way

138

INTERFERENCE

this is, I don't want us to get stuck, too." That he feared the water would return just as fast as it departed he did not mention to his brother, but Johnny seemed to be thinking the same thing because he didn't stray more than a few feet away.

In the brown-gray sludge, with the scattering of branches and weeds and plastic waste, the fish were hard to detect. Together they went with their poles, nudging and jabbing the uniform mess until they located spots that were softer than wood but harder than mud. They stabbed the things and brought into the bags not only fish but frogs, lizards, and more salamanders than they cared to count while a sizeable component of living creatures went directly to labeled plastic containers. The work was dirty and depressing, and in the short time it took them to fill their first bags they had gone quiet with strain. Halfway through filling their second bags, Jesse stepped onto a soft spot and was sucked up past his knees, and it was Johnny who pulled him out. So it went for the rest of the morning, with each brother rescuing the other, until their stomachs grumbled and they finally left the riverbed for lunch.

They were removing their snowshoes on the riverbank when Sarah's cruiser pulled up. She lowered her passenger window and bent toward them with two grease-stained bags in one hand. "Thought you two could use this," she said.

The men scrambled up the shallow embankment and lumbered tiredly over the gravel. Jesse took the bags, passed one to Johnny, and leaned deep inside the vehicle to kiss his wife. He refrained from kissing her in public whenever she was in uniform, but that morning—weighed with anxiety over bringing a baby into such a chaotic world—she suffered a panic attack that cramped her stomach and made her shake. Like the times before, her fear increased until Jesse pressed

139

ice to the back of her neck and whispered Elder Nikonha's affirmations to her. She could handle a gun, attend bloody crime scenes, go toe-to-toe with some of the most dangerous people in Canada, but it wasn't this which caused Sarah anxiety. Having lost her youngest sister in a car accident, it was the unpredictability of life itself. Advice from Elder Nikonha helped her through her worst times and with Jesse's support and a lot of sage tea, Sarah had gotten better over the years. Now pregnant, she couldn't take the healing tea, so when the bus crash claimed forty-two victims and Jesse was called out for too many wildlife incidents and Dan told her about Anabelle Cheever, the control over her anxiety slipped. And when the river suddenly disappeared, it vanished entirely with the water. Now as her husband kissed her, she wrinkled her nose at the smell and pushed his face away.

Johnny's head appeared beside his brother's in the window as he opened his bag. "Mushroom burgers. Right on," he said, and popped a French fry in his mouth. "Thanks. I'm starving."

"Do you have time to join us?" Jesse gestured toward the portable tables under a large oak tree near the walking path.

Sarah declined with a sigh. "Wish I could, but Falconer is hosting a news conference near the command station. I'm just here to keep things civil."

Chewing, Johnny asked, "That hot reporter going to be there?" A quick elbow to the ribs pulled him from the window, making him frown at his brother.

"She's bad news. Literally and figuratively," Jesse scolded.

"Just the way I like 'em."

Sarah rolled her eyes. "I would love to babysit you two, but I've got to run. Be careful out there, and, Johnny…?"

INTERFERENCE

"Yeah?"

"Smelling like that, *no* woman is going to want you anyway," Sarah said and drove on.

"Remind me about her sisters."

"Too good for you."

"All of them?"

"Maybe not Shar." Jesse took a bite of his burger.

"Isn't she ... didn't she die in a car accident?"

"Uh-huh."

Johnny wiped his mouth with the back of his hand. "Asshole."

"You asked for it."

A volunteer came by with bottles of water, and as they drank their attention swung to an area near the command station, where a draped podium had been deposited. Chairs were being organized into rows and sawhorses were pulled into a wide perimeter around the conference area. Four cruisers, including Sarah and Dan's, flanked the command station and gave the no-nonsense impression that disobedience would not be tolerated. The officers waited in their vehicles until a small SUV pulled up beside them, and out walked Mayor Falconer's communication manager, Nicole Lewis, dressed in a light gray suit. The day had significantly warmed since the morning, and yesterday's snow was now a dirty layer of slush that spotted Nicole's pants as she went to greet Dan.

"I should have worn black," she said and shook his hand.

Dan gestured to his own legs. "And they say fashion isn't practical."

Nicole pinched the fabric above her knee and shook her pantleg. "That's what's passing for fashion these days?"

141

"Touché." Dan put a hand to his heart, then turned toward the conference area. He walked beside her, explaining. "We've blocked the immediate area for journalists only, and you've already seen our outer checkpoint on your way in. Not too much trouble so far, just that bunch of quacks in alien costumes." He pointed past the perimeter where a costumed gathering with picket signs was accumulating.

"Uggh," Nicole moaned. "They were at City Hall today too. Can't you arrest them or something?"

"And let the aliens abduct one of *us* when they come? Not a chance. *Those* idiots are the ones they need to experiment on." He laughed.

"I'm with you on that one. All right, let's get to the schedule. Ada will arrive in twenty minutes. You can let the reporters in now, and would you mind also talking to our favorite friend again?"

"What'd she do this time?" Dan looked over Nicole's head to the line of vehicles waiting at the checkpoint, where Jessica Chung's red Mini Cooper idled at the front.

"The usual. She's pretty much camped out in front of Ada's house. Shoved a microphone at her children when they left for school this morning, asking if their mother has mentioned anything the city should know about."

"Christ." Dan pinched the bridge of his nose.

Nicole removed her vibrating phone from her pocket. "That's Ada. I've got to go. Thanks for your help, Dan." She tiptoed across the mud-soaked ground to a large, open-faced tent while Dan instructed his team to direct the reporters to the parking area. True to form, Jessica Chung sped past the checkpoint, the wheels of her car spitting up mud onto passersby. Then she stopped and was out of her car, her cameraman hustling to keep up. She hurried across the

142

roadway without looking. A horn blared and a van from CTV London slammed to a stop only a few inches away. She hit the hood of the van with her purse, swearing at the driver, and rushed onward to the seating area, taking a seat directly in front of the podium while her cameraman stood aside.

Seeing her sitting alone, Dan went over to her. He wasn't quiet about his approach, yet even when he was standing right in front of her, she pretended not to notice him as she dug inside her purse. She finally looked up when Dan cleared his throat. "I have the right to be here," she crowed at him.

"You do, and I'm not here to tell you otherwise, but you do have a responsibility to behave yourself, Ms. Chung."

She snapped her gum. "You mean *be quiet*."

"I mean stay where you're seated, do not approach the mayor, do not approach her children, do not trespass in the hospital, be a decent human being."

"Like your wife?" she retorted, knowing full well the sting it would cause. Jessica herself had covered the scandal. She'd even gotten an on-air apology from both Brandy and Shane before calling into question the police chief's investigatory prowess, as he was unaware of the ongoing affair.

Dan pressed his tongue to the roof of his mouth to keep himself from saying something he would regret. "Be good, Ms. Chung. That's all I'm asking." As he walked away, he thought he'd heard her murmur where *Dan* could go, but he ignored this.

Platoons of journalists assembled quickly as the sun peaked in the sky, and there was a thrum of conversation between them when Mayor Ada Falconer's silver Chevy Tahoe pulled to the side of the command station. She shut the engine and all four doors swung open to reveal not only the

143

mayor but Premier Henrik Madigan and two men in dark suits. Briefly, they looked at the crowd of reporters and stopped at the command tent, where they were given lanyards and shook hands with members of the coordination team. The feedback of loudspeakers being turned on fell over the crowd and they became quiet, waiting.

A few minutes later, the quartet made their way towards the reporters, with the Premier standing aside to let Ada take the podium. Cameras went on, microphones were readied, and from the back of the gathering, Nicole Lewis gave the thumbs up to her boss at the front. Ada tipped her chin and stepped closer to her microphone.

"Good afternoon everyone and thank you for being here. Over the last few days, our city has been faced with challenges never before seen. Only a week ago, in the Callingwood tour bus tragedy, we lost forty-two members of our community. They were mothers and fathers, sons and daughters, grandparents, neighbors, friends. Our hearts go out to everyone affected by this loss, and I'd like to take this opportunity to thank those of you who have supported them during their time of grief. To our first responders, from the bottom of my heart, thank you for your service to our community." Ada paused and her head swiveled above the seated crowd, then she continued. "Unfortunately, tragedy waits for no one. As you are all aware, one of our significant water sources, the Callingwood River, has run dry. I want to ensure all citizens of our community that we are working around the clock to figure this out as quickly as we can. I've met with members from the Ministry of Natural Resources and Forestry, the Ministry of the Environment, the Ministry of Agriculture, and the Federal Ministry of Public Safety, along with many provincial and federal emergency response

144

personnel. Here is what we know: the drainage or blockage is occurring at two locations, approximately seventeen kilometers north of the city and again eight kilometers south, at the Clarent's Bay and Albany Cove estuaries, respectively. To the north and south of these areas, the river continues as before, due in large part to a number of tributaries that unfortunately do not enter the demarcation points passing through our city. As you know, the section of the Callingwood River that runs through Garrett has drained overnight, resulting in the inestimable loss of aquatic life and their habitats as well as thirty-five percent of our water supply. Rest assured, our community is not in jeopardy of running out of water. Already, Lake Huron represents the bulk of our supply. Until we know more, however, a boil-water advisory will remain in place. We expect to have an update on this within the next forty-eight hours. On behalf of all Garretters, I want to thank Premier Madigan for his support as we work to restore our great city to its glorious self. Thank you." She drew away from the microphone and pulled her shoulders back, ready for the journalistic assault.

Cameras flashed and three dozen hands shot up, but it was Jessica Chung who leapt from her seat and shouted above the buzz of queries. "Ms. Falconer! Ms. Falconer!"

Ada purposefully pointed to a demure man in glasses and a red scarf in one of the back rows. He stood, forcing an indignant Jessica Chung to take her seat once again. "Ms. Falconer, Ched Bosswain from CTV London. I have two questions for you. With all the people on this, scientists and whatnot, can you tell us if they have any suspicion as to the cause of the drainage? Also, is there a timeline as to when citizens can expect the water to return, if at all?"

145

"Thank you for your questions. We are investigating a number of theories, but until I have concrete evidence, I prefer not to release that information. As for the river's return, I'm sad to say that your guess is as good as mine. We simply do not know the answer to that at the moment, but we are hopeful that it will return soon and take it as a good sign that only a portion of the river has been affected. As I've stated before, we will do everything we can to get to the bottom of this, for the good of our community. Thanks, Ched." Ada gave the reporter, the sea of reporters, her best commiserating, tight-lipped smile.

"Ms. Falconer!" Jessica Chung hopped out of her seat, getting a little too close to the podium for Dan's liking. He took a step toward her, but, seeing this and the ruckus it would cause on televisions across the world, Ada discretely pumped a palm beside her hip that told Dan to fall back.

"Yes, Ms. Chung," Ada said, though inside her civil mouth her teeth were clamped tight.

"Jessica Chung, CGTV. Mayor, there have been rumours that the city has been selling water from the Callingwood River for years, if not decades, and that you were personally warned by your advisors that the practice could cause supply issues, perhaps even what we are witnessing today. How do you respond?" Jessica's smug mouth pinched closed as she waited for Ada to answer.

No one noticed the rage that boiled up inside Ada. Her political career had taught her to kill her emotions, or they would be tied up and publicly hanged. She wouldn't let anyone, especially not Jessica Chung, kick that stool from under her, so Ada met the question, and Jessica's eyes, directly. "Ms. Chung, our city has never nor *will* ever sell our water. Our records are public, and anyone who has read them would

INTERFERENCE

know that there is not one iota of truth in your statement. Furthermore, you are welcome to tour our treatment facility any time you wish, with proper attire, of course." There was a smattering of laughter as many pairs of eyes zeroed in on Jessica Chung's mud-spotted white pants. "Next question?"

Color bloomed on Jessica's cheeks. Her nostrils flared. Ada's name rang from the lips of many reporters, but Jessica took another step forward so that she was only six feet from Ada's podium. Dan tensed, but then Jessica retreated, if only an inch.

"Last question, Mayor. The city's Fall Festival is one of the most popular events in Southern Ontario, something citizens and Canadians across the province look forward to every year. Are there any plans to cancel the festival, given the tragedies of late?"

Ada relaxed a little. "Good question, Ms. Chung. Our Fall Festival is a ninety-two-year tradition and brings thousands of visitors to our city every October. It gives our great community the opportunity to show the world our agricultural and artistic merits but—more importantly—proudly represents what we can achieve when we unite our efforts. Now more than ever I believe we need to lean on each other and come together with a positive, constructive focus. Our Fall Festival will continue as scheduled and I am happy to announce that this year, Premier Henrik Madigan and the Government of Ontario will partner with our farming community and our 4-H Club to make this year's festival even better. Premier?"

On cue, Henrik Madigan joined Ada at the podium, and she stepped back to let him speak. "Good afternoon. Thank you, Ms. Falconer. On behalf of the Province of Ontario—" he started, but then, pulling in from the street to the

147

gravel road, a horn blared. Again and again and again it sounded, with no apparent reason except to get attention. Heads turned away from the Premier toward the sound where a rusty old Winnebago glided past the checkpoint while scrambling officers smacked the sides, trying to get the driver to stop.

From the loudspeakers mounted to the roof came a man's steady voice. "The apocalypse is here! Prepare to repent and save your souls! Read your Bibles! This is the work of the Lord! Jeremiah line 50, verse 38: *'A drought on her waters, and they will be dried up! For it is a land of idols, and they are mad over fearsome idols.'* The water went with our innocence! Our sins make us thirsty, but we are quenched with the Lord!"

News cameras swung to the driver now, a mottled-faced middle-aged man with wild black hair and a chest-length beard. With a flat hand he hammered the outside of his door, where a large orange arrow pointed to a mural painted on the aluminum. There, a number of sheep were flocked around the Grim Reaper, but the Reaper had Ada Falconer's face. She was leading them through the gates of hell.

Dan yanked the radio from his shoulder, directing his team to the Winnebago, then ran toward it. Still at the podium, Madigan said, "This press conference is over." He and Ada were swept into Ada's vehicle by his security team.

"Don't burden your soul with their lies! Cast down your loyalty to false hope and raise up instead the—"

The loudspeakers squealed as Sarah got a foot on the driver's running board and yanked the microphone from the driver's hand. She leapt away as the man swerved and pushed the gas pedal. Faster the RV went, now spraying up gravel at chasing officers. Orders to stop went unheeded and,

148

INTERFERENCE

witnessing this savage departure from the news conference, cameramen hurried to catch the event on film. Dan raced toward the RV, gesturing for it to stop. From the back, from the sides, officers and security officials rushed to the madman, but it was Jessica Chung who planted herself in the middle of the road, just ahead of the driver. Her harried cameraman, filming from the side of the road, waved for Jessica to get out of the way, but she just quickened her report, her near-frenzied voice defiantly raving on. The driver hit his horn, warning Jessica to move. She stayed put. He pressed and held his horn; she dug her stilettos into the mud. The RV drew close, closer.

"Idol worshipper! The Lord won't save whores of Babylon! Get out of my fucking way!" The man spat out his window.

Too late, Jessica realized that the RV was not going to stop and, worse, that her shoes were stuck in the mud. She dropped her microphone, trying to pull herself from the muck. Tearing her right foot out of her shoe, she looked up to see her face reflected in the RV's front grill. She closed her eyes, bracing for death, when she was rocketed out of her other shoe.

149

17

In the brightly lit main-floor court of Garrett General's cafeteria, Greg Huxley poured his fourth coffee of the morning. Awake for the better part of thirty-four hours, he yawned at the carafe that was giving him trouble and shifted his cup to the next, where the full pot more adequately surged. He liked it black, but today he added sugar and cream and he was half-hypnotized by the caramel swirl of hot liquid and cold cream when he felt a gentle hand on his shoulder. Abe shook a plastic tumbler at him. "There's a hole in your cup too?"

"Big one," Huxley groaned, and took a blueberry muffin from a pastry basket, then both men sauntered to a quiet table near the window. They dropped into their chairs, exhausted, and sipped their coffees as they gazed at the sun-drenched walking path near the staff parking area where coatless pedestrians and scrub-clad employees enjoyed a late autumn warm spell. After a time, Huxley said, "That was something, huh?"

"You know, Hux, I stopped being surprised a long time ago, but this ... whatever it was ... makes me rethink science."

"Maybe we're dreaming."

"That would make more sense," Abe agreed, neither man openly willing to accept that they had just hooked up an

150

INTERFERENCE

electrified patient to a battery system and that, stranger still, the charge coming from Anabelle Cheever was almost nuclear.

After the clamps were secured to Anabelle's feet, the instant surge resulted in a brilliant flare of sparks, then forty-five seconds of darkness as the generators were overwhelmed. They were fumbling around for their flashlights when suddenly the lights turned back on. Their cellphones began ringing moments after with the same news: not only had Anabelle Cheever single-handedly charged three-hundred and fifty dead batteries in the space of a few minutes, but engineers calculated that she was generating enough energy to power the entirety of Garrett's significant industrial sector, should longer-term strategies need to be considered.

The situation was so incredible that Premier Madigan, who rushed to the city to tour the depleted river and was thus apprised of Anabelle's condition, requested a visit with her medical team. As though he wasn't busy enough already, Huxley convened a meeting with Adhira, Abe, Bruce, Kate, Premier Madigan, and Mayor Falconer before their press conference along the riverside. At one time, a meeting with Ontario's political elite might have tickled the doctors, but the theater of the meeting drew them away from their work and gave them headaches. Worse, Madigan's suggestion of provincial or federal command evoked the spectacle of a much larger circus that no doctor was prepared to endorse.

Now, as Huxley picked disinterestedly at his muffin, he said to Abe, "What do you make of her condition?"

Abe sighed. "On the record?"

"Of course not."

"God," Abe said simply. "There is no other explanation for an almost complete recovery as soon as that."

"You think?"

151

Abe put his tumbler on the table and, with his forearms on his thighs, leaned toward Huxley. He removed his glasses and wiped an accumulation of crust from the corners of his eyes. "Maybe a thousand years from now we'll know what we worked with today. A hundred and fifty years ago, we didn't even know that viruses existed. Now we know there are thousands, hundreds of thousands, potentially millions of them. Even the value of basic handwashing was severely underestimated. Now it's our first line of defense. My education has taught me to believe that all mysteries can eventually be solved with science, but my *experience* has taught me that science is the dominion of God."

Huxley couldn't disagree with this. His own professional experience was a sort of clumsy union of science and religion, but it was one he was comfortable with and often leaned on. That was why he'd always prayed when he was a about to lose a patient. And a time or two, he believed it worked. When Willie Shumacher, then eighty-four, suffered his second massive heart attack and was brought into the ER during one of Huxley's night shifts, the man's heart had already been silent for ten minutes. Only because Willie's distraught wife had to be dragged from the room by the hospital's security team, Huxley had worked on the man for longer than usual. Thirty-seven minutes later, after they had exhausted attempts with the defibrillator and shots of amiodarone and epinephrine were administered too late because of a snowstorm that slowed the arrival of the ambulance, Huxley was about to declare Willie's time of death. Outwardly, he sought the wall clock, but inwardly Huxley sought God on Willie's behalf. He had not yet pronounced the minute of Willie's death when Willie's monitor beeped and a little bump bulged the otherwise flat green line. Another bump followed and another, and then Huxley and his team threw themselves back at their patient with a vigor so instinctive it was as though God Himself was working through them. That was seven years ago, and Huxley had been invited to Ivy and Willie Schumacher's wedding anniversary dinner every April since.

The unexpected survival of an old man wasn't the first time Huxley had sensed a greater power working over him. No. Before Willie, there had been five-year-old Maddie Davis who had drowned in her family's pool. Another dead-on-arrival, the girl's lips and fingernails were ocean-blue and beyond Huxley's help so, while he played at trying to help the helpless child, he did the only thing he really could do—he prayed. And though he knew it was futile, he worked on the girl for longer than was reasonable, much longer than was even considered sane, and got the shock of his life when she sat up and hugged him. He was no miracle worker, but he wasn't so naïve as to believe that miracles didn't happen. They did. Anabelle Cheever's condition was only one such case.

When the sparks subsided and the lights returned and they chanced to touch Anabelle the previous night, they finally found what they were hoping for. There was still a slight buzz to Anabelle's skin, much like the prickle of a shock from dry socks when touching someone else's skin, but it was neither painful nor unbearable. They were finally able to work on her. First they had to turn her over and check for the bedsores they knew would be there. But there weren't any. Not a single one. Where there should have been several, maybe even a dozen, the skin on her backside was almost rosy with health. And when Huxley undressed the bandage he'd placed on Anabelle's head, he found a stubble of previously shaved hair just beginning to grow, but only the faintest wisp

153

of a scar underneath. The wound that he had operated on a week ago, piecing together the skull that was fractured like a windshield … was healed. He had touched the faint outline of the pink scar tissue underneath the stubble and wondered for the first time if he ever had any control at all. Now, as he looked at the craters beneath Abe's red eyes, Huxley said of God, "He sure has a funny sense of humor, doesn't He?"

"At least it's interesting." Abe nodded.

They were just finishing their coffees, readying for one last visit with their patient before heading home, when Adhira appeared at their table. She was wearing a dark green dress, and though she had fixed her makeup, the fresh eyeshadow and thick liner were not enough to awaken her face. The crescents of darkness under her eyes were crudely covered and gave her almost a cadaverous appearance. Still, she smiled brightly at them with newly glossed lips. "Gentlemen," she said, "I think I'm still in shock."

Abe smiled affectionately at his co-worker. "You *must* be. Here Hux and I are ready for bed and you are ready for a ballroom. Is the Premier returning? Or maybe the Prime Minister is making an appearance?"

Adhira shook her head. "Thankfully, no. It's just a lunch meeting. It's too late to cancel, otherwise I would." She said this half-heartedly, for beyond her puffed eyes was a glimmer of anticipation.

"I wish I were that young again," Abe said nostalgically. "Maybe I wouldn't need so much coffee."

"You did even then," Huxley reminded him. "You just didn't need as much sugar. Remember the surgical conference in Toronto when half our doctors got snowed away over the weekend?"

INTERFERENCE

"Ah," Abe scratched his chin, remembering. "You're right. Winter of '99. I had more caffeine than blood in my body until they got back."

Adhira checked her watch and set her purse on the table so she could put her jacket on. "Well, I'm off. See you two tonight?"

"Tomorrow for me," Abe yawned.

"Lucky bastard," Huxley coughed into his hand, and with droopy eyes the men watched the quick stride of Adhira's feet against the linoleum as she left the cafeteria.

Outside, the mid-afternoon sun had warmed to a miraculous heat, and Adhira was not more than ten steps from the building when she had to open and remove her coat. Gone was yesterday's snow, and the smell of barbeque was in the air. By the time she reached the restaurant where she was meeting Troy, she had broken out in a thick sweat, even with her air conditioning on. The makeup she had reapplied was now caked across her cheeks and her eyeliner had smeared onto the top of her eyelids, just beneath her eyebrows. She pulled a tissue from the box on her passenger seat, licked it, and was dabbing at her face when Troy appeared beside her door. He waved as she held a finger up for him to wait a moment. Troy nodded, stepping back while she hastily finished.

"Didn't mean to surprise you," he said when she finally opened her door.

"I'm so tired nothing could surprise me today," Adhira admitted honestly, and followed Troy to her favorite bistro near Garrett's only library.

Inside they sat at a booth near a ceiling-high bookshelf tucked into the back wall. The dimly lit space smelled of fish and hot tomatoes and, even at this early hour, many varieties of wine. Adhira declined wine and took coffee instead, then

155

ordered a smoked cheese salad while Troy ordered a tapas sampler with olives and skewered meats and pâté-topped crostini. The waiter was arriving with her coffee when she asked, "I was wondering, how is Sylvia settling in?"

"Snug like the last piece of a puzzle," Troy said with a half-hearted grin. "She doesn't like it, as you probably know but it's what's best for her, so I'm the bad son for a while." He shrugged, resting his arm against the back of his booth.

He hadn't shaved since she last seen him and as he sat across from her, Adhira admired the shadow on his jawline. She sipped her coffee and said, "I've yet to meet a patient who didn't think the same of their children when they have to make the hard choices. After a medical episode—whatever it is—patients always want to go home to what they know. I can't blame them. I'd probably be the same if it were me."

"Do you have children?" Troy asked.

Adhira shook her head. "Unfortunately, no. I haven't got anyone to put *me* in a home yet." No sooner were the words out of her mouth, Adhira cringed. "That was a terrible joke. I'm sorry. I'm so tired I don't know how to think straight anymore."

"No need to apologize. But if you're that tired, we can do this another time."

On cue their food arrived, and Adhira found herself with a mouthful before the waiter had even left the table. She swallowed this down with coffee and said, "My life is half exhaustion, half too busy to eat, and a smidge of sleep. I take what I can get when I can get it. You've got the best of me at the moment, I'm afraid." Looking at the man in front of her, something perhaps chiseled from giant hunk of testosterone, Adhira realized too late that she should have canceled their meeting. He smelled good, looked incredible, and said nothing offensive. *She* smelled like bedpans and looked and spoke like what was often found inside them. "You must get as busy as I do with your line of work, no?" she asked.

"I do," he said. "But only during trial. At least now, that is. Back when I was articling, I don't think I saw my own pillow for the first year. I slept on a chair in the file room so often that I got used to it; told myself that I preferred it to my own bed. It took my chiropractor four years to put me straight again, and even though I know I'd do it all over again if I had to, I'd like to think the students we have now are smarter than I was. There's only so long a person can live like that, or they start to go crazy. For me, that was when chugging a Red Bull had the same effect as a cup of camomile tea," Troy reminisced. "Your line of work is not as forgiving as mine, though. Losing a case is not the same as losing a patient, as much as some arrogant people out there believe. Speaking of which, I hear your patient had an interesting night last night."

"So much for privacy," Adhira groaned.

"Mostly the small-town telephone game." He shrugged. "It's always been like that here. It's part of the reason I was glad we didn't move here until my last year of high school, and even that was bad enough. Coming from Toronto, I was an alien to them. So I hit university as fast as I could and never looked back. That was normal teenager stuff, but a case like Anabelle's in a city that wants to know what you're eating for breakfast and what time you go to bed because there's nothing else to be excited about … it's just too big of a story to hide. Maybe in Toronto it could have been kept private— in a city like that there is always something strange happening. Strangeness is the fabric of the city. But here, a patient with"—he leaned over the table and whispered— "power … it will kill a person trying to keep a secret like that."

157

His eyes rose to the top of his sockets and he stared at her intently. For a moment, Adhira felt uneasy. She knew that Anabelle's secret couldn't be kept. As a whole, the city was incapable of it. But there was an innuendo not so much to *what* Troy was saying, but the *way* he was saying it that made her pull back from the table. She had never warmed to lawyers, even the long timers who defended the hospital against the fortunately rare cases of litigation. There was an aggression in their blood that Adhira didn't think could be nurtured out, so she had removed their type from her dating pool early on. Maybe it was her exhaustion that had made her consider Troy different from the others, and as she looked at him now she wondered if he were really that different at all. She said, "You say that as though it's on a billboard somewhere."

He bit an olive from a bamboo skewer, looking at her as he chewed. "Forgive me if I sound pessimistic, but it's what I'm paid to do. I just want you to be aware that situations like that tend to snowball before you even know the snow has been packed. As your legal team will tell you, it's in your best interest to keep a tight lid on her care and her recovery, even if the city needs a champion right now."

Adhira pushed her plate aside, feeling like a scolded child, though she had done nothing wrong. "Thanks for the advice."

"Take it," he said, and it was then that Adhira realized that whatever affinity that previously existed between them had grown cold. He rubbed his chin as though debating how to proceed, then said, "You took good care of my mother, so I'm here as a courtesy. Anabelle's parents have retained my firm for potential action against your hospital. We haven't filed the paperwork yet, but I thought you should know."

158

18

The air had grown from warm to hot by the time Troy left Adhira, open-mouthed, back at the bistro. After he'd made known the purpose of their meeting, she'd withered before him—and it was not without a hint of satisfaction that he watched her recoil as though she had been slapped. She had perfect cheeks for slapping, big and round, but to do to her what he had done to so many others would bring attention where he most needed privacy. Instead, he took her with his other skills; first slathering up her insecurities by fake admiration and coquettish banter, then slicing into the most tender part of Adhira: her profession. Of course, he pretended it pained him, but, really, the pain was more from unfulfillment—much like the kind he'd suffered as a teenager when the girls were too frigid to give him anything more than a dry rub. Now, having been in Garrett for almost two weeks, Troy felt that dark urge creeping up on him again, and it made him irritable.

He wasn't a rapist. No, that sort of thing was below him. The parting of already open flesh posed no challenge to him at all. His parents, or whatever deity commanded them, had bestowed upon him the kind of stature women, and even many men, gravitated toward. Troy was tall and lean but muscular. That he was unnaturally attractive became clear

159

every time a woman accepted a ride for which she never reached her destination. As he'd said to Adhira, secrets in Toronto were much easier to keep. In Garrett, however, there was no getting out of the spotlight, no matter how far in the shadows one hid. Its reach required all residents, even former residents, to act according to social norms, or be subjected to scrutiny. Troy knew that even small-town scrutiny could be dangerous, so here he was in a city that he didn't like, caring for a mother he didn't care for. Her stroke had come at the worst possible time. Not only was his office in the middle of acquiring Toronto's second-largest malpractice firm—Troy's own Baker & Chessington being the first—but he hadn't satisfied his dark urge in many months. It had begun to claw at him so that he couldn't concentrate on anything but. He felt he'd already shown the appropriate amount of assistance to his mother and was preparing his return to Toronto when he heard about the girl.

Anabelle.

It had come from the nurses at the hospital. Even when Troy had filled her vulnerable heart with the potential of passion, Adhira wasn't forthcoming about Anabelle's condition. Most doctors held their work in confidence, as Adhira had, but during one of his more burdensome visits to his mother, news of Anabelle's situation rumbled across the ward like an avalanche after a heavy snowfall. What most interested Troy was that the uniqueness of her condition suggested some kind of supernatural interference. Troy himself was not immune to belief in metaphysical power. The darkness that came to him when he was ten could only have been of another world, for it was definitely not acceptable in this one. It encouraged and empowered him to do things that he did not want to suppress, and he'd felt a kinship with his Dark

Friend ever since he killed his first cat. *Good boy*, his Dark Friend purred to him. *Now do it again.* He did. And by the time Troy was thirteen, in the junky neighborhood where he and his mother lived, there was not a single stray animal.

His teens were another story. During the time when weirdness could be passed off as the vagaries of adolescence, Troy had the shock of his young life when, deliriously excited in the back seat of his mother's car with Misty Alvarez one hot August night, he accidentally rolled up the window with his elbow and her hair got caught. Neither of them noticed that Misty's hair was trapped until she bent her head to kiss him. Moaning but not wanting to wreck the moment, Misty tapped Troy's shoulder and gently explained that her hair was stuck. By now, however, Troy was deep in his own mind, oblivious to reason. He held her wrists and pulled her closer to him, yanking her hair tight, tighter, so tight that a song might play if a violin bow was slid upon it. Then Misty's cries of ecstasy became cries of pain when his Dark Friend took over.

Never before had Troy succumbed to his Dark Friend when he was with someone. Until then, he had always managed to refuse his Dark Friend's entry into his psyche when he wasn't alone, but not for fear of hurting others. He repressed his Dark Friend because of what its discovery might do to *himself.*

That night in his mother's car was the first time his Dark Friend joined him in the presence of another, and it gave him a greater euphoria than he had ever known. Misty's distress hardened him until his erection was almost painful. Almost. Every time Misty screamed, his Dark Friend cheered him on, stroking those inner parts of him he kept hidden but were then very much alive, feeding him the way only his Dark Friend could. When it was over, Misty's eye makeup was

161

dripping down her cheeks, and her nose was leaking over her lips and chin. The quiver of her breath through her wet nose evoked a vulnerability that he found particularly appealing, and he told her how beautiful she was. Then he let go of her wrists and pressed the button that lowered the window. Some of Misty's hair had fallen on the gravel outside. More fluttered onto his mother's floor mat beside them. That was when Misty slapped him and flung herself out of the Corolla's open window, screaming.

He should have killed her. Instead, Troy threw her sandals out of the car, over the cliff, and drove off, letting Misty find her own way home. For a long time, he wondered if Misty would complain to the police. He didn't *feel* like a rapist. The first part had been very consensual, and Troy felt that the latter was just a rough extension of their intimacy. He didn't want to end up in prison, however, so he bided his time, waiting for the event to catch up with him, but Misty never did tell. He suffered no dirty looks from her friends at school, no angry appearance from her parents, no investigative phone call from the police. As weeks then months went by, when he'd gone on a number of boring dates—only so more girls could confirm that he was a decent human being—his Dark Friend's whispers once again became demands.

It wasn't sex his Dark Friend wanted. It was never sex, though sometimes it did start out that way. It was pain. It was fear. It was terror and agony and the slow crawl of death. His Dark Friend roared with approval when Troy was patient, shunned him like a child when he was not. There were rewards for making his Dark Friend happy. That thing inside him gave him strength and a level of cunning he didn't think any other person had. Now his Dark Friend wanted Anabelle. *Get her,* it told him. In the thirty plus years of their partnership, his

INTERFERENCE

Dark Friend had never demanded a specific death; any death would do. But the strangeness of Anabelle so tantalized his Dark Friend that Troy felt it salivating inside his head.

But how to get close to a protected woman? If his mother were still at Garrett General, he might have been able to figure it out. He could have seduced the hospital staff, perhaps even the uniformed officers he saw outside her door when he chanced an elevator ride up that way on the second night of his mother's stay. That close, his Dark Friend was almost frenzied with eagerness, and it was Troy who had to hold him back. It pained him to do so. When the elevator doors opened, Troy didn't expect his skin to burn or his eyes to water or his mouth to tremble like a lost hiker in a desert coming upon a mirage. But that's what it was. When those doors opened, the feeling that came over Troy almost crushed him to his knees. It was a drop of water on a dry tongue, a nibble of bread after a hunger strike, the bellow of a ship's horn to the shores of an almost deserted island. Whatever Anabelle was, it was what his Dark Friend wanted. No. It was what his Dark Friend *needed*.

Go back Troy. Dump your mother and go back! The voice inside his head ordered him as they drove to Southbridge. And if it weren't for the radio report on the river and the chaos that put the entire city on edge, well, he supposed he would have gone back and snuck into Anabelle's room. Reflecting now as he drove, however, he was glad he hadn't. The state he was in, his work would have been sloppy and sent him straight to prison.

He hadn't got to where he was by being sloppy, though. Troy had been a meticulous student ever since the first grade. Where other kids tossed their coats and books and bags around the cloak room in his school, Troy—always the last

163

one in and the last one out—carefully gathered his things and put them in their proper places. Even with that first cat he was careful, waiting until the winter when the stench wouldn't attract attention. And he'd only advanced to *people* when he'd gotten into enough of a rhythm with stray cats and dogs that he could keep surprises to a minimum. He learned that darkness, inner and outer, was his friend and that solitude was an even greater companion. Victims without partners or children or friendships were as easy as candles: a quick blow and you'd never known they'd been lit at all. He couldn't do this with Anabelle, of course. There were too many eyes, too many people enmeshed in her recovery. The whole city was rooting for her, for fuck's sake, so Troy had to abandon his preferred method of hunting and instead approach the only other way he knew how: with paperwork.

As luck would have it, he found Anabelle's father in the hospital cafeteria being badgered by Jessica Chung. A large man, William Cheever was taller than Jessica even as he sat eating a bowl of soup. Troy had come down for a respite from his mother's whining and saw the reporter shove a microphone between the man's face and his rising spoon. Unconcerned with the look of utter despondency on William's face, Jessica ordered her cameraman out from behind a curved metal art installation and told him to keep rolling no matter what. Calmly, William Cheever returned his spoon to his bowl, wiped his lips, and pushed back from the table. Heads turned and mouths gasped as William attempted to stand but fell back into his chair when Jessica leaned against him, demanding he give the city an update on his daughter and what was really happening in the ICU. Ordinarily, Troy would have left a situation like this alone. Unless it involved malpractice action, there was no benefit

INTERFERENCE

for his involvement. The scene was dark providence of course, and when Troy swept in to rescue William, he knew he had found his way to Anabelle.

Presently two blocks away from the Cheever's north-side bungalow where they would review their representation agreement, Troy wondered not for the first time what it was from Anabelle that his Dark Friend wanted. His is Dark Friend's urgency suggested to him that either Anabelle's otherness would go away or that something or someone else might want it too; and though he tried to push these thoughts aside, the latter wouldn't be suppressed. He sought an explanation from his Dark Friend. *Why her? Why now?* he asked the voice inside him.

Because, was his Dark Friend's only answer, coming in the form of a headache. A punishment for inquisitiveness.

Troy rubbed his temples, blinked, and slowed his speed as he finally pulled into the Cheevers' driveway. His quick penalty indicated to Troy that there was something his Dark Friend wasn't telling him, so he chanced one last question. *Are we alone?* he asked, turning the engine off. He felt a constriction inside him, as though his Dark Friend was trying to close up the spaces where Troy might discover the answer. Briefcase in hand, Troy waited inside his car, pretending to read a message on his phone but really seeing nothing at all because his vision suddenly blurred. Then a great expanding filled Troy, rushing through his bones, his bloodstream, his soul. His vision returned forcefully, and Troy saw with terrible certainty that there was another that wanted the same thing he was after.

No, his Dark Friend finally said. *We are not alone.*

165

19

On the long stretch of city-owned grassland between the Botcher and Fischer farms on the northeastern edge of the city, Garrett's fairgrounds were bustling with preparations for the Fall Festival. The previous week, a record eighty-seven tents had been erected and now organizer Perry Searles was busy confirming the would-be occupants with volunteer Dakota Cardinal as they wound along the path, checking paper place holders against their floorplan. As with previous layouts, they positioned the rides outside of the tented area, along the western perimeter, where the giant Ferris Wheel, Zipper, and coaster rides were large enough to draw attention to an otherwise isolated area of the park. Middle-sized rides—the Parachute Drop, Giant Swing, Giant Slide, Gravitron, and the stomach-flipping Kamikaze—abutted both the larger rides and those more suitable for toddlers and younger children. From this amusement area, festivalgoers would pass through a historic covered bridge to the tented area where the men now checked the boxes on their sheets. "That one's not right, Dak," Perry said to him, pointing to a large corner booth. "That's Darwin's Donuts, not Edna's Eatables."

Dak frowned, looking from his clipboard to the place holders, back to his clipboard. "I swear I had them right this morning."

"Isn't her son one of our volunteers?" Perry asked, reminding Dak that Edna's own husband had pulled the switcheroo on them the year before, *and* the year before that, too cheap to spend the extra hundred bucks for the better space. They had caught on, of course, but it hadn't stopped Edna from telling anyone who would hear that Perry and Dak were xenophobes and that the corner spaces had rats in them.

"We don't get paid enough for this crap," Dak said, returning their holders to their proper places.

"Smiles and bullshit ain't enough for you?" Perry joked.

"I get enough of that from my kids," Dak said honestly.

In truth, both his sons had grown to be fine men. Jesse had a reputable career with the city in animal enforcement, and Johnny had shown promise in law enforcement, but whether his younger son continued on the right side of the law was another story. Though his sons thought otherwise, Dak wasn't oblivious to Johnny's antics. Dak's childhood friend Dan Fogel was sure to keep him apprised of any encounters with the boys. Dak was aware of everything; from the time Johnny had crashed the quad he wasn't yet old enough to drive to the time Jesse, goaded by his classmates, had stolen five chickens from Roy Botcher's henhouse and let them loose in the locker room at Elliot High an hour before their senior team was meeting Garrett High in the basketball quarter final.

Dak forgave those misdemeanors in stride, accepting them as intrinsic to childhood, as his own father had when Dak himself was younger. Whoever the perpetrator, both boys listened to Dak's fatherly advice when they misbehaved, but it was Johnny's eyes that seemed to gloss over until the talks were over. The boys were grown men now, but it was no surprise to Dak to hear from Dan how Johnny got picked up for fighting at Shooter's and spent the night in jail over the summer. Dak feigned ignorance and didn't bail him out, believing a night in the slammer without them coddling him would do more for Johnny than another talk. Months afterward, with a glowing review from Dan for Johnny's summer internship, Dak became cautiously optimistic that Johnny was closer to maturity than to childhood.

He finished his round with Perry, satisfied that no other cheapskates had made switches, and they set toward the parade staging area where dozens of volunteers were clustered around a handful of floats.

Away from the shade of the tents, the air was so hot and damp that both men were layered in sweat once they hit Roy Botcher's driveway, where half the floats would eventually gather before their trip to City Hall and back. Panting, Perry aired the collar of his shirt and Dak rolled up his sleeves, wishing he had worn a t-shirt. "I tell you, Dak, I haven't seen an October like this since I was in diapers, and that was sixty years ago. It's so damn hot."

"That must have been crap you were feeling," Dak said. "It's *never* been this hot in October."

A strange look came over Perry's face and he slowed his stride to look at Dak. He spoke quietly, confidentially. "Snow yesterday, heatwave today. The river dryin' up. That bus crash. Those goddamned birds damn near breaking every window in the city. You get a funny feeling about all this?" Perry took one of his Nicorettes from his front pocket and began to chew.

Dak wiped the back of his neck with his sleeve. "It's strange all right."

"Strange? It's more than fucking strange, Dak." Perry's voice was a wild whisper, and Dak remembered that Perry avidly read the *Enquirer* for his weekly dose of conspiracy

168

nonsense. "Shit's happening here, Dak. You know the Feds are in town? Did you know that? There must have been twenty SUVs in the convoy I saw. Drove right by my house, Dak. Right by it, I tell you, and they weren't stopping for groceries. Something's going on, and maybe it's just Garrett, but maybe the whole damn *country* is going to get like this, maybe the world."

Dak looked at the horizon, where the sun was red and angry. He kicked at the gravel on Roy's driveway. "You want to know what I think, Perry? I think Nature's angry. I think she's mad at what we've done, and now it's her turn to get even with us."

Perry stopped walking. "Your Elder tell you that?"

"Don't need to hear from an Elder to know that we're destroying the planet."

"That's crazy talk. Nature getting even, now I've heard it all. You want to know what I think it is? It's aliens, if you ask me. They're doing some spooky shit here and it's all going to come out when we start getting beamed up for experiments."

"*Now* who's talking crazy?"

They were interrupted by the double beep of Jesse's horn as he pulled into Roy's driveway. The boys looked upset with each other, as usual, but they greeted Dak and Perry with the smiles that had always tugged at Dak's heart. To Dak's surprise, his own mother was in Jesse's back seat. He stepped to the car and opened the door for her.

"You three got some secret plans I don't know about?" Dak asked when they were all out.

"Go easy on her, Pops, she's had a tough morning. Aunty Hattie just passed away," Jesse said, rubbing his grandmother's back.

169

Mavis pulled a tissue from her purse and wiped her nose as Dak hugged her. "The devil's come to town, Dak," she whimpered. "The devil's here, I can feel it." Her shoulders trembled and Dak held her until her shaking subsided while the boys and Perry looked on.

"What happened?" he asked when he released her.

Mavis sniffed, dabbing her eyes. "She was fine yesterday. We had tea and she was perfectly fine. She was knitting a scarf for the snowman on the float and then ... then ..."

It was Johnny who finally explained. "She swallowed her CPAP hose while she was sleeping. Aunty Dorothy called Grandma this morning and she called Mom, so we picked her up." For seventy-two years, ever since grade school, Mavis, Dorothy, and Hattie had been best friends. The three had been through graduations, marriages, births, deaths, and divorces together. Dak himself had grown up calling Hattie and Dorothy his aunts, though there was not a speck of relation between them. They were also aunties to his sons and their kids cousins to Jesse and Johnny, a bond thicker than blood, so the news of Hattie's death brought a film of tears to his eyes.

"What do you mean, she *swallowed* it? Those things are attached to masks. They don't just up and go down your throat." Dak frowned, regretting that he'd left his phone in his truck, where he was sure there were many missed messages.

"Mom called Lionel and he confirmed it. They said it was a freak accident, that the hose might have been loose and went in when she rolled over or something," Jesse told his father.

Visualizing the misfortune, Dak's face went gray and his throat tightened. "I'm so sorry, Mom," he whispered thickly and took her to him again.

INTERFERENCE

They cried while onlookers pretended not to eavesdrop. The boys, too, joined in on their hug, and the family shared a moment of grief until Perry politely coughed.

"I'm sorry for your loss, Mrs. Cardinal. Mrs. Freemont was a wonderful woman."

"The best," Mavis agreed with a sniffle, squinting at him through the blaring sunlight.

"Johnny, fetch Grandma a pair of sunglasses, will you?" Dak instructed, and a moment later Mavis was wearing Johnny's own Ray-Bans, two sizes too big for her narrow face.

"I can check the floats on my own if you want, Dak. You go be with your family and we'll catch up tomorrow. I'll be fine," Perry said, grinding his gum as he worked out how much he had to do before he could leave. Lena would understand if he weren't home for dinner again. This time of year, a hot meal was something of a rarity for Perry, but it was a small sacrifice for the adulation he received. Had he chosen a more exciting career—in archeology or engineering perhaps—Perry figured he wouldn't need the action and excitement of the Fall Fair. But he had chosen accounting, so cold October food it was.

"Nonsense," Mavis said now, swinging her big bug eyes at Perry. "I'm here to help, and help is what I'll do. Hattie would have wanted us to keep going. I may be a bit teary, but I'll be fine. Just show me where the Southbridge float is and leave me be." Johnny's glasses slid down her nose, but she pushed them back up, waiting for directions.

"Are you sure—" Dak started and saw his mother's lips harden. Behind her, his sons shook their heads.

"Aunty Dorothy is waiting for her," Jesse said. "They're going to craft in Aunt Hattie's honor."

171

"I think that's a fine idea," Perry said gratefully. He pointed to the line of displays further down Roy Botcher's driveway. "Southbridge is the third one down, with the gray tarp around it. Lucked out with the weather this year that some of them are building their displays outside."

Mavis had already begun walking to the Southbridge display when she stopped and turned to Perry. She blew her nose into a tissue and stuffed it in her pocket, regarding him with a certainty that made Perry pull back. "It's not luck we're having, dear. It's the arrival of hell."

With that, Mavis fingered the dream catcher hanging from her necklace and rendered the accountant speechless. Perry left Dak to inspect the displays while Dak and his sons accompanied Mavis the short distance to the Southbridge exhibit. She released Dak's hand to remove her cardigan then clutched his hand tightly again before coming upon the only float concealed by scaffold-hung tarps. There was an open slit in the corner where two tarps met and Dak poked his head inside.

"Knock, knock," he said, gently drawing his sniffing mother inside.

The area was a whirl of activity with t-shirt-clad volunteers hammering, painting, stapling, sewing, gluing, welding, and bolting the makings of a formidable medieval scene. Small woodland creatures frolicked on a sparkling Styrofoam-carved ice castle. A lowered gate, made to look like iron, held an enormous red dragon braced for attack as it protected the smaller creatures behind it. Chester, barking orders to the eye-rollers around him, had his back turned to the entrance and so did not see them until Dorothy stood up from her work painting wooden trees and rushed to embrace Mavis.

INTERFERENCE

"We can't stop now. Where are you—" Chester started; but when the rest of the Southbridge retinue put down their tools, he swung around and offered a half-hearted condolence to Mavis, Dak, and the boys. "Terrible way to go," Chester said aloud, bringing a fresh wave of unease to the group. "Shouldn't use a machine like that if you're a nighttime traveller, but she's in a better place anyway."

Mavis' cheeks went red. Her eyes flashed wide, and her small mouth opened large and angry, but Dorothy quickly clapped her own hands to get everyone's attention.

"Now that Mavis is here, let me repeat what we've all shared privately. Hattie was a good woman. She was kind and funny and always, *always* helped whenever she could, never asking for anything in return. I'd like to dedicate this year's float to Hattie's honor. Let's make it the best we've ever had, for the best person we've ever known." She held up her paint brush, splattering a few green drops on her silver hair. Applause rose up the tarps and into the sky.

Chester tugged his sagging pants. "All right, then. Sounds good. Let's get on with it." No one did.

From behind the castle, where he had been adding glitter to the wet paint, Ed Norman stepped off the float. He took his time, cognizant of last night's strain on his pacemaker, and was breathing heavily when he finally reached Mavis. They weren't close, but through Hattie they had been friends, and he hugged Mavis until she squeezed him so tightly that his chest began to hurt.

"Sorry Eddie," Mavis apologized, only now remembering that the man had a pacemaker installed not long before. "I'm really not myself."

"None of us are," Ed admitted. Seeing Dak, Ed shook his hand. "Are you joining us today?"

173

"Wish I could," Dak said. "We're running through the entries, and then we're putting up signage for the route." Thumbing a finger at the boys, Dak added, "They'll be working on our entry the rest of the day, two behind this one, if you need anything."

With that, the group gathered Mavis. Confident she was in good hands, her progeny moved to an exit between the tarps. They were almost out when Jesse froze so suddenly that Johnny stepped on the heel of his shoe and Dak had to side-step to avoid both of them.

Suddenly filled with a darkness so overwhelming that it brought bumps to his flesh, Jesse shivered. There, demure in a thin, rose-colored blouse, sitting at a folding-table and knitting a small pair of mittens, was his former school crossing guard, Sylvia Baker. Her face had recovered some of its previous control, but her lips were still slanted as she talked to a woman whose name Jesse couldn't immediately recall. They were snacking from a bag of chocolate-covered almonds that Sylvia directed to the working side of her mouth but, as though Jesse himself had grabbed her arm, she dropped the almond she was holding and glared at him. Even from this distance, Jesse sensed a coldness in the woman, and when she stood and began limping toward him, Jesse found himself stumbling backward to the gap between the tarps.

"Jesse?" As he said his son's name, Dak felt a chill down his spine that made him uneasy. Through his t-shirt, he touched the outer edges of the medicine wheel hanging against his chest and intuitively fingered the white triangle that signified many things, including death. The piece grew warm beneath his touch, then burned so hot that Dak yelped, reached into the neckline of his shirt, and yanked off his necklace. It fell to the ground.

174

INTERFERENCE

Gaping at him, Johnny reached to pick it up.

Old, knotted fingers arrived at the medicine wheel first, and when Sylvia curled her hand around it, Dak swore he saw a thin tine of smoke curl from the woman's fist before she handed it back to him.

"Terrible heat today," Sylvia said, looking up at Dak with eyes that were a little too dark in the center, a little too white around the iris. "If I hadn't taken my earrings off an hour ago, they would have burned right through me like a hot knife through butter."

She spoke slowly, carefully annunciating her words to make sure they were proper. To make sure they were *human*, Dak thought, though why the idea came to him, he didn't know.

Swallowing the fear that bloomed up his throat, Dak accepted his necklace and shoved it in his pocket. It felt almost frozen against his thigh. "Thank you, Mrs. Baker," he said. Then, because both his sons had fled and he was standing alone in front of her, Dak asked, "You're helping out with the parade this year?"

Sylvia nodded, and as she and Dak spoke, Pandora rolled over the man, prodding and poking the magnified colors around him. He saw her; Pandora knew this with certainty. His older son had seen her too—past her weak layer of adopted flesh, through her brittle borrowed bones, to the essence of her immortal spirit. Their kind could, though in these modern times, with the growing detachment from spirit, they usually weren't sure what they were sensing. They only knew she was evil. They called her *calamity, corruption, suffering, catastrophe, the devil*, but were never close to the truth. Until now.

175

Examining the man that saw into her, Pandora wondered if he were any relation to the medicine man who'd driven her from her host in Africa. She understood there were curiosities around the world she hadn't yet discovered. As long as they posed no danger to her, she could let the curiosities be. But these two didn't seem harmless to Pandora. They were trouble, and trouble had to be disposed of. She knew these two would take effort; their heightened awareness made them anxious, and Pandora worried their penetrating energy might deplete her own as had been done by the medicine man. Reflecting on her current depletion, Pandora considered the failure of her entry into the city—a bumbling escapade reserved for novices.

She had lost something with Harold's death. The connection she'd had with him accorded Pandora a sense of belonging—the only time she'd ever felt that way—and when she felt the last tremble of his heart in that jail, there was a crumbling of her energy that could only be rectified with death. The bus crash should have revived her. The surge of forty-two souls from one plane to another should have made her whole again, should have remade her what she had once been—but like bark stripped from a tree, the act had made her thirsty and weak.

Only, she hadn't gone fully around the tree, had she? She hadn't felled it the way it was supposed to be felled. She'd left a filament there that kept the deaths from reaching her. A woodcutter with one last blow of the axe was an empty-handed woodcutter with a cold home. The last blow. The filament. Yes. Yes. *Yes! That* was her interference. The survival of a single passenger had siphoned Pandora's power, draining it like the river, isolating it like the electric surge, sickening it like the animals. She'd *never* failed to kill before,

INTERFERENCE

and her Maker was punishing her for it. With a certainty that filled her soul, Pandora knew what she had to do.

First, however, she needed her strength, and that required death. Hattie had done a commendable job of healing Pandora. She'd fought long and grotesquely, but her death was only a thin scab on a deep wound. Pandora needed more, so she waited inside Sylvia, picking at yarn with needles, until the volunteers were called to lunch.

20

Smoke rose from the grill in Roy Botcher's backyard, where he and his wife Gretchen readied the last complements to the annual volunteer appreciation barbeque. In years past, the covered fairground pavilion was used for the event, but the space was presently dedicated instead to a framework of pictures and devotions, memorializing Garett's recently lost citizens.

The day's heat had grown stifling, so the Botcher children passed around cups of iced lemonade while the volunteers found seats. Heaping bowls of potato salad, steaming corn, and smoked beans were put on a serving table alongside the back deck, and these were soon joined by platters of burgers, grilled chicken, brown-sugar pulled pork, and jumbo hot dogs. Perry waved to his grandchildren, already playing on the swing set, then found Roy scraping the grill and clapped him on the shoulder.

"My goodness, what a feast!" he enthused to the sweating chef.

Roy wiped his forehead with the back of his hand and continued cleaning the grill. "It's always so cold this time of year we never get the chance to do anything like this. Spaghetti or chilli. Chilli or spaghetti. We thought we'd do something different this year." In the field, one of the llamas yipped.

"It's always good, Roy, you know that," Perry told him.

INTERFERENCE

Putting his brush down and untying his apron, Roy looked down at the smaller man. "You mind if I say a few words before we eat?"

"Please," Perry nodded, though his stomach had growled so loudly he glanced at Roy's llamas, pretending the sound had come from them.

A few quick strides onto his deck and Roy stood above the waiting guests. He tapped a fork to the side of his pop can, and when the sound wasn't quite loud enough to get their attention, Roy hollered. "Before we eat, I would first like to thank each and every one of you for joining Gretchen and me at our home. It's a privilege we don't take lightly, and we are honored by your companionship, now more than ever." His usually steady voice quavered and there was a sniffling silence among the guests. Gretchen appeared beside Roy on the deck and held his hand, and Roy went on. "I lost three of my closest friends last week and more than a few neighbours. Now, I don't know about you, but I'm about done with this business. So let's eat up and pray for our friends and pray for our river, and let's make this the best damn festival the world's ever had. Amen." He mumbled the last word, unsure if he'd just delivered a sermon or a victory speech, but the words felt right.

"Not bad for an old farmer," Gretchen whispered in his ear as she hugged him. Her hair, red and still thick in a ponytail, tickled his nose. Roy sniffed, then the sound of applause hit his ears and rang across his fields. Old and young, the volunteers stood, whistling, clapping, cheering, their voices a collective totem of respect.

Not to be outdone, Chester hitched up his pants and was about to take a stand on Roy's deck to extol the virtue of hard work to the Southbridge collective, when the crowd

179

disbursed and formed into a quick line with their plates where Gretchen was already serving them. Roy patted Chester on the back and put a bottle of water in his hand so that Chester had something to squeeze.

While plates were being filled, Dak, Jesse, and Johnny stood away from the assembly, feigning interest in one of Roy's llama barns. Wary of the onlookers, the llamas straightened their long necks and stared at the men. Dak leaned his elbows on the fence, waiting for his sons to speak, but either they were disinclined or just as stupefied as Dak. Looking at the llamas, he said, "What the hell was that?"

Jesse's fingers slid down the length of his braid as he joined his father at the fence. "You tell me."

"You two got something going on that I don't know about?" Johnny asked, his face knitted with confusion. "*He's* tripping and running away, and you act like someone stuck a taser to you," he said to his brother and father. "The heat getting to you?"

"You didn't feel it, then?" Dak asked Johnny.

"Feel what?"

It was Jesse who spoke. He said only one word, but its vocalization made the men catch their breath so that there was no movement of air between them. "Flint."

A mixture of disbelief and terror clouded Johnny's face. Legends of the evil spirit who'd cut himself out of his mother had been taught to Johnny since ever since he could remember. Where other spirits supplied necessities like food, fertility, good weather, or strength, Flint instead was a taker, ravaging and damaging whatever he could, whenever he could. Flint's malicious association with death and darkness was no secret to the Cardinal family, nor their band, and it wasn't a rare occurrence that their Elders interceded to rid

INTERFERENCE

Flint from a struggling home. Johnny, young and detached from his spiritual self, hadn't yet had experienced the proximity of Flint's presence, but that didn't lessen his apprehension of hearing it now. He said, "In Mrs. Baker?"

They nodded at him, then Jesse said, "I felt it at the hospital, when those cats were running around. I should have said something then; maybe Nikonha could have done something about it."

"She still can," Dak maintained.

"You ever feel it like that, Dad? I mean, that *strong*? Nothing's ever gotten to me like that, nothing. I don't have a good feeling about this." Suddenly, Jesse felt so small and insignificant that a desire to take Sarah and leave the city shuddered through him.

Dak shook his head. "Nothing this strong, no. I suspect it has something to do with that crash and the river, probably those animals, too. It's not the first time things have gone strange around here. Before my time, Akśotha said there were ice floes on the Huron that poisoned many animals and people. Turned them all gray with sickness until her great uncle shot an arrow into a stone stuck in the ice. He told her it was the demon's heart."

"I've never heard that story," Johnny said, watching the slow approach of a coffee-colored llama.

"Stories have a way of bringing things back; they let the *settled* access us again, whether or not we're prepared to handle them." Dak pressed his lips together and picked at a splinter on one of Roy's fence posts. "I didn't want to give Flint an entrance."

"So what do we do now?" Jesse asked.

"We do nothing. We stay away and we pray. Don't go near that woman and don't let Sarah go near her either, you hear, Jesse?" Dak instructed.

181

But by then, Sarah had already arrived for the luncheon and was seated at a table between two leaf-shedding maple trees. On a much-needed day off, Sarah was easy to spot in her brilliant yellow sundress as she slid a plate of food over to Mavis, who looked none too eager to eat. Jesse waved at them, but their view to him was obstructed by a quick group of food-toting Southbridge residents aiming directly for the empty seats at Sarah and Mavis' table. Jesse's mouth dried when he saw Sylvia's pink blouse among the mix.

They were turning to beat the residents to the table when Johnny suddenly screamed. Like his father and brother, Johnny had been leaning on Roy's fence but was a little slower removing himself. With his attention on Sarah and his grandmother, Johnny hadn't seen the approaching llama rush toward him, nor had he seen the big jaw open wide or the crooked teeth clamp down on two fingers of his left hand. A flash of pain sped from his knuckles as the llama grinded its jaw and *chewed* Johnny's bones. Blood fell from the llama's lips, tears poured from Johnny's eyes, shrieks of gradually awakening horror erupted from many mouths, then Dak and Johnny ran to the fence. A number of saliva-flung expletives burst from Johnny's quivering lips then, as his brother and father reached his side, Johnny went limp against the top fence rail when the llama finally spit his severed fingers out.

By now, Roy, Gretchen, Perry, and Chester had reached the llama enclosure, the first two wrangling the offending animal into an isolation stable while the latter each fished one of Johnny's fingers from the dirt. "Ice! We need a bag of ice here! Quick! Hurry damn it! Hurry!" Chester ordered anyone who would listen.

INTERFERENCE

The disturbance-riled group gathered to the fence, gaping, gasping, groaning at the bloodshed. All but Sylvia Baker, who went on eating her beans.

21

Dan slammed his hand on the conference phone where he let his fingers lie for fear the black screen in front of him would once again light up with Mark Bennett's face. Never had he expected a time when the chief of staff from the Department of National Defense would demand his presence, but he had woken to the undeniable request and hadn't the energy in the early moment to orchestrate a plausible excuse. He'd scrambled into his too-familiar shower at the Sunset Motel, washed quickly and took the last of his clean uniforms out of the dry-cleaning bag, then rushed to the station to prepare his team for another shitshow. Sitting beside him now, his closest sergeant, Hoss Brander, groaned. "What if we just come back when this is all over?"

Dan buried his face in his palms and sighed. "Station vacation. I like the sound of that." Generally, Dan wasn't a man who lived for time off. He enjoyed his work even when things were ugly because he still held to the principle that he was a conduit of help. He'd felt this purpose in his bones as a new recruit and still all these later, even when his city had gone to hell and the Feds were on his ass.

Their impending involvement wasn't a surprise to Dan. Already, the city was full of outsiders, and Ada had warned as much when he and Boyce were in her office at City Hall, but it still grated on him. He went to sleep chief of police and woke up federal lackey, with many caustic levels above him. They'd given him a lengthy list of reports he had to file, no time to file them, and asked that he prepare space at the station for an operational contingent to oversee the station's activities in the proceeding months, should anything else of national interest arise. Presently he stood with the briefing binder his assistant Florence had prepared from the encrypted email they'd sent and considered tossing it in the trash.

Hoss drew a giant *X* over the notes he'd taken and looked at Dan. "I'm going to forget all this and let you tell me what you need me to do." The station's '90s-era air conditioner was failing miserably to maintain a comfortable temperature during the ridiculous heatwave and Hoss's shirt had sprouted a number of small sweat marks that darkened it.

Ernie Stiles, Dan's other right hand, nodded in agreement. "I'm with Hoss, Dan. They want that kind of work done, they can come and do it themselves, as far as I'm concerned." With his empty coffee cup in hand, Stiles pushed back from the table. Now over a week without a decent night's sleep, Stiles' own exhaustion showed in the twitch of his right eye.

"We're going to be good boys and do as they told us," Dan said respectfully. "They may be a pain in the ass, but— like it or not—we need them. Whatever's going on here isn't in my handbook and, the truth is, if anything else happens I'm not confident we'd have the resources to handle it. We need to play their game until things are stable enough to maintain ourselves. For all I know, a hurricane could run over us tomorrow and I don't want to drown before it starts, get me?" His men nodded and turned to leave. Dan stopped them. "Before

185

you go rushing into their paper dump, however, we need a welfare check across the usual sectors. I'd be lying if I said it wasn't an extensive list, but with the river and the heat and the animal attacks, there's a good chance some of our most vulnerable need assistance, at least assurance to know we're still here. I'd like your teams on it as soon as possible."

"It's going to hold up the reports," Hoss said..

"Let it," Dan told him. "People are more important than paperwork, whatever those assholes believe."

Respect reflected in their eyes. Dan dismissed them and went to his own office, where the air conditioning seemed to have died altogether. The apology chocolates he'd received days ago from the woman whose German Shepherd attacked his cruiser were now a wet puddle in the open box. Thankful that Marty had fixed the window so soon, Dan opened it now and let the breeze—a lesser kind of heat—percolate into his space.

He was just settling into his chair to begin the information gathering when his cell phone rang. Readying himself for another unavoidable summon, he tossed down his pen and ground his teeth until they crackled in his mouth. Reluctantly he looked at his phone, but the name appearing on the screen was much worse than he expected: Brandy.

"What is it this time?" he said.

"Real nice, Dan," his soon-to-be ex-wife answered. "We're still playing like that, are we? Here I am, giving you a courtesy call, and all I get is sass."

"You got hurt feelings, why don't you go see Shane about it? That's not my department anymore, remember?" The headache he'd managed to keep at bay now rioted inside him, and he popped two Tylenol into his mouth, dry-swallowing as Brandy went on.

186

"I heard you saved that reporter." Dan didn't respond, knowing his face had been all over the news since he'd tackled Jessica Chung away from that speeding Winnebago. She'd lost a shoe, but because of Dan she would live to buy another pair. "Did she *thank you* for it, Dan?"

The implication was clear and nasty to Dan's good senses. "I wouldn't have run so fast if it was you standing there." He didn't enjoy sinking to that level, but the insult brightened him a little.

"Grow up," Brandy snapped. "Do you want me to tell you what I called to tell you, or do you want to fight until I hang up?" She paused, waiting for Dan's retort, but he stayed silent, listening to the pop of her gum through the receiver. "Okay, then. Better. Now, what I have to tell you concerns Shane, but I don't want you to get all high and mighty like you do, hear me?"

"Go on," Dan said, if only to speed up the conversation.

"He's got an issue I think you should know about, given … everything … around here." Briefly, Dan wondered if she was going to tell him that Shane had given her an STD and that it would be wise for Dan to get tested, then he remembered that he hadn't slept with Brandy in so many months that he'd almost forgotten what sex was like. Still, he braced himself for such a revelation until Brandy said, "You know he's got a roofing business? Well, he told me that he's had quite a number of unusual calls this week. He gets these kinds of calls from time to time but never so many so close together, and never, ever as bad."

"What are you talking about?"

"You're going to tell me I'm reading too much into it, but I'm not, Dan; I swear I'm not. People all over the city have *things* in their roofs. Infestations like you'd never

187

believe. The Johnsons must have had three hundred mice eating through their attic. They had new shingles put on during the summer. It's not like they weren't taking care of their property."

"Maybe they didn't close the space properly," Dan reasoned. "Mice'll find a way in through anything. With the weather turning the way it did, they were probably just looking for a new home."

"And what about the bats?"

"Bats?" Dan asked, growing more alert.

"Loads of them in one of those apartment complexes near Mitton. Exterminators had to tear a huge hole in the roof, and that's when Shane got called."

Though he was not convinced, Dan said, "Could be a coincidence."

"Maybe, but then he got a call about snakes, and there were four about termites, and one hell of an earwig infestation in that crappy little nursing home where your grandpa used to be."

"Shane an exterminator now, is he?"

"I'm telling you, Dan, Shane said the roofs were *destroyed*. Not quick fixes, but full-on reconstruction work. There were so many termites at one property that the roof actually caved in. And there was a horde of cockroaches at another that broke through the ceiling right into someone's bedroom. You know the Pushkins?"

"Your parents' friends," Dan remembered. "They okay?"

Brandy's earring jangled against the phone. "Yes, thank God, but they've had to move out of their house while they take care of the spiders."

INTERFERENCE

Though it was stifling in his office, a chill swept up Dan's spine. "Spiders?"

"Uh-huh," Brandy confirmed. "They heard noises, so Andrey went outside to inspect and saw a whole bunch of heaves all over their roof. Their shingles were bunched up in places and he called Shane to come fix them, thinking it was the strange weather we're having. And—"

Dan interrupted, "This happen today?"

"A few hours ago. Shane sent a crew right away. They weren't up there for more than a few minutes when one of his guys nearly broke his back jumping off the roof. He said the heaves were *moving*, Dan, can you believe it? So he poked a shingle and they just came pouring out from a hole underneath. He was tied off, thank God for that, but he's got a bunch of cracked ribs. He said he'd rather have that than have ten thousand spiders crawling all over him." Silence fell between them while Dan digested the news. Finally, Brandy said, "I'm not lying, Dan."

"I wish to God you were," he told her, and sighed into the phone.

"Are you all right?"

"I have no choice but to be," he admitted. "Can you do something for me?"

"I'm not getting samples or anything, Dan. Please don't ask me to do that."

"No, no. Nothing like that. I'll get Jesse out to look at some of those properties. Maybe he'll notice—I don't know—a pheromone or something that's making the wildlife go nuts, but I want you to stay home, hear me? Stay home and stay away from the river and the hospital. Check your roof if you have to, but for God's sake, stay home until this all blows over, okay?"

189

"I didn't know you still cared," Brandy said, and the way she said it, a bit whiny like a teenager, made him realize her hold over him had softened. He cared, but cared a little less than before, though he'd never tell her that.

"Mind if Jesse gives Shane a call?" Dan asked now.

"Please," she said, and after taking Shane's phone number with a promise that only Jesse would contact him, Dan ended the call. He leaned back in his chair, messaged Jesse the particulars, and decided his paperwork would have to wait. Then Dan left the station for the short walk to his and Brandy's old church.

Nestled in what the locals called Old Town, St. Thomas was a tidy, gray brick blessing on an otherwise unkempt street. The once formidable heart of the city, Old Town had deteriorated with the death of its older residents and the exodus of its young. The first bank in Garrett—the Bank of Montreal—now housed a strip club and adult-video store. The old post office had turned into a vape shop and the original city hall, before its escape three blocks north, had since been subdivided into a pawn shop, a Payday Loan, and a tattoo parlor, from which St. Thomas was directly across the street. Dan ducked into a pizza shop holding its ground among the discredited, ordered a large pepperoni to go, and walked up the stairs of the church with his pizza fifteen minutes later. Through the open doors came the sounds of the pianist practicing, and Dan hummed the tune to himself as he headed toward Father Bonner's office.

"I smell Daniel Fogel," said the old priest through his partially closed door.

"I'm not sure I should be offended or pleased," Dan said, nudging the door open with the pizza box.

190

"Come closer and I'll let you know." Father Bonner grinned jovially. Taking in the shadows under Dan's eyes and the sheen on his skin, he added, "Actually, forget I said that. Come, sit and share your treasure while you tell me what's on your mind, Daniel."

He flipped open the box Dan set down and licked his lips. Dan laughed, recalling similar reactions when he'd visited and sought counsel before he and Brandy separated. While he'd never been an especially religious man, Dan grew to appreciate the principles of the church that Brandy's family introduced to him, so he continued to attend when he felt brave enough to be in the proximity of her parents, aunts, uncles, grandparents, and too many cousins to count. Respectfully they would wave and smile with downturned mouths, then gather around Shane as he assumed Dan's old position in the fifth pew of the middle row. Since the first and only view of Brandy and Shane's onscreen encounter, Dan avoided attending the after-service fellowship, instead preferring to visit Father Bonner away from the crowd. Pizza became their ritual.

"You look thin," Dan said without preamble.

Father Bonner waved his hand. "Busy times, you know. A bus goes over a bridge, and people need comfort. A river dries up and they need the sacristy wine." His own breath smelling faintly of whisky, Father Bonner sighed. "It's what I'm here for and I'm glad to be of God's service, of course, but I do wish it didn't take these kinds of things to fill the pews." He took a large bite of his pizza and closed his eyes, relishing the moment.

After a time, Dan retrieved glasses of water from the kitchen, already feeling the weight on him lift a little, and settled back into his chair, trying to suppress the pressures competing for action inside his head. "Thanks for this, Father," Dan said, finishing his second slice.

Father Bonner shrugged. "You've brought lunch, I should be thanking *you*. Tell me, besides the little concert Glenda has put on for us, what brings you to the company of an old man in the middle of the day? Something bothering you, Daniel? I know you were hoping for reconciliation ..." His voice trailed off.

"I'm past that, Father. You see she's—"

"With the little guy?" the priest's thick white eyebrows went up. "I do. I admit, when I see the space beside your wife, I find myself hoping that she'd ended it with that fellow. But then when I step up on the chancel, the little fella is still there. It's a mystery to me, but there it is. I'm sorry, Daniel." In truth, Shane was only a few inches shorter than Brandy, but the Father's comments warmed Dan, nonetheless.

"Not your fault, Father," Dan said honestly, then grew serious as he rested an arm on Father Bonner's desk. "And it's not why I came to see you. I assume you know the rest of what's been happening around here?"

The priest opened his palms, interlaced his fingers and rested them on his stomach. "I believe I might. Our community is quite the sharing bunch, as you understand. The crash and the river are common knowledge, of course, but I've also heard something rather peculiar about young Ms. Cheever. My instinct is to dismiss the talk; a rumor spread does not make a rumor truth, understand, but I would be lying if I told you I didn't somehow believe it, Daniel."

"May I confess something to you, Father?"

"Of course."

"I haven't read the whole Bible yet. I've been meaning to, but I'm still on the Old Testament."

INTERFERENCE

"It can be tricky, yes," Father Bonner said. "That's why I always suggest beginning with the New Testament. It's easier to digest until you get your sea legs, if you get me."

Dan sipped his water and finally arrived at the purpose of his visit. "I suppose I was wondering what the Bible says about all this. Is there something in the pages I haven't read that might, I don't know—"

"Explain all this?" Father Bonner offered helpfully. Dan nodded. The Father took a napkin to a speck of pizza sauce on his lip. "I'm expected to say there is an answer for everything in the Bible, and for the most part that's correct. As to the electrification of a young girl, there's no specific reason I could give that might satisfy you. I'm afraid that the apostles didn't have that one in their manual." He crossed himself and Dan did the same. "But when you finally get to read their works, you'll see that they all speak of the will of our common enemy."

"The devil?"

"Who else?" When Dan didn't respond, the old priest said, "If you believe in one, you must believe in the other."

"I'm trying," Dan confessed.

"Do you have a better explanation? I might add I have heard of the animal attacks as of late and the problems the little fella is facing with his roofing business, not to mention the mysterious turn in the weather. I'll refrain from calling it the apocalypse, as I'm not sure quite *what* it is, but I do not believe it to be the will of God. I fear the *other* has settled into our little town and just does not want to go away."

"I feel ridiculous for asking this, Father, but is there an exorcism or something you can do?" Dan blushed.

"I can do better than that," Father Bonner said. "I can pray. I can get the congregation to pray. I know it sounds simple, but it's rather not. There is *power* in prayer, Daniel.

193

You must *thrust* your faith to God, all of it, because even a little doubt opens a door to the other." The old priest put a hand on Dan's wrist and squeezed it gently. "I suspect it's not the answer you wanted, Daniel, but it's the only one I can give. We'll do our best."

"Thanks Father."

"Now, may I confess something to you?"

Dan smiled. "Please."

Father Bonner turned to look out the side window, where an accumulation of fast-food trash had scattered over the parish green. He frowned. "I'm an old man, Daniel. I've encountered a lot in my time, so there is little that surprises me. The river is a curious thing, but not altogether shocking. I've seen waterways come and go, most not quite as suddenly, though there was a drilling incident I remember—Lake Peigneur, if I recall correctly—that managed the reverse. Woke up a lake, went to bed a small sea. Though rare, these things happen. I believe that even Ms. Cheever's condition will eventually be explained; as human education is still in its infancy, we don't yet have the tools to figure it out. Maybe I'm wrong, maybe it's the devil, maybe it's a mystery that will never be solved." He fiddled with a string on his sleeve, then said, "The animals, the weather; plagues come and go, but lately I've been having *dreams*, Daniel, terrible dreams. They shock me awake and keep me up. If I manage to fall asleep, my dream begins where the last one ended, like a dark narrative insisting I follow to the end." His hands shook slightly, and Dan saw a genuine fear fall over the priest's face.

Dan said, "What kind of dreams, Father?"

"Have you—" Father Bonner hesitated. "Have you decided what presence you'll have at the Fall Festival?"

"You think something is going to happen there?"

"I do," the priest replied.

22

In the early evening hours, a strange wind began to pick over the city, and the warmth that had settled like a cattle brand began pulling away. A slight chill now wound over the streets so that windows were closed and sweaters were donned and fireplaces were lit.

With her back to the wind, Adhira snuck a few puffs of her cigarette and dashed it out with her shoe before flipping up her collar for the walk through the parking lot into the hospital. She didn't enjoy coming on her time off, but that wasn't the reason for her displeasure. After a nap and a long bath, she'd decided that the news of the Cheevers' pending litigation against the hospital couldn't wait the few hours until her shift actually started. As a doctor, she'd long known that bad news was best delivered in person, so here she was to deliver it, exhaustion and all.

She scooted through the sliding doors, deciding to drop her purse and jacket in her office, when she spotted Abe, jacket in hand, on his way out.

"You're early," Abe said, yawning.

"And you should be sleeping by now."

Abe shrugged. "There was a little movement with our patient. I thought she was going to wake up."

Adhira raised an eyebrow. "You didn't call."

195

"Because you would have run here like you did now. Why is that, anyway? Did Huxley call you?"

"I don't understand, Abe."

The doctor tugged on his coat. He spied the swaying of trees through the window and fastened the buttons all the way to his neck. "She moved a finger, if you can believe it."

"You saw this?"

Abe nodded. "The nurses first reported it a few hours ago, but Hux and I weren't convinced so we waited by her bed until she did it again. And there it was. A little twitch of her pinky."

"Myoclonic?"

"Possible," Abe said, "but we don't believe so. Movement was slow, more like she was scratching a cat than jerking. Go see for yourself. Once that finger got going, it hasn't stopped. If I wasn't so tired, I'd have stayed at her bedside just to watch that little finger move. Quite the sight." He bid her a smooth shift, then hunched further inside his jacket as the doors slid open and the wind assaulted him.

After a quick detour to the cafeteria, Adhira rode the elevator to her office, sipping a large hot coffee. She dropped her purse and jacket on her desk and decided to pay a visit to Huxley before they saw Cliff. She had just stepped from the elevator onto the fifth floor when Huxley dangled a Kit Kat in front of her face.

"I'd say we celebrate with champagne, but the vending machine is out." When she eyed him curiously, Huxley added, "Abe called me after he saw you. Told me to send your ass home to sleep for a few more hours so you don't scare the patients." He opened the package, broke the bar down the center, and gave Adhira half.

196

INTERFERENCE

"You don't look so hot either," Adhira said, breaking a stick from her chocolate bar. "As much as I'd rather be getting my beauty sleep, I'm here to talk to Cliff. He still in?"

"Not sure," Huxley said. Watching her disinterestedly nip at her favorite snack, he asked, "What's the problem?"

"I need a need a day-maker before we get into it."

She sighed, relieved that Huxley didn't insist she explain. For seventeen years, after a shift together when a screaming woman arrived at the ER with intense abdominal pain, *day-maker* had been their code for cases that made them smile. That particular case had stuck with them not only because the patient had been unaware that she was thirty-nine weeks pregnant and deep in the second stage of labor, but the soon-to-be mother was an avid astrologist who insisted her sign prevented her from pregnancy, even as the baby was crowning. While they both agreed that "But I'm a Libra!" *was* a better code, their professional oath required that patient interactions be treated with confidentiality and integrity, even in matters that made them laugh until their sides hurt.

Huxley whispered, "This beats Libra. We might need a new code after this." He finished his chocolate bar as he accompanied Adhira to the intensive care unit.

"It *must* be good if you're thinking about a decision like that."

They washed at the sink and Adhira couldn't help but feel a pang of excitement. Days ago, she'd thought Anabelle's death was only a matter of time. Now Anabelle was not only approachable but exhibiting non-myoclonic movement. It was a small victory in the tragedy tornado that had hit the city, and Adhira gladly welcomed it. The week had been hell; one of the worst in her career, but as they drew toward Anabelle's

197

bedside and Adhira saw the color back in the young patient's face, she was struck by a moment of gratitude so severe her eyes prickled with tears. Adhira looked up at the fluorescents, trying to keep her weeping at bay, then her eyes swept fully over Anabelle, from the fresh bandage on her head, to her clean gown and sheets, and lastly to that moving finger. Had the movement been as constant as Abe suggested, Adhira might have suspected limb dystonia and tested Anabelle's basal ganglia function, but it was random and slow, so she made a mental note for further investigation if it persisted.

"Incredible, isn't it?" Huxley said quietly, watching the slow swirl of Anabelle's left index finger.

"Never thought I'd see it," Adhira agreed, eyes unblinking, afraid to miss the movement. Anabelle's thumb tapped the bed once, twice, and then her middle finger dragged a short line in the sheets. Although she didn't want to ruin the moment, it occurred to Adhira that Anabelle's potential recovery would present additional challenges, of which she now reminded Huxley. "What if we can't release her?"

Huxley drew his lips into his mouth, thinking. "We'll get to that. We got this far, didn't we? I don't know about you, but I wasn't expecting us to be where we're at today. Baby steps, just like we tell our patients."

Adhira knew that was the logical process, but nothing about Anabelle's condition was logical, and it brought the greatest worry she'd ever felt for a patient. She sighed. "We didn't train for this."

"No, but I figure if we ever want to freelance as electricians, we might have options." He nudged her gently and was rewarded with a small smile.

Afterward, as Huxley updated his patient reports, Adhira came to collect him for their short journey to Cliff's office on the second floor. She knocked gently. "Time? Kathy said he's leaving soon so it's now or sometime tomorrow."

Huxley tossed down his pen. "Nothing like a good tantrum before I leave for the night. Why not?"

He cracked his neck and stood, then followed Adhira down the quiet halls. Earlier, Adhira had apprised Huxley of the Cheevers' lawsuit, so Huxley had prepared himself accordingly. He'd run through a litany of scenarios in his head, most involved the throwing of a stapler; all involved the bulging of the many veins on Cliff's neck. In the current social climate, where Cliff's behavior could easily land him in the stocks of public discontent, the CEO was smart enough to temper his rage in public, but he still miserably failed in private. Cliff had success with others, as Huxley had seen with the rest of the staff, but for reasons unknown to Huxley, Cliff appeared uninterested in the same caution when it came to Adhira and himself. Malpractice suits in Canada weren't especially uncommon, but at Garrett General, in a city where the community mostly adored its practitioners, litigation was rare. When cases did arise, however, Cliff went ballistic to the point that Huxley himself had strongly considered taking valium before appointments with him.

As they walked, Adhira slipped a small tablet under her tongue. "We do what we got to do, right?"

"And I thought we were friends," he whined, until Adhira drew from her pocket a small bottle of lorazepam and pressed one of the tiny white pills into his palm. It wouldn't work immediately, but it would give him something to look forward to while Cliff's rage boiled over.

Outside the CEO's closed door, the doctors stopped. "Namaste and all that shit," Huxley said to Adhira, smoothing the front of his shirt.

S. L. LUCK

"May the force be with you," she responded, lifting her breasts while staring ahead at Cliff's door.

They tapped fists and Adhira's hand rose to knock when both of their pagers went off at the same time. "What now?" she groaned, checking her pager, that archaic but functional institutional tether, when she realized that Huxley had already withdrawn and was using the phone at Kathy's desk.

"Can you repeat that, please?" he said, gesturing Adhira over. She waited beside him, trying but unable to hear the voice on the phone. Huxley finally hung up, still in shock.

"What?" Adhira asked him now. "What happened?" A cold certainty ran through her that the news was going to be terrible, that it was going to exhaust whatever strength she had left, that whatever it was meant death.

Instead, Huxley said, "Anabelle's awake."

200

23

His dreams were of a lipless woman in a never-ending night. He'd come upon her in the mist in the shadow of a hill of bones, where she pounced on him and begin feeding. The sickly sound of his own bones being consumed terrorized him more than the pain itself. And he woke, screaming, in his old bedroom.

Johnny sat up. In an antique rocking chair in the corner, Dak wiped the sleep from his face and went to his son's side. The cool of a wet cloth against his forehead eased Johnny's panic, but still he looked at his father with fearful eyes. His young son's face, scarred with fear, preternaturally grown old in the hours since they left Roy's farm, brought a fresh stab of anxiety to Dak, but he smiled warmly at him now.

"It's okay, Rabbit, I'm here," Dak cooed to his son, using the nickname they'd given to Johnny when he was four, after he'd whipped his older brother in a race around the house, crossing the toilet-paper finish line with the carrot he'd forgotten to spit out still dangling from his mouth.

Johnny's eyes swept over the familiar desk light and onto hockey figurines in the soft glow of its cone, then to the comforting blue hue of his jersey-decked walls. He let out a little puff of relief then finally looked to his father, who was rubbing Johnny's forehead with his thumb.

"It hurts, Dad," Johnny whimpered, raising his bandaged hand, where the slant of two missing fingers the doctors had been unable to attach was obvious to both.

"It's time for Tylenol anyway," Dak said, thankful the codeine was mostly managing Johnny's pain. He drew a pill from the prescription bottle and gave it to Johnny with a glass of water.

Johnny swallowed the pill and settled again. "What time is it?"

"Almost six. You got a few hours at least." Dak patted Johnny's leg. "You want some breakfast?"

Though his son's eyes were puffed and signs of exhaustion were playing out all over his face, Dak knew that Johnny hadn't managed more than a spoonful of soup in almost two days. Looking at him, a grown man yet somehow small and childlike, with all the heat pressed out of him, Dak felt guilty for appreciating this stolen time with his youngest son.

He said, "I can fry up some sausages, if you like."

Just then, the smell of bacon hit them, and they heard the clang of faraway dishes being put to use.

More to appease his father than out of any real hunger, Johnny followed him to the kitchen where his mother was already many steps along in their breakfast. New crescents of darkness hung beneath her eyes, and her normally smooth, biscuit skin had taken the dry sheen of clay. On the table she'd set a plate of cut fruit and tomatoes, individual containers of yogurt, and a multi-compartment server with several varieties of nuts. Seeing them come into the kitchen, Wendy brought a stack of pancakes to the table and gave Johnny a gentle, one-armed hug with the hand that wasn't holding the spatula. "Just in time," she said cheerfully, pulling out a chair for Johnny as though she'd been waiting hours for his arrival. "Sit, sit."

INTERFERENCE

Dak kissed his wife, silently sharing his concern through a locked stare, then took a seat beside Johnny. "Smells incredible," he said appreciatively, and was glad to see Johnny agree and look eager to eat. Soon, a plate of bacon, a tray of sausage, half a baked ham, a bowl of scrambled eggs, and a dish of hash browns were placed before them.

Johnny's tired eyes widened. "Shit, Mom. You feeding an army?"

"You could say that. We've got three more to feed for the next while. Coffee, dear?"

Dak held Johnny's cup out for him while Wendy poured.

"Save some for me," Jesse said. He and Sarah came up the basement stairs, both in robes. He ruffled his brother's hair and snuck a piece of bacon before sitting down. "You look like shit, Bunny."

"Tell me again why you're married to him?" Johnny asked Sarah, who was pouring a glass of orange juice.

"I ask myself the same question sometimes," she said, watching her husband indiscriminately pick from the plates and stuff his mouth.

Johnny frowned. "So, you're my protectors now or something? Are we expecting a llama invasion anytime soon?"

The room grew quiet until finally Wendy, turning off the stove, said, "Tell him."

Holding hands beneath the table, Sarah and Jesse quietly consented with a nod to Dak.

The others waited while he set his coffee down and looked at Johnny. "We've asked your brother and Sarah and your nephew or niece to stay with us until this all blows over. We need to stick together—"

203

"You're pregnant?" Johnny gaped at Sarah. She nodded and patted her still flat belly. He began to wonder how much he'd missed during the fog of the last two days as his father went on.

"You're going to be an uncle," Dak confirmed, "as long as we get through this. It's not my news to tell, but I'm telling it because it underscores what I've got to say next. I'm not sure how much you remember of what happened at the farm, but we believe that your injury was only a diversion. When everyone rushed to the llama pen to see what was going on, a few of the children were left unattended." He paused, letting the severity of words settle over his son. "Two of Perry's grandkids died. They were found at the play set."

He did not elaborate, though the lowering of his eyes caused Johnny to press him for details. Dak's undesired recollection materialized with the tightening of his jaw and the flaring of his nostrils. In his lifetime, he'd seen terrible things. His volunteer efforts at the local shelter had inured Dak to the torments of homelessness, addiction, violence, and the gut-wrenching mental afflictions that attended most of its patrons. And though he'd grown a self-protective, case-hardened detachment out of necessity, it crumbled to dust when he saw those taut swings and those two blue faces in Roy's backyard two days ago. The boy was only four. The girl only eight.

"I'm sure you'll find out later, but I'd avoid it, if you can," he said. His fingers were pressure-white around his cup.

Johnny, surprised by his own appetite when he'd first seen the spread his mother laid out, set down his fork, sure he'd never be hungry again. "Was it Flint?" he asked when no one would meet his eyes. "It was, wasn't it?"

"We think so," Jesse told him. "She was the only one sitting at the picnic table near the swing set when it happened.

Her back was to the pen, and she would have seen the kids twisting the ropes—" Suddenly Dak coughed, and Jesse's explanation stopped.

Observing the dawning horror on her younger son's face, Wendy took the empty chair at the table. She was serious when she turned to him. "We've asked Nikonha to come. She will tell us what to do. Right now we all just need to eat so we can be strong when the time comes that we *need* to be strong."

She plucked a strawberry from Dak's plate and deliberately bit down while the rest of them pushed their breakfast around their plates. When the food was eventually collected and put away, Wendy had to force the fridge door shut with her hip to keep it closed, and she released them all with a stern warning that they'd better eat more for lunch or she'd start storing it beneath their bedsheets.

Jesse and Sarah showered and dressed while Johnny fell into an uneasy, medicated sleep. Dak used this time to sneak to his office in the basement and check his gun cabinet, explaining to Wendy that he had paperwork to do. From the look in her eyes, he knew she wasn't convinced, but she pretended for his sake as much as her own and dismissed him with a kiss and a tight, prolonged hug.

The small window afforded little light, so Dak switched on his desk lamp, as he wasn't quite ready for blare of the pot lights. He'd taken a mug of coffee with him, and this he set down as he sought comfort in the familiar paintings his mother had bestowed on him in her will almost a decade earlier. Harmonious plumes of reds, oranges, and yellows patterned fields, suns, animals, and people. Dak took in their unity and peace and let their messages wash over him as he prepared to defend his family.

Calmer now, he went to the closet and opened the doors. He expected his gun cabinet to have somehow vanished, but it was still there. His finger drew from memory the code and punched it into the keypad, then Dak opened the safe.

Just then, something banged against the window; a dwindling remnant of the windstorm the city had been enduring for over two days. If the death of two children wasn't enough, the city had been hit with fierce winds that toppled trailers, overturned streetlights, peeled siding, felled trees, and knocked down six billboards and the neon displays for Garett's only McDonald's and two of its Tim Horton's.

At the sound, Dak turned and peered at the little square above his desk. He pulled the blinds up. A scattering of leaves and loose twigs whirled across the back sidewalk, but nothing else of significance—so Dak returned to his task.

Back at the cabinet, he removed each of his rifles and looked them over. He was checking the safety on his Browning when the window rattled. Again it screeched and clacked within the pane until Dak was sure it was going to explode in on him. He set the rifle back in the case and quickly locked the safe, all the while bracing himself for a sudden spray of glass. But the moment he closed the closet doors, the window went still. A cold tine of fear rose up his spine, and he involuntarily shuddered with the certainty that Flint had seen him with his guns.

The doorbell rang.

Jesse's heavy footsteps sounded up the stairs, and Dak pulled the blinds closed, realizing that the heaviness in his chest was the pounding of his heart. His fingers trembled and he had the rusty taste of blood in his mouth from biting the inside of his cheek, but now he steadied himself and concentrated on slowing his breath. If Wendy saw him like this, she would know he had been visited. She was already a mess worrying over Johnny and her upcoming grandchild, so Dak took a moment to collect himself. He smoothed his hair, rubbed color into his cheeks, and got his tobacco pouch from his desk. Then he went to greet Nikonha, who was removing her wet boots at the front door.

"Dakota." The old woman halted the removal of her shoes and opened her arms wide. She rose onto the tips of her toes to reach around his shoulders, holding him warmly like a mother. Then Nikonha pushed a wrinkled cheek to Dak's chest and pinched her eyes shut, listening, and released him with a wary smile. "We have much to talk about, Good Fish." She eyed the tobacco pouch in Dak's hand. "Should I leave my boots on, then?"

Wendy, who had been standing aside, slid Nikonha's jacket back onto the shorter woman's shoulders and retrieved her own from the front closet. She slipped one more time into the room of her sleeping son and, content that that she wasn't needed, joined them in the small garden.

The wind was unkind to them, lashing at their legs, whipping dust into their eyes, chilling their bodies through the thickness of their jackets, as though Flint was trying to push them back into the house. Seeing Nikonha's sparse hair flip about, Dak offered to get her a hat, but she waved his concern away. The Elder smelled the wind, tasted its poison on her tongue, felt its clutching fingers, and set about her task with an expediency that put the others at ease. From a duffel bag she'd carried on her shoulder, Nikonha drew a prayer blanket that she quietly laid on the worked-up rows of earth. A wild draft twisted up the fabric until Sarah and Jesse hurried stones onto the corners.

The Elder sat and set a large shell on the center of the blanket. Four containers were then positioned above the shell. The others huddled close, trying to block the wind as Nikonha drew pinches of tobacco, sweetgrass, sage, and cedar from the containers and put them into the center of the shell. A puff of mixed medicines swirled upward as the incensed wind worked to stop the ceremony, but Nikonha ordered the group to open their jackets and fill the spaces between them. They were to beat Flint together or not at all, and the others obediently opened their coats and leaned inward, forming a makeshift teepee.

The first match Nikonha struck went out the moment it ignited. Then the second. The third. The fourth. Each time a match was struck, wind tore into the top of their teepee and snuffed it out. Leaning further toward each other, shoulders touching, faces a breath away, they helped Nikonha thrust her prayer upward. She struck fire. The medicines began their slow burn, and Nikonha wasted no time retrieving the eagle feather from her bag to smudge herself, Dak, Wendy, Jesse, and Sarah. Up and down the feather circled the medicine's smoke onto their faces, their bodies, while Nikonha beseeched the Spirits for their physical, and mental strength. They renewed themselves like this for some time, until finally the medicines had burned out and their ashes were returned to the earth.

When they retreated from their gathering, the wind had fallen quiet. Dak helped Nikonha to her feet and carried her bag inside, where Wendy prepared cedar tea and a snack of moose meat and strawberries. Before they sat, Dak showed Nikonha to the bedroom. His injured son was now awake and attuned to his phone.

"Little Elk," Nikonha greeted Johnny, and proceeded to retrieve the contents of her bag.

As Johnny pulled himself up, pain lanced the stubs where his fingers used to be, and he sucked in air to keep himself from swearing in front of Nikonha. She deftly repeated the outdoor ceremony for Johnny's benefit. With his good hand, Johnny welcomed the medicine his Elder was guiding toward him, and by the time the ceremony was complete, Johnny felt better than he had in days. "Miigwech Nikonha," he said a little tearfully, and the curtain of wrinkles on the old woman's face drew apart as she smiled up at him. In the corner, Dak sniffed.

"We will get through this, Little Elk," Nikonha said to Johnny, patting his knee with an arthritic hand. She squinted at him. "Rabbit, Elk, boy, man, not so little anymore, and not so easy to knock down, am I right?"

Johnny held up his bandaged hand. "What's two fingers when I got eight more to fight with?"

A chuff of laughter came from Dak. They saw Nikonha out of Johnny's bedroom and into the kitchen, where their tea was already poured for them. The tea was sweet and tasted of the earth, and as they sipped from their mugs and picked at the berries and moose meat, Nikonha was apprised of the family's encounters with Sylvia Baker, who they all suspected was hosting the spirit Flint. Though Dak did not relay the incident in the basement to the group, he suspected that Nikonha understood, as she held his eyes intently.

Once all had spoken, Nikonha spread her elbows on the table and leaned forward against her folded hands. Though she spoke quietly, the sound carried from her mouth was that of time itself, of the crashing of waves, of ancient winds over high mountains.

She said, "When I was a girl, they took my friends, my brothers, my sisters, my cousins. I'd go to play, and there would be another empty swing, another unattended net, until there was no one to play with anymore, and I was alone. I remember being scared that they were coming for me, but they never did. They never did." She pointed to a crevasse of skin on her neck. "This is from when my best friend was taken from me. A piece of my whole. This"—she felt a divot on her arm— "was the presence of my baby brother." She touched her chin, tapped her cheek, rubbed her ear, patted her nose, her forehead, an eye. "My big sister. My uncle. My neighbor. My niece. I bear their scars, but I am still intact. Pinch me," she ordered Wendy, who knew not to refuse. Wendy gently pinched a flap of skin on Nikonha's wrist. Nikonha said, "Still here, even with the pain, and that is how we defeat our other enemy, Flint." An old fist formed in front of them, thin-skinned and scarred. It was the strongest fist any of them had ever seen. "In your head and your head and your head"—she pressed a warm finger to each of their foreheads— "know that we are together even if we are apart. Go inside there, let the Spirits in, and never be alone. We need an army of warriors to send Flint back to before he was born." Five pairs of eyes viewed the Elder with awe. "We will call all the Elders," Nikonha told them, confident in her plan. "And say goodbye to Flint."

24

In the dark of his mother's musty living room, Troy wrestled with a need so great he trembled. A film of withdrawal sweat covered the entirety of his body, so he'd shucked his clothes and sat naked on the couch with the curtains drawn, waiting for the stage to pass.

He'd known it was coming. Months without fulfilling the desires of his Dark Friend, it was inevitable that he'd be punished. The small ache that crept up his leg and settled on his shoulders became a full-body cramp that gripped him until he had to run to the toilet, where things were squeezed out of every orifice he had. Then his skin boiled. Then it froze. Then it burned again. His nose ran. His eyes watered. His mouth twitched. Even after the productive meeting with Anabelle's parents, his Dark Friend showed no appreciation for the gains Troy had made. There was no gratitude for their gratefulness, no leniency for their willingness to thrust their daughter's welfare onto him as though Troy alone could save her, Troy alone could fix her. His relationship with the Cheevers would lead to rapture, but the prolonged process enraged his Dark Friend, and he felt its petulance with every spike of pain, every stab of anticipation.

How long had it been? Three months? Four? He reached for the memory, drew it from the place where he kept his secret things, and unwrapped it now. Late night. After the Runnymede Library had closed. A foggy Tuesday. One of the many nights Troy had stayed late at the office, so his presence in the shadows along Bloor could be rationalized. A departing storm had emptied the streets. There were few that had seen him and none that had caught him wedged between a concrete wall and a thicket of bushes in the messy lot of a home under construction.

His fortuitous dip down Ellis Park Road was a last-minute decision. He waited there a few minutes before he spotted a woman he had seen coming from the library a short time earlier. Heavy book bags hung from the crooks of her elbows, and her attention was attuned to her feet as she lowered her face away from the rain. She practically walked right into his arms, and it was only after he'd placed his hand over her mouth that the woman understood her reading days were over.

Remembering now the huffing of her breath against his fingers and the spill of blood from her ears, Troy wished for another easy elimination that would satisfy his Dark Friend until he could get to Annabelle without ruining his life. Garrett was crawling with law enforcement, and over-vigilant locals were already pouncing at anything that moved. There was no easy solution. He knew his delirium was dangerous; he knew his eagerness could make him sloppy, but he also knew that if he didn't try, his system would shut down. Reason would abandon him. Tact would escape completely. If he didn't satisfy his urge soon, it would consume what made him human and turn him into an animal. He shuddered.

The lights of a passing car swept through a slit in the curtains and fell on a collage of pictures on the living room wall. Pictures of his mother and her friends. Pictures of his mother and her dog. Pictures of his mother and him, when he was younger and obedient. The light passed but Troy stood and went to the wall, sliding his fingers over the frames, over the glass, over his mother's face from memory. *She would do for now*, his Dark Friend suggested. Troy was indifferent. *You have access*, his Dark Friend purred inside him. *And you don't love her anyway.*

"I don't love anything except you," Troy said to the empty room. His Dark Friend's suggestion wasn't something he hadn't thought of before. It was always there; it was his first thought as though it had been born with him, but it didn't give him pleasure because—young as he was when he'd first recognized the presence of another inside him—Troy was smart enough back then to know he needed his mother. But he didn't need her now. *Go on*, his Dark Friend advised, and Troy took from the wall a picture of his mother. He squeezed the frame until the glass broke. Still he crushed, more, more, until glass sliced his fingers, his palms, and his own blood fell onto the floor. It stemmed his headache, and the pains he'd suffered for the last few days began to ebb away. Another sweep of passing lights drew across Troy's naked and bloody body and his wide, grinning face then left him in darkness once more.

He left the living room and padded to the kitchen, where for the next twenty minutes he pulled shards of glass from his hands. His Dark Friend's new admiration inoculated him from suffering, so even though several of the cuts were deep, the procedure was painless.

Troy wrapped his hands in kitchen towels and poured himself a bath. He preferred to visit the hospital as a clean man, a sane man, a man who'd simply tripped over a cat when he went to fetch a midnight snack and found himself with the broken pieces of a family treasure in his hands. The

213

water turned red once he entered the bathtub and soon the things below the surface were indistinguishable in the dimness, but he lay there until the water ran cold, thinking.

By all means, his mother was not an easy choice—perhaps the worst he could make—but his Dark Friend's insistence made his suffering over Anabelle tolerable, so he was determined to try. He dressed carefully, reminding himself that his godlike stature in Toronto's legal community was no accident. He'd gotten to where he was with prudence and an expanse of logic that bordered insanity, and he would employ those skills to do what he had to do.

He drove to the hospital in the shadows of the night, leaving his window open to feel the sharpness of the air against his freshly bathed skin. His story required the appearance appropriate to a man near shock, so Troy let the wind mess his hair and blanch his skin. When he arrived, the towels he'd earlier wrapped around his hands were soaked through, and though there was only a heartbeat of irritation on his palms, he looked in the mirror to ensure the face he was about to present was the one expected. He frowned at himself, drew the corners of his lips down in a grimace of fake pain, and began to quiver, as though all his times at trial had been preparation for this moment.

The air outside was cold, and though the earlier wind had somewhat subsided, a new breeze fought vainly against his march to the emergency door. It pushed hard at him, until his body was slanted against its backward thrust, but he drove his body onward to the squares of light emanating from the building. Looking now at the patients and visitors clustered together trying to sneak a cigarette outside, Troy noticed that none of their pants were flapping and none of their gowns were waving beneath the bottom of their jackets.

INTERFERENCE

The Canadian, provincial, and municipal flags standing sentinel on a landscaped grassy rise at the front of the hospital hung, immobile, down the poles that held them, and not a single leaf or wrapper of gum carried past him as he walked.

The night was still but for the action around Troy. The thrum of resistance in the cool air was attuned only to him. His eyes swept up to the top floor of the hospital where he knew Anabelle Cheever lay, and he wondered if the presence he felt was hers.

You feel that? he asked his Dark Friend now. *She doesn't want us here*, came its reply. *Already resisting*. Troy grinned slyly, for the first time appreciating the game they were about to play, then he staggered through the doors of the hospital.

He was attended to quickly, and before long he was rushed from the reception desk past a clot of indignant would-be patients who groaned dramatically while Troy and his nurse walked by as though his passage renewed their suffering. A woman clutched her stomach and shouted at the nurse that she had been waiting for hours while a man, slumping and slobbering over the trail of dried vomit on the front of his shirt, barked drunkenly to everyone in the waiting room that you had to be good-looking to get help. The mother of a red-faced baby beside the drunk leaned away toward the wall, and Troy was sorry he hadn't had a seat far away from the man to relinquish to her. There was still a smidgeon of decency left in him.

He relayed his false story to the attending doctor, who efficiently removed three shards of glass Troy hadn't seen, and expediently sewed thirteen stitches—six on his right, seven on his left—in varying parts of his hands. The doctor would have been suspicious if Troy explained he didn't require freezing, so he accepted the needle and pretended it felt better while the doctor worked on him.

A short time later, with his hands bandaged and decently numb, Troy thanked the doctor and retraced his way through the same waiting area. Only the mother and her baby were gone. In her place, a gargantuan man with tattoos covering most of his face seemed to be the keeper of the room's peace, for each time the drunk tried to speak, the tattooed man jabbed the other's foot with the heel of a crutch.

Feeling a strange kinship with the kind beast, Troy inclined his chin; an infinitesimal gesture, but the beast paid no notice, and Troy departed the hospital, ready to see his mother. Even with his previous parting words and parking lot abandonment, the costume of injury would endear him to her again because no mother, not even his own, wanted to see her child suffer. He would feign pain and let her dote on him until her defenses were down and his strike would come unnoticed.

As he stepped off the sidewalk into the parking lot, an old minivan sped past Troy and screeched into a stall. A moment later, William Cheever scuttled out of his car carrying four bags of fast food, each from a different restaurant. He spotted Troy almost immediately, greeting him with unmistakable joy. "Troy!" he called, hurrying toward him with his bags. "Troy! I was going to call you! You'll never guess what happened! She's awake! Oh, she's awake and talking and wants *food*. Can you believe it?" He shook his bags in the air, and two French fries flew out.

The unexpected news sent a rush of heat though Troy and he stifled a shudder as he looked at William Cheever. "A miracle." Troy smiled at the man. "Thank God for that. How is she feeling?"

William's shoulders popped upward. "She's not walking yet, but the doctors say that will come, if they can figure out the ... you know." He let the statement hang. William's eyes

INTERFERENCE

fell on Troy's bandaged hands. "I'm sorry, Troy. I'm so worked up these days, with Anabelle and everything, I'm not thinking straight. What's it now? Two o'clock in the morning and of course you shouldn't be here in the parking lot talking to me. What happened? Are you okay?"

"Cat tripped me on my way to the kitchen," Troy told him. "They're not so far off when they say midnight snacks'll kill you." His little huff of laughter made William lower his bags and give him a sympathetic whistle.

"Broke my toe when my own damn cat did that to me last year. He became an outside cat after that." William chuckled then looked down at his bags. "You get your snack after all that trouble?" Troy said he did not, hoping William would extend an invitation, which he promptly did. "If it's too late for you," William said, "say so, but if you're still hungry, why don't you come see Anabelle with me? She's the only one on the floor, and they've been pretty lax with the visiting hours since she woke up. We've told her all about you. I'm sure she'd love to meet you."

"I don't want to impose …"

"Nonsense!" William said, guiding him along with a bag-ladened hand. "She got Susan to get her a coffee, so she'll be up for a while yet. Says she doesn't want to sleep, and right now that's fine with me. As long as she's here, you know?" There was a catch at the back of his throat.

They took the main entrance, and Troy was grateful to avoid the emergency waiting area. Here there was only a scattering of people: a middle-aged man rolling his intravenous pole toward the vending machines, two nurses talking quietly over cups of tea on a bench near the water wall, and an old woman consoling another woman weeping on her shoulder. Through all this, the smile had never left William's face. He

217

had his daughter back, and not even this depressing sweep of hospital life would change his gratitude.

In the elevator, William watched the ascension of lights on the control panel with unrestrained enthusiasm. Almost immediately, the bigger man in his heavy jacket, against which leaned bags of hot food, started sweating. Troy offered to ease the burden in William's arms, but William politely refused, nodding toward Troy's hands. "You got your hands full already," he said. "But I'm sure they stitched you up nice and you'll be good as new before you know it. They're good people around here, you know. Makes me feel sort of bad about the lawsuit." His eyes sidled away from Troy as spots of color touched his cheeks. "They *did* do everything they could, given the circumstances, and between you and me, I don't think a bigger hospital would have done anything different. They might have bigger and better facilities in Toronto, but with the amount of people they tend to, Anabelle wouldn't have been a priority like she was here. The way she was—you know, with the electrification and everything—I wonder if she would have been too much trouble for them, taking a whole floor in a city that size. If I'm being honest, I think they would have let my girl die rather than take up all their resources."

His voice trembled, and Troy sensed that if he pressed the lawsuit right now, William would crumble. Not only would it make Troy seem insensitive, but it would engender suspicion that he definitely could not afford. He wouldn't give up because as of this moment the lawsuit was his only way to Anabelle. Biding his time was his only option. As long as he wasn't dismissed, there was still hope.

Troy said, "They were amazing when my mother had her stroke. She wouldn't be recovering like she is if she didn't get the care she had here. One of my partner's fathers suffered a stroke a few years ago, and I remember the hell that poor guy went through. They discharged him too quickly, and he ended back in the hospital off and on for maybe four months. All the rehab programs were booked up, so they had nowhere to put him. He had a homecare nurse that visited twice a week, but it wasn't enough to keep him going. He deteriorated so fast that by the time he was able to get into a program, they couldn't help much." He looked at William, who was listening intently. "I think there is something to be said for small communities, you know?"

The elevator doors opened and the men stepped out onto the quiet floor, with Troy following slightly behind William. *There! There! THERE!* Get her! Get herrrrrr! His Dark Friend salivated inside his head, and Troy did his best to shield his outward senses to his Dark Friend's frenzy. He rolled his tongue over his teeth, swallowing the surge of saliva in his mouth.

"That hospital smell gets you every time, don't it?" William laughed.

"I'll never get used to it," Troy said, and wiped the corners of his mouth.

"That was quick," said a thick-set nurse, smiling up at them from her desk. She eyed Troy delightedly as most women did, and he gave her his most innocent smile. With effort, she peeled her eyes off Troy. To William, she said, "She's been surfing on her iPad since she woke up. Your wife's been trying to keep her away from the news, but you know how kids are. Tell them not to do something and it's the only thing they want to do." She wrinkled her nose.

William held up his bags. "This'll keep her mind off it," he said confidently, then added, "Our ... friend ... was just leaving as I was coming in. Mind if he pays a quick visit?"

219

The request was unnecessary because since Anabelle had woken up, the Cheever family had the floor to themselves and would continue to do so until the electrification issue was resolved, but William insisted on signaling his respect for the team that had saved his only child.

The nurse, whose nametag read *Tammy*, glanced at Troy's hands. "Tripped over a cat," he said to her unspoken question.

"You two go on in, and mind your balance, you hear?" She winked at Troy.

"Oh!" William said suddenly, turning back around. "Almost forgot! Bacon double cheeseburger and curly fries for you." He set a bag on Tammy's desk and removed her food. Avoiding Troy's eyes, she tucked the items behind her computer screen with an embarrassed murmur of thanks.

"Enjoy." Troy tipped his chin to Tammy before William led him away from the nursing station.

The distance from the desk to Anabelle's bed was only a few strides, but as they approached the only room that was lit, Troy felt as though he'd just crossed the span of a desert. Outside the glass walls, his heart pounded and his body ached with a thirst he hadn't realized he was capable of bearing without succumbing to death. When William tapped on the sliding glass door, Troy was struck by a paralyzing fear that he wouldn't be able to control himself. Before this, he'd always been able to tame his Dark Friend when required, so his inability to shut it out now brought an agonizing worry that made him nauseous. "You all right?" William whispered to him.

"I've never done well in hospitals."

"A burger will help that, I think." William smiled, and then the glass door slid open and Susan Cheever was blinking up at Troy, confused.

INTERFERENCE

"I was in the neighborhood," Troy said, holding up his hands with a small laugh.

Susan's maternal instincts drew her toward him and into a tight, breast-crushing hug. "Oh! Oh, you poor dear! What is with this city these days? No one can get a break. Come, come in. She's awake and she's excited to meet you. You tell him she knows about him?"

"Yes dear," William said, entering the room. When he finally stepped aside, Troy's eyes fell upon Anabelle.

Though he'd somehow expected his treasure beyond all treasures to present a formidable appearance, the girl was small and birdlike. In the Cheever home, Susan had practically thrown pictures of Anabelle at him. He'd seen her as an infant, white-skinned and cherry-haired, splashing in her grandmother's tub with plastic farm animals, and again as a toddler with fuzzy pigtails, squeezing a golden retriever. He'd seen her dance recitals, at birthday parties, at school plays, at church. Troy had seen the space of her first lost tooth and the scrape of her first bike ride. Susan had teared up talking about Anabelle's first slumber-party, last heartbreak, and the pride they'd felt watching her accept her high school diploma at her graduation ceremony the previous year. So he knew to expect large green eyes and a saddle of freckles across her small nose, and he knew that her injury would have emaciated her already thin body. None of this was surprising. What was surprising was that when Anabelle first spotted Troy, he felt her see right into him.

Rubbing Anabelle's arm, Susan said, "This is Mr. Baker, honey. Remember we told you about him?"

"H—" Troy started, then cleared his throat. "Hello Anabelle," he finally managed. He did not offer her his hand, afraid the contact would prove too irresistible for his Dark

221

Friend, knowing the Cheevers would suspect his injury as the reason. "It's Troy, actually. Please call me Troy." He swallowed and watched her eyes follow the slide of his Adam's apple, then he took a chair William pulled up for him and sat. Anabelle did not take her eyes off him.

"I convinced him to come up for a snack," William told his daughter, setting beside her a small box of donut holes, a bag of fries, a cheeseburger, and a personal pizza.

Susan chortled with laughter. "You'd think she's a giant, trying to feed her like that." The relieved parents began nibbling at their food, but Susan's brows knit with concern. "You okay, dear?" she asked, patting Anabelle's ankle. "Are you tired? Dad can pack the food up for later if you'd like." Concern flitted over William's face as he chewed.

Anabelle shook her head and finally laid her iPad down on her stomach. "No, I—I'm fine." Her pinky finger twitched, then to Troy she said, "You don't have a cat."

His Dark Friend squealed. *What fun! What fun she will be! Can you feel it, Troy? Can you? Can you? Can you? Take her and take all. Take her and take everything. She's it, Troy, she's IT. The one I have been waiting forrrrrrrr!* He felt his Dark Friend work through his blood, his veins, his—No! No! Troy squeezed his legs shut and covered his lap with his hands, pressing with his wrists until a jolt of pain deflated him. All this in seconds. Then he fought his Dark Friend's push with the blocking of his mind. Onto the path that lay between his Dark Friend and Anabelle, Troy shoved the memory of his tax returns and the tying of his shoe. On went his haircuts, his belt size, the color of his mailbox, the final question on his bar exam. He congested his mind—the singular space now a thickened miasma of random thought, anything, anything to keep him calm, keep him sane. His heartbeat a thunderclap in his chest, Troy forced a sympathetic smile.

"I have two cats actually," he lied to the girl who had read him, knowing she would know.

"Brain injury," William said.

"But she's already healing faster than they thought she would," Susan interjected, as though saying so made it irrevocable. "Show him your head, honey," she instructed Anabelle.

Obediently, though with eyes locked on Troy, Anabelle tilted her head to reveal a shortened patch of red hair a few inches slantwise from her ear. Already, there was no discernable scar or bruise or scratch that would have indicated the girl had tumbled off a bridge in a tour bus.

"Isn't it incredible?" Susan beamed.

With a mouthful of burger, William said, "Blows the mind, doesn't it? Once they figure out the other stuff"—he gestured to the wires extending from her feet— "she'll get discharged."

"Is that right?" Troy remarked, calming himself with great effort.

"I'll be out soon," Anabelle said tonelessly, her finger swirling around her bedsheet. She bumped the pizza and it fell facedown on the floor. Susan gave a little cry as both she and William reached to scoop it up. And while their heads were turned away from their daughter, Anabelle's eyes fell to Troy's lap.

25

The fifth floor of the hospital was a nest of quiet. Gone were the percussions of monitors and the whispers of ventilators. Absent were the unconscious sounds of doomed patients; no longer were last rites chanted in haste beside disconsolate mourners. There was a pause in the dispirited procession of the living who dragged themselves past the nursing station, away from the soon-to-be-dead. The temporary reprieve from the loud quiet accorded the two nurses on duty a weightlessness that eased the strain on their shoulders, relaxed the muscles in their necks.

From Anabelle's room their chatter was easily heard, and it was not without effort that Anabelle kept from laughing at sexual escapades gone wrong or weight loss ventures gone worse. Her company having departed hours ago, they supposed she was asleep, but Anabelle had never been more awake.

She felt no pain, nor was she suffering from isolation or what they called *survivor's guilt*, though she supposed the curiosity around her survival would accompany her to her grave. If asked, Anabelle believed she could fling her covers away and dash out the doors, such was the rapidity of her recovery. Were it not for the wires, she felt she could even return to college in London, but somehow Anabelle knew she should do none of these things right now. Her time in the fog had told her so.

The deep-throated belly laughs of a nurse conjured the memory of her grandfather, living large and letting everyone know it beside her on the bus that day. How happy he had been to be showing her off, and how happy her grandmother was, pretending to be annoyed with it. "Let her be, Earl." Her grandmother elbowed him then. "You're embarrassing her."

And though color had spotted her cheeks and she'd hidden her face behind her hands, Anabelle had felt a hundred feet tall as her grandparents bragged about her to their friends, who then inquired about her relationship status to pass along to their grandsons. She'd celebrated her nineteenth birthday the week before with a party thrown by her parents and a pub crawl organized by her friends, so she was still suffering from a raging hangover when her grandparents surprised her with the casino trip.

Anabelle wasn't averse to spending time with her mother's parents; in fact, she enjoyed their banter. Where her father's parents seemed to diminish with age, retreating from social and physical activity, substituting friendships with doctor's visits, Grandpa Earl and Grandma Gingy seemed to expand through time. They gathered people like fridge magnets, accrued experience like passport stamps, welcomed adventure wherever and to whomever it took them. Reflecting now on the enormity of their lives, Anabelle was somewhat consoled that her grandparents had lived that way, but she would give anything to have them back.

Lying in her bed, listening to the nurses' overly loud exchange of secrets, Anabelle knew she would never forget her grandparents' selflessness. When the SUV hit, their quick exchange of fear went to Anabelle, only to Anabelle, and when the wind bashed the carriage and the passengers flailed about, it was her grandmother who shouted, "Help her, Earl!" By the time the semi pushed them over the guardrail, both her grandparents had removed their seatbelts and were cocooned around her, pressing their bodies to hers, frantically shouting their love to each other, to her, their prayers a united plea for help. In that terrible moment, their fear was for Anabelle alone, for she had heard their resigned declarations of love, saw their goodbyes in the steadiness of their eyes as they locked on each other. Then they were gone, and Anabelle was submersed in fog.

There was no pain when she entered the fog, nor was there recollection of the crash or anything that ever existed before the fog. It was like being born in an underlit room: disorienting in its foreignness but otherwise sedating. Her body, light with movement and exempt from the restriction of gravity, passed through the suspension of space and time as a cell would in an infinite body, going everywhere and nowhere at once. She didn't know whether her first feelings were instant or if they sprouted somewhere in the ellipses of time, but they came and they were additive, the effect of fertilizer on a plant. Beneath the net of fog, Anabelle bloomed. She became something she hadn't been, evolved from her human seed into something stronger—and with terrific power.

Unfolding her new self, Anabelle had pressed the canopy above her until she burst through the protective web and emerged with the knowledge of what she had become. It was then, when she rose above the shelter of the fog, that Anabelle first sensed the existence of otherness that was not human but toying with humanness as cats would butterflies; batting one about until life was exhausted, then onto the next. There were not one of these *things*, but *many* sourced from the same evil, and she felt their gaze upon her as she rose from the mist, their individual ambitions now yoked against her.

As her consciousness flooded back, she worked to retain their memory, fearing that she would forget that she was in danger outside of the fog. Anabelle forced their names through her fingertips, tracing the letters of their names. *Pandora. Dark Friend. Flint. Lamashtu. Lilith. Mavet. Azazel. Bael. Pocong. Shinigami. Daeva*'s animals, *Ariton*'s water. *Ala*'s weather. These and more, her fingers remembered with movement etched into her sheets, and when she finally woke, her fingers did not let her forget.

Anabelle's first certainty upon waking was that she had gained something with that crash. Her second was of the peril she faced because of it. She woke in fear not because of the recurring thoughts of her grandparents acceding to death as they hovered over her, and not because of the screams of terror as bones cracked and skin split, but because Anabelle had suddenly become the object of *demons*. The accident had splintered one of these things like a chip from a stone, severing its power, and somehow Anabelle absorbed its loss. Now they all wanted it, as though Anabelle were some sort of competition and her death was first prize.

When she'd first opened her eyes two days ago, she'd felt them in her room, fluttering like midges over her skin, touching, testing, and one by one she dug into her new power and flicked them away. But their tongues had tasted and they returned, more, more, until her room was bursting with them, sliding over her body and beating each other back at her bedside. A great compression of terror crippled Anabelle until she understood that the testers and the tasters in her room were only understudies. With their report,

227

stronger, meaner, more terrible chiefs of hell would come, and Anabelle was determined to be free of the hospital before then. Intuiting the need for a measured escape so they wouldn't realize how strong she was, Anabelle feigned exhaustion to her doctors, to her parents, even alone in her room because she knew they were watching. Watching. Always watching.

To her doctors, her medical reports were nothing short of a miracle. Her skull had healed. The delicate sponge of her brain showed no sign of past trauma. Her hair had defiantly sped back, its uneven length noticeable only with a close face and the squinting of eyes. They didn't know she willed her body to heal, and they didn't know she had worked the job of a conductor, opening and closing the circuits within her body to determine how her new self worked. They thought the surge the hospital experienced late last night and early that morning were issues in the mechanical room, something from the generators, or the unpreparedness of Lakehead Power. But it was not that. It was Anabelle piloting the mechanisms of her new self. She found she could squeeze her energy out and pull it back in. In, out, in, out, in … in … in … but not yet enough to be disconnected from the ridiculous tangle of wires attached to her ankles.

The whisper of shoes brought Stephanie into her room. "You're up!" the nurse exclaimed cheerfully.

"Morning," Anabelle murmured, drawing a pinch of empathy from the nurse's face.

Stephanie's eyes scanned the monitors. Then she peeked at Anabelle's healed headwound in case it had sprung back open, and changed one of her intravenous bags. "How are you feeling today, my girl?" she asked. The endearment was a collective one, for once the ward was cleared of other patients and Anabelle became their sole concern, the nurses took it upon themselves to care for her as they would for their own children. For not only was Anabelle the city's hope, but a small-town hospital's triumph, and the nurses shone with pride every time they were near. In the short time since she'd woken, Stephanie had become Anabelle's favorite nurse, indulging in gossip with Anabelle like an old friend. She reached for the cord to the bed control, and the steady whir of the motor elevating Anabelle's head broke the silence in the room.

Anabelle tried to ignore the invisible things lurking behind the nurse, beside the monitor, at the foot of her bed. *Flick. Flick. Flick.* She warned them away. "I could use a coffee," Anabelle admitted. "But not the cafeteria crap. I'm too young for heartburn."

A smile touched the nurse's lips. "I hear you," Stephanie said. "I don't know what they put in it, but I don't believe it's fit for human consumption. Gets the job done, that's about it. Shift change is in twenty minutes. Want me to get Zadie to pick you up a Starbucks on her way? Your parents must've gotten us a hundred so far. This one's on me." Things swirled around the oblivious nurse like dark and destructive ozone.

Clamping her eyes against the nightmares around her, Anabelle said, "I'd marry you for a latte."

"I think you'd upset that friend of yours," Stephanie joked, busy with Anabelle's urinary drainage bag. "Tammy told me he seemed quite taken with you." She swiped the air with her hand. "Seems a bit old, but when you look like that, age is just a number, right? I tell you; I haven't seen a man like that since my friends took me to Vegas for my bachelorette party twenty years ago. Men of Australia, or something like that, I think the show was called. Only those ones had nothing above their necks, couldn't spell stupid if it were printed for them, there were so many spelling mistakes on these love notes they wrote. I mean, looks or no looks, it should be a crime to sell a postcard that isn't spelled correctly, know what I'm saying?" Stephanie squealed with laughter. Against her will, Anabelle joined in. "But your guy, that *friend* of your family's"—she air-quoted with her fingers— "you see it in his eyes, don't you? That thing that says he could tear you apart, reciting Shakespeare or even the dictionary the whole time and … mmm! You'd just love it." Stephanie gyrated her hips without embarrassment while the invisible things around her silently growled.

Anabelle knew that it was no secret her parents had retained Troy Baker to represent the family in a potential lawsuit against the hospital. The trio of doctors that tended to Anabelle ordered the nurses not to permit him access without their presence since his impromptu visit early that morning, much to the disappointment of the none-too-quiet nursing staff. With the interest in her case and the scrutiny of governments, law enforcement, and news media around the world, the unit had adopted the requirement of a sign-in sheet to track visitors, along with strict instructions to bar a number of people on the doctors' list, where Troy was second only to Jessica Chung.

Since Troy's hands were bandaged, Anabelle's father had taken it upon himself to sign the lawyer in when he'd visited, but intentionally omitted Troy's last name to avoid an uncomfortable confrontation. As per protocol, Tammy should have cross-referenced Troy's name with those on the prohibited list, but she was too smitten to remember. The commotion from the nursing station when the doctors

INTERFERENCE

discovered he'd breached their defenses would have woken Anabelle if she were asleep, but she was alert and just as rattled as they were, only for different reasons.

Sure, the lawyer was hot. Perhaps twenty, twenty-five years older than Anabelle herself, Troy presented an irresistible, fuckable front. She had been with only two men: the first on her seventeenth birthday with her boyfriend Andrew—whose too-eager, misdirected javelin spears to the areas *beside* her vagina almost made her swear off sex—and her current boyfriend, Robbie, who never gave her an orgasm. Robbie wasn't bad looking, but neither was he *Troy*, who Anabelle believed could wet the panties off any woman he chose without even touching her. Were she not aware of what Troy was, Anabelle might have even considered imagining his face on Robbie's body next time she was with him, but she knew—and *what* she knew was terrible.

He entered her room as death enters the departing, sponging up light, and it took some effort for Anabelle to pretend she didn't notice. Her parents coddled the man like a son, bandaged up the way he was, but she wasn't fooled. Her new senses warned her against him, spooling through her brain garlands of grotesque imagery that made her already delicate stomach turn sour. Until then, the darkness in her room was unembodied, smokes of another existence, but the personification of evil at her bedside with her parents was another story.

"You all right, honey?" Stephanie asked her now, patting her leg.

Anabelle gestured to her ankles. "Would *you* be?"

Stephanie's sharp shoulders dropped slightly. She glanced behind her to see if anyone was listening, then said, "I can't say that I've ever had electricity coming out my ass,

231

S. L. LUCK

so I can't relate, but given the circumstances, you're doing well. You know what I would do if I were you?"

"Zap all your ex-boyfriends?"

"That, of course, but you do realize this is a money-maker, right? All those networks wanting interviews, I'm sure once you're out of here you could make a small fortune just telling your story. Maybe even pay for college."

"Hadn't thought of that," Anabelle said sullenly.

"Aw, now," Stephanie said, "You're going to get out, just wait and see. They won't keep you up here forever, though if I'm being selfish, I have to say I enjoy having you. It's never this easy up here."

Anabelle frowned. "Were any of the others up here?" she asked a bit hesitantly. "I mean I know that … that I'm the only one, but did any of them make it here?"

The nurse shook her head. "A few made it to the emergency room, but that was it."

"Were any of them like me?"

"You mean the electricity?" Stephanie asked. When Anabelle nodded, the nurse said, "No, but that doesn't mean it wouldn't have happened to them. You didn't get like this until *after* Dr. Huxley sewed you up. Scared the living hell out of everyone, but you're here now and that's all that matters." She fingered a coil of Anabelle's hair. "Never thought I'd be working with electricians on a patient, but the Lord does surprise sometimes, doesn't He?"

So does the devil, Anabelle thought, determined to get out of the hospital as soon as she could.

26

By the time Ed escorted Dorothy and Evie to the seats Chester saved for them, the Blundy and Ashurst Funeral Home was packed. Though death was no stranger to Southbridge, Dorothy had been inconsolable that morning, and it had taken Ed and Evie a great deal of time to coax Dorothy out of her robe and into the dress Evie loaned her for the occasion. Like other assisted-living homes, Southbridge retained a small, low-floor transport bus with a wheelchair lift that the non-driving residents used for daily activities, somber and otherwise. Their patient driver, Joe, was used to delays, so when they finally managed to get Dorothy onto the bus, he still greeted the latecomers with a smile. The others behind him, however, were not so kind.

"You planning on standing the whole time, dearie?" Ada Tilbury asked testily while Dorothy boarded.

"Move your goddamn purse, Ada, and let the woman sit," Maria Lewis shot at the cranky woman.

Ada's old lips clamped into a tight pucker. "I'm just saying that there are others to think of. We've been sitting here for almost an hour, Doris has been holding *it*, waiting for you to come. *She*,"—Ada wriggled a finger at Dorothy—"should be more considerate."

Doris, who'd been sitting behind Ada, blushed a deep red. "I'm fine, Ada. It's not a big deal." Her embarrassment suggesting that her urgency had passed, Doris looked out the window at the falling flakes of snow.

"Let the woman alone." Behind Dorothy, Evie scowled. A relatively new resident, Evie was still learning to navigate the variety of personalities at Southbridge, but already she disliked this woman. "Here, hun, sit here," she said, guiding Dorothy to the empty space beside Albert Humphrey, who was patting the seat to welcome her. And perhaps it was the solemnity of the day or the sourness of the interaction that made her do it, but Evie proceeded to bump Ada's purse onto the floor with her rear, then took the seat it vacated, settling down with a triumphant grin.

"Excuse me!" came the indignant squawk from Ada's parched windpipe. She began to rise, then saw the grimacing faces around her urging composure. Grunting, Ada sat back down with splayed elbows, nestling like an angry bird. The women seated, Ed took the space offered at the back between Willie and Anton Forbes, the only pair of sibling residents.

"Looks like we're ready to go, folks," Joe called to them over the intercom, and when the bus pulled away from the parking lot, Dorothy once again began to cry.

At the church, Ed and Evie ushered Dorothy down the aisle of mourners while the throaty bellows of the organist's pipes were setting the mood for the coming gloom. From the open mahogany trusses to the gold-flecked carpet, sniffs and sobs and exchanges of grief hovered over the congregants and weighed on their hearts.

Seated at the front were Hattie's five children, gray themselves, to whom Hattie's long life was of little consolation as they wept on the shoulders of their spouses. Behind

234

INTERFERENCE

them were a platoon of grandchildren and great-grandchildren bearing Hattie's dimples, uncomfortable in their clothes and pulling at their collars and sleeves. Smaller children, oblivious to the obligations of grief, tickled one another and had to be settled by their parents, only to start again once their elders weren't looking. A small boy's insistence that he needed a snack was hushed. A small girl's insistence she needed the bathroom was abandoned once a candy bar was placed in her hand. To Ed's great relief, he found Chester in a middle row near the aisle, guarding their spaces with a splayed leg on the bench.

"I pretended I couldn't hear it when they tried to take your seats," he whispered with a laugh and set his leg down.

Ed, already tired from the day's activity, gratefully sat beside him and accepted a tissue offered by Chester. "Just in case," Ed said, and tucked it into his hand.

"Me too, please." Evie sniffed.

The crowd quieted as Father Bonner made his way to the podium. He tapped the microphone and the muffled sound of the speakers being turned on rang throughout the building. "We will begin in a few minutes, once our ushers have brought chairs for those of you standing at the back. In the meantime, we ask that everyone take their seats and turn off their cellphones." He stepped back from the podium and clasped his hands respectfully, waiting while extra chairs were distributed. Ada Tilbury had just managed to sit when the high timbre of the organ's pipes signaled to the crowd that the funeral was about to begin. At the sound, Hattie's two daughters and three sons stood and made their way to the back of the room, one after the other, in a single, somber line. Children were hushed, phones were silenced, and the congregants rose to their feet, turning inward toward the aisle.

235

Two white-gloved ushers opened the interior doors and clicked the doorstops in place, the insignificant taps of metal pins being positioned sounding large and foreboding to all who could hear. Then Hattie's flower-adorned coffin was rolled down the aisle while her adult children walked reverently behind to fresh concussions of sorrow. In front of the altar, the ushers turned Hattie's encased body, then removed five roses from a wreath on top and presented one to each of her children.

Hattie's youngest daughter, Marianne, was the first to bend and kiss the coffin. She pressed her cheek to the cold metal casing above her mother's face, then drew her lips in to keep herself from wailing. The crowd stood while Hattie's remaining four children wept, kissed, and rubbed the thing that would take their mother into the ground. Shuddering with sorrow, they united for a brief embrace, then returned to their seats beside their waiting, worried spouses. While a melancholy hymnal was played, four ushers distributed tissues to those without. Reflections on Hattie, on private mortalities, spread through three hundred despairing minds, and the funeral was ready to proceed. Restored at the podium, Father Bonner said, "Please be seated." The sound of three hundred people sitting was a solid drumbeat of obeyance.

What followed was ninety minutes of prayer, of recollection, of gratitude, and of heartbreak. That Hattie Freemont was loved was undeniable. The testimony to her greatness was registered on all of them. Skimming the room, scanning familiar faces old and young as he and Evie soothed Dorothy, Ed appreciated the full house on Hattie's behalf. To his right were the Cardinals, whom everyone in Garrett knew through their philanthropy. To his left was Police Chief Dan Fogel, alone, seated two rows in front of his ex-wife Brandy and her current boyfriend, whose unfortunate public sexcapade still drew public attention, as presently seen by the whisperers and pointers around them. There was the Fischer family and the Boyd family, the Beechers, the Penners, the Widlows, Roy and Gretchen Botcher, and many, many others. Doubly troubled and standing at the back as though he were at any minute about to sprint away was Perry Searles. The man who'd just lost two grandchildren to Ray Botcher's swing set looked ghastly with despair.

Leaning against the wall beside the doors Hattie had been rolled through, Perry's entire body seemed to sag. The pouches previously under his eyes now sank over his cheeks. His slack mouth emitted unrestrained whimpers, then sobs, then great gusts of grief, and the congregants felt the tearing of Perry's heart in their own chests. More than a few people had to be held together by the others around them. When finally the opening chords of the departing song came, Perry stepped back to allow the coffin and the familial procession to exit, then Ed blinked and Perry was gone.

It wasn't until they left the chapel and collected themselves to Blundy and Ashurst's banquet room for the after-service luncheon that Ed saw Sylvia sitting beside one of the hall's many windows at an empty table, sipping coffee.

"Mind if we join you?" Ed asked politely, though Evie and Dorothy were already pulling out chairs for themselves.

"Please do. I ran like the devil to get it, so I think I've earned some company." She laughed, the glint in her eyes coming, going, coming, as Pandora peeked outward from inside.

The women settled while Ed fetched a tray with coffee and cookies. "Something to tide us over until lunch is ready," he said, distributing cups.

237

Opening a packet of sugar, Evie said, "It was a lovely service, wasn't it?"

"Hattie would have been proud." Dorothy sniffed.

A film of humanity hung like a wet towel over the sclera of Sylvia's eyes and—temporarily compassioned—she turned to Dorothy. "Living on the other side of the city, I didn't know her as well as you, but I know she would have loved it, dear."

"Did you see Perry?" Dorothy asked Ed.

He nodded. "I can't imagine what that family's going through. I'm surprised he came."

"He came for Dora's sake. She and Hattie used to knit together. She wanted to be here but she's with their daughter, planning the funerals. Oh, God, that poor family. Losing their children." Dorothy's breath caught, and her steady hands began shaking.

Evie dabbed the drips under Dorothy's cup and lowered her hands onto the other woman's wrist. At Evie's touch, the anguish Dorothy had been keeping inside suddenly burst and she buried her face in her hands and cried. Sylvia looked on, her face blank.

"The Lord only takes the good ones, but how hard it is when he does," Evie said. At this, the corner of Sylvia's mouth twitched.

They worked to console Dorothy as the banquet hall filled. With smeared makeup and raw noses, the congregants entered: first acquaintances, then friends, then family, attending in increasing rank of intimacy with the deceased. Unleashed children raced around tables, fought each other for food, and picked at their bodies without parents near to shame them. Soon, the room was bustling with activity, and when Mavis Cardinal finally excused herself from the gathering room where she sat with Hattie's children, most of the seats had already been taken. The brightness of the banquet hall was a refreshing relief to Mavis, and she took comfort in its liveliness as she poured herself a tea. Her sons and grandsons helping in the kitchen, Mavis wandered around the room until she spotted a seat beside her old friend Ed. Seeing her come, Ed raised a hand to Mavis and pulled out a seat to welcome her.

"Thanks, Eddie," Mavis smiled at him as he shuffled his chair aside to make room. She put her tea on the table, then purposefully stepped over to Dorothy and hugged her from behind. Dorothy squeaked with a fresh wave of sadness until Mavis put her head to Dorothy's. "Remember what Hattie said about this?"

Dorothy nodded. "No pity." Then tears of laughter sprang from her eyes and she said to the group, "She told us she wanted a party when she died. She made us promise we would drink and dance until our feet fell off." Against her will, she smiled. It was an easy promise to make when they were decades younger and Hattie was still alive, but the certainty that Hattie's wishes hadn't changed made her suddenly sit up straight.

Mavis squeezed Dorothy's shoulders and kissed her temple. "That's exactly what we're going to do. We're going to close this place down, then we're going to go somewhere else and dance a groove into the floor. I have Advil and runners in my bag for both of us. The boys will drive us anywhere we want to go." Considering the size of the bag Mavis had stuffed under the table, there was no doubt as to its contents and Dorothy chuckled, the brittle coating around her heart softening a little, resigning to the factions of loyalty.

"How are you doing?" Ed asked when Mavis finally sat beside him.

"Terrible, but I have to remind myself that we were lucky to have had Hattie as long as we did, when others aren't as fortunate," she confided. Her next words came out so quietly that the others leaned in to hear. "Let me tell you something, Eddie, those kids … that was no accident. Children don't go hanging themselves on swing sets, and a woman doesn't just swallow a hose. You hear what they got Jesse doing?" Ed shook his head, so Mavis explained. "They have him checking out people's *roofs* now. Birds, insects, *things* are crawling into people's roofs like the flood's coming again. Tabitha's grandson had spiders crawling all over him when he woke up. She said they were even in his *diaper*." Mavis shuddered. Three of the four others at the table recoiled as they imagined the baby boy, helpless against an arachnid mob.

"They like to come inside this time of year," Ed reasoned.

"One or two, maybe, but not *thousands* of them, Eddie. Jesse showed me a picture, and it made my hair whiter. They had to hire extra help for Jesse and the city had to get exterminators on contract. The boys have been at fifty homes already this week, and not a single one of them was normal." She fingered the dream catcher hung low on her chest and the look she gave Ed made him lose his taste for the coffee he was drinking.

He set down his cup as though it had gone bitter. Given his decades as a congregant and volunteer at Holy Redeemer, these were the times Ed was expected to rationalize God's will or offer some speck of wisdom to comfort the bereaved and the downtrodden. And if Bessie were alive, perhaps he could reconcile the heavenly plan with the instances of late, but as time without her withered on, Ed increasingly struggled to believe her old adage that God was all things good and all things right. He said to Mavis, "There have been quite a few hurricanes this season. Maybe the animals are affected. Farmers get pest invasions all the time." Dorothy and Evie nodded.

Mavis' small mouth puckered. "There's trouble, Eddie, trouble like we've never seen. The devil's come and I think he likes it here."

Evie seized the cross hanging from her necklace. Dorothy's hand went to her lips. Ed drew back from the table and looked away from their faces to the plate of cookies, though he found no answers there.

Dorothy said, "It *is* the devil. It *is*. It must be."

"What could you do about it if it was?" Pandora's voice came to them through Sylvia, key-minor syllables resounding from the high winds of hell.

Though they did not know why, the other women tensed as though they'd come upon a phantom in a dark alley, and the strangeness that came over them caused them to nibble at their cookies for a spot of sugar to brighten them. Ed, however, was suddenly stirred by apprehension and began sweating in his suit. With his palms slickened and his thin white hair sucked to his scalp by dampness, Ed had the peculiar feeling of being observed like mitochondria under a microscope. Sylvia, he saw, was looking at him, waiting for an answer. Casually she repeated, "What would you do if it was the devil, Ed? Run away or fight back?"

"Fight, of course." The answer had come at once.

Sylvia's nostrils flared. Then Ed felt it. The muscles around his pacemaker constricted. The ancient tissues of his heart palpitated. A glacial cold gripped his veins and drew blood away from his head to protect his heart. He felt faint. He—

241

"Mavis!" Coming from the kitchen with a tray of baked pasta, Wendy Cardinal called out. On hundreds of necks, heads swiveled to see her toss the dish onto the buffet table and hurry toward her perplexed mother-in-law. Some of the blood came back to Ed's head and the blackness that threatened to overtake him subsided enough for him to see Sylvia's pallor flicker from liver-gray to subtle peach, back and forth, back and forth, like a cadaver interchangeably being sucked of blood, then injected with it. "We need you in the kitchen," Wendy implored Mavis, her eyes flashing to Sylvia. "Come, Mom. We need your help. We need it *now*." The chatter of three hundred guests stopped. Remembrances halted on tongues, water glasses were held in wait, dripping noses were neglected, and even the play of children was slowed, slowed, because all sensed that something was happening.

In the new quiet, Mavis regarded her daughter-in-law with confusion. She looked past Wendy to the buffet table. "Are we out of food already?" Then, because of the seriousness on Wendy's face, Mavis rose from her chair and collected her purse.

Through the window to the back kitchen where Dak, Jesse, and Johnny were laden with platters ready to be brought out, Sarah's gasp made them look from the food they were trying to balance to Mavis, who was standing beside Sylvia Baker. "We just need you to come," they heard Wendy say, for Mavis was so weighted with bewilderment that her feet did not move.

"Why, Wendy, you're shaking," Mavis touched her daughter-in-law's cheek to steady her.

"Are you all right, dear? Maybe you should sit." Evie patted the lone unoccupied seat between herself and Sylvia, whose lips moved in soundless whisper, and whose black tongue only Wendy and Ed could see.

"I—" Wendy began and bent over in a sudden spasm of pain.

Platters were tossed, bowls were upended, and trays of food were abandoned to the floor as Dak and the boys ran. Wendy seized her stomach, threw her head forward and vomited on Ed's shoes. Sylvia winked at Ed and he, too, felt her terrible fingers touch the coil of his intestines. *No, no you don't*, he feebly pressed outward at her from inside, employing that part of himself that still talked to spirits. Her quivering, chanting mouth ruptured into a smile. *You don't like to play, Eddie?* She planted her words inside his head while Sylvia's body mechanically moved to help Wendy like all the others. *Play with me, Eddie.* Back and forth, back and forth, her color went, but the crowd was oblivious. *Play with me.*

What ... are ... you? Ed directed to the devil woman. In response, she tugged his bowels. Ed lurched forward in a gasp of pain. *Help me, Lord*, Ed pleaded, then Psalm 23 burst inside his head. *Though I walk through the valley of the shadow of death, I will fear no evil ...*

The devil-thing's laughter seeped inside him like lethal mold. *Using Him whenever it's convenient for you,* she cackled. *Think it will work?* She scratched his insides. Ed yelped and flared his silent prayer to God.

The next moment, Dak was beside Wendy and the boys were ushering Mavis away from the table. Sarah, who had come up behind them, said to the mob of mourners-turned-spectators, "There was a bad batch of chicken. She had a bite in the back with us before she came in." Men in suits and women in dresses gathered around the table to help and soon Sylvia was guided aside so the table could be cleaned.

Ed instantly felt better. Pointing at his vomit-covered shoes, he said to the onlookers, "I inherited my father's weak stomach. Always makes me sick to see other people sick." Wendy, being escorted away by Dak, gave Ed an apologetic grimace. To Dorothy and Evie, Ed said, "If you don't mind, ladies, I'd like to give my shoes a quick wash."

"Of course, Eddie," said Evie.

"You sure you're fine?" Dorothy touched his arm.

Chester pushed himself through the crowd. "Let me through!" he growled at a woman who'd been refusing to budge. She harumphed indignantly and bumped him with her rear before turning away. "I can't leave you alone for one moment, can I, Eddie?" Chester helped him to his feet, scowling at the other man's shoes. "What the hell happened to you?"

"A touch of food poisoning," Ed replied. "Not mine, however." Chester's nose wrinkled in disgust.

"He's got a weak stomach." Sylvia winked from the corner.

"Attention, everyone," Hattie's oldest son, Clifford, said. He tapped a microphone mounted on a podium beside a projector screen that was now unrolling from the ceiling. His bald head was patterned with the shadow of a window lattice, and he squinted as a bright spot of sun hit his eyes. Shuffling sideways, Clifford said, "As you've seen, we're having a slight issue with the food service, but as Mom would have wanted, we are going to carry on and celebrate her life. We've ordered from Mom's favorite pizza place, and it should be here within the hour, so please bear with us. In the meantime, please help yourself to desserts and drinks if you're hungry, and we'll begin a video we've put together that celebrates how special she was. Thank you." He turned the microphone off as his mother's favorite songs bloomed through the speakers and a close-up picture of her face as a younger woman appeared on the screen.

The murmur of conversation resumed while the presentation was paused to give the guests time to return to their seats. One of the ushers who had been at the service now wheeled out a mop bucket and set to cleaning up Wendy's mess. Two Blundy and Ashurst attendants swept everything from their table into the tablecloth, which one then bundled away while the other expediently washed and dried the table before spreading a new tablecloth on top. The entire operation had taken minutes, but to Ed felt like hours as the devil-woman glared at him from behind Dorothy and Evie.

He took Chester's arm and whispered, "Stay with them, Chess. They're having a really hard time, and you know how to cheer everyone up." He pulled away. Chester expanded with importance and strode to the women. Then Ed conducted himself to the men's washroom.

It wasn't until he was alone that Ed began to shake. He waited until one of Hattie's grandsons departed the restroom, then removed his shoes, using a wet paper towel to wipe them. In the oval mirror, the sight of his own face caused him to drop one of his shoes, and his hand went to his quivering mouth. He'd known the devil only once before, when Bessie was taken from him, but never had he seen his flesh, never had he felt him inside his head. *What just happened?* Ed wondered. Splashing water on his face, he looked past the glass into himself and questioned his sanity. It would be a reasonable assumption that dementia had come at last. But amid his paroxysm of pain, had he not seen Wendy regard Sylvia with the same terror he himself experienced? No matter how much he tried to convince himself otherwise, Ed was sure there was a moment when Wendy's eyes locked on his own that they exchanged the indelible awareness of evil. He sighed. Whether it was the devil's trick or old age, Ed knew he was in trouble.

245

A short time later, convinced of the likely deterioration of his mind, Ed emerged from the restroom to find Dak Cardinal leaning against a wall, waiting for him. The other man, normally a vision of health and optimism, looked worried. Apprehension was grooved into his forehead and his jaw was so tightly set the muscles near his ears spasmed beneath his skin. Dak said, "Just checking to see how you're doing, Eddie. I keep a spare set of work boots in my trunk, if you want them. They're not fancy or anything, but I think they'd do the trick."

Ed looked to his own feet as he stood sockless in the cold leather of his shoes. "You got a pair of socks in there? About now, I'd take anything you have. When you get to my age, anything but wool feels like cement."

"Sure do," Dak said. "It's not too cold outside, if you'll join me."

Ed tipped his head to peek inside the banquet hall, relieved to see that Chester was still with Evie and Dorothy, watching with the others the film that had begun playing on the screen. "I could use some fresh air," he said, and followed Dak down the carpeted hallway to the glass-encased foyer and out into the cool October afternoon. As pledged, Dak opened the back door of his truck and produced a pair of socks from a storage net behind the seat. He gave them to Ed, who accepted them appreciatively.

Dak closed his truck and began fidgeting with his keys. "I've known you how long, Ed? Forty years?"

"Unless you've aged in reverse, it's fifty-three," Ed corrected him. "Your mother used to sit for Bessie and me before you were even born, if you remember her telling you."

"That's right," Dak gave a little chuckle, and the silence between them stirred the recently settled parts of Ed's stomach.

"How is Wendy?" he asked.

INTERFERENCE

To the left, to the right, Dak glanced around the full parking lot to ensure they were alone. He lowered his head. "Except for her nerves, it's like nothing ever happened. Once we took her away from your table, she immediately felt better, Ed. No pain, no nausea, nothing. It's better for everyone else to believe the excuse we gave, but ..." he hesitated. "There's something strange going on, isn't there?"

"If you're asking if I think it was food poisoning, Dak, I do not believe anything of the sort," Ed said to facilitate Dak's revelation. "I'm an old man, Dakota, and the things old men say are not always believed. But let me tell you this, either dementia decided to throw a surprise party inside my head at the very moment your wife got sick, or I sat with the devil today. I'd be committed to an institution if anyone knew I said that, but more likely they'd just slip me some pills like they do to all my friends. I don't care. It's the truth. I know what I saw, and I know what I felt. That *woman* was inside my head."

"She was in Wendy's head, too," Dak told him.

"Why do I get the feeling this doesn't surprise you?"

The doors to the funeral home opened and a cluster of middle-aged couples filed out, already lighting their cigarettes. Dak took Ed into his truck where they would not be heard. Through the windshield, they watched the smokers fill their lungs with lethal relief. Neither man would meet the eyes of the other while a tide-surge of disclosure rushed from Dak's mouth.

Ed, who'd seen much in his years yet still considered the curiosities of the world a mystery, did not doubt Dak. Instead, he shifted his arthritic hips and turned to face him. "What do we do now?"

And while Dak told him, and while Hattie's life scrolled before two-hundred and ninety-seven guests, a single set of eyes watched Dak's truck.

247

27

Three kilometers downstream from Garrett's water treatment plant, Dan Fogel exited his cruiser and stepped onto the hiking trail that linked the city's adventurers to Sarnia in the west and London in the east. Not yet sunrise, the morning was crisp with cold. Hoarfrost clung to the trees, the grass, and the bottom of the depleted river, so that everything was glittering white except for the splashes of blood recently gushed by the city's third homicide victim of the year. In the dimness of the awakening day, Dan spotted Sarah, pen and notebook in hand, talking to a pair of sobbing witnesses. With his arms wrapped around the woman beside him, the man trembled as he looked from Sarah to the body he'd found, now covered beneath a yellow tarp. The woman mewled when Sarah prompted her to speak, so Sarah motioned to an EMT to check the woman for shock. Before long, both the man and the woman were sitting in the back of an ambulance, while a technician took their blood pressure.

As was his custom, Dan did not directly go to the body. He preferred instead to circle it, looking for clues, watching, seeking, feeling the area that would become his focus. Sarah waited for Dan to finish his routine while she oversaw the completion of the containment perimeter. By the time he'd

INTERFERENCE

made his way over, splinters of unfiltered light were slicing through the treeline, and Dan had to put his sunglasses on.

"You're not going to like this one, Dan," Sarah warned him as he knelt beside the body.

"I never do." Dan squatted and lifted the tarp to peek at the woman's face. He groaned. There, discarded beside a copse of leafless trees, a young nurse lay still, the black-purple bruises of strangulation evident around her neck. Dan knew this woman as one of the ICU nurses at the hospital, though he could not place her name. What bothered Dan, besides the senselessness of her death, was that not only had someone strangled the woman but stabbed her as well, as though the perpetrator wanted to be sure she was dead.

Dan had attended to more than his share of murder victims, so he was unfortunately familiar with the psychology behind the secondary abuse. It heavily suggested the act was intentional, and that the killer knew the victim. Random acts of violence did not often lend themselves to the kind of brutality inflicted by former lovers, neighbors, friends, or family. Sometimes the savagery suffered by victims of serial killers suggested kinship, but this was usually dismissed once a pattern was discovered.

"Do we have a name?" Dan asked.

"Tammy Elizabeth Cormoran, age twenty-eight. Reported missing by her roommate when she didn't return home from work last night." Sarah read through her notes, some from the witnesses, some from dispatch not fifteen minutes ago. As evident from the scrubs the victim wore, Sarah added, "She's a nurse at the hospital."

"Was a nurse," Dan corrected, gently setting the tarp back over the nurse's face. "Are you getting the feeling that we're in some kind of last survivor's game? I don't know

249

about you, but I'm sick of all this." He gestured to the entirety of the space around him.

"It's a shitty time for everyone, Dan," Sarah agreed. As close as she was to Dan, she preferred to keep a barrier between her work and personal life, so he did not know about her pregnancy or Flint or the arrival of hell to their beloved city. He suspected the latter, as every citizen did in some way or another, but still she did not feel comfortable bridging the conversation with him, for fear he would deem her insane. Looking at the pouches under his eyes, she said, "You get any sleep last night?"

"About an hour. Is that a nap or a blink? I don't know any more. I tell you, Sarah, when this is all over, I'm promoting you to acting chief, then I'm going to fly somewhere with no clocks and I'm going to sleep for a goddamn week. And if you call me, I'll fire you."

He dragged his hands over his face and rubbed color into his cheeks as she threw her pen at him. He picked it up and stood. The evidence technicians arrived, parting their way through the gathering crowd. Dan frowned, remembering his conversation with Father Bonner. There was no doubt the old priest was disturbed. The dreams he'd shared with Dan were not of this world, but from somewhere in the periphery of evil. It was obvious that Father Bonner expected Dan's skepticism, and he was visibly relieved to have Dan listen without doubt, without interruption. Why would Dan disbelieve if he couldn't explain it himself? In the church office, incredibly unsurprised at Father Bonner's confession, Dan had been possessed by a terrible kind of apprehension—and the little sleep he had managed since then was filled with nightmares.

INTERFERENCE

Against his professional judgement, Dan ordered a significant contingent to patrol the upcoming festival. There was no known threat, but still he couldn't push aside the terrible dread the priest stirred in him. With the incidents of late, the contingent could be justified as a necessary precaution, and Dan hoped it proved to be just that.

A tsunami of flashes, shouts, and hollers suddenly swelled around the perimeter. A mob of national and foreign reporters rushed for answers, screaming to be heard, with local Jessica Chung leading the pack. Ignoring their cries, Dan said to Sarah, "Let's interview the usual list first. Family. Friends. Colleagues. She got a boyfriend?"

"I'll check," Sarah said, noting Dan's orders.

Glancing once more at the yellow tarp, he cleared the tightness in his throat. Then, because Dan was not convinced the victim knew her murderer, he added, "Reach out to Jan Boyden and see if she can give us any clues to who this monster is." The head of Toronto's Homicide Unit, Jan Boyden had worked with Dan and his predecessor many times over the years, more for the larger city's sake than Garrett's own, and he knew that if there was a sniff of any similar crime anywhere in Ontario, Jan and her team would know of it.

"Dan! Dan!" Jessica Chung called. "Over here! Chief Fogel, here! Here!"

Against his will, Dan's eyes slipped eastward, where the thin reporter was stumbling and staggering in front of twenty others pushing from behind. The woman was braced against a crush of elbows and chests and the none-too-delicate prick of recording equipment. Had the perimeter been an actual wall, Dan figured Jessica would be crushed, but like a cockroach continue to live.

"Chief Fogel, *please!*" she shouted again.

251

"You want me to handle it?" Sarah asked.

Dan shook his head. "What's another headache? I got it."

He sighed and strode toward the throng now vibrating at his approach. As he got closer, the ravenous group surged against the police tape until it broke. Without the flimsy barrier, they fell inward over each other, pretending they had not seen such a device not moments before and so crept forward until three of Dan's constables sped to contain the area. The fracas lasted less than a minute, only until Dan raised his hand and warned them in a booming voice that there was plenty of room in Garrett's jail cells. So advised, they fell back grudgingly but remained elbow to elbow, watching, shouting.

"Chief Fogel! Is this a homicide?" one reporter yelled. "What can you tell us?"

"Should residents be concerned about a murderer on the loose?" the one beside him shouted, thrusting a microphone over the newly erected police tape.

"Our sources say it's a nurse. Can you confirm?" belted another.

The speed with which news travelled wasn't surprising to Dan, but the audacity of its messengers never failed to disappoint him. He ignored the questions and was about to return to his cruiser when he noticed that Jessica Chung had been jostled off to the side and was waving at him. Frowning, Dan realized she was not in the heels and form-fitting suit he was used to, but in jeans and sneakers. Her long hair up in a messy ponytail and without the dark stain of lipstick she normally wore, Jessica looked almost innocent as he walked past her. The effect was jarring. "Please, Dan!" she begged beside a cruiser that had been set up as a blockade.

"I don't have anything for you, Ms. Chung," Dan said. "You'll have to wait for the conference with all the others. If you don't get run over, that is."

His reminder made her flinch. "I'm not here for that. I wanted to thank you," she said, biting her lip. "I just need a minute."

Seeing one of their own stealing Dan's attention, the sea of reporters began drifting toward them, so Dan lifted the tape attached to the cruiser and invited Jessica in. Quickly, she ducked beneath his outstretched arm and stood beside him, fidgeting. "Don't make me regret this, Ms. Chung. They're apt to start rioting soon, so let's make this quick." Next to him, she looked small and as tired as he felt. "Something wrong?" he asked.

Jessica looked down at her feet. "No, I—" she hesitated as her peers closed in. "I'm not here for the story, Dan. I'm here because I've been trying to call your office since the news conference to thank you for saving my life, but they wouldn't put me through." She held up a hand when Dan started to speak. "I'm not knocking you; I know I deserved it. The pressure of my job is hell sometimes, but it's no excuse to behave the way I do. I know that. When that van was coming toward me, it's like I could only think about the story. I *had* to have it—and it almost killed me. That's what this job does to you. It makes a person not who they really are, but that's not who I want to be. It's not. You didn't just save my life, Dan, you *changed* it. I just came to tell you that."

Of all expectations Dan held, Jessica's declaration was not one. "You're not a reporter anymore?" was all he could think to say.

She shook her head. "I'm taking some time off. They gave me a leave of absence for a few months, so I promise I won't bother you for a while. And even when I go back—*if*

I go back—I promise I'll be different. I don't want to be that person anymore." Wind blew a loose strand of hair over her face and she tucked it back behind her ear. Then she did something that woke him more than the coffee he'd inhaled an hour earlier: Jessica Chung rose on her toes and hugged him. "Thank you," she whispered into his chest, then quickly stepped back.

Realizing his arms were stiff at his sides, Dan relaxed. "You're welcome Ms. Chung."

"Jessica," she said.

"Jessica," Dan repeated. "Well, you're welcome, Jessica. I'm glad it worked out for you."

"Who do you have to sleep with to get information around here?" a reporter behind the tape sniped, jealously eyeing Jessica.

Perhaps it was the godawful last few weeks or the lack of sleep or his increasing realization that he had no control over the happenings of the world, but Dan turned to the woman who'd been his adversary and asked her for coffee when she felt up to it.

"I figure a little bit of friendship is what this world needs right about now, don't you think?" he asked, looking away from her to the tarp-covered body not thirty feet off. Without hesitation, Jessica accepted Dan's offer and left him, bewildered as to the providence of life. Disappointed reporters called after him as he returned to Sarah, who had resumed her interview with the two witnesses.

"Excuse me for a moment?" Sarah politely asked them, and when they acquiesced, she stepped away to talk to Dan. "What did the bulldog want?

Dan smiled. "She wanted to apologize. And thank me for saving her life."

INTERFERENCE

"Saw God, did she?"

"I don't know about that, but I'm not going to dismiss someone who wants to change their ways." He tipped his chin toward the two witnesses huddled together near the ambulance. "They give you anything that can help us?"

"Doubtful," Sarah said. "They were the only ones around. They might not have even seen her if the wife didn't stop to tie her shoe when she did."

"Until we know what we're working with, let's keep an eye out. I know we're tight already, but we can't have folks worried if they're going to make it home or not." Dan pinched the bridge of his nose to quell the sudden caffeine crash in his system.

"We'll make it work," Sarah said.

They stood for a time, observing the activity near the nurse's body, doing their best to filter out the racket from the reporters, feeling the day's new wind sting their faces. Again, Dan returned to Father Bonner's dream. He said now, "If you don't feel comfortable answering, forget I said anything, but could you explain to me how dream catchers work? Is it literal or figurative?"

Sarah had never spoken to Dan about her spirituality, but neither did she shy from wearing the jewelry or endorsing the symbols of her culture. "A bit of both, actually," she told him, watching his gray-streaked hair flap in the wind. "Are you having bad dreams?"

"These last few weeks, I'm not sure I'm even awake, but I'm not asking for me. I have a friend who could use one; at least I don't think it could hurt, could it?"

She was heartened that he didn't dismiss the power of the protective charm she dearly valued, but something about the way he wouldn't meet her eye made her say, "There's

255

been a high demand for them lately. You're not the only one who's asked about it."

"Oh?"

"If I tell you, you're going to think I'm crazy."

"Nothing could make me do that, unless you started rooting for the Leafs."

Sarah's smile was uneasy. "No, nothing as bad as *that*. But we've had maybe a dozen people call asking us to make dream catchers for them this week. Roy Botcher, Jack Fischer's wife—I forget her name—Boyce Swinkley, Phil Beecher, a few doctors at the hospital; even the mayor, but don't say anything about it." Dan made a zipping motion at his lips, then Sarah continued. "I don't know what's happening, Dan, but it's like they're all having the same dream, or parts of it. It's not normal, you know?"

"Any ideas on what's causing it? Off the record. No judgement, I promise."

"My culture challenges us to seek connections in our relationships, not just with others but with—especially with—the earth. We honor Mother Nature, and so we are always learning from her. If something is wrong, Mother Nature lets us know. The river. The animals. The weather. Even that patient and the bus crash. I think it's all her way of warning us. I don't know if your friend's dream is the same as the others, but I think there's evil here, Dan. I couldn't write it up in a report, and you wouldn't want me to record all the things I've seen and heard lately." She held up her palms when he cocked his head, "Not that I'm keeping anything from you, Dan. I'm not. But I'm not sure you'd want me writing about the devil, that's all I'm saying."

"You think it's the devil?" he asked.

"I know it is," Sarah said.

256

28

With three days to go before the opening of the Fall Festival, the communal kitchen at Southbridge was full of residents. The sun was still tucked beneath the hills when the ovens went on, so that a few hours later, when Ed finally woke from a fitful sleep, the dining room was bordering on hot and smelling of bread and cookies and several kinds of tarts.

Dorothy hurried a cup of coffee and a donut to Ed's table, and there he sat, still waking, watching as dough was rolled, pies were filled, sauces were stirred, jams were canned, and buns were stuffed. Around him, the typewriter clicks of knitting needles sounded as women finished their projects, and a faint smell of glue passed Ed's nose as decorative artwork was completed. Though the day opened with prayer on her behalf, not even the murder of a young nurse could quell the residents' excitement. Until yesterday, the fate of the festival had been uncertain, with several community members speaking out against the appropriateness of celebration given the recent atrocities. In rebuttal, Southbridge joined nursing homes and schools across the city in entreating the mayor to support the fair's continuation, not only for the mental well-being of the city's beleaguered residents, but as a testament to the city's endurance. It was only after Dak Cardinal, stepping in for Perry Searles, pledged to lengthen the time

S. L. Luck

allotment for the mayor's opening speech, that the event was finally confirmed.

Ed sat still among the explosion of activity and searched for the devil-woman. No longer would he call her Sylvia, at least to himself, and it was with great relief that he found her absent from the kitchen and wouldn't have to speak her name. He sipped his coffee, trying to rid himself of the after-taste of evil. Overnight the nasty thing had come into his head. *Ehhh-ddie*, she whispered inside him as he lay alone in his bed. *Eddie, Eddie, Eddie, come see me, Eddie. Won't you come see me?* That she could speak inside him brought such a sudden convulsion of terror that Ed had wet himself. *Little boy has wet his pants, has he? Oh, ho, ho, ho, better change, Eddie. I can smell it already.* He jumped out of bed and shut his door. *Knock-knock, Eddie.* Her voice surged inside him, and for the rest of the night, each time he began to relinquish himself to sleep, the devil-woman knocked. He could only assume she'd busied herself with invading someone else when at last she allowed him to sleep. That had been three hours ago.

Feeling the buzz of caffeine, Ed picked at his donut. Before long, Chester rushed in and Ed felt the outside cold breezing off his jacket. He slapped Ed's table and sat down; the wisp of hair covering the top of his head fluttered then settled. "We're going to win it this year, Eddie! Four times in a row. Simpkin can kiss my rosy-red ass if he thinks he's getting that ribbon. I can't wait to see the look on his face when he sees our float. I've got a fifty on it. Easiest bet I've ever made." The thrum of excitement pulsed through the man's entire body so that, sitting across from Ed, Chester bobbed forward and back, forward and back, twitching his knees in a squeaky, restless jig. "What's the matter, Eddie? Ticker okay?" He patted his own chest.

258

INTERFERENCE

"Bad sleep."

"Wait until you start shitting yourself every time you fart; we're not too far off from that, you know." Chester's lips pursed and he looked away from Ed to the pies being pulled from the oven.

The disgusting bodily function that awaited them was the least of Ed's concerns, for he wasn't entirely sure he'd live long enough to experience further penalties of old age. He said, "You hear about the nurse near the river?"

Chester nodded. "Orest's granddaughter. Terrible."

"He's at Akerdale, no?"

"For a few years now."

Ed pushed his donut aside. "I'm starting to think there's not a safe place in this city. In here, out there, people dying everywhere."

"It's not safe anywhere," Chester agreed. "Never has been, Eddie. It pays to be oblivious sometimes, doesn't it? It's so much easier that way." He pulled Ed's donut toward him and took a bite.

You look like hell, Eddie, a voice soundlessly sprouted. With his cup halfway to his lips, Ed froze. There, coming into the kitchen with Evie on her arm, was the devil-woman. She didn't look at him, but she didn't have to. Ed felt her crawl inside his skull. *Cat got your tongue, bed-wetter? Talk to me Eddie. Talk to me.* Summoning the ancient, disciplined part of himself that restrained his mind, Ed pushed her away. As if nothing were happening, bakers continued baking, sewers continued sewing, crafters continued crafting. Tying on an apron, Sylvia chatted amicably with the other residents while the devil inside her barged into Ed's mind. *Oh, I wouldn't do that, Eddie. Want to see what happens when you don't play nice?*

259

Chester howled. Ed's eyes swept from Sylvia to Chester, who had dropped Ed's donut and was now holding his temples. "Christ Almighty! It feels like I just got stabbed in the head." Evie dusted the flour from her hands and hurried to their table. "You okay, hun?"

Eddie.

Chester groaned, rubbing the sides of his face with two fingers. "Must be a muscle spasm or something—"

Eddie.

"Want some Tylenol, Chester?" Albert Humphrey asked.

Eddie.

"I think it's passing, Alb—"

EDDIE!

In an eruption of agony, Chester's arms shot out. Ed's mug flew across the room and smashed into Flora Quimby. A surprised squeal came from the old woman's bright-pink lips and she dropped her knitting while two of her tablemates began dabbing at the coffee stain down her floral-patterned back. Bakers and crafters and handymen and handywomen converged around Chester. Again he cried as the others tried to ease his pain, unaware that nothing could help him.

ENOUGH! Ed's command ricocheted around his interior until it hit the devil-woman.

That tickles, Eddie, wafted her response.

Behind him, Evie was rubbing the base of Chester's skull. "This works wonders for me whenever I get a headache," Evie explained, digging her knuckles deep into Chester's loose skin while the others looked on. "How does it feel?"

"I think it's working," Chester moaned. "Keep doing that. Oh, God, please keep doing that. My head is starting to feel better." Evie did, and soon the crowd dispersed back

INTERFERENCE

to their stations, reminded that the golden years sometimes proffered more dirt than anything else.

What do you want? Ed asked the thing inside his brain.

Call me Pandora, Eddie, she purred.

Ed flinched.

"You getting a headache too, dearie?" Evie asked, easing up on Chester's neck.

"Just stretching, no need to worry about me," Ed said.

Liar. Pandora flicked him.

Stifling the sting she inflicted behind his eyes, Ed rose. "I don't know about you, but I could use another coffee. Evie? Chess?"

Get me one too, Eddie.

What do you want? Ed again inquired as he collected a tray from a rack at the end of the counter. He took three mugs and a small carafe and brought it back to his table. Pandora tapped his ear drums, rubbed his nasal cavity, felt his cerebellum.

"You're supposed to get it in the cup, Ed," Chester said.

Ed stopped pouring and let Evie take the carafe from his unsteady hand.

"I think you boys have had too much excitement this morning." Evie filled their cups. "Once this festival is over and things get back to normal around here, both of you should think about a nice little trip to Florida; spend the winter where the weather won't make you crazy. Worked like a charm for me last year. You boys want some pie?"

"Wish I could," Chester said. "I got to get back to the grounds. Float's done, but with Perry away, we've got a shit ton of extra work to take care of. Sorry for the language, Evie."

261

"I raised five boys; cursing is their second language," she waved his apology away.

"Sylvia!" Chester waved across the room at the sandy-haired woman who was removing cookies from a cooling rack, using tongs to put them into cellophane bags. "Going to start decorating this afternoon. Pick you up after lunch?"

"I'll be ready." She nodded and began closing the bags of cookies with red ribbon.

Evie put a hand on Ed's wrist. "Why don't you come with us? Even if it's just so that you're not sitting in your room. The days after *anyone's* funeral, it's not good to be alone. I remember my father telling me that when my mother died forty years ago. You have to keep people around you if you want to heal." *Like a scab on a wound*, Ed thought, but said nothing. "Dorothy's napping, but she's coming, too. You can watch us do the front entrance."

Join us, Eddie.

Fear for his friends overrode his concern for himself. If he stayed home, Ed worried that he wouldn't be able to help them, should the need arise, so he picked up his cup. "No coffee for me, then. I'll need a nap if I'm going to make it through the day." He rose and carried his cup to the dish bin over the garbage station, then made for the hallway.

You murder that girl? Ed inwardly intoned as he passed Sylvia without looking at her.

Instead of answering, she conveyed the images of her kills with Harold through the projector of Ed's mind. *You should try it sometime, Eddie. Cleans the pipes.*

Ed's stomach turned sour. Hurrying toward his room, he hoped that Pandora's reach would peter out like a faraway radio signal, but still he could feel her probing him like a tongue. *What do you want?* he asked once more.

262

I have a job for you.

Not interested. Ed passed the nursing desk and waved to the two attendants on duty.

I didn't ask if you were interested, Eddie.

He turned the handle to his room, entered, and quickly locked the door behind him. "Go to hell," he said aloud, spinning his sharp old eyes around to ensure he was alone.

Already there, and you will be too if you don't listen to me. I have some birds that need caging, Pandora cooed. *One Cardinal, two Cardinals, three Cardinals, four … better make it five and six or you're out the door. Baby makes seven that's not going to heaven.* From beneath his bed and inside his closet and behind his bathroom door and in his head, her evil throat rang high with laughter, resounding off the walls like an eerie symphony. Ed's bladder loosened. He hurried to the toilet, sure that the devil-woman was lurking behind the shower curtain, but she was not there.

Unsteady on his feet, he clutched the safety railing on the vanity, then sat to urinate. "Help me, Lord," he whispered to the ceiling.

Pandora shrieked. The mirror shattered. Ed clamped his eyes shut as glass exploded on him, buffeting the exposed parts of his skin. He felt hot blood flow from a rupture above his eye. *Leave Him out of this, Eddie. You can beg for forgiveness after you take care of the Cardinals. There's a—*

NO! he refused, shucking his glass-covered clothes, then collected his robe from the door hook, all the while fighting the lunacy inside his head.

There was a banging at his door. "Mr. Norman? Are you okay, Mr. Norman?" came Georgia's voice from the hallway.

The tiles in the bathroom began rattling. *Cage my birds Eddie—*

263

NO! Ed raged inside himself.

"Mr. Norman? Open the door Mr. Norman!"

The ceiling panels started to vibrate. One of the boards crept open, then two, three, five, seven, until the black skeleton of the roof was disinterred, and Ed was staring up at the corpse of death itself, with no beginning and no end, but everything, everything, contained in a wet and masticating mouth. *CAGE MY BIRDS!* Pandora roared through the ceiling's rotting teeth.

Ed screamed.

"Mr. Norman! I'm coming in!" Keys rattled in the door.

"Dear Lord, I beg you to destroy my enemy..." Ed prayed to the Father of his past.

The mouth's black tongue snaked toward him. *Cage my birds!*

"Dear Holy Lord, NO!" Ed shouted into the maw of evil.

The door to Ed's room banged open. At once, before Georgia's small face cleared the barrier of the wood, the demon dissipated upward, the ceiling panels shifted back into place, and the tiles stopped rumbling.

"Mr. Norman!" the glasses hanging from a string around Georgia's neck swung wildly as she rushed to the bathroom door where Ed stood, trembling and bleeding. "My goodness! What happened?" She cast a confused glance at Ed's mirror, which lay shattered over the floor. Georgia led him to his bed, where she tended to the cut above his eye.

He said, "I must have closed the door a little too hard. By the time I got to the toilet, the mirror was coming down." He glanced behind the nurse to the bathroom, where nothing but the broken glass was amiss.

264

"I told those boys we needed a maintenance check in here, but they never listen to me." She shook her head. "You know what this means, Eddie? It means those lazy butts owe you one. You want Sonja's old room? They're almost done the renos in there. They gave it a good update so it's not so … like a hospital, I guess. TV's built right into the wall, and it's got a bigger kitchenette than the one you have. Loads of light. White and shiny cabinets. The waiting list is full, but with what they've done to you, I'm sure it's yours if you want it. You want me to tell them?"

Though he was sure Pandora would find him anywhere he went, the idea of extra space between himself and the body she inhabited sounded good to Ed. "I don't want to upset anyone," he said meekly to his favorite nurse, knowing she would insist.

"Nonsense, Eddie. You deserve it. Plus, if anyone gets their knickers in a knot, I'll just tell them I had the final say. Let them deal with *me*." She snorted and pulled back from his face. "Well, now, it's not as bad as it looks. Thank God for small miracles, huh, Eddie? Let me get you a Band-Aid, okay?" She patted his leg and glided out of the room.

Alone, Ed expected the devil-woman to come terrorize him again, but he was relieved to find her absent. He waited for Georgia while the activities of the hallway rustled past his room. Residents were retiring to their beds for their after-breakfast naps or returning to the kitchen and common areas to continue their festival preparations. In the frame of his door, a tall, blond man carrying a bouquet of flowers appeared. The man stopped and turned to Ed. His beguiling face summoned no recognition on Ed's part, but still Ed tipped his chin in a gesture of greeting.

"One more over," Ed heard Georgia say from the hall-way. Then she was beside the man, ushering him over to Sylvia's room.

The man waved a bandaged hand to Ed, then he was gone. Waiting for Georgia, Ed was again troubled but not entirely sure why. He picked the last flecks of glass from his arms, thinking, considering, deconstructing the last few days until Georgia scurried in, bursting with gossip. She drew a Band-Aid and tube of ointment from her pocket and sat beside him on the bed.

"You'd think everyone in this building's on Flibbies they way they act around that man."

"Flibbies?" Ed asked, wincing as Georgia cleaned the cut above his eye.

"Sorry, Eddie. Of course you wouldn't know. Fliban-serin, it's like female Viagra. Get's you all hot and bothered, if you know what I mean. I'm not on 'em, but I know a few women who are, and they act just like the ones cooing over Mrs. Baker's son. Practically foaming at the mouth like they've never seen a man. And at *their* ages," she said, click-ing her tongue against her teeth, then applied ointment to the bandage and stuck it above Ed's eyebrow.

"She's got a son, then?" Ed asked.

"A hot one, apparently. Not for my liking, though. I like a man with meat on his bones. My first husband was too skinny. Shouldn'a married him. It wasn't until I met Martel that I got what I needed. Skinny boys want you to be skinny like they are, but you never will be, you know what I'm say-ing?" Ed didn't know, but he nodded anyway. Georgia stood. "We'll get the glass cleaned up right away; don't try to clean it yourself, hear me?" She wagged a finger at him and pulled a broom from the closet, sweeping the glass into a pile just outside the bathroom door so he wouldn't step on it in case he needed to use the washroom again. "Tell me something, Eddie," Georgia said as she reached the door to the hallway. "Before I opened the door … it sounded like you were talking to someone in here. Am I hearing things, or did that actually happen? If you don't tell me the truth, I'm going to watch you like a hawk to make sure you're not going to go Frederic on me."

The reference to a former resident who had developed late-onset schizophrenia and begun conversing with his own feces drew a laugh from Ed. "While the conversation *may* be more scintillating than what a man usually gets around here, I haven't gained any more friends, fortunately. I was praying the building wasn't going to come down on me; maybe a little too loudly, though. I'm fine, Georgia. Promise."

"You can never pray too loud, Eddie," Georgia said warmly. "Someone will be up here soon to take care of the bathroom, but I'll let you rest. If you need anything, just give me a holler." She closed the door.

Briefly, he thought of taking an Ambien, but besides the fact it would make him drowsy for most of the day and he needed his wits about him at the fairgrounds, he figured Pandora wouldn't let him sleep anyway. Had he been younger, Ed supposed he would have been afraid to sleep with the devil circling him, but with Bessie gone and little to keep him on the top side of the earth, he did not fear for his life. The opposite, in fact; he very much welcomed death—just not at the hands of the devil-woman. Bessie would have wanted him to fight, of course, and for *her* he would.

Exhaustion crashing in on him, Ed pulled his blanket from its tight tuck under the mattress and drew his legs onto the bed. He closed his eyes, waiting to be invaded. The trick of his situation was that even if she wasn't around, Ed expected her to be—and so panic thrummed under his skin and made it impossible for him to relax. He turned onto his stomach, his side, his back, trying to will himself to sleep even if only for a few minutes, then sat up. *The devil has a son*, he reminded himself, wondering if the man knew what was inside his mother.

29

Ten feet away from where Ed Norman jittered on his bed, Troy entered his mother's room. He had expected it to smell of piss, but instead it reeked of the rotting-rose smell of her overpowering perfume. Breathing from his mouth, he figured he preferred the piss to anything that smelled of the woman who'd birthed him. It reminded him of his childhood, when she would come at him like a gnat, trying to love him, trying to suffuse him with empathy and compassion and bear warmth where it could not exist.

Satiated after his recent kill beside the river, Troy knew that optics required him to play the part of a good person, so here he was: if not a model citizen, a model son. The nursing staff shouldn't have allowed him in her room, but Troy was born with a convincing face, and when she saw the flowers in his bandaged hands, the older female nurse practically threw herself over the counter to help him, leaning on him to direct him to his mother's room. The pressure of the nurse's breast against his arm left a sweat mark on his jacket, but it was a small price to pay for unfettered access to his mother's new life. Hell, he could even drop the flowers and leave. The only thing that mattered was proof of his normality.

He'd gone far down the hall by the time his Dark Friend told him to stop, then cranked his head to the bleeding old man sitting on a bed. *Kill him, Troy. Kill him!* his Dark Friend immediately instructed, and Troy felt the rare twang of repugnance emanating from his companion. What was it about this small man that his Dark Friend did not like? Of course, his Dark Friend liked nothing, loved no one; it was not in his nature, but his Dark Friend's prudence as of late waned more often than Troy was comfortable. *Haven't you had enough?* he sniped to his Dark Friend as the old man stared back at him. His insurrection was repaid with a tug at his stitches, and he grimaced before being pushed along by a not-so-gentle nurse who didn't care what he looked like.

"Your mother's on her way. We called her down from the kitchen. She'll just be a moment. Why don't you get those flowers in a vase while you wait?" The small nurse gave him an unimpressed once-over as she nudged his mother's open door with her hip. "Top cupboard to the left of the sink, but if it's not there, just ask for one at the nursing desk." Without waiting for Troy's response, she swiveled on her heels and left him.

Get her too, his Dark Friend said snidely, and Troy couldn't help but smile to himself. He stepped inside his mother's new home, noticing that he did not exist in her space. The pictures and figurines he'd earlier brought to the admissions administrator, more for his benefit than his mother's, were dumped among chintzy yellowed doilies, books of gardening-themed crossword puzzles, and bottles of prescription medication. Nowhere were pictures of Troy as a child or as a teenager or as an adult, and that suited him just fine. No reason to pretend unless there was a good reason to. He found a vase where the snotty nurse said it would be and began filling it with water when his Dark Friend suddenly shrivelled inside him like a worm under a magnifying glass. Troy turned.

INTERFERENCE

"You've got the wrong room," his mother said. The parts of Sylvia that still remained human regarded her offspring with a mixture of affection and indignation, though with the memory of him discarding her in the parking lot not two weeks earlier, the latter sentiment mostly overrode the first.

"Am I that bad, Mother?" Troy frowned and turned off the tap. He put the flowers on the counter.

"You're not that *good*, Troy," Sylvia said, and Troy noticed that while her speech had improved, her attitude had deteriorated.

"You seem better. Was I so wrong to want that for you?"

"You're going back to Toronto then?"

Troy threw his hands up. "Can't a son visit his mother without a lecture?" Then, because she had shrunk away from him, he said, "No, Mother, I'm not going back yet. I'm taking care of the house like I told you, and I've got some work that might keep me here a while longer."

"Oh?" Sylvia drew two cups from the cupboard and set the kettle to boil, then she shuffled to the recliner. Looking at her son, she was overcome with the uncomfortable feeling that her life had been misspent.

Meanwhile, Pandora released Sylvia and went to investigate whatever was inside her son. He'd always been an asshole, and so Pandora felt an invisible kinship with him—but now that she had killed Hattie and the two Searles children and taken a nice little bite out of the Cardinal boy, her injuries were beginning to heal and her perception again broadened. She was stronger; not quite her old self, but neither the emaciated, withered remnant she had been when Anabelle first scourged her power. That day in his mother's kitchen when she was blocked from inspecting Troy,

271

Pandora reasoned it was her deprivation that made her incapable of doing so. Now she saw her inability for what it was: another like herself. Her hackles rose high, expanding outward until the room was full of her might and the *other* inside Troy sizzled and retracted in on itself. The clamping of his insides caused Troy to squirm.

"You've never had a case here before. Has something changed?" Sylvia asked. If he were a different son, she might have hoped for a more permanent return, but since her admission she had been unable to ignore the neglect many of her neighbors suffered from their families. It made her unwilling to force a relationship that just wasn't there.

Ignoring the pain in his side, Troy opened the cupboards until he found the strawberry tea his mother liked. He dropped a bag into each of the cups she'd taken out. "I've been retained by a local family," he said vaguely.

"Which family?"

"Can't say, Mother."

"I hear you've been spending time at the hospital."

"Don't push, Mother."

Her son's ventures around the city were almost impossible to conceal. Even in Southbridge, where women were far past their prime, exploits of the handsome lawyer found their way to Sylvia's ears, no matter how she tried to avoid them.

"It's the *electric* girl, isn't it?" she asked.

Pandora turned to their conversation.

"Is that what they're calling her?" The kettle whistled and Troy went to grasp the handle, but the pressure pained his hand.

Sylvia rose and took the kettle from him, frowning at the gauze wrapped around his palms. She poured water into their cups, leaving Troy's on the counter, and carried hers back to the recliner where she extended her legs. After a time, she inquired about his hands.

Dark Friend, limping inside him, urged Troy to leave, get away, rush anywhere else, but he took his cup and drank the hot liquid to soothe his cramps. "You always told me not to walk around the house in the dark. I supposed this is what I get for not listening to you. I tripped over that rug at the bottom of the stairs, and that picture of Lucy on the grass broke my fall." His hands spread wide to pre-empt her worry. "The picture's fine, just the glass is broken, but I've already got it in a frame shop so you should have it back in a week. Want me to bring it here?"

"I'm not staying, if that's what you want to know."

"I'll put it where it was, then."

Like a foreign wind, a thought drifted through Sylvia's mind and her blank eyes swept to the window. The late morning was still bleak and gray. "It's boring in here. You're so far away you didn't know how busy I was before my stroke, but I was, Troy, I really was. I was learning to dance. Did you know that? There's a ballroom group for seniors. I only went to a few classes, but it was fun. Oh, how we laughed." She drummed her fingers on the side of her cup, her vacant face elsewhere. "I took up painting, too. They encourage us to do that here, but it's not the same, maybe because the people don't change or that they do, I can't figure it out, but it's ... I guess depressing is the right word."

"It'll get better," Troy said.

"Will it, though? I wonder. I think if I had something to occupy my time, something that I loved, maybe, or even just something ... I don't know ... *interesting* to do or think about, I could come to like it here."

Pain lanced his ribs, and Troy squeezed his abdomen to try and push it out; but his mother had just given him an opening, so he pressed on. "What are you suggesting?" he groaned.

"You'll think I'm crazy."

Troy had little time for her game, but like a good son who hadn't just strangled and stabbed a nurse on the riverfront, he said, "No I won't. Tell me what would make it better. We are on the same side, Mother. If you need anything from me, just ask it."

Sylvia twisted a button on her sweater. "Well, if I got the chance to meet the electric girl, I'd be the talk of the town around here." She didn't look at him as she spoke. Instead, she held her mug and twirled her button, a little more, a little more, until the fabric around it began bustling into a tight swirl. "Gossip is the first hobby of everyone around here and if I had something to talk about, I might consider staying. It's a silly thought, I know." Pandora maneuvered whimsy and hope into Sylvia's face, resting her tongue while they waited for Troy's incredulity to pass.

Dark Friend's feeble attempts to reach Troy did not succeed. Troy said, "You've never asked to meet a client before."

"You've never put me in a home until now."

"This, again?" Troy looked at the ceiling. He would do anything to escape his mother's clutch on him, but given the current status of her health, his full emancipation required her to be attended to by anyone but himself. He did not want nor need to be dragged back to Garrett every time she fell or suffered a seizure or—God willing—a fatal episode of some sort. Until the latter happened, permanent placement was his only hope of severing their miserable tether to each other. Professional inappropriateness aside, however, he didn't see an organic avenue where he could propose such an introduction, should he feel the need to extend his mother the courtesy. He said, "I can't introduce you to my client, Mother. There are rules against that sort of thing. The family needs their privacy."

Sylvia shrugged as though she didn't really care about meeting Anabelle Cheever. "Of course you can't. It's silly of me to ask. It's just that it gets lonely in here. It would be nice to have something to chat about besides our aches and pains. That's all they do here, Troy. And once the festival is over, there won't be *anything* to talk about. Ah, well. Once I'm out of here, I won't have to worry about being bored anymore, I suppose." A glint passed over her pupils.

Troy went to the window and turned the wand to let in more light. "It seems like your rehab is going well."

"And I have you to thank for that," Sylvia said. It was the most honest thing she'd said.

The sudden urge to vomit overwhelmed Troy and he excused himself to use her washroom. Glassy-eyed, Sylvia flicked her hand to indicate he was welcome to get sick wherever he wanted; it didn't matter, it didn't matter, nothing mattered but the girl. She didn't hear Troy's indrawn breath as he rushed past her or the bang of his knee against the door when the handle turned too slowly. Then he was in, whamming his back against the door, panting, sweating; his stomach, now lungs, now heart, now head, all reeling, spinning, shriveling from their casings, going inward like liquid down a drain. He lurched over the toilet and retched, expecting something, anything to come out, but his heaves were as empty as his heart.

Get ... out ... Troy, Dark Friend pleaded. His insides constricted, and Troy thought for a moment that his Dark

Friend would spill from his mouth into the toilet and that he would finally get to see the thing that was inside him—but the water was unchanged.

On the rare occasions he got sick, it wasn't medication that soothed him, it wasn't rest or tender care that healed whatever broke him down. It was the memory of his hunts. They recharged him; the extinction of another filling him with energy, vitality, strength. Sitting back on his knees, wiping the sweat from the back of his neck, Troy turned to the memory of the nurse. His Dark Friend inched toward the memory like flowers toward the sun, and together they remembered Troy's fortune in the nurse coming along when she had. He thought that perhaps *she* had been following him, for when he left the hospital after meeting Anabelle and drove to the river to release his tension, Tammy had appeared not ten minutes later.

It wasn't until he read the news reports that he realized he'd come upon the route that she'd taken home for years. Even in the middle of the night, Tammy felt safe enough that she carried no pepper spray, no personal alarm, no weapon to protect herself. He'd seen her coming toward him as he stood looking out over the water, and he pretended to have trouble lighting a cigarette with his mangled hands. Their earlier introduction had kindled what she assumed was a kinship with him, as many people naively would. When she saw him struggling, she rushed to help.

She was so taken with him he could practically smell her pheromones. It wasn't until his hands were around her surprised neck and pain shot through his palms that Troy realized the previous delirium that had anesthetized him had worn off. One, two, five stitches in his dominant right hand ripped open but still he squeezed, crushed, mangled. There was no blood, of course, just saliva and snot and tears ejected in the ninety seconds it took for the nurse to stop struggling. When he laid her down, looking left, right, all around him, Troy took his pocketknife and put it to her skin.

Dark Friend squirmed, livelier now with the sip Troy gave him. Rasping, his Dark Friend tried forcing Troy to his feet. *Leave before she gets us. Before she gets ME...*

"I don't understand," Troy said aloud, leaning over the sink.

He turned on the tap and splashed his face until his cheeks stung. An image came to Troy then, but it was faded, like an underdeveloped photo. He toweled his face and focused on his friend's blurred subliminal message. It looked vaguely human. Troy tried blocking out the noise of his own heart, his own breath, any outside noise so he could understand what was being told to him, but the more he concentrated, the more the image seemed to shift and escape his comprehension.

"Are you okay in there?" his mother called from the other side of the door.

"I'll be out in a minute," Troy grunted back. When he eventually extracted himself from the security of the bathroom, his Dark Friend hissed at the reunion with his mother.

In her faraway voice, Sylvia said, "I heard a girl got murdered yesterday."

"I heard about it on the radio this morning. Poor woman."

"Yes. Poor woman," Sylvia robotically agreed. "They say she was one of the electric girl's nurses. Did you know her?"

Visions of the nurse's terror leapt to Troy's mind: her frightened eyes, her bulging veins, her open mouth gaping like a fish out of water. "I'd have to check my files. The name doesn't ring a bell."

277

"*Did* they release her name?" his mother asked, latching onto a detail Troy couldn't confirm.

If they hadn't released the nurse's name yet, Troy realized he'd just incriminated himself. Gooseflesh spread over the entirety of his skin. "I thought they did, but maybe not. I had a terrible sleep last night." He held up his hands to her to illustrate the point, but her blank eyes were fixated on the wall behind him.

Sylvia's mouth opened and her lips moved on Pandora's volition. "Hmm. It's not good news, but it's something to talk about, I suppose. It's something interesting, though, isn't it? My son might have known the murdered nurse. People around here would find that exciting. *Very* exciting." Her lips curled into a smile unbecoming to the harmless woman he'd previously known her to be.

"You can't talk about that, Mother. It's not appropriate," Troy said.

"Since when did you ever care about being appropriate? At least with me, you haven't been." Then his mother's distant eyes pounced on him. "Everyone will want to hear about it. I'll be the talk of the town around here. There's a woman here who likes to gossip more than your Aunt Vida, even, and you know what her son does? He's a police officer. I'll bet *he'd* want to know that you knew the murdered nurse. They say that no detail is too small. At least that's what they say on those murder mystery shows."

"I didn't say I knew her, Mother—"

"And you're a lawyer yet, so maybe you can help them, huh?"

"Mother—"

INTERFERENCE

Sylvia's hands clasped together as Pandora sang with her lungs. "My son knew the murdered nurse. My son knew the murdered nurse. My son knew—"

"Did you miss your medication today?" Troy glanced at the door to ensure it was still closed.

At once, her damning song became a chant, became a call, became a yell. Spittle flew from her raving mouth, and Troy rushed to quieten her with his hands. She bit him. Again, her teeth dug into the gauze, scraping what stitches hadn't already ripped open, sending a fresh wave of pain into his tender hand. His own goddamned mother had bitten him! Only because they weren't at home, he resisted urge to cover her nose, too, and press, press, press.

Her muffled cries broke from the edges of his palm. "*Ma! Saa! Nuuu!*" Gibberish. Gibberish. "*Ma! Saa! Nuuu!*"

Troy leaned over and spoke to her ear. "You have your way, Mother. I'll do what I can to get you that meeting."

Like nothing had happened, Sylvia instantly relaxed. Gone was the maniacal glimmer in her eyes and the ambush in her throat, so Troy removed his hand from her mouth.

"Shut the blinds for me, will you please? I'd like a nap now," she said sweetly.

Already working on a plan to make the introduction to Anabelle Cheever, Troy left his mother in darkness.

279

30

Anabelle did it. After countless attempts, after overloading the batteries she was attached to, after nearly shocking her own heart and singeing the hair on the nape of her neck, she finally managed to rein in her current. She knew not only because the hum that accompanied the flow of her energy toward the floor had vanished, but also because she felt a fullness she'd not yet experienced since awakening; something akin to the satiation of a fed craving.

Now, days since she'd woken, and after examinations by a team of doctors and electrical engineers from across the country, Anabelle again stunned her caregivers, who were reluctant to detach the wires.

"You just want to keep me to lower your power bills," she told Doctor Huxley, who studied her from the corner of the room.

"We might keep you forever if we could actually figure out how to do that."

"Funny, Doctor."

"All joking aside," Huxley said, "I can't explain your recovery. As I told your parents, you check almost every box you need for discharge. Every diagnostic test we've done on you came out squeaky clean, but we haven't got you walking yet."

"It's hard to walk when you're chained up like this," Anabelle slid a leg out from under the blankets to show a makeshift manacle on her slender foot.

The doctor's eyes, still amazed by the feat, widened appreciatively at the genius contraption. "If I hadn't just operated on your brain and you hadn't just charged all the batteries from our wrecking yards, I'd give you a clean bill of health and kick you out the door; with respect, of course. But at the moment, my fear is two-fold. First, if we remove those wires, I'm concerned about a relapse in your recovery. I don't know that whatever phenomenon that made you a real-life version of Electra Girl won't happen again. Secondly, I'm not only responsible for your safety, but for the safety of my staff and our other patients as well. I won't compromise either, but I also understand that we can't hold you forever. I'm saying that we've got to proceed slowly, for everyone's benefit."

Anabelle crossed her arms, aware that the doctor didn't see the demons that lurked around them. She tried to shut out the forked tongues and black eyes and sharp claws, but as her time in the hospital wore on and her room became infested with evil, it became impossible to ignore their threat to her safety. The weaklings she saw when she first awoke were nothing to what now prowled beneath her bed, along the walls, against the ceiling. They were bigger, darker, meaner, and sometimes when they got close she could feel them breathing on her. Now that she was able to retract her energy, she couldn't risk using it to fend the creatures off, for fear her caregivers would notice she was still electrified. That would be catastrophic to her plan. As long as she was confined to the hospital, Anabelle was an easy target, and the realization that she had to save herself bore heavy on her mind. She looked at her oblivious doctor and the monster circling his throat.

281

"If you don't remove the wires, I'll do it myself," she said.

Huxley held up his hands. "Let's not be hasty. I promise I'll do my best to get you out of here as soon as possible; all I'm asking for is a little time."

"But I'm not electrified anymore; there's no reason to keep me here," Anabelle protested.

"We need to be patient, Ms. Cheever—"

"Am I under arrest?" she asked Huxley, and when she saw him flinch, she knew that *arrest* wasn't the right word. Of course it wouldn't be. She'd done nothing wrong. No, she wasn't being arrested, she was being *detained*, possibly by the men and women in dark suits that sometimes congregated around the nursing station, asking questions about her condition.

The doctor laughed uneasily. "You watch too much TV, Ms. Cheever. The things you're suggesting don't happen in real life. I promise you; we are keeping you solely for prudence purposes."

Only, what had happened to Anabelle didn't normally happen in real life, either. Huxley couldn't refute that, nor could he refute the growing and mysterious contingent that visited her room and asked questions she didn't want to answer.

Anabelle drew up her knees and tapped the screen of her iPad that lay on her lap. The news report she'd been reading appeared on the screen, and she turned it toward the doctor. "Is this the stuff you say doesn't happen in real life, Dr. Huxley? I don't mean it to sound the way I know it's going to sound, but aren't there more important things to worry about than me?"

Huxley's eyes swept over the image of the yellow tarp covering the body of nurse Tammy Cormoran. While they hadn't publicly revealed her name yet, it became obvious she was the victim when she didn't appear for yesterday's shift, and this was then confirmed by the investigating officer who'd already interviewed a handful of hospital staff before the day was done. His face went white. "That's different."

"What's different?" Dr. Tanti's upbeat voice came from behind Huxley, and he turned to see Adhira and Abe, charts in hands, ready for their daily check-ups on their famous patient.

"We're talking about important things," Anabelle told them, and flashed her iPad to the two doctors, enlarging the picture so that the nurse's body filled the entire screen. She knew she had no reason to revive the tragedy, but the juvenile parts of her that demanded retribution for her incarceration drove her to flash the image to the people who had saved her. Their faces fell.

"She was valued member of our staff," Adhira said stiffly, and the eavesdropping nurses at the station desk erupted in a fresh wave of sobs.

Abe's lips clamped together, and he sighed heavily through his nose. "She cared for you, yes?" Anabelle murmured an acknowledgement. The doctor was not prone to chastising a patient, but the indignance Anabelle conveyed caused him to scowl. "Then you must be thankful for her life, as we are. Put that picture away, please." She did.

Adhira lowered herself onto the edge of Anabelle's bed. "I take it he's told you we can't release you yet?"

"There's nothing wrong with me."

Adhira put her folder down. "You're right to be upset, Anabelle. If I were in your position—"

"You're *not* in my position."

"No," Adhira concurred. "I'm not. But *if* I were, I'd be upset, yes, but I'd also do whatever I could to speed my release. I hear you've been reluctant to answer our questions."

283

Anabelle ignored the shadow of a demon that jumped onto Dr. Tanti's lap.

"I don't like talking to them," Anabelle said of the suited mystery people who pretended to empathize with her but really only wanted to run tests, tests, and more tests.

Adhira leaned in and said in a lowered voice, "I don't like talking to them either."

"They're not really doctors, are they?" Anabelle asked, and the look the doctors exchanged was all the answer she needed.

"I know this is not an ideal situation, but if there's anything we can do to make you more comfortable—within reason, of course—just name it. Sometimes a different meal or a visit from a friend can make all the difference. We had one guy insist his dog stay with him, and we made it happen. I know it probably seems like it, but we're not heathens, Anabelle. We do want to make this easy on you as long as you're here." The female doctor patted Anabelle's ankle and rose with her file.

From the back of his hand, Abe whispered, "*Says* the heathen who took the last cup of coffee this morning."

"First come and all that." Adhira smirked.

Pleasantries more or less settled, Huxley left the other doctors to do their work. The two nurses on-duty outside of Anabelle's room were wiping their faces as he approached. He offered the women his shared sympathies and instructed them to keep a close watch on Anabelle, for fear she might try to remove her attachments. Then he rode the elevator to the third-floor staff room, where he took his lunch bag from the refrigerator. The savory smell of his wife's beef stew soon seeped through the seams of the whirring microwave, and Huxley inhaled the comfort of home as he looked out the picture window at the snow-flecked trees along the empty walking trail. He'd used the path many times, as the majority of the hospital staff did, and wondered now if they still felt safe doing so. Would they alter their schedules to avoid walking in the dark? Would single walkers pair or even triple up? Or would they avoid the trail altogether, afraid of being victims themselves? The hospital would need to address their anxiety, and Huxley hoped Cliff had the mind to dig deep into his latent reserve of empathy. The CEO was capable, he knew, but *willingness* was another obstacle altogether.

The microwave beeped to signal that his lunch was ready but still Huxley stood, looking at his faded reflection in the window. His formerly dark hair was now mostly gray, and the fullness of face that he'd enjoyed as a young athlete and student was now isolated to banana-shaped puffs of skin beneath his eyes. He was not old, but getting there, something Tammy Cormoran would never get the opportunity to do. A long timer at the hospital, Huxley had seen many hires, advancements, and even retirements, and his memory took him to Tammy's nervous first shift, when she'd changed the gangrenous dressing of a geriatric patient only to go squealing from the room right into Huxley when the woman's toe fell off. He'd reassured her, then, that her reaction did not make her a bad nurse and relayed the story of when he was a resident and told the wrong woman that her husband had died in surgery. The story made her feel better and endeared her to him for the rest of her shortened tenure. He sighed heavily against the glass, knowing that her death would sit on him like a stone.

He left a patch of breath fog on the window and took his stew from the microwave, sitting in the corner away from a cluster of nurses where he could be alone. Though full of flavor, his food was tasteless to him, and he mechanically ate while his brain tried to compartmentalize the events of late: the bus crash and animal attacks, the drying of the Callingwood River, the strange weather, the electrification and subsequent de-electrification of Anabelle Cheever, the Searles children's deaths, Tammy's murder. Together they made no sense; apart they were no less peculiar. He wondered if he were dreaming, but his dreams were another story.

Last night, Huxley had woken screaming and Karen had had to shake him to get him to stop. Only, at the time he couldn't remember what he had dreamed about; he'd just felt a terror that pervaded every part of his body and every part of his mind. Normally, Huxley didn't have dreams, or if he did, he didn't remember them. But for the last week he felt traces of illusion when he woke, like a patient waking from surgery, aware that something had happened but unsure what that something was. Chewing his food, Huxley couldn't shake the feeling that he'd somehow been *worked* on.

Karen would suggest therapy, as she was a therapist, after all, or a heaping dose of the Good Book, which she insisted healed whatever therapy couldn't. He wasn't averse to either, but Garrett was too small a city for the luxury of secrecy, and he knew that his personal *and* professional integrity would suffer if he talked about his newfound fear of sleeping, so he kept his concerns to himself.

He was just finishing his stew when the door swung open and Abe and Adhira walked in. Both doctors were engaged in laughter, and as they drew to Huxley's table in the corner, Abe said, "We've decided we're moving to Fiji and we're taking you with us."

"Sounds good to me," Huxley said. "What's the occasion?"

INTERFERENCE

Adhira said, "Cliff's moderating a roundtable group where we can talk about our *feelings* with him. He sent an email a few minutes ago."

"Damn me to hell," Huxley said. "Just when I thought I'd heard it all."

Abe retrieved his and Adhira's lunch bags from the fridge and both sat across from Huxley, unpacking leafy salads and sandwiches. Adhira's phone rang and, after peeking at the screen, she silenced the call. She bit into her sandwich while Abe reported on his examination of Anabelle.

"Unless we move to Fiji, I've got—what—ten years left before I retire? In that time, I think I could circle the globe and still not find anything stranger than this patient. She defies logic. She comes in like a lightning rod and now she's idle as a rubber mat; tell me I'm dreaming, Hux," Abe said.

"I think we all are," Huxley told him.

Abe pushed his salad around his bowl, eventually forking a cucumber, which he now pointed at Huxley. "I tell you; someone's playing with us. Maybe God, maybe aliens, but someone's having a hell of a time shoving us across their gameboard."

"You believe in aliens, then?" Huxley asked Abe.

The doctor shrugged. "Of course. Spirits. Angels. Aliens. It's preposterous to think we're the only capable beings in the entire universe. Humans are egocentric, so it fits our mindset to believe that everything that occurs happens *only* to us. Why couldn't there be electrified beings six thousand light years away? And what if that's *normal* over there? Why can't the same phenomena happen on some other planet? How long ago did we first think the Earth was round? Something like twenty-five hundred years. That's a blink when it comes to the universe but eternity to ourselves, no? Centuries

287

from now, maybe a millennia or two, we might have an answer for everything that confounds us now." He nipped his cucumber off his fork and chewed thoughtfully for a moment. "You know they're sealing her file?"

Adhira's phone rang again and without looking at the screen, she pressed a side button to set it to vibrate.

Huxley frowned. "How can they do that? We have almost a hundred doctors collaborating on it, not to mention the electrical group."

Abe said, "Not anymore. Cliff's orders. From now on, it's us, him, and whoever is holding his neck."

"You're a big boy, Abe, you can say balls," Adhira chimed in.

"Big boys don't need to say *balls*, Doctor Tanti." Abe winked. "They operate on them."

"You're a cardiologist," Huxley said.

"Heart, balls, same thing."

"Children." Adhira rolled her eyes, her good humor leaving when her phone vibrated against the table. The other doctors looked at her. She shoved her sandwich aside. "You want to talk to my parents, please be my guest."

"You should just make your parents happy and marry whoever they want you to marry. That's what I tell my daughters, anyway, but it doesn't seem to work. Abby's with a painter and Molly's guy thinks he's going to get rich playing video games. Deadbeats." Huxley's groan was shared by many fathers across the world. "Who are they to think they get to choose, huh?"

"Just because I'm Indian doesn't mean my parents are arranging my marriage. They're very progressive, I told you."

"Why the avoidance, then?" Abe cut in. Older than Adhira by little more than a decade, Abe regarded her almost as

INTERFERENCE

a daughter and so liked to counsel the younger doctor in matters of life and love, regardless whether she sought his advice.

"They want me to come to Puja with them."

"Puja," Huxley said, twisting his face. "Remind me what that is again?"

"It's one of the ways Hindus worship. Garrett doesn't have a temple, so we do it at home. We ask for guidance or assistance, express gratitude, ask for protection ... like you two do but to our gods and goddesses. I have my own shrine at home." Her phone rang. She ignored it.

"And it bothers you that your parents want you to do this?" Abe asked.

"It's complicated."

"Any more complicated than a human battery?" Huxley said.

"Definitely not that complicated. It's not *Puja* I'm avoiding. They want me over because my dad's been having dreams about me lately. They think I'm in danger or something. He's got my mom all worked up about it, and now they won't leave me alone. They've been calling me non-stop all morning." She sighed. "He's probably just been into the spicy food again. It gives him nightmares."

"Prayer never hurt anyone," Abe said honestly.

"I've been dreaming too," Huxley admitted openly for the first time. It came out quick, like a breath pushed out of him, and he felt his heart clench as he waited for their judgement.

There was the sound of metal chairs being dragged across the floor as the group of nurses packed up their things and disbursed. Abe waited until the last one was out the door before he put the lid on his half-eaten salad and leaned closer to the other doctors. "I think they're premonitions," he whispered. "I'm going to tell you something and if you ever repeat

289

it, I'll deny it and I'll never bring you anything from Mara's bakery again, understood?" Two nods responded to him, and though the room was empty, Abe Nkosi looked around to be sure. He said, "I've been dreaming, too, but it's not just me; five of my patients are reporting the same thing. You know how they get emotional after surgery? Well, this week I've had to send the chaplain to four of them and prescribe anxiety medication for another."

"Post-operative anxiety," Adhira interjected. "It's common—"

"I do not need a lesson in medicine," Abe banged the table with his fist. "Sorry, but I need you to understand. We are all having the *same* dream, Adhira. And I have to pretend that what they're telling me is normal, but it's not. It's not. At first, I thought it was a coincidence, that maybe I'd said something to my bypass patient, or she to me and that I subconsciously picked it up. But then a second, a third, a fourth … this week I've been more psychologist than surgeon and now I'm thinking that *I* should be the one in the chair. It's like they are telling me my own dreams, but—"

"About the fair?" Huxley interrupted. Abe flinched.

Confused, Adhira asked them to explain.

Huxley said, "I'm not sure what to tell you. I don't remember much when I wake up, but I get this feeling that something's going to happen at the fair. I don't know why— it's like, when I try to remember it, it just goes farther away. Weird, right?"

"What has your father told you about his dreams?" Abe asked Adhira.

She shrugged. "He won't give me details; says they'll scare me too much."

INTERFERENCE

Abe packed his containers back into his lunch bag and held it against his body. He said, "We are doctors, so we are supposed to follow evidence, yes?" They nodded. "We are dreaming because our bodies are trying to tell us something, warn us against harm, perhaps, and I believe we should listen to them. After all, it wasn't just science that kept us alive for two hundred thousand years, but *instinct*. We don't write that in our charts or report about it to the boards or discuss it with our patients, but it is always there, embedded in us, inseparable from the human condition. In Africa we have this saying that all you need to know is *that you know,* and that is enough. It is the first and greatest protection and it's never wise to dismiss it." He was talking with his hands now, gesticulating with his fingers to articulate his point. "In all matters, caution is our ally, and I don't think this is any different. Adhira, go do Puja with your parents. We must protect not only our bodies, but also our minds. I'm going to see my pastor after work and I suggest you do the same, Huxley. No harm in that, and if it protects us, all the better. As for the fair—Abe let out a slow breath— "now, this is just my opinion, but I get the feeling that we won't have time for that because we are going to be needed *here.*" He emphasized the last word, and the chill it sent through their bodies made each doctor squirm.

Adhira whistled and pushed back from the table. "Well, this was a fascinating conversation, but—" At once, all their pagers went off.

Overhead, the speakers sounded with a tinny female voice on the hospital's public announcement system. "Code yellow, fifth-floor, female, age nineteen, five feet two inches, shoulder-length red hair. Code yellow, fifth-floor, female, age nineteen..." the voice repeated three times.

291

The doctors left their lunches and ran out the door. "We need to split up!" Huxley ordered, directing Abe to the north stairwell and Adhira to the west. He ran to the east stairwell, and then the doctors were climbing, rushing up, up, fast, faster, exploding onto the fifth-floor hallway, Adhira ahead, shouting at the nurse on duty.

"Where is she?" Adhira yelled.

The young nurse stuttered at the three panicked doctors. "I—I—"

"Where is she, dammit?" Huxley slapped the desk.

The woman, Claire, drew her lips from inside her mouth where she had been biting them. "Stephanie was getting us a coffee; she was only gone a minute and then a call came about Tammy ..." Tears welled in the nurse's eyes.

Abe removed his glasses and pinched the bridge of his nose. "Did you see where she went?" Claire shook her head, so Abe used the phone at her desk to call security.

Meanwhile, Adhira and Huxley rushed to Anabelle's room. Adhira picked up one of the attachments that had been secured to the girl's foot. "Looks like she just pulled it off."

Huxley dragged both hands through his hair. "She warned me she was going to do it. I should have taken her seriously. This is my fault."

"A nineteen-year-old girl like a monkey in an exhibit, being poked and prodded by strangers; it's definitely not your fault, Greg. I would have done the same thing if I were her."

"What do we do now?" Huxley asked.

"We find her," Adhira said.

31

Morning gloom spread over the gathered parishioners in Holy Redeemer's fellowship hall so that even with the east wall fashioned entirely of windows and all the lights turned on, the room was dismal and more than a little depressing. An emergency intercession by the ladies' prayer group, which consistently brought seven or eight dedicated parishioners, now hosted fifty-seven women, many of whom had never before stepped foot inside the church. Father Robert Pauliuk customarily gave the group the freedom of the church and let them tend to their meetings without his interference, though they did welcome his visits and counsel whenever he appeared. There was such an edge of unease in this large group, however, that today he offered his assistance to Julia Fowler, the meeting leader.

"Either they all know something I don't, or they think we're offering a buffet today," he joked to Julia as they returned to the stacks of chairs along the back wall.

Julia's pink cardigan flapped loosely against her hips as they walked. "When Nancy called me last night, I thought we might expect a few more ladies today, but not this many. I'm happy to share the word of the Lord with them, Father, but this is just too many for me. Do you mind staying?"

"Of course," he said.

293

She was visibly relieved. "Thank God. I was racking my brain trying to figure out what to say to them."

Father Pauliuk added his chair to the row being built. "May I ask what has furnished us with this turnout today?" His eyes swept over the fidgety women who were now taking seats. "I'm assuming it's not good news, by the look of them."

Julia placed a chair next to the one the priest set down and together they returned to the back wall. "I don't know, exactly. A few women contacted Nancy about their husbands, and she suggested we meet. It snowballed into this." Her gaze fell over the crowd.

Seeing the tension on her face, Father Pauliuk pulled Julia aside where they wouldn't be overheard. "There's something happening with the men in our city?" he asked her quietly.

The thought came to him that the long-standing application for another strip club license had finally been approved by city council. As it had occurred when the exotic dance club *Mounds* opened some seventeen years earlier, the church's women's auxiliary experienced an uptick in enrollment. By all means, Garrett's men weren't immune to transgression, but in Father Pauliuk's experience the swell he saw today foretold of a collective, pre-emptive strike against future infidelities.

Julia read into his question, and a blush showed fierce on her pale face. "No. Sorry, I shouldn't have said it like that, Father. It's just that some of the ladies were concerned about … you're just going to think I'm silly saying it … but apparently, they've been having *dreams*; nightmares, or something. I guess one woman got talking to another and they all got talking to Nancy. It's not just the husbands, Father; some of their daughters and sons are having them, too."

Julia's white hair rustled as she turned and gestured to a tall black-haired woman clutching an empty bottle in the front row. "Marta is refusing to leave without holy water."

The preacher's eyebrows went up. "That bad, is it?" At Julia's nod, he added, "Well, let's not keep them waiting."

It was his habit to address the group as one of their own, preferring to keep his involvement as informal as possible to foster an environment likely to engage conversation and garner trust. Today was no different. While last coffees were poured and last seats were filled, Father Pauliuk lifted a chair, brought it to the front of the room and sat with his tumbler of tea. He said, "Can everyone see me all right? It's a big group for a circle but if you'd rather—"

"We're fine like this," came a woman's irritated voice from somewhere in one of the middle rows.

There was a murmur amongst the crowd, with audible shushing and orders for respect, but the Father went on. "Well, that works for me, then. Feel free to move your chairs, if you wish; we're all family here, so please make yourselves comfortable. First, I'd like to thank our prayer leaders, Julia and Nancy, for arranging this meeting. There are many new faces here today, and we welcome you with our hearts and with the great blessings of God." The women he knew acknowledged their new counterparts with smiles and hand pats while the others looked on nervously. A handful of new recruits appeared relieved when he spoke, as though the extension of God's grace was the very thing they had came for.

"Now, for those of you who are unfamiliar with our church, our service times are posted on the bulletin board in the front vestibule. You do not have to be baptized to attend, and you may participate only as much as you wish. We extend our assistance to you at your leisure. Also, while I am honored to be so kindly received by our ladies' auxiliary, please note that it is not my intention to intrude or bore you; you'll get enough of that in my sermons." The laughter he hoped for rang out and he saw the tension slowly ebb from their bodies. Jaws unclenched, fingers loosened, shoulders settled. "Julia asked me to speak today but before we get to that, I'd like us to pray."

The sign of the cross was made by most of the assembly, with one confused woman tapping her forehead and then spiraling her finger down her face. They lowered their heads.

"Dear Heavenly Father, we pray that you lift up our gathering into your merciful care. Bless our friends, old and new, and grant us the wisdom to attend with love our fellowship today." A chorus of *amen* finished the prayer. Father Pauliuk clasped his hands together. "Now, ladies, let's see if I can be of assistance. I understand there are some concerns—"

The same woman who had interrupted him earlier stood up. She wore an untucked flannel shirt and chewed her gum loudly as she spoke. "We need an exorcism, Father Pollock." He ignored the mispronunciation of his name, letting the woman say what she'd come to say. She flicked her bleach-damaged hair behind her shoulders. "I saw it on TV. The devil was possessing this girl and they got a priest to take it out of her. She was real crazy-like until they splashed some holy water on her and it sizzled, you know, like bacon in a frying pan." The woman popped her gum and added, "She was better after they did that."

"Ah, I see," the good priest replied, wondering if he was being put-on by the woman. "You believe the devil has inhabited your ... husband?" Father Pauliuk ventured cautiously.

"You're goddamn right I do," she said, and when the woman beside her nudged her leg, she said, "Pardon the language, Father."

"And why do you believe this?" he asked.

"He screams in the middle of the night like I've cut off his ..." She hesitated. "What I mean to say is that he's having nightmares, Father. And he's so scared of them that you'd think the house was burning down."

In the second row, Tina Medley raised her hand. "Go ahead, Tina," Julia said from her chair near the coffee station.

"Gerald's been dreaming, too," Tina said with a catch at the back of her throat. She fidgeted with her necklace. "He's usually a sound sleeper, but lately he gets up in the middle of the night and I have to hold him to calm him down. Our doctor said it's probably just stress from all the things that have been happening around here lately, but then I had the same dreams Gerald was having. We—we wake up at the same time and we're *screaming*, Father, we're screaming and it's horrible, just horrible." Her lips quivered.

Marta Ramos rose from her chair, cradling her empty bottle. "I have them too. We're all having the same dream, Father. My daughters won't sleep in their rooms anymore; they've been sleeping in my bed for five days. It's been hard on the kids lately, you know, so I thought that's what it was. At first, they couldn't really explain their nightmares to me, but then Emilia said something about a lot of people getting killed, and when she said it Gabriella started to cry because she had the same feeling. Ted thought they might have snuck and watched one of those horror movies we don't like, but ... but then I had nightmares too. Something's not right, Father." The bottle shook in her hands.

297

From the back row, a small voice tried to be heard over the gasps and whimpers. Father Pauliuk stood to instill order. "Please, we need calm if we're going to solve this. Let her speak."

A gray head rose just barely over the others. Mabel Wimbrey's wrinkled face, trembling with Parkinson's, was compressed with fear. "Archie had a heart attack." A rush of women reached toward her, but Mabel went on, "They say he's going to make it and for that I am thankful. I know he wasn't in the best health to begin with; we're not spring chickens like many of you, but he had those dreams, too. He woke up with such a fright, he was sweating and then his color went; his poor heart just couldn't take it. He had those dreams and they almost killed him. It was the dreams, Father." A tear squeezed from her eye and she used the hand not holding her cane to wipe it from her cheek. She sat back down.

Consternation puckering his face, Father Pauliuk said, "How many of you are having these dreams?" Two dozen hands rose. "And how many of your friends or family members are having this dream?" The rest of the hands went up. "Are they similar?" Every single head nodded. He couldn't deny the possibility of a demonic presence in their small city, but neither could he be sure that the convergence of catastrophe hadn't somehow triggered the psychological response they were experiencing. Truth be told, he wasn't sure *what* their identical experiences implied, but he was determined to find out. That he was in front of believers and skeptics alike required more of a measured approach, for he knew the skeptics would seize any opportunity to repudiate whatever solution he put forth. He said, "I thank you for sharing your concerns with me and I promise to do my best to help you, with the grace of God. We must remember that *all* things are

298

possible through the Father, and that we will get through this if we rely on his strength and his wisdom." He pointed to his right, where Julia had rolled out the rack of Bibles they used for fellowship events. "For those of you who don't have them, please—" As he was speaking, movement from the corner of his eye drew his attention to the entryway, where his former parishioner and bookkeeper, Ed Norman, stood. Father Pauliuk finished his instructions to the group and asked Julia to cover for him for a few minutes while he excused himself, ignoring the huffs of indignation from the gum-popping woman as he went to greet Ed.

"Ed, what a pleasant surprise," the priest said.

He shook Ed's hand and then pulled him in for a quick hug, realizing only when Ed's face was near his own that Dakota Cardinal was standing right behind them. He released Ed and greeted Dak, then led both men down the hall to his office. Much like the overfill in the fellowship room, the men's appearance was unexpected, and Father Pauliuk was unsettled not only by the timing of their visit, but because neither man was a parishioner. Ed's attendance had dwindled then stopped altogether after the death of his wife, and Dak wasn't a believer in Jesus per se, though he and his family did believe in a higher Creator, as was common in his culture. Other than through Dak's charitable endeavors, he wasn't sure how the men knew each other, so his curiosity was etched on his face. "I've already had too much coffee this morning, but I can bring you some if you'd like."

They declined his offer. "I know I haven't come in a while," Ed started, but the priest put up his hands.

"No need to explain. I'm glad to see you, Ed. How have you been?"

Ed patted his breast. "I have some new hardware."

299

"Pacemaker?" Father Pauliuk asked.

"Uh-huh," Ed said. "And it's a good thing I do, otherwise I wouldn't be here to tell you what we need to tell you." His eyes confirming trouble, Ed frowned.

"You know you can talk to me, Ed. You too, of course, Dak."

Dak pursed his lips, readying himself for a difficult conversation. "May I close the door?" he asked Father Pauliuk. The priest nodded.

When the room was secured to their liking, Ed said, "I'll let Dakota tell the story. Maybe you can tell us what you make of it. You'll understand why I asked him here once you hear what he has to say."

Dak, who was familiar with Father Pauliuk more from the tragedy of the parish fire two decades ago than from casual acquaintance, said thoughtfully, "I appreciate your hospitality, Father."

"My pleasure." The priest smiled, appreciating Dak's courtesy.

"I know you're wondering why we've come to you today, but we felt that with the parallels in our spirituality, you might help. Our Elders are of the same mindset; they believe unity through all faiths is the only way that we are going to get through this."

"Please tell Nikonha I said hello," he said to Dak, fondly remembering several community clean-up events where he'd worked alongside the woman.

"I will," Dak said, offering him a slight smile before seriousness once again overtook his face.

Though Dak was an easy conversationalist, his next words were awkward on his tongue and more than once he eased his explanation to ensure he neither exaggerated nor understated his report. Eventually, as Father Pauliuk listened attentively and Ed nodded on encouragingly, Dak got into a rhythm and revealed everything he knew about the devil-woman, from Jesse's first encounter with her in the hospital to the smoke rising from her hand as she handed Dak his medicine wheel, to Sylvia's proximity when Johnny's fingers were bitten off by one of Roy Botcher's llamas. He finished with the episode after Hattie's funeral, when both Wendy and Ed had seen her black tongue, and when she had spoken inside Ed's own head.

Father Pauliuk, who had been silent while Dak spoke, now looked wide-eyed at Ed. The older man shuffled in his chair, and when Ed regarded his old friend and spiritual guide, he saw terrible worry on the preacher's face.

"I wish to God it wasn't true, Robert," Ed said. "I wish I could blame it on my heart, I wish I could blame it on old age. That would be a blessing, of all things, but I don't believe it is. That woman came to me in my own room, in my *head*." His eyes shot to Dak.

"It's okay, Ed. He needs to know," Dak said.

Ed shifted in his seat. "Honest to God, Robert, she was in my mind, demanding I … I take care of Dakota and his family. I can't say exactly how she expected I do this, but I know exactly *what* she wanted me to do. She has intentions on them. Evil intentions, Robert. I feel she is targeting them because they all seem to sense her. Nobody else but them, and now me, I suppose." Then Ed relayed the incident in his room in its entirety, leaving nothing out.

"A woman just asked me to perform an exorcism," Father Pauliuk explained after Ed was done, if only to verbalize the complexity of his thoughts. "She believes her husband has been possessed by the devil. Everyone you saw in that

S. L. LUCK

room has been affected by similar nightmares. I don't know what to make of it, but I don't believe it's good. When my wife died years ago, I believed it to be the devil's work, and perhaps it was, but I do know that what happened then is not the same as what is happening now. However much it pained me, my grief did not invite the devil into my head nor encourage violence against others. Have you shared your experience with anyone else?"

Ed shook his head. "Only Dakota."

Father Pauliuk leaned on his elbows. "Good. I appreciate your candidness, Ed. Something like that would be hard for anyone to admit. To be honest, if Dakota hadn't explained what he had and if I didn't have a room full of people suddenly demanding holy water, I might have suggested the advice of a doctor. I say this because my feeling is that there *is* something amiss here. I believe you, Ed, and I need you to understand that if you share this with anyone else and it gets to the staff at your home, they might insist on medicating you, which could potentially expose you to more danger or leave you unable to protect yourself if she comes again. That said, you need to do what you feel is right to protect your health. Understand?"

"Your feelings align with mine, Robert."

"What can you tell me about the dreams everyone seems to be having? Do either of you know anything more of it?"

"I know that all of a sudden everyone wants a dream catcher. Our phone is ringing off the hook. We can't make them fast enough," Dak said.

"There's a few down my hall that started screaming at night," Ed said. "They don't say what it is, but I know."

"Sylvia?" Father Pauliuk asked. "Do you think she is causing their nightmares?"

302

Ed shook his head. "No. Not her. The thing *inside* her. I have no reason to believe this except that I do: I think Sylvia and the thing inside her are two different entities. You know how you can sense evil, Robert? Well, sometimes I sense it from Sylvia and sometimes I don't. It's like the evil comes and goes like a switch being turned off or on. I don't know that she's aware of it, either. Maybe she is. Maybe I'm wrong."

They watched as Father Pauliuk absently touched his collar. The band of white standing stiff like armor around his neck contrasted starkly against the blotches of anxiety that appeared on his skin. "I'd like to confer with my colleagues, if that's all right with you. Like Nikonha said, I do believe unity is our best defense against this beast."

Dak said, "There may not be just one demon, Father. We think there could be more than just the devil-woman."

The preacher frowned. "More than one?"

"The nightmares people tell us about seem similar except for the method in the violence," Dak explained. "Some people say something's going to happen with the river. Some say it's the weather that's going to get us. A few have suddenly developed fear of their pets. We're fostering two dogs, a hamster, and a bird because their owners are now petrified of them. You see, Father, the end of these nightmares is the same: people die. But the *way* they die is not the same. I'm not sure what the Bible says about that, but in our culture, it indicates interference by different spirits."

A long rush of air pushed out of Father Pauliuk's nose. He said, "Whether there's one or many of them, demons report to the devil, and we have to do whatever it takes to stop him. With things pointing to something happening at the festival, I think it should be cancelled. Dak, you've been on the committee for years, do you think you can convince them to reschedule it until we figure this out?"

"I'll bring it up to them, but I don't know what their appetite will be to change anything.

A few days ago, I had to practically beg the mayor not to cancel it. If I ask her to do it the day before it's supposed to kick off, I doubt she'll listen to me now."

"Will you try?" Father Pauliuk asked.

Dak inclined his head. "I have to. It won't be easy, but I'll do what I can. I think the dreamers will be on our side; they won't be hard to convince. It's everyone else I'm worried about. People need something to look forward to, and with all that's happened here lately, I think we've got a real fight on our hands if we're thinking of taking away the only thing that gives them hope."

Unable to stop himself, Father Pauliuk said, "It's not the only thing that gives people hope." He looked at the crucifix mounted above his door.

"Sorry, Father. That's not what I meant." Dak blushed.

"I know. You're right that the festival has come to symbolize hope for many people, and I know that the court of public opinion won't look favorably at the city or the committee if you succeed, but I think you might help save a lot of lives, if what we suspect is true."

"And if they won't cancel it?" Ed asked. "What do we do then?"

The silence between them intensified in their ears so that each man heard only his own heartbeat, only the expiration of his own breath. A long-suppressed terror once again rose in the preacher. He said, "We must exorcise the demons."

"An exorcism?" Dak looked at Ed, who appeared completely unstirred by Father Pauliuk's proposition.

The preacher held up his hand. "We administer minor exorcisms on a daily basis. We expel evil during baptisms, for example, and for this I have the latitude to perform as I must.

But if what you're saying is true—and I have no doubt that it is—then I must talk to the bishop and get his permission to conduct a major exorcism. Our complication here is that major exorcisms are a much longer process. It can take months or even a year of careful investigation before I would be granted approval, if I were the one to perform the exorcism."

"But we don't have that kind of time, Robert," Ed complained.

"I don't believe so, no," the Father agreed. "But I will do my best. In the meantime, it's important to remember that evil reacts to good like smoke reacts to clean air; it tries to smother it and poison it. I think that the more we gather and pray the spirits out, the harder it will be for them to stay. We need to choke them out with prayer. And I'm not suggesting only Christians do this, Dakota." Outside, a cluster of clouds settled on the sky and the priest's office was filled with shadows. Looking at the apprehensive men in front of him, the good Father's faith intensified, and he said a silent prayer for their safety.

They made plans to speak again in the afternoon, and Father Pauliuk saw the men out before returning to the Fellowship Hall. In the short time since he'd been with Ed and Dak, the group had grown, swelled to what he estimated to be over a hundred women, and even a few children. Julia was reading the words of Joseph from Genesis 40:8. "*They said to him, 'We have had dreams, and there is no one to interpret them.' And Joseph said to them, 'Do not interpretations belong to God? Please tell them to me.*'" He applauded her appropriate selection, even though only half of the fidgety group seemed to listen.

Seeing Robert return to the room, the gum-popping woman muttered, "It's about time," loudly enough that every bowed head turned to him.

305

"Ah! I see that Julia has blessed you with Genesis. This is what we need to do. We need to take our dreams and let them be interpreted by our all-knowing Father."

His thumb rested on his bent index finger, and he used this triangle of flesh to expound his guidance, turning it and waving it for emphasis, while one hundred heads followed his hand like kittens to the red end of a laser. He did not broach the matter he'd discussed with Ed and Dak, but he did assert the need for both prayer and caution while he formulated a plan to help them. With the Fall Festival commencing the next day, he advised Julia's group to avoid the fair grounds and then extended the entirety of the church for their purposes until their dreams subsided.

"We will keep our doors open through the night; we only ask that you be mindful in cleaning up after yourselves. I don't mind clearing furniture, but my back isn't what it used to be. I will be in and out of the building as I confer with my counterparts, but let's plan to meet later today. How does seven sound?" There was a murmur of consensus, and he left them to plan the potluck Julia and Nancy had suggested.

He went now to the chapel, where the familiarity of the space never failed to soothe him. Clasping his hands behind his back, he walked the length of the nave then stopped to look up first at Jesus, hung high and center, then above at the stained-glass saints continuing sentinel to the ceiling of the apse. He was overcome by a great tide of emotion that made him shiver with love, and he put himself before them as a man hopeful of victory on their behalf. Reflecting on the task ahead of him, his knees began to tremble and he steadied himself on the altar until the feeling passed. He turned to the Bible that lay open on the altar and began to read, fortifying himself with the word of God. He calmed himself this way until, a few minutes later, his cell phone rang. It was Father Bonner.

306

32

Mayor Ada Falconer wasn't an afternoon coffee-drinker, but here she was, nearly five at night, on her fifth espresso of the day. The ugly buzz of too much caffeine gave her a headache, so she reached for the bottle of Advil in her desk drawer only to find it empty. She sighed and pinched the tender flesh between her thumb and index finger like her yoga instructor had taught her, but the pressure did little to ease the pounding inside her head. It was the worst month of her life. She had never had to meet with families of deceased citizens, but now there seemed to be a steady stream of them, demanding answers, alternately wetting her shoulder with their tears and then blaming her for causing them.

The young nurse's family had been the worst of these encounters. Grief bleating through his trembling lips, Tammy Cormoran's father accused Ada of being so consumed with media attention that she failed in her sworn duty to protect the city. He didn't care that she'd solicited assistance from other cities to patrol the area, he wanted his daughter back and he swore that until he was reunited with Tammy in the afterlife, he would make Ada's life a living hell.

If that weren't bad enough, her rushed entry to the office this morning had been exacerbated by a horde of protesters who threw mud at her until her security team scooped her into the building. Even then, she heard the shouts. "New mayor now! New mayor now!" a group of knit-hatted twenty-somethings shouted. "Garrett's had enough! Garrett's had enough!" a competing cluster of middle-aged men and women yelled. Her escape inside inflamed the mob, and they shrieked and bellowed louder, until their skin turned rage-purple and their chanting, angry mouths sprayed wetness on the windows. She could almost feel their spit on her neck as she hurried away from them.

Hunkered inside her office for the better part of the day, she resisted looking outside—but each time she did, the mass was bigger and the signs were meaner. *Justice for Tammy! Bring Back Our River! Garrett Stinks! Don't Take Away Our Festival! Festival = Freedom. Don't Let Our Kids Down! We Are Not an Experiment! Attention Whore! Not Even Your Husband Likes You!*

During her twenty-three years of working in various municipal and provincial offices, she had seen her fair share of demonstrations, but never before had they been so hostile, never before had their attacks been so personal. Worse: because the city was already bursting with journalists, the insults against her were splashed across national and international news networks. Her husband, who—it turned out—*did* like her, saw the signs on TV and proceeded to call every hour to ensure she was safe. Such was his worry that Ada even spent the better part of an hour she didn't have begging him not to come and "kick some lowlife ass," as he so eloquently put it.

Her only saving grace, if it could be called that, was that Jessica Chung was suspiciously absent from the charge. Ada didn't know what to make of it. Presently, she turned on the foot massager under her desk and let the machine knead her

INTERFERENCE

tired feet. Ada was just closing her eyes for a moment of peace when her communications manager, Nicole Lewis, scrambled in.

"Unless it's good news, I don't want to hear it," Ada told her, wishing she hadn't had that last espresso.

Nicole slipped a single sheet of paper onto the desk, pushing it toward Ada with one finger. "I think you're going to like it," she said, then leaned forward with an enthusiasm that piqued Ada's interest.

Ada peered at the paper. The message was printed on a pattern of *confidential* watermarks. "You've *got* to be kidding me."

"Nope. As long as you're on board, it's a go. Isn't it great?" Nicole's bracelets jangled against Ada's desk as she pulsed with excitement.

On any other day, Ada would have been thrilled by a visit from the Prime Minister, but at the moment it felt like a surprise inspection. Already there was intense scrutiny over everything she did; she did not want nor need his eagle-eyed retinue combing over the city.

"Dial it back for me. Since when did our Prime Minister become interested in our festival?" She used her toe to turn off the massager and slipped her unsatisfied feet back into her shoes.

"Since Anabelle Cheever broke out of the hospital," Nicole said, waiting for the news to settle in.

"What are you talking about?" Ada's eyes swung to her desk and mobile phones, and she cringed at the unheard messages lighting in their electronic corners. Something as important as Anabelle's escape should have crossed her desk the old-fashioned way—in person or conveyed through her secretary, Carla. Next time, she would tell Carla to staple it

309

to her goddamn head if she had to. Ada frowned. "And sit down, already; you're making me nervous."

Nicole sat. "I thought you heard."

"I would have if somebody thought to tell me."

"I'm sorry, I—"

"Just get on with it."

Her enthusiasm obliterated by Ada's annoyance, Nicole was careful with her explanation. "It happened yesterday morning. Apparently, her father picked her up at the 7-11 down the street from the hospital. The nurses didn't know she was gone until Anabelle was already home."

"Good God," Ada groaned.

"It's not like she wasn't better," Nicole reasoned. "Her recovery might've been posted on the internet, for all her parents talked about it. I can't blame them for wanting her home. If my daughter were being held like that, I probably would have done the same thing."

"You're not saying her parents were in on it ..."

"How else would she have gotten home with all the security around the hospital?"

"She wasn't a prisoner," Ada said, for no reason other than to vocalize a half-truth.

For the sake of Garrett's endangered ICU unit, the hospital's medical team had kept her apprised of Anabelle's condition, so Ada knew the voltage running through the girl's body had ceased. But the knowledge didn't lessen her fear that, once at home, Anabelle would begin lighting up the city like a human Tesla coil. Ada also knew there were a great many eyes from the federal administration monitoring Anabelle's case that wouldn't be too pleased to have an *asset*—as they once inadvertently called Anabelle to Ada—on the loose.

310

Nicole crossed her legs and leaned back against the chair. "The Cheevers believe she was. Her father went on record with the *Gazette* just this morning and made a statement that she was being held against her will, if you believe it. Apparently, their lawyer was with them when her doctors showed up at the house and tried to return her to the hospital, but by then the family got the press involved and there was no way they could take her back without making it look like she wasn't being arrested. People would have lost their minds, Ada. She's the miracle survivor. Half the city thinks she's some kind of saint."

A long sigh escaped Ada's lips and she reached for her sparkling water, thinking as she drank. There was no lessening the tragedy of the nurse's murder, but Ada was painfully aware that had she not additionally been dealing with the fallout from Tammy Cormoran's death, she wouldn't have missed news of Anabelle's escape. After a time, Nicole removed her suit jacket and hung it on the back of her seat. Ada noted small sweat stains on Nicole's blouse and recognized for the first time since she had sat down that they were both victims in the same storm.

Ada asked, "How much of this was on the news?"

Nicole shook her head. "Jane Fresley gave me most of it," she said of the Prime Minister's director of communications. "Shifty as they are, they knew they'd be blamed if Anabelle was forced to go back, so they made a deal with the family to allow the team to access Anabelle in exchange for her *freedom*." Nicole's fingers air quoted the last word.

"*Team* meaning what I think it does?"

"Medical, scientific, military, the usual when you've got something weird going on," Nicole said. "And that brings us to the festival. They want to make a splash of her recovery;

311

use it as an endorsement of our technological and intellectual superiority. Wave the hell out of that flag to all the immigrants they think are going to pay off our debt. It'll make him look good; for a while anyway."

Rereading Jane Fresley's letter, Ada knew there was no refusing the proposal. The Prime Minister was coming to Garrett tomorrow morning, where he expected the parade to open with his motorcade, in which he would ride with Anabelle Cheever. Ada's lips fluttered as she blew out her frustration.

"I thought you'd be happy," Nicole said.

"Ecstatic," Ada said, sarcasm oozing out of her. "It's just not a good time right now. People are jamming our help lines because they're worried their water is going to run out. Boyce has got his hands full trying to contain the animal attacks. He's only got two guys and they're busting their backs running around the city. One murder and now there's a rumor spreading we've got a serial killer on the loose. And the protesters aren't just going to go away if we ask them nicely." She threw up her hands.

Nicole stood and went to the window. Two floors down, the smaller gathering she'd earlier elbowed her way through now overtook the entirety of the square. There were banners, signs, flags, cardboard cut-outs with Ada's face and devil horns on them, megaphones, adults, children, teens. The vast majority of the signs vocalized support for the festival, even threatening violence if it was canceled. At the outer rim of the square, however, there stood about a dozen people holding a long banner. *This Is Not the Time to Celebrate*, it read. Beside it were two elderly women struggling with oversized signs of their own. Their *Shame on You* and *Change the Date* signs clipped each other as one of the women stumbled against a bicycle rack.

INTERFERENCE

Looking down at the square, Nicole said, "Most of this will go away once the festival starts. Once they get their beers and their ciders and their cotton candy, there's not going to be a whole lot of protesting. It might be another story afterward, but these people just want to have a little fun, Ada. And they want to know that their city and their government are looking out for them. I think a visit from the PM will solve a lot of our problems."

Ada knew that although outwardly Canada had an unresponsive relationship with demonstrators, they were increasingly being silenced and criminalized across the country. If any of the city's residents ended up in jail because of the PM's visit, it would only infuriate them more, and doubtless they would blame her. When she was little, her mother always told her that the best escape from between a rock and a hard place was to find the weak spot and break right through with a hardness of her own; but when the rocks pushed right back—what then? Ada figured she'd have to choose who she could tangle with most successfully. It certainly was *not* the Prime Minister.

She said to Nicole, "Tell Jane we're delighted to have him, and to let us know if there's anything they need. You're going to coordinate this on our end, then?"

"I've already sent her the information on the staging area and the parade route."

"Dan's aware?"

"He will be," Nicole said. "Now that you're on board."

"I had no choice," Ada said, and dismissed Nicole to begin the inane task of conferring with the Prime Minister's Office.

Alone at her desk, Ada ordered a Greek salad with chicken to be delivered to the security office on the ground floor, wishing she were instead at home in her pajamas with

313

a glass of red wine near the fireplace. She called her husband for her hourly safety check-in. They both knew she would be late again, and Mathew offered to pick her up when she was ready, but Ada declined. If the city was going to jeopardize her safety, it was damn well going to pay for a security detail to see her safely home. She didn't tell Mathew about the special visitor coming tomorrow; she would do that later in bed and let Mathew give her a reason to stay faithful. Ada was already looking forward to it.

A short time later, her desk phone rang, the little red light indicating a call from the building's security department. Her stomach grumbled as she picked up the receiver, expecting that her dinner had been delivered, but instead her head of security, Joseph Weber, asked if she was expecting visitors. Ada said she wasn't and was about to leave it at that when Joseph said, "Can you spare five minutes, Mrs. Falconer?"

"For whom?" Ada asked, wondering who was sly enough to convince Joseph to ask.

"There's four of them, ma'am," Joseph said. "I've got two priests, Dakota Cardinal, and another gentleman. What's your name, sir?" There was a muffled reply and then Joseph reported, "Ed Norman. They say they are waiting on Dan Fogel too."

Two priests walk into a mayor's office ... Ada thought to herself and directed Joseph to have one of his men accompany them upstairs once Dan arrived. She stretched while she waited, leaning her head toward each shoulder, arching her spine in, out, exercising her breath to gain a few moments of peace. Already, the sky outside was dark, and Ada wondered why the meeting couldn't wait. She wasn't particularly religious, so she would have had little issue declining their audience, but if Dan Fogel was part of the group, Ada knew that it would be wise to listen to whatever they had to say.

Her salad was brought up shortly after and she took a few quick bites before there was a knock at the door. Her assistant Carla had already gone home for the evening, so it was Joseph himself who poked his gray head in. His glasses slid down to the end of his nose as he regarded Ada apologetically.

"I appreciate you seeing them, Mrs. Falconer. I just couldn't say no to Father Bonner; we've been going to his church for decades. Tabitha would have killed me."

"No problem, Joseph," Ada said. It was her desire to maintain close relationships with all her staff, so she knew Joseph's wife Tabitha sometimes leashed him up so tight that he couldn't so much as fart without her permission. A vulgar metaphor, she knew, but no less true. Joseph thanked her again and brought Carla's chair into her office so the five men would all have a place to sit.

"Thank you, Joseph," Ada said as he left.

A minute later, Dan Fogel entered, his normally attractive face now fatigued and dappled with shadows. He waited until the other men were seated before he took his own chair to Ada's left, next to the window. Beside him sat a priest in suit and collar that Ada didn't recognize. One chair over was the priest Ada knew as Father Robert Pauliuk of Holy Redeemer, who had suffered the loss of his wife in a fire two decades ago. Next to Father Pauliuk was Dakota Cardinal, whom Ada knew through his leadership in the community. The white-haired stranger on the end was fixated on the picture of her family vacation in Jamaica the year before.

"Beautiful children," the man croaked.

"I had to bribe them with toys to get them to smile for that one," Ada recalled of the time that now seemed ages ago. Five pairs of eyes fell on her chicken salad, so Ada closed the lid and pushed it aside. She said, "I tell my staff not to eat at

315

their desks because no job is so important that you can't take a break, but I think there's an exception for when your city is going to ruin, no?"

Dan held up his palms. "No judgement. We came unannounced anyway." He looked to the other men as if hoping they would speak, but when they didn't, Dan said, "We don't want to keep you, Ada, but there's something we'd like to discuss with you."

"Sounds ominous. Has there been another murder?"

It was the priest beside Dan who spoke. "Not yet."

"Oh?" Ada's stomach suddenly soured, and she took from the small beverage cooler near her bookcase a can of ginger ale. Only the old man accepted her offer of a drink, and Ada passed him a bottle of water before returning to her chair.

"When you hear what they have to tell you," Dan said, "you'll understand that I'm here unofficially. I can't put what they're saying on record because, truthfully, I don't believe it would help any; if anything, I think it could cause a lot of trouble. But I have no reason to doubt them, Ada. None at all. There's been too many incidents these days that we have no answers for. You know it yourself."

"I'm listening," she said, and then each man took his turn explaining his own account of events.

For nearly an hour, Ada listened first to Father Bonner, then to Father Pauliuk, then to Dakota Cardinal, and finally to Ed Norman while Dan Fogel watched them attentively. Occasionally, Ada would glance at Dan to confirm what she was hearing was true, and Dan would nod on and tip his chin to the man who'd made the disclosure. Ada heard of Sylvia Baker, whom they all referred to as "the devil woman," and of her reaching into their heads and into their dreams. She heard of congregants terrified to sleep and of residents

INTERFERENCE

fortifying their homes against demons, and of their agreed recommendation that the Fall Festival be postponed until events in Garrett normalized.

Only, it wasn't really a recommendation. The men before her were absolutely convinced that something terrible was going to happen at the festival, and they were adamant that the only way to prevent calamity was to take away its venue.

When they were finished, Ada asked Dan, "Can't you just arrest her? Isn't there something you can book her on?" Immediately, Ada felt foolish, probably appearing as though she'd watched too many late-night cop dramas, but in the immediate moment she felt it was the most reasonable solution to their problem. This way, they could not only contain their concern but also preserve the city's dignity as one that didn't acknowledge the occult.

Dan said, "I wish I could, but I have nothing to go on. We're not in Salem, and it's not the seventeenth century when we could try her for witchcraft. Unless there's a sudden rise of puritanism, there's nothing we can hold her for. Thanks to the extra support we have right now, I was able to double our patrol for the festival; but if you ask me, I'd rather not have to be there in the first place."

Ada absorbed their alarm, felt it creeping up her tired feet and settling in for a long stay in her already overstimulated nervous system. She leaned back in her chair and folded her arms beneath her breasts, letting out her bottom lip to blow air at her bangs as she looked at the ceiling. The men waited for her to speak, and when she did, Ada found her voice a little unsteady. "I can't expect it was easy for you to come see me, but I want you to know that I'm glad you did. Anything that affects our citizens is important to me ..."

317

Sensing the political niceties were a precursor for their letdown, Dak said, "I've been running things since Perry's been away with his family—"

"Please pass my sincere condolences to his family," Ada interrupted.

"I will. I'm sure he'll appreciate that. I'm grateful for your time, Mrs. Falconer, but I get the feeling that you're not onboard with our proposal. I know it's a lot to digest, and a lot of it doesn't make much sense, but that doesn't make it false. With all due respect, I can't in good conscience let the fair go on, whether or not you agree with us."

Ada blinked at Dak. "Are you saying *you'll* cancel it if I don't?"

"I will," Dak said, his confidence unnerving Ada just a little too much for her liking.

"I'm sorry, Mr. Cardinal, but last I understood, *I* run the ship around here. Whether the festival is going to proceed or not will be entirely of my doing, as I'm sure there will be a hundred other people lining up to take your place if you find yourself unwilling." Ada gestured to the window. "Look outside if you don't believe me. Our citizens want their fair. They want something to take their mind off the terrible things that have happened, and I'm not about to take it away from them. I don't mean to sound harsh, but there are other entities at play here besides some woman planning a trick. We've got a very capable and competent police force, and we've been fortified by equally capable and competent law enforcement partners. If something were to happen, we would be more than prepared to deal with it. Now, if we understand each other, I have work to do."

Ada made to rise, but Dan held out his hand as if to stop her. "Wait a minute, Ada, there's no need to get like that. You know me. You know I would never bring something to you that I didn't believe in myself. You have to believe me on this one. I know it sounds crazy, and I know that what we're asking you to do is going to cause a lot of headaches around here. But it's what we need to do to keep people safe. If I'm wrong, well, then that's on me. I'll take full responsibility for this one; resign if I have to." The other men swelled with admiration for Dan, and he took in their collective respect and gave it right back to them. "We're not some ragtag bunch of troublemakers, Ada. You've got the best citizens in the entire community right in front of you, begging for you to do the right thing. It would be wise to listen to them."

"I'm sorry, Dan, I just can't do it. I want to believe you, and I'm not saying I don't, but how would it look if I tell people they can't enjoy a day out with their families because we're scared the boogeyman is going to get them? The media would have a heyday with that one."

"It's not like that, Ada," Dan argued.

"It's exactly like that," Ada said, ignoring the priests' frowns. "But it's not the only reason I won't make that call. Because I respect you and because I know that you'll keep in confidence what I'm about to tell you, you need to understand that my inclination *is* to do exactly as you suggest—as I *was* prepared to do a few days ago, mind you—but now my hands are tied. Right before you gentlemen came in, I was informed that the Prime Minister will be opening our parade."

The men gasped. Father Bonner and Father Pauliuk crossed themselves, Dak reached for his medicine wheel, Ed's hand went to the soft flesh above his pacemaker, and Dan buried the lower half of his face in his steepled fingers. "You have to tell them it's canceled," Dan said. "There's no other way, Ada. He's in real danger here. You can't let him come."

319

"I have no choice," Ada said. "They're already making arrangements. If I tell his team not to come because we feel something bad is going to happen, they'll ask me to back it up—and if I try, they'll have me *committed*. I'm just as frustrated as you are, but we've got to work with what we've got. Whatever the size of your team tomorrow, double it again. With his protection detail, that should be more than enough."

"I told you, Ada, we've already done that," Dan said.

"And I told you to double it again," she countered.

Already, Dan was calculating how many additional officers he could pull, but the numbers were grim. "We don't have the manpower, Ada."

"*Get* the manpower," she ordered. "And keep me updated if anything changes."

Then Ada shook each man's hand. It was Father Pauliuk who held on a little longer and offered her a blessing, which she ashamedly accepted. The touch of the preacher's hand suffused her with a guilt so deep she stifled the shudder rising to her shoulders. She wished she could give them what they wanted, but what they wanted was career suicide. After busting her ass to get where she was, Ada simply wasn't about to let it go, nor was she willing to make the city a public spectacle more than it already was. As she saw the men out, she thought she heard one of them say, "Lord have mercy," and realized uneasily that it came from neither priest.

33

In homes, in apartments, in condominiums, on the streets, a disquiet fell over the city. Streetlights and porch-lights spilled onto vacant spaces, upon which a short time earlier residents had rushed, preparing for something that poked at their anxieties for no particular reason, except to the dreamers.

Believers in Buddha, in God, in the Creator and in a great many spirits and gods and goddesses were compelled to pray. Puja was repeatedly practiced by Garrett's Hindu population. The city's Anglican, Lutheran, Catholic, and Baptist churches hosted impromptu evening services to soothe Gentile souls, and even Garrett's lone synagogue was full of anxious Jews.

Even so, residents anticipated the next day's festival with an exultation not experienced since Fauville tour bus number 587 plummeted from the Callingwood Bridge on that windy morning three weeks ago. Meticulous routes through the fairground were drafted by children eager for their annual carnival rides, candy, and games, while astute parents crafted their own methods for spreading the fun on limited budgets. This year everyone was willing to spend a little more.

Having been rejected by Ada, Dak returned home, where Nikonha was waiting with his family, while the others returned to Holy Redeemer to plan. There lurked a malignance in the outside darkness that the Cardinal family was unable to evade, so they took their ceremony to the living room and opened a window to let the unwanted energy out. Soon, smells of cedar, sweetgrass, sage, and tobacco reassured the Cardinal family and their Elder.

Rising from her prayer blanket, Nikonha said to them, "I've spoken to our knowledge keepers. We will gather at sunrise tomorrow to purify the fairgrounds. It's the best we can do."

Sunrise ceremonies were usually a great comfort to Dak, for they were the times when he reflected with gratitude on the many blessings in his life. When the boys were younger, they sleepily attended all of Nikonha's ceremonies, and though their attendance somewhat dwindled as they grew into men, Dak knew the experience was part of who they became. The ceremonies had prepared them well. Though as he looked at their worried faces, he only hoped it was enough.

Nikonha stayed with them, reflecting, beseeching the spirits for protection, cleansing the bad energy around them until her voice began to crack and her eyelids became heavy, and she could stay no more. Dak offered Nikonha his and Wendy's bedroom, but she declined. "I need my bed if I am going to have strength tomorrow, and so do you," she said, touching his arm tenderly and accepting their hugs until she finally departed.

Full of worry, each member of the Cardinal house spent the rest of the evening imagining everything that could go wrong, while on the other side of the city, in Father Pauliuk's office, Father Bonner deflected Dan's apologies for Ada's decision.

"You did your best, Daniel. If it weren't for you, I fear she wouldn't have blessed us with her presence in the first place. At one time, our collars would have granted us the

INTERFERENCE

freedom of kingdoms, but these days it seems we need a hall pass just to get from A to B. I know I'm being facetious, but it is what it is sometimes. As long as we rely on the Father, everything works out." He smiled weakly at Dan.

Just then, Julia entered carrying a tray of sandwiches and juice boxes. The low-heeled pumps she'd worn earlier had been replaced with a pair of fuzzy pink slippers, and she had changed into an ankle-length floral dressing gown and peach-colored robe.

"Don't mind me, gentlemen," Julia said. "I figured if I'm going to be here all night, I might as well make myself comfortable. Here, we've got some sandwiches and juice for you. They're still fresh and you look like you could use them. Please help yourself."

Father Bonner and Dan began unwrapping tuna sandwiches.

"How many do you figure we have now, Julia?" Father Pauliuk asked, poking a straw into his juice box.

"Last count was a hundred and seventy-six," Julia told him. "But they're still trickling in."

"And how many are staying the night?"

"As far as I know … *all* of them, Father."

The men stopped eating and looked from Julia to the other priest. "All … of them?" Father Pauliuk asked.

Julia nodded. "They've brought their own blankets and pillows and quite a few have air mattresses and sleeping mats, so it's going to be one big slumber party." Her eyes squinted into little half moons as she grinned. "Nancy's son opened the school and lent them all of their gym mats too."

"Thank you for coordinating this, Julia. Please let them know we'll begin vespers about ten minutes late."

"I will, Father," Julia said.

323

"I suspect I'll have the same to look forward to when I return to my own parish," Father Bonner said when Julia left. "A blessing, for sure, but not without its challenges. Praise the Lord." He finished his sandwich and turned to Dan. "Will you be joining us this evening?"

Dan shook his head. "I wish I could. When I was a boy, you'd never keep me from a slumber party, especially in such good company, Father, but I have to figure out my schedule now. I have no idea how I'm going to do it." He sighed. "You know the story of the loaves of bread and the fish?" Both priests nodded. Dan said, "Well, if there's a way we can make a thousand constables out of a few dozen, I'd be happy to hear about it."

Father Bonner brightened. "That's exactly what we're going to do."

"I don't understand," Dan said.

The older priest's white eyebrows crested so high in his forehead Dan thought they just might fly away. "We are going to create our own army, Daniel. We are going to gather the believers across the city and thrust our prayers against the devil-woman and every other brute out there. You have your guns and your vests to protect you, but the first layer of protection will always be God. There are one hundred and seventy-six soldiers of God in this building, and more coming by the minute. I believe there are hundreds, if not a thousand more people in our city that will lean on that impenetrable power tonight. They might not know why, but that doesn't matter. All that matters is that they *do*. We will take care of our flocks tonight and we will prepare them for whatever is going to occur tomorrow. I say we put out a call to prayer just before the festival starts. Maybe right after the parade, when everyone will be gathered together." Father

Bonner slid aside the cuff of his sleeve to peek at his watch. "I will do my best to fortify our troops during vespers and again in matins, but let's set a place to bring everyone together. Does the staging area work? Robert, the Botchers are members of your church; do you think you could ask Roy if he'll allow us that space near the greenhouse? We've only got an hour between the end of the parade and the opening of the fairgrounds. Thirty minutes should be enough."

"Of course," Father Pauliuk replied. "Good plan, Alistair. I know a lot of folks have been working hard on their floats, but I think we're up for battle if we try to convince them they don't need their cinnamon donuts or coasters afterward. Especially now."

Father Bonner nodded. "We'll have to do our best."

Dan stood and tapped Father Pauliuk's desk. He said, "Well, I'll leave you to it. Let's hope it all works out tomorrow, huh?"

But as Dan walked out, Father Pauliuk and Father Bonner looked at each other, certain that hope was not enough.

34

The red fingers of the sun began touching the horizon just as volunteers were finishing their preparations for the annual Festival Flapjack Breakfast under the big white tents on the northern edge of the fairground. At the beverage station, seven silver urns of coffee were arranged beside carafes of steeped tea and cartons of juice and milk, which Perry Searles gloomily nudged together to keep them from falling off the crowded tabletop.

He filled his thermos with black coffee and surveyed the space around him, his trancelike grief thwarting demands for perfection typical of him. He'd left his clipboard in his truck, and he didn't care to retrieve it; the loss of his grandchildren weighed so heavily on his soul that he cared for nothing any longer. Previously the smell of bacon being cooked just a minute too long or the vision of syrup drips on the freshly dressed tables would send him into a hair-pulling tizzy, but now he regarded these imperfections placidly. They could burn the food and smother the tables, for all that Perry was concerned.

From behind, Dak clapped Perry on the shoulder. "You okay there, Per? I think we've got it under control; you can go if you want."

INTERFERENCE

Dak's touch seemed to tug Perry from somewhere so far away he wasn't sure Perry would ever respond. Then Perry said, "Nah. Dora's coming with Catherine and the baby. They don't want to be alone. The fresh air will be good for them." His hand went to the back of his head to smooth down thin vestiges of graying hair.

"Kevin coming?" Dak asked of Perry's son.

Perry shook his head. "Haven't been able to get him out of the house since the funeral. He's taken a month off work, but I don't know if he'll ever be ready to go back. I try to get him out, but he doesn't want to see anyone, you know? God, I wish it had been *me* instead. They were just kids, dammit, they were just kids." Spittle flew from Perry's mouth as he tried to contain his anguish. Dak squeezed his shoulder, letting him cry.

Outside the tent, conversation buzzed as the line began to build. Perry wiped his face. "I'd like to let Dora and Catherine eat first, if it's all right with you, Dak. They don't need everyone staring at them the whole time."

"Of course," Dak said. Perry began to step away, but Dak reached for his arm. "Perry?"

"Yeah?"

Too late Dak realized that he didn't know how to broach the subject of Sylvia Baker or the thing inside her in a manner that would make Perry believe him. He didn't care about feeling foolish; he just did not want this man to suffer any more than he already had. "You know I wouldn't lie to you, right Perry?"

Perry turned around and blinked at him. "About what? Something wrong, Dak?"

"I think you should take your family and go. Have your pancakes, eat up and all that, but I think it would be wise to leave right after."

327

"Are you saying we're not welcome? I know my absence has created a pile of work for you, but—"

"It's not that, Perry. You did all the heavy lifting for months; you did a hell of a fine job, so there wasn't much for me to do. It's just—now hear me out before you say anything—I have a bad feeling about today. I know it sounds strange, but … you and I, we both believe in a higher power, don't we?"

"I'm not so sure anymore," Perry admitted, more depressed than curious about where Dak was leading him. "I did, or maybe I still do, but when you have your guts pulled out of you like we did, it's hard to believe in anything. If there *is* someone up there"—Perry jerked a thumb upward—"then they're sure playing one hell of a sick joke on us."

"You ever think about it the other way?" Dak ventured cautiously. "What if all this is because of someone else? Someone evil. If we believe in good, then we can't deny the bad, can we?"

Perry frowned. "You're goddamn right it's evil. I don't know what you're getting at, Dak, but I'm in no mood for a theological discussion. If you have something to say, say it and let me be."

Dak drew from Nikonha's advice to hear beyond words if he wanted to understand Perry's heart, so he knew there was little he could say that would help his friend feel better. At last, he decided to be honest. "Something's going to happen today, Perry. I don't know what, but I feel it in my soul. And I'm not the only one. All around the city, people have been dreaming about it, the *same* dream in a thousand different heads. I personally know of two churches that were full last night because people are terrified. Our Elders, they're sensing something too, and whatever it is, it's not right. I'm not sure what it all means, but I couldn't live with myself if I didn't tell you about it and something bad happened."

Perry stepped back. For a moment, Dak thought he'd angered him, sure that what he was telling Perry had crushed the last traces of his strength. Instead, Perry's gray eyes bore into him with new alertness. He said, "Catherine's been having nightmares. Or she *was* having them. The docs gave her drugs and she's been doing better the last few days; now she says she doesn't remember her dreams any more but before … before they were awful. We figured it was because of the kids, you know. Anyone would have nightmares after something like that."

"What were her nightmares about?" Dak asked.

"She wouldn't tell us. But now I wonder." Perry looked at the entrance of the tent, where his wife, daughter-in-law, and remaining granddaughter were walking in.

"Eat and then get them out of here," Dak warned Perry again.

"I think we'll take it to go," Perry said, no longer in the conversation, already with his family. He dashed behind the serving table for Styrofoam containers while his curious wife mouthed her confusion to him.

Satisfied he'd done what he could to protect Perry and content with the steady progress of breakfast being cooked and distributed to the hungry crowd, Dak took leave and hustled to the pavilion a field's length away. There, under the cedar roof, Nikonha had gathered sixteen Elders, already accepting their medicine. A haze of smoke traveled up their shoulders, necks, faces as Nikonha's eagle feather circulated in front of them.

June Good Leaf's small chin and high cheeks were pink with cool morning air. She bustled up her scarf to keep from aggravating her arthritis, but the wind found its way to her skin in other areas, pinching her here, poking her there until she couldn't help but shiver. Seeing June struggle, Dak removed his jacket and covered her small body, insisting that his sweater was all he needed. Between Wendy and the boys, he found his place.

They crowded in on him, sharing their warmth, and Nikonha's eagle feather appeared in front of Mavis, then Sarah, then Jesse, then Johnny, Dak and Wendy. The family purified their souls, extending their peace outward as far as they could to rid the area of bad energy. When it was over, Nikonha collected her prayer blanket.

Edward and Lillian Leveque, married for fifty-nine years, strode as fast as their failing hips would take them toward Nikonha, wanting to speak to her first so that they might also be the first to sit. June's short fingers, clasped around a jar of freshly made crab apple jam, stretched to Nikonha, who graciously accepted the gift. Edward produced an eagle feather of his own from a leather pouch near his hip, the tremor in his blue-veined hands jittering the feather until Nikonha gently received it in her open palms.

"The eagle doesn't fear." Edward's deep voice carried throughout the pavilion. "We must be like the eagle." The others around him nodded their agreement. Now he addressed Dak and Wendy. "I felt the evil you are talking about. They waited until my head was bowed and my eyes were closed and then they *went* for me." Edward pulled up his coat sleeve, where an angry red welt was braceleted around his wrist. "They tried to pull me down, but I was stronger. I shook them off with my determination. There is a war approaching, and we cannot run from the battleground, Dakota. June and I will stay here as long as you need us."

Cherie Farmer, Russell Honyoust, and Georgina Poodry, whose eyesight began deteriorating three decades earlier, requested closer inspection of Edward's wrist. He instantly obliged by thrusting his arm under their noses. Their intake of breath was felt among all of them, like berries from the same vine. Collectively they soured, doubling their attention to the invisible things around them, agreeing to stay nearby should they be needed while Dak returned to his duties at the breakfast tent.

Across the field, Dak walked with his sons. He couldn't help but reach for them, appreciating how fine they'd turned out to be, knowing he'd give his life to protect them. Usually they blushed at his attention, but now they accepted his arms on their shoulders, and it was wild-timing Johnny who said, "I love you, Dad."

"You planning on going somewhere?" Dak asked, frightened by the deeper significance of Johnny's declaration.

"Not for a long time."

"Good." Dak squeezed him.

Just before they got to the tent, they embraced. They hadn't had a group hug since the boys were toddlers, and the memory of his sons clamoring over each other in their pyjamas to get at him constricted his throat and drew tears from his eyes. He held them tight, knowing the lone silhouette standing just outside of the pavilion was Wendy, watching them from afar. He waved. When she waved back, he let their boys go. "I'll only be in here for a little while," he told Jesse and Johnny, wiping his face. "I'll meet you at the staging area once I'm done but, I beg you, if you see that woman, stay the hell away from her, you hear me?"

"I'm not going anywhere near her," Johnny said, holding up the hand with two missing fingers.

"We'll keep an eye out," Jesse told his father, and they parted.

331

35

In the back area of the breakfast tent reserved for volunteers, Anabelle groaned as yet another gaping woman begged her parents to let her take a picture of "Garrett's miracle girl." Her father explained that Anabelle would rather be left alone, to which the woman acquiesced by indecently snapping a picture over his shoulder anyway. Anabelle figured that by the time she finished breakfast, her picture would be tucked inside every cellphone in the city, but she went on nibbling at her food, furious that her continued release had been predicated on a PR stunt. As far as Anabelle was concerned, she was voting against the attention-hoarding asshole in the next election, and she brooded on this as she choked down her pancakes.

The call from the Prime Minister's office two days earlier had surprised her parents, but little surprised Anabelle anymore, not even Robbie's sudden devotion. They'd been seeing each other exclusively for only a few short months, and Anabelle had yet to declare her love for him because she didn't love him, and maybe never would. Only, since she'd been released Robbie insisted on declaring *his* love for her. Over and over and over again. His puppy dog sadness when she didn't respond likewise annoyed Anabelle to the point that she unintentionally zapped Robbie when he tried to rub her back.

Though he squealed in pain, she felt not even a little guilty when she told him the electric blanket they were lying under must have been defective. Adoringly, Robbie believed her.

Now, as he sat beside her with his hand on her leg, she didn't mind his attention. The bitches with whom she'd graduated high school congregated at the closest table, eying Robbie ravenously, if only for his proximity to the most famous person in the city. Lauren Hunt, Meg Wilmingdon, and Addison Farrah—all in a constant state of preening in case members of the media arrived—winked at Robbie, then waved ingratiatingly with their pinky fingers at Anabelle whenever they could catch her attention. Anabelle made a point of waving to everyone *behind* the sycophantic trio, going as far as shaping a heart with her hands and raising it to Clara Piggle, the sweet but desperately nerdy trumpet player in Garrett High's choir assembly.

Through it all, Anabelle could not ignore the evil beings around them. The ones that had surrounded her in the hospital now collected here, hissing and scratching on the table, on diners' laps, around ankles, on top of their food. The black pits of their eyes were trained on Anabelle, only on Anabelle, following her every movement, her every breath. They knew her secret and, like every boy in her eleventh-grade class, wanted to excise a singular piece of her power for the authority it bestowed.

As she had in the hospital, Anabelle zapped these creatures, presently doing so with a cough, a sneeze, a scratch, so that the working of her fingers was unremarkable to all who should see. Since her release, she'd practiced her new skill whenever she was alone and came know the depth of her reach. She knew, for instance, that she could fry Addison Farrah's long blond hair or melt Meg's ridiculous sunglasses like

333

an egg cracked on the top of her head if she wanted to. Small advantages, but no less appealing.

On a small stage in the adjacent tent, Garrett's own Ten Fingers from Heaven began their first set of the day. Lead singer Sidney Hayes bid the volunteers and parade participants a glorious morning, then her smooth, rhythmic voice suffused her listeners with a serenity not experienced in weeks. Cups were cradled to chests, ears were lifted to melody, and a great many shoulders swayed between first and second helpings. It wasn't until her mother tapped her hand that Anabelle realized she was speaking.

"Huh?" she asked.

"I said 'Dr. Huxley is asking how you're feeling'." Her mother gestured to the doctor sitting at the end of the table.

He was so quiet Anabelle had almost forgotten about him, and she gave him credit for his discretion. It was obvious the doctor was as uncomfortable with babysitting Anabelle as she was because he made a considerable effort to minimize his presence. Until this morning, his visits had been scheduled at her home twice daily to ensure there was no recurrence of what he called "her curiosities." His examinations were thorough but brief, and not once had he suspected she still had more energy in her body than an atomic bomb. She didn't know *how* she knew this, only that in the middle of the night when she couldn't sleep, she had wandered onto her back deck for some fresh air and—with the city sleeping and no one to spy on her—Anabelle had targeted a maple tree five blocks away at the bottom slope of their community. With a twitch of her finger, she'd obliterated the fifty-foot tree into a splintering of toothpicks.

"Anabelle?" Dr. Huxley asked now. "Are you okay?" He rested his fork on his plate but made no move toward her.

INTERFERENCE

Anyone looking on might think of the doctor as a concerned uncle or older relative, and for that she was grateful.

"I'm fine. It's just a lot to take in," she admitted. "I was just thinking about how my grandparents loved this pancake breakfast. My Grandpa Earl always brought his own syrup with him. One cup syrup, one cup whisky, together in a flask. He said it was the only way real men ate pancakes." She laughed and her parents joined in.

"That's right." Her father pounded the table with his fist, recalling his father-in-law trying to get him drunk on syrup at the festival breakfast each and every year.

Huxley looked down at his plate; his own pancakes were suddenly less appetizing. "I'll never look at pancakes the same way again," he said.

William clapped Huxley on the back. "Next time you're over, we'll make you some with the *real* syrup."

"It'll have to be a warm day so I can walk home," Huxley reasoned. Then he said to Anabelle, "After being stuck with me for so long, it must feel good to get out, huh?"

"It feels weird," she agreed.

Huxley nodded. "That's normal. I haven't had a patient yet who spent as much time as you had in the hospital and felt normal returning to regular life. The feeling passes before you know it. And once you don't have to see my ugly mug every day, you'll feel even better."

His paternal smile warmed her. "You know, you're not so bad for a doctor."

"I'll tell the others you said that," Huxley joked. "All kidding aside, you're a hell of a trooper, with all we put you through."

Robbie's hand rose from her leg and slipped around her neck. "She's amazing, isn't she?"

335

Inside, Anabelle cringed, suppressing the urge to zap Robbie's stifling hand into the next province. She realized their breakup was inevitable, but it was too much work for her to consider at the moment. She had other demons to wrestle, the real kind, and she didn't need Robbie complicating things any more than they already were. "I'm just glad it's over," she said to Huxley, leaning forward to eat over her plate so that Robbie would be obliged to release his grip on her.

Susan said, "We're all glad it's over, hun." She touched the small hairs at the base of Anabelle's ponytail. "Dad and I were thinking that after the festival is over ... what do you say if we all go on a vacation somewhere? Get away from it all for a few weeks. Hawaii might be nice, or somewhere more exotic like Spain or ... oooo! You've always wanted to visit Greece. We can book the trip this week. What do you think?"

Anabelle's desire to travel conflicted with the demands of her education; she was already three weeks behind. The university had been gracious enough to allow her an exemption on her midterm exams as long she completed the assignments she'd missed, even offering a tutor to help get her back on track. They, too, knew the world would be anticipating her return to school and were doing everything they could to accommodate Canada's golden child.

Although Anabelle was ready to return to her studies, she knew the endeavor would be impossible with the spirits lurking everywhere she went. They debated the idea until Dr. Huxley said he would talk to the school and try to work out an arrangement for Anabelle to complete the remainder of the semester remotely. As far as her parents were concerned, this was a brilliant idea, and they began discussing their travel plans. They didn't know that as they deliberated between

Bora Bora and Athens and Waikiki and Barcelona, Anabelle couldn't help but wonder if she would live the rest of her life like a human insect zapper.

She was sipping the latte Robbie had brought for her when a cramp caused her to wince. She dropped her fork and turned to the entrance—where the nurse-killer appeared. Lauren, Meg, and Addison's attentions went instinctively to the handsome lawyer, who was shaking the hand of a departing Perry Searles. The group of swooning middle-aged women huddling nearby stepped aside to let Perry out and Troy in when Anabelle realized that on his murderous arm was the hand of her old crossing guard. A rush of whispers muffled the sound of the music while an interior wind was produced by the sudden fluttering of eyelashes, the constriction of stomachs, and the expansion of breasts. Inattentive husbands and boyfriends, sensing the gale force of foreign masculinity, scrambled to fill their partners' plates and cups to keep them from wandering too far.

Hoping to avoid Troy, Anabelle stood and made the feeble excuse that she wanted to relax before the parade, but it was too late. Her father's thick arm was already up and waving Troy and his mother toward their table.

"Sit for five minutes and then I'll come with you," her mother instructed with a gentle hand on her wrist. Reluctantly, Anabelle returned to her place beside Robbie, who wrapped a protective arm around her waist. This time she didn't try to force him away.

In a few short moments, arrangements were made at the table. Plates and bodies were hastily shuffled, and Anabelle was squished against Robbie's lap by the time they were finished. Her new self sensed Troy's movement toward the table like the pull of a magnet. Then he and his mother were lowering themselves onto the plastic chairs directly across from her. A voltaic panic rose from her toes to her intestines to the spongy flesh of her lungs until every part of her was on edge, fully charged. Clutching her empty coffee cup, Anabelle pretended to sip, if only to have something to do while she tried extricating the unwanted vision of Troy's hands around the nurse's neck. Around him, the demons receded to the periphery, still there but impelled away like pepper water from soap.

Anabelle noticed that at the sight of the lawyer, Dr. Huxley grew noticeably uneasy. Politely nodding a stiff greeting, the doctor tried to hide his animosity by keeping his mouth full so Troy wouldn't be compelled to speak to him, and Anabelle made a mental note to insist her parents discontinue the lawsuit against the hospital. She didn't want or need any money. She only wanted to be as far away from Troy as possible.

"I see you've brought company," Susan said warmly of Sylvia, whose overly made-up face shone bright with peach lipstick and heavy matching blush.

Troy smiled at his mother. "She's never missed a year."

Clutching her wicker bag, the old woman said, "I hope I'm not intruding. I haven't gone out much since my stroke, and Troy was kind enough to offer to take me today." The duality of her voice—warming like freshly-baked oatmeal cookies yet chilling like a tarantula on the back of a neck—turned Anabelle's stomach. From left to right, Anabelle watched to see the others' reactions, but her parents and Robbie seemed enamored with the grandmotherly apparition. Dr. Huxley, though, stopped chewing and tilted his head as if he hadn't heard quite right.

INTERFERENCE

"Not at all. Not at all" Her father waved the woman's concern away. "Glad you could join us. You know, your son has been so helpful to us since the accident, meeting us at all hours. I worry we've got him too tied up, but I suppose over a good breakfast like this isn't the worst time to chat."

"A man's got to eat," Troy said, and Anabelle felt that pull again. "Speaking of which, I better get us some plates before it's gone. What would you like, Mother?" The old woman did not turn to Troy but kept her eyes on Anabelle, the parting of her mouth to give her order like the tremor before an earthquake.

"Hey," Dr. Huxley said now, absently glancing at his watch. "It's time to check our patient. She's got to be in top shape for her big debut in an hour. We'll scoot over to the medical tent, if that's okay with you, Anabelle?" He stood, waiting.

In a flash, Sylvia's hand shot across the table and clamped down on Anabelle's arm. Her mother, father, and Robbie were all looking at the doctor and so missed the woman's panther-like reflex. "Do stay a while, child. Don't let an old woman spoil your morning. We will be gone before you know what's happened." The weight on Anabelle's arm was absurdly heavy, and she would have zapped it off if it weren't for the risk of exposing her power.

Sylvia exuded such elderly vulnerability to her mother that Susan said, "Just a few minutes more, Doctor?"

"I've been directed—" the doctor started.

"Nonsense," Sylvia said with a congenial croak.

He looked from Anabelle to Sylvia, back and forth, weighing how much he was prepared to argue with the woman who, for reasons he was unable to articulate, gave him the creeps. Just then, Troy returned to the table, and

339

with him, many sets of eyes. Huxley relented, preferring not to engage with an elderly woman in front of a crowd.

"I can spare five minutes," he said, and sat back down.

"Wonderful," Sylvia said, the dragging of her hand from Anabelle's skin rough like sandpaper. She began nibbling at her food while Troy maneuvered his fork and knife with his bandaged hands.

"How are the hands, Troy?" William asked.

Troy turned his palms upward. Everyone at the table inspected the clean white gauze. "I'm not a ball player, so I can't complain. My fingers are fine. Palms are a bit itchy, though."

"A sign of healing," Huxley offered, noting that though they were attempting to appear otherwise, the mother-son duo was attuned to Anabelle's every movement. Their parted lips seemed to suck at her far-away exhalations. Huxley watched Anabelle's oblivious parents make polite, if guarded, conversation with the lawyer. Everyone at the table knew Anabelle would be riding in the Prime Minister's motorcade during the parade, and it was quietly discussed that Anabelle should get his autograph for her remaining grandparents, who would be thrilled. Again, Huxley looked at his watch.

There was a slight movement near Sylvia's waist, and Huxley suspected she'd elbowed her son, because Troy suddenly said, "If you don't mind, doctor, I'd like just a minute with my clients. I can walk Anabelle over to the medical tent right after, if you'd like. We won't be long."

Immediately Anabelle paled. Perhaps because it was his job to evaluate the human body, or perhaps because he was alert to a change in his patient since Troy and his mother had arrived, Huxley caught a faint push of perspiration on Anabelle's cheeks and a slight quiver on her lips. In the days since

INTERFERENCE

she'd been released, Anabelle appeared the epitome of health and vitality, but now she appeared to suffer—and from what, Huxley wasn't sure. His experience had taught him to take changes in a patient's health seriously, an understanding doubly important given Anabelle's experience and his orders from the government. Frowning, he said, "I'm sorry, but it can't wait any longer." When he saw Troy's ready objection on his face, Huxley added, "I have my orders. I hope you understand, Mr. Baker."

"Of course," Troy acquiesced. "We'll finish up here and walk her back from the tent. I have just a few questions. It won't take long, Anabelle."

Anabelle's stomach turned as her parents dumbly, naively nodded their approval of Troy's plan. Then she followed Dr. Huxley away from the table.

36

The late October morning was appropriately cool outside the breakfast tent, causing Huxley and Anabelle to pull up the collars of their jackets while they walked the short distance to the first-aid station in the small white tent near the middle of the field. The grass released its dew against their feet, and soon their shoes were glistening with moisture. Already Anabelle's color had returned, and she again seemed the flourishing young woman Huxley knew her to be. Without turning to him, Anabelle said, "You didn't need to examine me now, did you?"

"Not for the reasons they think," Huxley said, shaking his head. "But I can't discount that I felt you were uncomfortable there for a moment. Were you?" When Anabelle didn't respond, he slowed his pace. "Look, I'm sure I'm not your favorite person right now, but you need to understand that we did everything we could to protect you. Between you and me, I think it's good that you're home now. I'd have preferred you not to force it on us, but it certainly expedited things, and I think for the better. I can't see that there's anything wrong with you, Anabelle, but I'm wondering if there's something strange between you and those two that might cause you problems." At this, her eyes swept to him. "I won't try to convince you to not sue us. That's completely your decision and you have the right to do that if you want to, but my instinct tells me your reactions at the table have nothing to do with that. Am I correct?" The tightening of her jaw confirmed Huxley's suspicion. Quietly he said, "You know that everything you say to me is confidential, right?"

"To everyone?" Anabelle asked. "What about those guys in suits? I'm sure they'd have something to say about that." She soured at the memory of the secretive agents who were more interested in her condition than even her parents.

"They're not here, and I'm not recording this. In fact, let's say I might just forget everything you tell me by the time it comes out of your mouth."

She dismissed his offer. "You'll think I'm crazy."

"You should hear the things I hear sometimes, but you can't because it's private, like I told you. And nothing you say could make me think you're crazy. After all you've been through, you'd have a right to be, but you're not. You haven't begun talking to chairs or anything, have you?" Huxley asked. Anabelle shook her head. "Well then, I'm all ears if you have something to say."

The big red cross at the first aid station hung in front of them. A plastic window in the front of the tarp let them know that there were people inside. "If I ask them for privacy, what are the chances we'll talk?" Huxley asked.

She hadn't shared her secrets with anyone so far, so her doctor's offer was beyond tempting, especially if he was legally bound not to share them with anyone. It was exhausting keeping her knowledge to herself, draining her almost as much as brain surgery had, and Anabelle felt that if she could release even a little of that pressure, she might finally be in a better mind space to solve her problems. Demons swirled around the doctor as she considered him. "What's my guarantee that you won't say anything?" she asked.

S. L. LUCK

Huxley thought and drew his cellphone from his pocket. "Would it help if I showed you my NDA agreement? I might have a copy in my email somewhere."

"It's a good start," Anabelle said, half-convinced.

"How 'bout I tell you a secret of my own, then? Something that nobody else knows, and if it got out, it would end my career. Would that work?"

He hadn't known he was going to say this until he said it, but Huxley surmised that it was the only way he was going to get her to talk. It wasn't exactly true that no one knew his secret, for he'd told his wife in a middle-of-the-night confession decades ago—and though he'd spoken not a word of it since that day, he never forgot how good it had felt to unburden himself in that moment. Furthermore, he didn't believe that Anabelle would divulge his secret to anyone, since he had saved her life in the operating room. After witnessing the peculiar duo, particularly the mother who seemed for some reason not of this world, sharing his secret was a chance Huxley was willing to take.

Anabelle said, "You don't have to."

"Are you going to tell?"

"No."

"Then I will," Huxley said and pretended to tie his shoe should Troy and his mother be watching their pause outside of the first aid station. "I watched another doctor remove the wrong kidney from a patient and said nothing about it. It was early in my residency, and I was on call. That means I have to be not only available but also sober. Back then I dabbled a bit with substances I shouldn't have, so I was terrified that if I reported the doctor, they would find out that I was high." His breath came out of him heavy and long and when he looked back up at her, Anabelle saw that color had flushed his cheeks.

344

"Did ..." Anabelle started.

"He survived. The kidney was put back in before the guy left surgery, but there was a hell of a lot of coverup. I haven't had a drop of anything since."

Just then the tent flap opened, and a man with an official-looking lanyard stepped out. "Can I help you folks?" he asked.

Huxley drew out the documentation he'd received from Canada's chief public health officer and explained his need for privacy inside the tent. Understanding dawned on the man's face. He looked at Anabelle as would a young hockey player seeing Gretzky for the first time and immediately stepped aside. "Of course. We haven't had any patients yet this morning, but that'll come once the fair opens and those crappy rides start jiggling people about. It's all yours." He poked his head inside and called his three co-workers to join him for pancakes. They happily obliged. Huxley pushed aside the door flap, and he and Anabelle disappeared from view.

As Huxley performed a cursory examination behind one of the several partitions, Anabelle whispered, "It wasn't your fault."

"If I'd been clean, it wouldn't have happened," Huxley admitted honestly. "Are we going to talk, Anabelle? If we are, we don't have much time."

She bit her lip and revealed her memories of the fog. The doctor listened carefully, and because he didn't ask her questions or betray any emotion besides interest, she told him everything except that she could obliterate a tree from a mile away. That was one secret she wouldn't share with anyone.

Anabelle packed her story into the tidy space of a few minutes, and when she was done, Huxley was so overwhelmed he had to sit. "May I?" he pointed to the space beside Anabelle

345

on a cot. She nodded and he slumped down, the invisible weight on his shoulders now making him crouch him like a much older man.

"Are you okay, Dr. Huxley?"

He sighed an affirmation and said, "I'm just trying to figure out how to report a murderer to the police without appearing like I'm still on drugs. I'm not saying this because I don't believe you, Anabelle. There was something about that woman that didn't sit right with me, more than even him, and my instincts have never served me wrong. But I'm not sure what to do with this information. If it's okay with you, I'd like to call my friend on this one; he's with the police department." He held up his hands. "I promised you I won't say anything, and I won't, but this is a guy I can talk to about things without having to go into too much detail. I'd like to have him keep an eye on both of them. Is that okay with you?"

Anabelle's ponytail jostled against her back as she nodded her agreement. "Thanks for listening," she told Huxley, but before Huxley could respond, Troy was outside the door flap, asking for her. She had to concentrate to keep her bladder from releasing—and when she looked at Huxley, he saw not fear but outright terror on her face. "I can't go with him. Please don't make me go with him. Please."

His text message to Dan was instant. *Need help quick. Come to first aid tent. I'll explain later. Tell no one. Hux.* He left Anabelle shaking on the cot, and went to the entrance flap, sticking his head out to see Troy and his mother waiting like two wolves for Red Riding Hood to start her journey. "Almost done. A few more minutes and I'll send her out," Huxley told them, and whether it was because of the wide dilation of their pupils or the obvious stifling of their anticipation, the hair on the back of his neck stood up.

346

INTERFERENCE

"The poor dear isn't sick, is she?" From the crumpled crevice of her grandmotherly mouth, Sylvia's voice slithered outward, testing for traps, for truth; the way her knotted hands coiled around her wicker bag, constricting, suggested an underlying power far beyond her appearance.

Huxley seized on Sylvia's remark. "She's taken a bit of a backslide in her recovery today," he said. "It's possibly just exhaustion, but I'd rather rule some things out before I send her back. We won't be long." Then, without giving them the opportunity to protest, he closed the flap and returned to the cot. He checked his phone and saw Dan's two-word response: *Five minutes.* To Anabelle, he said, "Here's what we're going to do. If I insist on walking you back, they'll know we're wise to them. See that space there?" Anabelle's eyes followed the doctor's finger to a sliver of light between the grass and the bottom of the tarp. "I'll pull up the tarp and you slip out there. Keep going until you reach the parking lot. Here, take my keys. I'm the red Corolla in the nearest row beside a small black cargo trailer. Get inside and leave if you see them coming."

"But—"

"If anyone asks, I'll pretend you slipped out when I left you behind the curtain. I'll tell them you're overwhelmed, so it won't be a hard sell." He squeezed Anabelle's fingers round his keys. "You have a cellphone?" When she nodded, he had her enter his number on the screen and send him a test message to ensure they could connect outside of the tent. Huxley eyed her with grave concern. "You're going to be all right, you hear? Whatever this is, we'll figure it out."

Anabelle hugged him, and if he felt the electricity pulsing through her body, he didn't let on. Then Huxley peeked around the partition to confirm Troy and Sylvia were still on the other side of the plastic window, but when he turned to tell Anabelle, she was already gone.

347

37

It was only by luck that Dan saw Huxley's message. On site since long before the sun had risen, he'd toured endless stretches of field, investigated every alley that fed onto the parade route, scrutinized every checkpoint, every obstruction, and every millimeter in between. Working with the Prime Minister's security personnel, Dan leaned on their numbers to bolster his own team and ensure eyes were everywhere, so he was confident in his coverage during the parade. No one could so much as sneeze in Garrett while the Prime Minister was in attendance, but Dan knew that afterward would be a different story. The moment the man left, his contingent and every appropriated operative would abandon their little city to fend off a danger few people knew anything about, and it was this that had kept Dan awake long past midnight. His short sleep hadn't even rustled the sheets before the alarm on his phone woke him, and it was the same alarm he was just about to set for a nap in his cruiser when he saw Huxley's message.

Cursing Huxley's timing, Dan flipped down his visor. What he saw in the mirror was a ghost of his former self. Not only had he lost the ten or so pounds he'd gained since Brandy left him, but maybe even a few more. The resulting thing in front of him was a blob of ashen skin as attractive as

348

INTERFERENCE

a punctured blister. He rubbed his eyes, slapped color into his cheeks, and exited his cruiser at the surprising clip of his younger self. As long as he'd known Huxley, the man had never distorted necessity, so his message caused Dan to call upon long-disused muscles to speed from the gravel road at the opposite end of the field to the first aid tent.

On his arrival, Dan saw Sylvia Baker and her son standing outside. Knowing what he knew and presently trying to hide it was the most difficult task of his entire policing career, but he hadn't risen to his post by being inept. A master negotiator and as inscrutable as the Kryptos outside the CIA headquarters, Dan flexed his strengths as he explained to the scrutinizing duo that he had business inside the tent and asked that they move away from the door.

"Problem, officer?" Troy asked, hovering much too close for Dan's liking.

"Wouldn't tell you if there was," Dan said sternly. "Step aside, please."

The old woman's eyes flickered black, and when her thin lips split into a smile, her corrupted teeth were the disinterred gray of another time. Then she was everyone's grandmother again, with sweet half-moon eyes atop the friendly plump of smiling cheeks. "Of course. Thank you for your service, officer," Sylvia cooed to him, and for a moment Dan suspected she was trying to hypnotize him, but he shook the feeling off and left them to find Huxley pacing behind a partition in the tent.

"Tell me," Dan said without preamble.

"Are they still out there?" Huxley whispered. Dan nodded, and the doctor's arms folded across his chest as he considered how best to warn Dan about Sylvia and Troy. He said, "I'm going to need you to not ask questions—"

Dan stopped him and tipped his head toward Sylvia. "If it's about her, I already know." Huxley's eyes, so wide now that Dan could see all the tiny blood vessels around the doctor's irises, beamed in disbelief. "I'm saying this so you'll know I'll believe you, whatever you tell me."

Huxley, bound by his professional oath and his respect for Anabelle, told Dan he felt that Sylvia and Troy were a danger to Anabelle and asked if he had the capacity to monitor their movements, should they attempt to approach her. In turn, Dan summarized what he'd gathered of Sylvia from the Cardinal Family, Ed Norman, Father Pauliuk, and Father Bonner.

"I have nothing to report on her son, though," Dan said as he concluded.

For a moment, Huxley thought back to his using days, when a whiff of sevoflurane would sweep his cares away. Given what Dan and Anabelle had told him, he almost wished for it now. He said, "Tammy Cormoran. You have *that* on him. I can't tell you how I know, or even if it's true, Dan, but I don't suspect I'm wrong about this. You've got to keep an eye on him."

In the silence that followed, the synapses in Dan's brain made the connection. Dak was adamant there was more than just the devil-woman to contend with, but Dan didn't think it was going to be the woman's own goddammed son. Again, none of this could be officially reported, but Dan knew it would be wise to share with the rest of the group. He would have to designate an officer he didn't have to Troy, someone experienced enough to keep the sharp-eyed lawyer from knowing. His overnight research on the family led Dan to understand that Troy wouldn't be easy to fool, but who to designate with the task? He considered the few officers that

INTERFERENCE

wouldn't ask questions, against his will settling on the only officer who knew the truth of the situation: Sarah Cardinal.

Just then, Huxley's phone rang. "I thought doctors drove nice cars," Anabelle said to him.

"Obviously, you're okay," Dan retorted, and checked his watch.

"I owe you one, Dr. Huxley."

He said, "You can wave to me in the crowd. I'm going to send my friend Dan to come and take you to the Prime Minister's team. He's in uniform, so you'll know it's him. Call your parents and tell them they came and got you after your check up. They don't need to be worrying about you." Hearing Huxley's instructions to Anabelle, Dan gave him a thumbs up, and Huxley added, "You're going to be heavily protected during the parade, but you'll need to listen to whatever Dan tells you to do afterward. Do you understand?"

"I'll listen," she responded.

"Everything's going to be okay," Huxley assured her.

From the other end of the line, Anabelle asked, "Are they still there?"

Huxley held his phone to his chest and stepped out from behind the partition to peer at the plastic window. When their presence wasn't obvious, he went to the door flap and scanned the field outside. Sylvia and Troy were gone.

351

38

Pandora seethed. She had been a hair's breadth away from the girl who'd stolen her power, so close she could smell the sugar from the girl's latte on her breath. By now, Pandora should have regained her strength, but she was still the inferior version of herself because the bitch had parried Pandora's every thrust, every lunge.

The thing inside Troy, as strong as a snowflake, stood oblivious beside her while she and Anabelle tested each other. Their forces locked, but it was Anabelle's will over Pandora's, fighting like a much bigger opponent, that settled their round. This was how Pandora discovered that what she had lost those few weeks ago was amplified in Anabelle. Worse, the bitch didn't even break a sweat when she outsmarted them, concentrating her energy inside the tent while she escaped to make Pandora believe she was still there. *Clever kids get killed*, she brooded, wondering how the cop had arrived so fast.

Alarmed by the officer's appearance, Troy dragged her away the moment the man went inside, and under the impression they were returning to the breakfast tent, Pandora went obligingly like a feeble old woman. When Troy marched her past the tent, however, it was clear he would not be taking her back. "Our visit is not done yet, Troy," she allowed Sylvia's infirm voice to say.

352

INTERFERENCE

"She's busy, Mother. The doctor is with her and then she's in the parade. You had your time." He picked up speed so that she had to take two steps for his every long one, and soon she was scuttling beside him like a maimed dog.

"Slow down, Troy."

"I don't want you to catch a cold, Mother. Let's get you home," he said, directing her toward his Mercedes, his grip tight on her arm.

Pandora sensed the juvenile fear of the being inside Troy. The coward didn't want to get caught. It was so attached to Troy that it compelled him away from capture. She, too, used to do that with Harold, but only because his capture had meant the end of his life. But things were different in Canada. If Troy were convicted of murder, for the nurse or the others he'd killed, the most he could get was a life sentence behind bars in a Canadian penitentiary. They wouldn't force poison into his body like would have happened to Harold had Pandora not ended him first, so she saw no reason to hurry.

"Let me go," she pleaded in Sylvia's elderly voice as a group of young families approached.

When concern rose on the adults' faces, Troy donned the look of a worried son so convincingly that their concern turned to pity. Wrapping an arm around her waist and leading her away from them, he said, "She forgot to take her medicine. Don't mind us. We're still adjusting." The families all hurried off without another look back. Pandora slapped Troy's hands. He pinched the droopy skin on Sylvia's side and doubled his efforts to haul her to his car. "Don't make this any harder than it has to be, Mother. You had your visit, now it's time to go home."

353

Pandora reached inside Sylvia's son now to where the other like herself was and squeezed. Troy winced but kept his pace. *Last warning*, Pandora cautioned Troy's other and stung it. She was countered by tight fingers around the back of Sylvia's neck. There was the mumbling sound of the thing trying to converse with her, but it was too inferior to breach Pandora's psyche. She let it curse in its indecipherable primitive language and made her decision. Retracting from Sylvia's spaces, she allowed Troy to lead her to his car, wobbling beside him as an old woman would. "I'm tired, Troy. Why am I tired?"

Surrendering the hold on her neck, he said, "It's been a long day for both of us."

Nearer now to Troy's car, Pandora daubed the sheen of senility onto Sylvia's guiltless face and turned the woman's head to look at her son. "Have I ever spanked you, Troy?" she asked. He responded with the electronic beep of his car unlocking. "I don't remember ever striking you like other mothers did to their children back then. I should have spanked you."

"You need a nap," Troy said, and held the passenger door open until she was tucked inside. Relishing in its deluded dominion over the being in Sylvia, Troy's Dark Friend stroked the tender filaments of Troy's ego while he started the car.

They were pulling out of the parking lot when Pandora inflated Sylvia's lungs and vented through Sylvia's mouth. "How many people have you murdered? Tell me, and maybe I'll go easy on you," she said.

Dark Friend's hackles rose within Troy and caused him to wring the steering wheel. Pandora wasn't averse to murder, of course, but she was averse to the power it bestowed on its perpetrators. It made beings like herself stronger, and Pandora simply could not have that. Not at all.

"Talk to me," Pandora commanded, and Troy's hand went to his throat where confession began pouring out of him.

"N-nine-nineteen," he stammered against his will.

"Child's play. I'm at over four thousand. Let's see if you scream like they did," she growled.

Then her skin began to bubble and dissolve in a flash of acid smoke, and his mother's liver-spotted skin grew dark, darker, until it was the ash-grey slag of death. Her short hair stretched and spidered toward him, coiling around his wrists, his feet, so that he could not remove his foot from the gas pedal. Troy screamed. Dark Friend hissed. Pandora cackled and pressed Troy's foot further down. The Mercedes sped down one city block, two, three, the sound of the accelerating engine a roar inside the vehicle but barely a whisper to confused onlookers who sprang out of the way of the little old lady and the maniacal man behind the wheel.

"You should have taken me back, Troy. You didn't take me back, so now I'm taking you."

Sylvia's eyes sucked inward, and when Troy looked at his mother's face, he saw two spectral chasms swirling above her nose.

"What are you?" Troy cried. "What the hell are you!"

"I'm your Mother."

Pandora's black tongue slid from Sylvia's lips and split into a serpentine cable that brushed against his ear. Her ancient fingers worked open the healing cuts on his hands and dug deep until she found the shuddering thing inside him and dragged it out. Outside the protection of his body, Dark Friend squealed and writhed until Troy vomited at the abominable vision of what came out of him.

355

"Please—" Troy begged. "No more. Please."

"Do you love me, Troy? Do you love your mother? Say you love your mother, and I'll make this end."

Pandora razored into Dark Friend until it, too, begged her to stop in its underdeveloped tongue. The sound of chasing sirens gave Troy sudden hope, and he yanked his foot away from the gas pedal and onto the brake. The car did not stop.

"Naughty boy," Pandora growled again and thrust her might onto the gas pedal until it touched the floor. Then she pitched the wheel left, away from the sirens, toward a grove of oaks. "Say you love me, Troy. Say you love your mother!" Pandora roared.

"I—"

And then the Mercedes rammed into a tree.

39

In the breezy, gray-dressed air, ten thousand citizens abandoned their sadness and welcomed the spell of anticipation as they spread like garland on sidewalks, in windows, on designated intersections, along the dried banks of the Callingwood River. Children clutched bags for the scavenging of treats and parents gripped tumblers of coffee or stronger drinks, enjoying the ageless experience of unrestrained glee. Temporary barricades erected during earlier hours were now abutted by eager bodies large and small, with a peppering of much smaller faces perched high onto shoulders of parents.

In the staging area between the fairground and the western edge of Roy Botcher's farm, meanwhile, Fathers Bonner and Pauliuk prepared for a post-parade intercession, uniting their Catholic and Anglican parishes, respectively, along with the clergy and congregants from six other local parishes. In all, there would be representation from the Catholic, Anglican, Baptist, Orthodox, and Presbyterian communities, and the two men took comfort in their ability to rally their members on behalf of God. They shared a short prayer and strode over the looped length of floats, marching bands, vintage cars, fire trucks, farm tractors, dance troops, community groups, horse riders, and law enforcement.

Approaching Southbridge Retirement's entry, they waved to Ed as he stepped down from the platform to greet them.

"You shared our plan with the others?" Father Pauliuk asked, gesturing to the dozen or so residents settling into their positions beside a big red dragon hunkered in the middle of the platform.

Ed said, "I shared what I could. You'll have their support, Fathers." The way he sighed concerned his former spiritual leader, who frowned.

"How are you feeling, Ed?"

"Like I'm fighting the devil. I think I'm going to need a new pacemaker after this."

Robert put his hand on his old friend's shoulder. "He only gives us what we can handle," he said, reminding Ed of Ed's own advice to him when their parish suffered a catastrophic fire decades ago. The advice, and much prayer, saw both men through the ordeal, though it was only Robert whose belief hadn't wavered since then. He said, "Roy's been kind enough to allow us the use of his home should we need it today. Maybe you'd like to lie down before we gather?"

Ed shook his head. "I'm all right, Robert."

Robert craned his neck to inspect the Southbridge float. "Is she with you?"

"No," Ed told him, scanning the populated field for sight of a woman he preferred not to see. "She left early this morning. I don't know what to make of it."

"The devil doesn't like to make things easy for us." Robert sighed.

Behind the Styrofoam castle wall, Chester raised a ruckus among the residents. "Where the hell is Eddie? I told him to get his goddamn ass in place. We're about to go—oh!

358

INTERFERENCE

Forgive me, Fathers!" The excited blush on Chester's cheeks paled to white and he hurried off the platform to atone for his outburst. "I didn't know Eddie was with you. Please excuse me; I'm having a heck of a time trying to get everyone together." He swiped the sweat off his forehead and looked apologetically at the men in cloth. "You ready, Eddie?"

"We'll see you later," Father Bonner said and left Ed to contend with Chester, who, out of earshot of the priests, lectured Ed for wandering away.

Chester was not, however, out of range of Evie and Dorothy, who fell on him with mother-bear defense on behalf of their beloved Eddie. It was their incensed rebuke, heard a great distance away, that generated a much-needed chuckle from the two men. They carried on, grinning silently through their apprehension until they came upon the Cardinal family's woodland entry. There, on a long trailer bed, the family had assembled taxidermied bears, beavers, and moose on a small moss-covered meadow. The animals were making pies that scrolled along on a conveyor belt Dak had installed the week before toward an imitation stone oven built by Johnny the day after that. A banner on the side of the trailer proudly advertised Cardinal & Sons Construction, though it was widely known that the company relied on Dak's efforts alone, at least as far as the family was concerned.

Wendy was using a staple gun to reattach a corner of the banner when Father Bonner tapped her shoulder. Startled into a scream, she flung the stapler backward. She spun around and saw him. "Father! Oh my goodness I'm sorry! Did I hurt you?"

"Serves me right for sneaking up on you," he said, rubbing the sting from his side.

359

Nikonha's gritty old voice said, "Give him some credit, Wendy. He's tougher than he looks." She came from behind the moose and took Johnny's hand as he led her onto the ground. "Old friend, how are you?"

"It's good to see you, Nikonha," he said, reciprocating the strength of her embrace.

The Elder released him and poked at his wrist. "I haven't seen you since your spill; how is your arm?"

Long-serving volunteers at Garrett's only community soup kitchen, the priest and the Elder's kitchen appointments coincided precisely every six weeks, and it was on the most recent occasion that a new volunteer had inadvertently knocked a boiling pot of soup onto the floor. The resulting splash caught the newcomer's leather boots and a good portion of Alistair's left wrist, not badly enough for a hospital visit but enough to keep him awake at night. It was only when Nikonha knocked on his door with a jar of what she called "special honey" that he was able to rest comfortably.

He slid back the sleeve of his coat and presented a faint pink scar on his wrist. "Much better, thanks to you." Nikonha smiled.

Returning from a last-minute inspection of the ready participants, Dak said to the other men, "Any sight of her?"

Robert and Alistair sighed the contrary just as the timer on Dak's phone went off, signalling the commencement of the parade. He dragged his fingers down the side of his face, reluctant to leave his family but required at the starting area to oversee the opening.

"Go," Nikonha ordered, gently nudging Dak. "We've got it from here," she said and turned to the band of Elders seated on the Cardinal family float.

INTERFERENCE

There was June Goodleaf, Lillian and Edward Leveque, Cherie Farmer, Russell Honyoust, Georgina Poodry, and several other wise faces that reassured Dak more than he was prepared for. A small hitch rose up his throat. Wendy hugged him and he promised to meet them along the route once he ensured the parade monitors had everything under control. A moment later, with the Elders ready, the priests off to prepare, and the participants and spectators nearly frenzied with anticipation, Dak drew his whistle from the string around his neck and blew it three times.

The parade had officially begun.

40

Driving the lead car in the parade, Dan felt somewhat comforted that Anabelle was cocooned by security in the Prime Minister's motorcade directly behind him. One of the few locals apprised of the Prime Minister's visit, Dan knew she was in safe hands. Anabelle, in turn, was comforted by Dan's offer to have her parents ride with him.

Now inching away from the starting area with William and Susan Cheever in his back seat and Greg Huxley in the front, Dan smiled and waved through his open window to the crowd. The wide-eyed adoration of candy-coated toddlers did not alleviate the unease that crept through him and he proceeded slowly, slowly, with the cruiser's lights flashing, simultaneously monitoring his rear-view mirror and off-handedly fluttering his fingers to no one in particular. A glance in Huxley's direction verified the other man's disinterest in the parade.

"Ooo! I bet she's having the time of her life back there!" Susan Cheever said of her daughter, saluting the spectators. She'd received Dan's invitation to ride in his cruiser as though she was being received by the queen herself, so Dan made the last-minute effort of sounding his siren when he collected them and watched her light up. The world was going to hell, Dan reasoned, so why not have a little fun on the way out?

INTERFERENCE

"She's probably forgotten about us already," William joked. He and his wife fell into a companionable discussion about which social media channel they would post the pictures of Annabelle with the Prime Minister on and who would get the first phone call so they could gloat about it. William's cousins over in Sarnia seemed like a good option, though they both agreed that Susan's ridiculously pretentious sister in Toronto might be a better choice.

Huxley and Dan quietly disengaged themselves from the conversation and, satisfied the couple weren't listening, Huxley asked, "Any ideas for what we're going to do when this is over?"

Dan spied the Cheevers' preoccupied faces in the mirror. "Shut the city down and move to Reno."

"I'm coming with you," the doctor said.

"You can monitor my liver."

"I've had worse jobs."

They moved on, gliding past new faces while Susan and William tossed miniature chocolate bars from their windows. The rise of tiny faces at the approach of Dan's cruiser—rivaled only by the shock of their parents at the sight of the Prime Minister sitting atop the back seat of a heavily guarded Mustang convertible next to Garrett's own Anabelle Cheever—never wavered.

Proceeding at a crawl, Dan led the hundred and seventeen entries away from the fairground, past the eastern slice of the Craig Valley golf course, the jammed parking lot of the city's upscale retirement village, the newly renovated Gilford Boutique Hotel, the Callingwood Baptist Church, and the stroller-lined frontage of the city's most expansive lowrental apartment district.

363

Their nerves stretched tight, Dan and Huxley searched for Sylvia's face among the crowd, both men believing they'd spotted her beside a sleeping toddler, a yawning grandfather, amidst a gang of candy-scavenging kids, but they knew this was her trick, and they imagined the black tunnel of her throat rumbling with laughter at their hysteria.

Huxley let out a long push of air. "This is ridiculous," he said after a time. Dan agreed and kept the gas pedal at an even five.

They were beginning their turn in front of the Garrett Gazette when the radio on Dan's shoulder buzzed. "222, this is 137, over," came Sarah's steady voice.

"137, code 10-12, over," Dan responded, informing Sarah that there were passengers in his cruiser who could overhear her communication.

There was a brief pause, then Sarah said, "We have a 10-50 at the north entrance to the Callingwood Gardens walking trail. Subject is 10-45, over."

Dan eased onto the brake pedal. Huxley's eyes swept to Dan while Susan and William, oblivious, tossed more candy and leaned out their windows to wave back at their daughter.

"10-9, over," Dan instructed and waited for Sarah to repeat the message that Troy Baker had been killed in a motor vehicle accident. When she repeated the communication, he relayed his own encrypted message asking if she needed immediate assistance, but Sarah declined. "Do we have a 20 on the female?" he asked.

"Negative," Sarah said.

Dan spied the clock on his dashboard and explained that he would arrive once the parade was over, approximately in thirty minutes, then ended the communication. Were the fatality that of an innocent citizen, Dan would have been

364

INTERFERENCE

compelled to rush to the scene, but he felt no hurry now, especially because a hasty departure would attract too much attention. Before the Prime Minister's security team could react to his delay, Dan once again pressed the gas pedal and continued leading the entrants north along the river-facing promenade, where a wind-battered memorial for the tour bus victims had been erected on a twelve-foot stretch of fence.

"Everything all right?" Huxley asked once he confirmed the Cheevers weren't listening.

Dan said, "One down, one to go."

"Her?" Huxley responded without looking at him.

"Uh-huh."

Huxley drummed his fingers on the window frame. "Why don't I feel happy about that?"

"Shit situation," Dan reasoned.

When they reached the memorial, Dan slowed to a stop. Here, there would be a ten-minute delay while the Prime Minister publicly paid his respects. A sixty-foot perimeter previously cordoned off gave the Prime Minister a wide berth when he and Anabelle stepped out of the Mustang, but he waved generously to the distant spectators before clasping his hands together and proceeding to the promenade.

Riding in the second to last vehicle of the Prime Minister's motorcade, Mayor Ada Falconer soon joined their doleful observation of the forty-two laminated faces affixed to a weathered scrap of plywood. The wooden borders above, below, and between each picture were filled with messages of sympathy and there were a number of moldy-looking teddy bears and rotting floral arrangements stapled on the edges of the board. Several crosses below the sign stood sturdily in place with bricks on their bases, most of which were covered by a layer of deflated balloons, plastic flowers, rain-dimpled cards, and dozens of candles with spent wicks. A matching pair of *World's Best Grandma* and *World's Best Grandpa* coffee mugs at the base of one of the crosses sprouted wires with pictures of several children, all with the same brown eyes and the same dark hair.

The lowering of the Prime Minister's head prompted Ada and Anabelle to do the same, but behind the dark lenses of Anabelle's sunglasses, her eyes were everywhere but on the memorial. To her left, to her right, over the promenade fence and onto the depleted riverbed, she looked for the woman, but the area was teeming with demons that clouded her vision. Beside the Prime Minister, at Mayor Falconer's feet, on the shoulders of every plain-clothed Mountie in and outside of the perimeter, malignants of all shapes and sizes lurked and scrabbled about like ghostly spiders on Anabelle's unsolicited web. It was the greatest collection of evil she'd seen to date, no doubt because their scouts had delivered news of her power. With their many legs and their many arms and their many heads, the superior beasts wheeled around Anabelle, jabbing for possession, but her invisible breath stung them, and her clasped hands imperceptibly struck them until they fell still. Inside, her energy thrummed.

The crowd grumbled as a mob of opportunistic reporters seized the riverside pause and scurried in front of bawling children and furious parents. There was a flash of cameras and a thrust of outstretched microphones and a burst of pleading from overly made-up journalists for the Prime Minister to turn around. Such a fuss they made that Anabelle wondered which evil was worse. She was reflecting on the good fortune that Jessica Chung wasn't among them when the Prime Minister touched her shoulder. He didn't say anything but continued to stare straight ahead. Anabelle let his self-serving gesture continue until at last he tilted his head upward and blinked dramatically. His eyes were dry when he swung around.

"Over here! Prime Minister, over *here*!" came an immediate shout.

"Ms. Cheever!" came the second.

"Wave, Charlotte, wave!" said a mother who, not to be outsmarted by the aggressive press corps, carried her daughter over an unguarded stretch of fence, deep onto the desiccated bed of the Callingwood River. When the unsuspecting Prime Minister waved to the pig-tailed toddler in the mother's victorious arms, a crush of parents hurried to the riverbed so their offspring, too, could see Canada's leader. Bottoms were scooped over the promenade fence, more were maneuvered through gates further on, all for a glimpse of someone who would forget their faces before the hour was done.

With cameras recording his every movement, the Prime Minister's manicured fingers swept out in benevolent greeting to the future voters. An aide tried to sway the tarrying leader back to the Mustang, and there was an overt showing of her watch before he acquiesced. Effecting a winning smile and a vote-grabbing wave, he finally turned.

Grateful the farce was almost over, Anabelle sighed and was about to return to her spot in the back of the Mustang when a gust of wind blasted over the riverbed. Yanked from the hands of children, a trio of balloons—red, yellow, white—were whipped upward where no amount of squealing could recover them. Collars were drawn up, and a great many eyes squinted against the wind that gusted here, there, this way, the other, so brutally violent that the realization came that not just the political affair was over but so was the parade.

A team of men hurried their leader into the SUV behind the Mustang while a lone agent, slanted against the gusts, offered his hand to Anabelle. A spike of wind forced his hand

367

back. Again he reached for her and was not so much forced as *ejected* away from Anabelle. In the cruiser a few feet from the Prime Minister's motorcade, Susan Cheever let out a squeak of fear. Out her open window, she reached for Anabelle and was caught by her seatbelt.

"Anabelle!" she screamed. "Anabelle!"

"It's a goddamn tornado!" William cried from the backseat, pointing north to a spiraling column of black air rising from the adjacent marshland and advancing toward them.

He fumbled with his seatbelt, but Dan and Huxley were already out of the cruiser, steaming toward Anabelle. Once more, the wind lashed out. The locks on Dan's cruiser depressed and, like a toy car, it was shoved out of the perimeter toward the last car in the Prime Minister's motorcade, where it blocked the advancement of the parade. The cruiser touched the front bumper of the Suburban and came to a rest.

On the other side of the riverbed, the spinning column grew wide, spreading its deadly limbs outward while it drilled a path of destruction toward little pig-tailed Charlotte and the twenty-seven other families sidled next to her. Mothers and fathers and children screamed while, one by one, each vehicle in the Prime Minister's motorcade sped away.

"Where is she? Where the hell is she?" Huxley whirled around.

Struggling against the gale, Dan worked a hand around Anabelle's waist and tried to pull her back to his cruiser when Anabelle raised an arm and pointed across the river at the bottom of the column where a figure was materializing in the vortex: a little old lady with a wicker bag.

"Oh God! She's gonna get killed!" shouted a man who was unable to look away during his sidewise scramble onto the back of an idling truck. "That old lady is done for!"

368

"What the hell?" Dan shouted, realizing for the first time how skeptical he'd been.

Following the direction of Anabelle's arm, Huxley's mouth fell open. "It can't be!"

There was a mad clambering of parents bumping each other as they raced to get off the riverbed when young Charlotte's mother suddenly stopped. From her feet to her knees to her hips to her teeth, the ground shook her body, shook her little girl. The other parents stopped shoving each other long enough to sense the terrible tremble rising in their own skin, in their own children, and their fear turned to outright terror.

Back on the promenade, there was not a single spectator. The idling floats succeeding the Prime Minister's departed motorcade were now abandoned. Strollers and wheelchairs and blanket-strewn wagons deserted the sidewalks and now there were just Dan, Huxley, and Anabelle and Anabelle's frantic parents trying to escape a car that was being battered by wind-swept banners and gale-extracted siding. One, two, three blasts of air corralled the occupants back toward the center of the river. The little old lady, who by all common sense should have been shucked into the swirling mass above her, bore the storm impassively and continued her purposeful stride in Anabelle's direction, clutching her wicker bag with her two small fists against her stomach. All this Anabelle saw and more, so much more, for the tornado was not just a weather phenomenon but a cataclysm of evil housed within a towering, tempestuous demon.

As Sylvia stepped onto the opposite riverbank, a roar erupted from beyond the western bend in the river, and Anabelle knew with brutal certainty that the river would soon be dry no longer.

S. L. LUCK

"S-she's filling the river!" Anabelle stuttered to Huxley and Dan. "She's going to drown them. We need to get them out!"

"Christ have mercy!" Dan groaned and made for the riverbed. Huxley rushed after him.

Give it to me, Pandora pressed onto the electrons around her in an attempt at atmospheric morse code.

Anabelle received the message and returned one of her own. *Leave us alone.*

Return what you've stolen, and I'll go away, Pandora transmitted.

If it were as simple as giving the devil-thing her power back, Anabelle would have done it, but her parents had raised no idiot. First, she wasn't about to leave herself vulnerable, and second, she didn't believe the woman would go away if she did. No. The devil-thing would kill her, would kill others, and Anabelle was not about to allow that. *Go away*, Anabelle broadcasted back from the promenade.

Then the little old lady that was not an old lady dropped her wicker bag and a tendonous, many-tentacled creature issued from its opening. It waited at the old woman's feet like an obedient pet. *Meet my Dark Friend, Anabelle. His home was ... lost. But you have space in there, don't you? Plenty of room for two. If you don't give me what you've taken from me, my Dark Friend is going to move in, and I don't think you'll like his baggage. Give me what's mine, and we'll go away.* At this, the writhing creature at her feet rasped its approval.

No, Anabelle refused. Westward, there was a thunderclap of something gushing in their direction and then they saw it: a wall of water five meters high raging toward the corralled children and the corralled parents and Huxley and Dan.

370

"Son of a bitch!" Dan howled, driving his body against the wind to push a father and the two children in his arms up the embankment. Behind him, Huxley dragged the pig-tailed Charlotte and her frantic mother toward the shore. Neither man was going to make it.

Last chance, Pandora intoned through Sylvia's blackened mouth. The water rushed near; so near that the hopeless parents on the riverbed now closed their children's eyes against the fate that was upon them. Resigning themselves to their doom, Dan and Huxley locked eyes in a last gesture of mutual respect. Then they braced themselves.

Anabelle thrust her arms outward, commanding every proton and electron as far as she could reach. With all her might, she steered them away from the shuddering parents, away from the trembling children, away from Huxley and Dan and up, up, up to Sylvia and the sky-thing that was Pandora. The old woman did not flinch. When the water hit, she drew it up into the twister and lashed spikes of rain onto their faces and bodies. The creature at Sylvia's feet slithered up her leg and waited for instruction. Anabelle pushed, driving the outer bands of the vortex backward, more, more, until the people on the river bottom were freed of Pandora's grip. Then they ran.

Pandora roared. Sylvia's arm whipped sideways and the giant wire-framed turkey from the Garrett Grocery float went whizzing across the sky. Again Sylvia's arm shot out. A tuba went by. Then two Canadian flags. A rainbow flag. An inflatable Air Canada airplane. A driverless tractor still attached to a hay wagon. Then a miniature hockey rink on a trailer. With Dan in the front and Huxley in the back, the terrified families were led back onto the promenade, where they bulleted toward their vehicles and drove away. The men returned to Anabelle just as the river filled.

"Holy God, look!" Huxley cried and pointed at the sky. There, a hundred feet above, was a moose, a beaver, and a bear making pies. With the lightness of a feather, the Cardinal family float barrelled toward Anabelle and Huxley, but Dan yanked them down just in time. The float crashed against the memorial.

"Give me back my power!" Pandora shrieked in a voice everyone could understand.

Something rolled against Anabelle's foot, and when she looked down there was a *World's Best Grandma* mug with a broken handle beside her shoe.

"Is that smoke?" Dan called through the furor.

He raised his nose to the air. Huxley and Anabelle did the same. The scent was unmistakable. Drifting from behind one of the promenade's several art installations were the scents of cedar, sage, sweetgrass, and tobacco. Joined by the Elders, Dak, Wendy, Jesse, and Johnny helped the medicine forge its path.

Pandora howled as the medicine abraded her outer bands, then she thrust herself outward and it wasn't just floats coming at them, but cars and eighteen wheelers and boats recently winterized.

"Give me my power!"

Anabelle pushed the onslaught back and countered with her own. One, two, ten light poles speared toward the little old lady. Pandora flicked them away and drove her Dark Friend at them. Anabelle crushed it mid-air. Whatever it was disintegrated in a flash of black blood and fell into the raging river.

From an alley between a bakery and an insurance brokerage, Father Pauliuk, Father Bonner, and Ed Norman emerged, riding a golf cart. Ed was driving while, reading from their Bibles, the priests performed their first major exorcism. Holy water was flung from the golf cart, and Anabelle propelled every drop across the river.

A shrill cry resounded throughout the sky. "Give me back my power! Give it to *ME*!" Then the bands of wind unfolded, lengthening into giant serpentine jaws that struck high out over the water, slashing at Anabelle. Smoke rose, holy water splashed, and the distant prayers and devotions of citizens of many faiths across the city united for a common purpose. Pandora squealed. One of her claws shot out, and when it drew back over the water, Ed Norman was no longer in the golf cart. He was sky-high in the grip of hell.

"Do something!" Huxley cried.

"Oh my God!" Dan gasped.

"Lord have mercy!" the priests pleaded in unison.

High above, with his stomach clamped tight and the soulless eyes of evil bearing down on him, Ed reached for the part of himself that still believed and found that—through his hiatus—the Unchanging remained unchanged. He looked down at the Fathers, and then his eyes swept skyward to where Bessie was waiting for him. Then, for the first time in many years, Ed Norman prayed.

There was a wail of pain, another and another. Efforts were doubled, tripled, and Anabelle converged all her strength, all her energy, every prayer, every plea into a great and singular core and thrust it at the beast. A stomach-emptying howl erupted over the city. Pandora's limbs struck out, and one connected with Dan's head. He crumpled to the ground beside Anabelle. Rushing to Dan, Huxley dodged Pandora's strike. The next one sliced his shoulder.

Anabelle looked at the two men now collapsed at her feet, toward Dan's cruiser where her parents were buried in wind-blown rubble, and up at Ed Norman's strange grin as he mouthed something not to the devil-woman, but higher up to the sky. Anabelle drew power from the earth, from the sky, from the water, and fused it with her own.

Then Anabelle attacked.

41

Silence followed the thunderclap. The tornado that wasn't a tornado dissipated and was swept away by an agreeable breeze, and when the first chirp of returning birdsong sounded over the river, Anabelle, exhausted, dropped beside the officer and the doctor and found that they were still breathing.

Huxley opened his eyes. Hearing the pitch of sirens in the distance, he clutched his bleeding shoulder and sat up. "You had all that in you?" he said.

Anabelle nodded. "Are you going to tell?"

"Hell, no. I know what you're capable of. But just don't use it on anyone else, okay? If you ever get mad at your boyfriend or something, don't fry him. Promise me that."

"I promise."

Ambling over to Dan, Huxley winced, and a fresh gush of blood rippled down his fingers. Anabelle gasped, but Huxley waved her away. "I'll be fine. Go check your parents. Go or I'll buy a goddamn billboard with your face and your electric hands on it." She hurried away.

Hearing her daughter shout her name, Susan Cheever called out from an opening in the rubble. A moment later, Dak, Jesse, and Johnny were at the cruiser with Anabelle, working to extricate her parents from beneath the towering

375

pile while Nikonha and Father Bonner hurried to Huxley and Dan. The Elder touched Dan's limp fingers as Father Bonner anointed the unconscious police chief's forehead and beseeched heaven for a miracle. Father Pauliuk, meanwhile, fixed his eyes on the body of his old friend floating face down in the water.

42

It was a rare day when Jessica Chung was a welcome guest at Garrett General. On the third floor of the hospital, where Dan was recovering from a minor cervical fracture and a concussion, Jessica, in an over-sized sweater and jeans, carried a small vase of flowers past the nursing station and ignored the glares.

Since Dan saved her life, the epiphany of her behavior had come upon the reporter like an illness, and she knew it would take her a long time to recover. Restitution was the remedy, or so her therapist suggested, so here she was, paying respects to her new friend. She had dabbed a little perfume behind her ears, and this is what Dan smelled as she gently hugged him.

"I like the new you," he told her.

"I like the new me, too," she responded, blushing, and that was as long as they had together before Sarah and Jesse came in.

"You look like hell, boss," Sarah smiled, giving a dutiful once-over to Jessica, who took the cue and stepped respectfully aside.

"How are you feeling?" Jesse asked.

Dan rubbed the skin on his wrist. "Alive. How's your dad?"

377

"Running his ass off trying to keep the doomsdayers away from the gates."

"Come again?"

"That asshole who almost ran her over is out on bail. He's got his Winnebago parked near the front gates, harassing people with flyers. *Tannin's Tornado*, they're calling the storm. There's about seven of them shoving pictures of a sea monster in front of kids, telling them the monster is going to eat them if their parents don't take them to church." Jesse's frustration came out in a long, lip-rumbling breath. "These idiots sleep all day in their parents' basement, but they sure know how to hustle when they put their greasy little minds to it."

"Are we doing anything about this?" Dan asked Sarah.

"The usual, but Roy's also got a load of manure that's being redirected as we speak." Sarah gave Dan a sly grin.

"You're going to be a great mother," he told her.

They were enjoying the overdue pleasure of laughter when Huxley knocked on the door. "I was going to make a ward exception and blow an airhorn in here, but the nurses already changed you once, and I didn't want to torture them again. How's the head?"

Their eyes fell on the sling hanging from the doctor's neck. In the days since he'd been stitched up by one of the newer surgeons at the hospital, he'd gotten used to his temporary limitation, but still his bandage seemed to glow against the dark red fabric of his sweater.

Dan said, "I'm feeling so good that I'm beginning to think the only reason you're keeping me here is so I don't go to Reno without you."

Huxley laughed. "I don't need two hands to take all your money in poker—but, no, it's not *me* holding you here.

INTERFERENCE

Adhira tells me you haven't gotten any smarter with that whack. She says you've been begging to be released?"

Sarah smacked Dan's arm. "Whatever happened to 'health should be your number one priority'? So much for walking the talk." Dan shrugged.

"Anyway, it's not like you can go back to work the second you're out of here," Huxley told him. "You're going to need weeks to recover, possibly a few months. You take it easy for that long, and I'll book the tickets to Reno myself."

"Ever hear the joke about squeezing money from a doctor?" Dan said, but the punchline was heard only by Jessica, for that was when a gurney carrying Sylvia Baker was wheeled down the hallway past Dan's door.

Jessica said, "You all look like you saw a ghost."

A ghost wouldn't have turned his insides to mush or made his recovering shoulder hurt with memory, Huxley thought, but didn't dare share this in front of Jessica. "If Jesse hadn't found her when he did, that woman *would* have been a ghost," he said, and they all looked at Jesse.

In the aftermath of the madness, and with emergency services yet to arrive, Dak assumed command and sent his sons to the water to recover Ed and to look for any signs of Sylvia. So it was Jesse who found the devil-woman, curled up in a fetal position, with her toes and her bottom in the shallow water of the opposing shore, peacefully asleep. His father's teachings that all life has value overrode the temptation to leave the woman there and let her drown. He reluctantly hoisted her small body onto a stray sign floating nearby and brought her to the pavilion where police cars and ambulances were arriving. In the proceeding days, he learned that she had been diagnosed with a brain injury so severe that she would require around-the-clock care for the rest of her

379

life, however long that would be, and it was obvious to Jesse that they were all as conflicted as he was.

He said, "I'm just glad it's over," and squeezed Sarah's hand. They continued this way, secretly recalling Annabelle's terrific power, and Jessica pretended not to notice their shared awe.

While secrets were being kept in the hospital, Father Bonner and Father Pauliuk were each returning from exhausting meetings with their archbishops, where both men shared their riverside experiences in full. It was Father Bonner who, having also been granted forgiveness for performing a major exorcism without permission, now carried a tray of coffee and a box of donuts into Father Pauliuk's Anglican parish.

"Thought you could use some company," he said, and put the donuts on the desk.

"You're one of God's miracles, you know that, Alistair?" Robert said, retrieving a coffee.

"He puts me where I am needed. How did it go?"

"The Lord is my strength," Robert said. Alistair nodded and they let silence wash over them as they ate.

After a time, Alistair said, "What day is the funeral?"

"Day after tomorrow. I know the passage of a soul to heaven should be a time for celebration, Alistair, I know this in my soul; and I know Ed longed to reunite with his wife, but I must admit this one is difficult for me."

Alistair nodded sympathetically. "That's what makes us human, and that is okay, Robert. Can I offer any assistance?"

"Dan tells me the pizza near your parish is pretty good."

"Another miracle," Alistair Bonner replied, and they relaxed in the consolation of small wonders.

43

Over the soft white sand of Barbados' Carlisle Bay beach, William Cheever padded barefoot with three strawberry daiquiris toward the white umbrella under which Susan and Anabelle lounged. It was the dead of winter back in Canada and the Cheevers were happy to escape the punishing cold. His Irish skin a little crispy from an application of expired sunscreen, William winced when his shirt slid across back as he leaned to deliver their drinks, but he smiled with gratitude that his daughter was still alive. He sipped his daiquiri, still unable to forget the helplessness he'd felt when he was trapped in that cop car while a hell of a freak storm almost killed his only child.

In hindsight, he was glad he hadn't seen any of it, for he suspected those nightmares would have been much worse. At least he could sleep believing Anabelle was tucked safely under the art installation with the Elders like she told him.

As far as Anabelle was concerned, William saw that the longer they spent on the island, the more she seemed to relax, even enjoy herself. Of course he wished her swimsuit covered more than just the essentials, but William expanded with fatherly defense each time a potential suitor went leaping away.

Behind her sunglasses, meanwhile, Anabelle let her father enjoy his superiority while her fingers twitched.

Thank you for reading my work. If you enjoyed the story, please consider leaving a review online at your favorite store.

Connect with me at:

www.authorsluck.com

Twitter: @Author_SLuck

Instagram: @authorsluck

Manufactured by Amazon.ca
Bolton, ON